God of Sparta
A Demon of Athens Novel

Martin Sulev

Copyright © 2020 Martin Sulev
All rights reserved.
ISBN: 9798611476048
Cover by damonza.com

THE DEMON OF ATHENS SERIES

TYRANNY
GOD OF SPARTA
SHADOW OF THEBES (2021)

For my mother, who instilled in me the wonder and joy of stories.

MAPS

GREECE AND THE AEGEAN

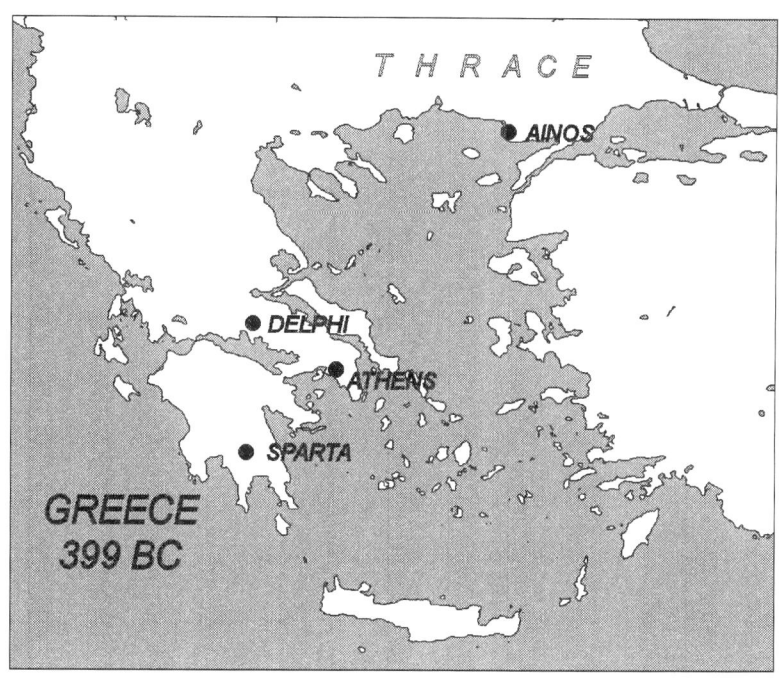

DELPHI AND VICINITY

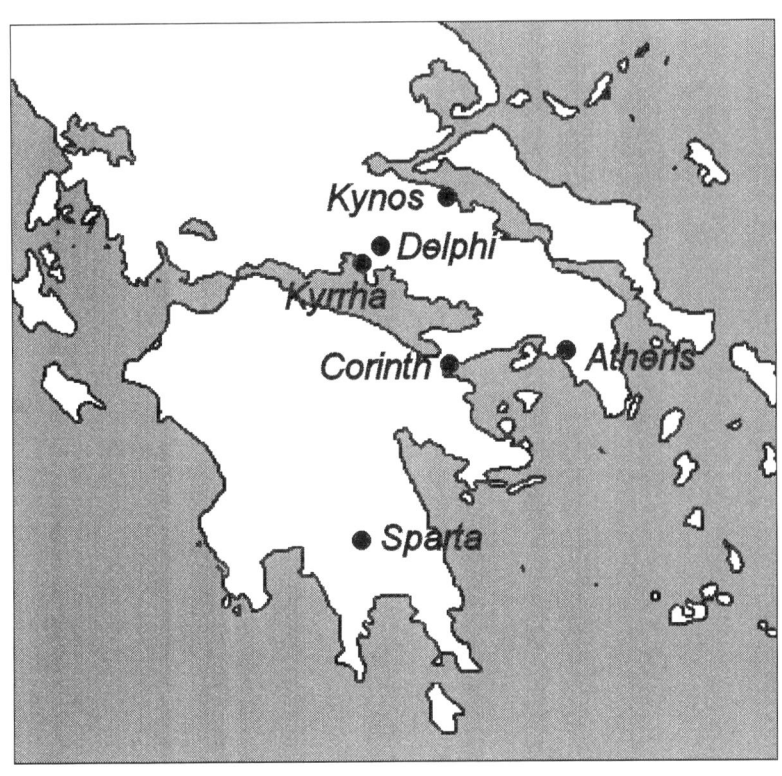

NORTHEASTERN AEGEAN AND THRACE

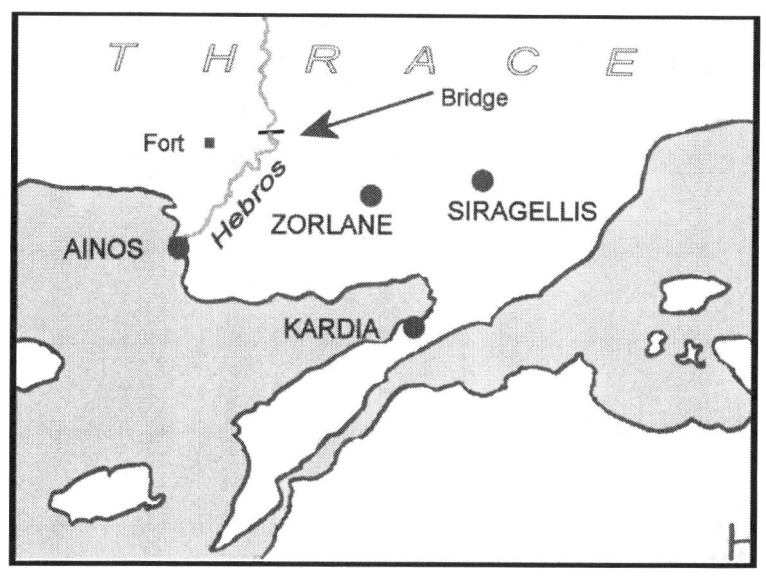

A NOTE ON SPELLING

For various reasons, transcribing Classical Greek words into English can be quite a challenge. In this book, I have used different conventions in different situations for different reasons. For familiar places such as Thrace and Sicily, I have tended to use conventional English spelling to avoid confusion. In many Greek names, however, I have used "k" instead of "c", as in Alkibiades and Perikles, to better approximate the original pronunciation or Greek spelling. In yet other cases, I made rather arbitrary decisions regarding a particular name (Thrasybulus rather than Thrasyboulos, for example) because I thought it looked nicer on the page. All that is to say, I apologize in advance if my spelling choice in a particular situation differs from what you yourself might have chosen.

M.S.

PART ONE
MORTALS ΘΝΗΤΟΙ

Μισῶ δ'ἅπαντας τοὺς θεούς, ὡς οἶσθα σύ.

I hate all the gods, as you know.

I turned my back on them long ago. For this I became known as the Blasphemer. The Godless One. The Demon of Athens. But I tell you this, Athenian: they are titles I bear with pride. Not since I was a youth have I offered wine or flesh to the unworthy deities of Olympus. Nor has a prayer passed my lips in these many years, for I would rather die a free man than prostrate myself like a slave at the feet of a god and beg for aid. The gods are petty and vindictive. They neither reward virtue nor punish evil. I curse them all.

But I save my greatest enmity for Apollo. His father, Zeus, is lofty and distant, unknowable even to the other beings who populate the ranks of immortals. Poseidon, though capricious and easily roused, is content to govern his watery realm and those who dare to venture there. The third brother, the dark Hades, is patient, knowing that in the end all mortals will become his subjects. The other gods, powerful as they may be, tend to their own matters: Artemis in her glades and forests, Hephaestus at his forge, and the thief-god Hermes scurrying about the heavens like the weasel he is.

Apollo is different. The golden-haired god meddles in the affairs of men, Greeks and barbarians alike. From the ends of the earth seekers of prophecy come to his temple at Delphi to ask the god for

3

guidance in matters both great and small. Through his oracle he whispers into the ears of kings and commoners, influencing their actions while dissembling his true motive of sowing discord and strife among mortals. Many believe Apollo to be the ally of mankind, but he is not. He is their adversary. He is the great manipulator. And like all gods, he is cruel.

And like many, I, Daimon, son of Nikodromos, suffered when the radiant god turned his burning gaze on me. But, being a fool, I let the Furies drive me forward and I fought him nevertheless, heedless of the destruction it inflicted on those I loved.

For I have another epithet, less spoken now but no less true than my other names.

Some men call me *O Theomachos*.

The God-Fighter.

CHAPTER 1

The men in the camp were already dead. They just did not know it yet.

From my hiding spot behind a line of pine trees I watched the camp come to life with the rising sun. The bandits cooked their breakfasts or just shuffled about, blinking away the last remnants of sleep. A late riser crawled from his tent. One of his comrades pointed at him and said something, causing others nearby to laugh. The man waved a groggy hand at them and wandered in my direction. Ten paces away from me he stopped and hiked up his tunic. The pattering of his morning piss went on for an age. If the man had bothered to look up, he might have seen my green eyes staring back at him. But he did not. The bandit dropped his tunic, turned, and headed back to rejoin his fellows.

The bandits' camp was nestled in a depression formed by three hills and was sheltered by dense stands of pine. It was well away from the nearest pass, making it almost impossible to find unless one was searching for it. But I had been looking for their refuge for some time and now the men inside it were going to die.

I touched Tibetos on the shoulder and my oldest friend nodded. Needing no further instruction, the former slave slipped away to pass the word along to the others to attack on my signal. In the meantime, a flicker of unease passed through me as I considered the doomed men.

It was a large band, nearly fifty men. We had only thirty fighters, but that is not what bothered me. We had dealt with bandits before. The end of the great war with Sparta had led to a plague of such gangs of landless men. Mostly they were miserable lots, groups of escaped slaves or desperate men and their families, driven to brigandry out of poverty and want. Some bands were more formidable collections of former soldiers and mercenaries who, like me, had known nothing but war for their entire lives. The easy plunder from preying on travellers and isolated farms was a much more attractive prospect than a life of poorly-paid drudgery in the city. My men and I had dealt with them all, making the borderlands of Attica safe.

But these men were different. Unlike most bandits, they did not prey on isolated travellers close to their home base. They were constantly on the move, attacking well-protected trading caravans and farmsteads. The damage done, they would vanish into the mountains, only to reappear in another location to rob and kill again. They had frustrated my efforts to wipe them out for almost a year. But they had made a mistake and now they would pay for it with their lives.

Bad luck would be a fairer description than mistake. The bandits had raided a farm only three days earlier. They had slaughtered the inhabitants and put the house and outbuildings to the torch. By chance, we had been close enough to see the thin plume of smoke from the burning farm rising in the distance. We found the defiled corpses of the farmer, his wife, and their three children scattered around the charred remains of the farm, a feast for the crows. Even the slaves and livestock had been slaughtered and left to rot in the sun.

We were too late to save the farmer and his family but not too late to avenge them. Traces of the raiders' passage still fresh, the bandits had been easy to track to their current base. Now they were trapped like fish in a net.

I brought my fingers to my lips and blew three shrill whistles. On cue, twenty javelins lanced through the air from three directions and rained down on the men below, skewering and wounding a dozen bandits before they even knew what was happening. "Pick your targets!" I heard Tibetos shout. My group of ten men remained silent behind our screen of trees as javelins and slingshot continued to maim and kill.

It has been my experience that battles almost never go according to plan, but this was one of those rare exceptions. We were the *peripoli,* rangers tasked with guarding the borders of Attica against the enemies of Athens. My men were trained to work together and they closed the trap with practiced skill. The bandits, to their credit, reacted quickly, confirming my suspicions that they were mercenaries or former soldiers. They seized nearby swords and spears and took cover among the tents and rocks, denying Tibetos and his skirmishers easy targets. At the same time, they were pinned down, and if they did not move, they would be picked off one by one.

Tibetos and his men emerged from the trees, as did the squads led by the veterans Telekles and Stachys. The assault converged on the enemy from three sides. Our fighters in front had spears and light, hide-covered shields. Behind the front rank, slingers whirled their weapons, waiting for the chance to loose a bullet on an exposed limb or head.

When men are frightened, there is little difference between them and animals. Just as a shepherd uses his dog to steer his flock of sheep or goats this way or that, so too can men be herded like unthinking beasts. I was the shepherd now. Hemmed in on three sides, the bandits turned and fled in the only direction left to them. Towards me.

"Now!" I shouted.

I broke cover along with nine more of my fellows and we launched our javelins. I have never been skilled with javelins, but even I could not miss. So close and exposed were the fleeing bandits that they might as well have been the bales of hay our young recruits used for target practice. The volley of deadly missiles left more of the enemy writhing on the ground with wooden shafts protruding from their bodies and limbs.

Already thirty of the bandits lay dead or wounded, while the others looked about, dumbfounded by their predicament. Except one.

"Charge them together!" the leader shouted, pointing his sword in our direction. He was in the centre of the camp. He was tall and muscular, almost as large as I was. His accent was unmistakably Spartan. "Charge the weakest side!" he roared.

His plan might have worked. Our line was loosely strung out. Had they run at us en masse, they would have surely broken through. As it was, however, the Spartan's men still had not recovered their wits. My weapon was already free from its scabbard. "Kill them!" I shouted and I sprinted towards them.

In truth, I did know if my comrades were with me, but it mattered not, for the *aristeia* filled me. I was young and fearless. Rage and battle-joy flowed through me as I cut through the bandits as a ship's prow carves through water. The blue-tinged metal of my rhomphaia flashed like sunlight reflecting off waves. The gracefully-curved Thracian blade was named Whisper and she sent two men to the Underworld before they had even moved. I was dimly aware of my comrade Mnasyllus off to my side. The ox-like warrior roared as his oversized *kopis* sword cleaved through flesh and bone.

The already-fraying courage of the remaining bandits snapped. They threw down their weapons and fell to their knees, begging for mercy. Only the Spartan did not yield.

"I want the leader alive!" I shouted, pointing at the Spartan. "I want him alive!"

The Spartan howled in frustration at the collapse of his comrades' will to fight. "Cowards!" he screamed at them.

"Throw down your weapon!" I shouted at him.

Instead, the Spartan charged at me, bellowing a war-cry. Many men fear the Spartans and they are right to do so, for the Spartans are relentless and deadly fighters. But they are men who bleed and die like any other. I suppressed my urge to run and let the Spartan come to me.

It was a reckless charge. I could have impaled him on my blade, but that was what he wanted: to die with honour in battle. I needed a prisoner. His sword hacked down towards my shoulder in a blow that would have cut down to my heart had it landed. But it did not, for at the last possible instant I flipped my grip on my weapon and stepped into the attack. I jerked the pommel of the rhomphaia up and punched it into the Spartan's jaw like a boxer's uppercut. He reeled backwards and collapsed like a defeated brawler, his sword tumbling away from his limp fingers. Tibetos and the others leapt on the groaning Spartan and bound him before he could regain his senses.

Blood-lust still surged within me. My chest heaved and blood pounded in my ears. With effort I wrestled down my rage and came back into myself. The remaining prisoners were herded together with the bloodied Spartan. We had not lost a single one of our own men. "Search the camp!" I ordered.

Tibetos glanced at me. I nodded and he and some of the others fanned out, dispatching any wounded bandits with a spear-thrust. The moans and whimpering of dying men decreased until the only sound was that of my men pillaging the camp.

A pile of assorted booty grew at the centre of the clearing. Weapons and armour fell with a clatter as they were added to the rising pile of arms. Among the swords and spears were many of the forward-curving *kopis* swords favoured by the Spartans. They were heavy, inelegant butchers' weapons made for hacking through shields, armour, and bodies: simple but effective tools, as the Spartans had proven so many times. Not a few coins were discovered, amounting to a small hoard. The haul was considerable and each man would receive an equal share, fair compensation for their service to Athens.

Tibetos approached me, each of his hands bearing an item of interest. "These are from the leader's tent," he said, jerking a thumb at the bound Spartan. The first item was a bag containing a few hundred silver tetradrachm coins. "Look at them," Tibetos said, pouring a jingling trickle of the shiny coins into my palm. A handful of freshly-struck Athenian owls stared back at me. There was hardly a mark on them, not like the battered coins that one usually encountered in the market. It was possible that they had been stolen from a merchant, but it seemed more likely to me that the Spartan had received them directly from someone in Athens.

"There was also this," Tibetos said, handing me a wooden rod. I turned the object over in my hands. It was the length of a man's forearm and had a hexagonal cross-section, with six flat faces running the length of the rod. It was a *scytale*, one of a pair of identical rods used for reading coded messages. The principle was simple enough. A strip of leather was wound around the baton and the message written vertically along the faces. When unwound, the letters on the strip became a string of seemingly random letters. But when the recipient rewound the strip around his own identical baton, the message would reappear. Spartan soldiers often used them to relay orders, but they were not something I would expect to find in a bandit camp.

I put one end of the rod under the Spartan's chin and forced him to look at me. "What does a weasel-shit robber need with a *scytale*?" I asked. "Who possesses its twin?" The man's hard black eyes bore into me. His hair had been cropped short, but I knew that at one time he had worn the long, braided locks of a Spartan warrior. "Who are you, Spartan?" I asked. He stared past me in contempt, so I kicked him hard in the gut. Tibetos and Telekles jerked the gasping man back to his knees. I repeated my question.

"I will see you in Hades, Thracian," he spat, his Spartan accent clear.

"I am Athenian," I said. His assumption that I was Thracian was a reasonable one. My mother was a Thracian and I had the green eyes and long, flaming hair so common among those people. Thracian mercenaries were common enough and I wore Thracian armour and wielded a Thracian weapon. But my father had been an Athenian general, a *strategos*, and as much as I belonged anywhere, I considered myself Athenian as well.

I leaned down so that my face was a foot's length from his. "Perhaps you know of me. My name is Daimon, son of Nikodromos." The Spartan's eyes flicked up towards mine in a flash of recognition. And fear, for I had sent many of his country's finest warriors to the Underworld. But the man regained his composure and resumed staring straight ahead.

I held the message rod in front of his face. "Who do you communicate with? Why would a goat-dropping of a mercenary like you be receiving coded messages?"

The Spartan sneered at me. "Untie me and fight me and perhaps I will tell you."

I was tempted. When I was a youth, I was rash and would have accepted his challenge. There are times when a man must rise to such a contest and be seen to display his courage and prowess, to show the enemy they are not his equal. But there was no need to fight a beaten man. And I was under no illusions. The Spartan would never talk. "Get them up!" I said, turning away.

"Coward! Shit-eating Athenian coward!" the Spartan yelled at my back. I ignored him.

We interrogated the rest of the prisoners, but there was little they could offer. There were a few men from Sparta, but they were not the elite Spartiate warriors like their leader, just common foot soldiers. There was a Theban and two Corinthians, traditional enemies of Athens, and five from Megara, which was no surprise, for if an honorable man has been born in Megara, I have yet to meet him. There were also two men of Athens.

"Keep those two alive, along with the Spartan," I said, looking at the Athenians in disgust. "Kill the rest."

The remaining bandits cried and begged for mercy. But they died quickly, for I take no pleasure in taunting or torturing prisoners, a lesson my father had inculcated me with from an early age. But the men in the forest had murdered and raped their way across Attica. They had earned their deaths many times over.

"Take what you can carry," I called out to my men.

Laden with booty and with our three prisoners roped together like livestock being led to market, we left the camp and the dead bandits for the scavengers. By the late afternoon we had descended to the plains of Attica to the north of Athens. The fields were ripe with the first summer grain crop, and olive trees and vines were already heavy with fruit, their scents mingling with that of the dust thrown up as we tramped down the well-worn track that passed as a road.

We came to a crossroad that I knew well, for our patrols often passed that way, as did many farmers and travellers going to and from Athens. The convergence of the track-ways was guarded by a wizened oak tree whose great gnarled branches reached out like an old man's fingers high above, providing a shady rest-spot or a place to take shelter from winter rains. The ancient tree belonged to no one. It is most likely still there, though I have not passed that way for many years. It had borne witness to the ravages of Spartan armies and the Persians before them, yet remained untouched by axe or fire, perhaps because the invaders recognized the power of the place and thought it better to leave well enough alone.

The oak was a place of worship. Tiny, crudely-carved idols hung suspended from the reaching branches and empty dishes and cups ringed the base of the great tree. They were the remnants of prayers for a successful birth or the recovery of a sick ox, for such things mattered to simple folk eking out a life in the hardscrabble lands of Attica. Some of the votives were for Zeus and the other Olympians, but far more were appeals to the local spirits that had dwelt in springs and trees and soil since the beginning of time. The educated class of Athens would have scoffed at the offerings, regarding such things as little more than the superstitious beliefs of ignorant farmers. But the locals knew the importance of keeping the resident deities happy, and so, the ancient covenants persisted. Today, I thought, as we approached the tree, we would honour the spirits with something more substantial than wooden statues or cups of wine.

"Time for a rest!" I barked, and in the shadow of the great tree we found much-appreciated respite from the blazing sun. The men passed around their water-skins and chewed on dried meat and stale bread from their kit-bags. None was offered to the prisoners. The Spartan glared at me. I ignored him.

The horizon rippled with the heat. I squinted at a distant shape that flickered in and out of view in the turbulent air. Presently the shape resolved itself into a cart pulled by two oxen. As the cart drew closer, I saw that the driver was a burly farmer with a youth sitting beside him. When it reached the crossroad, I stepped out in the middle of the track-way. The cart creaked to a halt. The farmer and the boy sat stiffly on the raised bench at the front of the cart, their wary eyes watching me as I approached.

I patted an ox's back as I passed. "They're fine-looking beasts. Where are you going today?" I asked, peering in the back of the cart. There was not much, just a few amphorae and covered pots. "Returning from the city with your son?"

"Who wants to know?" the farmer asked, putting on a gruff voice. From his sun-beaten face, his gaze darted nervously to the small horde of armed men who had risen to their feet to watch the encounter.

"We are the *peripoli*," I said. "We are returning to the city from a patrol."

The farmer's body relaxed visibly. "By the gods!" he said, taking his wide-brimmed hat off and fanning himself with relief. "I thought you were them marauders been camped out in the mountains. They pillaged three farms last month alone!"

I pointed at the prisoners. "This is what's left of them."

"What?" The farmer frowned in disbelief. "That sorry lot?"

"The rest are dead. You can sleep without fear tonight. Spread the word to your neighbours."

The farmer nodded agreeably. "I'll do that. Have no worries, young ..." His voice trailed off as he searched for a way to address me.

"My name is Daimon," I said. "Daimon of the *peripoli*."

The farmer's eyes widened in recognition. He swallowed hard. "I'll be sure to tell everyone. Zeus be with you!" he said hurriedly. He lifted up the reins, eager to put distance between us.

I reached out and took hold of his wrist. Not violently, but my grip was firm enough. "What is your name, O Farmer?"

"Smikres," he said.

"Smikres," I said. "I need one more thing of you."

"What's that?"

"To witness justice."

Rope is a very handy item to have, a point that was drilled into me by Lykos, the *peripoli* captain who taught me to be a ranger. Every patrol, he said, should have rope among its supplies, It can be used for tents, scaling walls and other obstacles, and a hundred other situations that might arise. This was just one such occasion.

Timonetus, one of the more agile members of our band, clambered up the oak tree. From his perch he caught the three ropes we tossed up to him, draping them over the sturdiest limbs so that their looped ends hung down at neck height.

The two Athenians died quickly, for I had Mnasyllus yank down on their kicking, suspended bodies to snap their necks. It was more than they deserved. The Spartan we left until last.

I put the loop of rope over his head. "You will not enjoy a soldier's death," I said.

"Eat shit, Athenian!" he said, and spat on me. But his actions could not completely mask his fear. All men fear something, even Spartans, who fear dishonour more than death. I took hold of the other end of the rope along with Mnasyllus and Tibetos. "Eat sh – "

His final words were cut off as his feet left the earth. He kicked and jerked. His face grew dark and his eyes threatened to burst from his head. Shit and piss dripped down his legs. His swollen, purple tongue lolled from his mouth. It was a terrible death. But the Furies, the spirits of vengeance, whispered in my ear. Their poisoned tongues recalled the defiled bodies of the children the Spartan had left rotting in the pounding sun a few days earlier and my heart hardened against him.

The sunburnt skin of the farmer Smikres turned a few shades paler. "Tell your neighbours that justice has been done here," I told him. He nodded weakly and stumbled back to the cart.

"Come on, boy!" he managed to choke out.

The youth turned to join his father but hesitated. He looked me in the eye. He was a lanky lad, perhaps fourteen or fifteen years old with dark curls and wide eyes. A life of farm labour had made him strong and he would surely fill out even more in the coming years. "You are truly Daimon of the *peripoli*?" he asked suspiciously. I nodded, wondering what ill-rumoured deeds had reached the boy's ears along with my name. But the boy surprised me. "Thank you," he said. He held out his hand. "You are a *daimon* for us. Like your name!" A *daimon* is the spirit of a dead warrior that protected the living in their times of need. The boy's comparison was more apt than he knew. I was a warrior, certainly, and though my body still breathed, the heart that beat within it had been without life for many years.

I shook the boy's outstretched hand. "You look strong. We can use lads like you in the *peripoli*."

The boy beamed, but then shook his head. "My father would never allow it!"

"Then go with your father," I said. "He is a wise man,"

The boy hurried to join his impatient father, who began beating his oxen into motion with a stick before his son had even taken a seat. As the ox-cart trundled away, the boy turned and waved one last time before disappearing over a rise.

We left the bandits suspended under the great oak tree. The swinging corpses served as a warning to those who would harm the people of Athens as well as a reassurance to Athenians themselves. Athens may have been weak, but her borders were still protected by the *peripoli*.

And by a demon.

CHAPTER 2

Athens is a small place.
Not in size, for the city and its surrounding lands constitute the greatest polis in Greece. In sophistication, too, the city itself makes upstart Thebes and dour Sparta seem but as backwater villages on the edge of nowhere. Nor does Athens lack for people, for the streets teem with men of all classes and vocations: the wastrel scions of aristocratic families; barking merchants and traders; wary yeoman farmers in from their fields to vote in the assembly or serve on a jury; and the myriad landless citizens who loiter about drinking away their daily wages. And slaves. Countless slaves of every station running about the streets, hauling their masters' loads, shouting at anyone who hinders them in their tasks, and shirking those duties whenever possible.

And despite this great, seething mass of people, Athens is like a small village. It is not possible to spend any amount of time walking its crowded, reeking streets without eventually encountering all manner of acquaintances, be they friends or enemies. Even when names are unknown, faces are recognized and noted.

Citizens and slaves of Athens are also, as a rule, small of mind. Jealously and pettiness manifest themselves as a thousand dramas every day in a never-ending contest to scrabble higher up the dung-heap of wealth and influence. The players are all united in one thing, however, and that is their disdain for outsiders, whom Athenian citizens almost as if by natural right consider inferior. Outsiders like me.

It counted for little that my father had been elected as a *strategos* five times. That I had slain the tyrant Kritias and helped restore democracy meant even less in the minds of many. My success in rebuilding the *peripoli* and protecting the borders of Athens made me tolerated at best, for I served some function at least. But my mother had been a Thracian slave, which meant I was denied my birthright to be a citizen. In the courts and in the assembly, even the poorest labourer had more rights than me.

Thus, on that day, returning from just having hanged the Spartan, I should have been more careful. Had I not drawn attention to myself, the people of Athens and I could have persisted in our normal state of mutual resentment. But I have always suffered from pride. I should not have let it rule me.

I should have known better.

IT WAS NOT MY INTENTION to cause trouble.

I did not want to cut through the agora that day, but my journey had been a long one and I was tired. The dust of the countryside clung to my skin like a second tunic and my empty stomach would not cease its rumbling complaints. I could have visited Thrasybulus in his home had I been more patient. But word was that the most powerful politician in Athens was at the *bouleuterion* on the west side of the agora. I would go to the council chamber and report to Thrasybulus about the bandits and their Spartan leader and be gone once again to shed my gear and quell my hunger. It should have been a simple matter.

It was a bad decision, for the gods and Fates conspire against me endlessly. If Tibetos had been with me, he would have steered me clear of any conflict. As it was, my level-headed friend had returned to the *peripoli* compound in the port of Piraeus with the rest of the men. I was alone.

Beside the southern stoa at the edge of the marketplace, I paused to take in the scene before me. As on most days, the agora thrummed with the activity of the rich and the poor and slaves. Vendors, money-lenders, speech-writers, barbers, slaver-dealers, healers, sausage-sellers and more competed for business, filling the air with their hoarse calls as they sought to lure customers away from their competitors. Under the cries of the merchants and hucksters was the murmur of more tempered discourse, for the marketplace was as much a hub of debate and socialization as it was a place for trade. Groups of men clustered on steps or in the shade of monuments, discussing the business of the day, engaging in vociferous debate, or catching up on gossip or rumours.

There was something else in the air besides the normal odours and clangour of commerce. I had grown up prowling the agora, picking purses and pocketing anything that would fit into my tunic, much to the displeasure of my father. This familiarity with the beating heart of the city allowed me to sense the mood of the agora as a sea-captain's instincts warned him of the subtle changes in wind and waves. And now it was as if a stone had dropped into a pool, sending its ripples in all directions. Whatever it was, it was not my problem. I would see to my business with Thrasybulus and be off.

Taking a deep breath, I prepared to wade into the sea of humanity. A voice stopped me. "Stranger! Can you spare an obol for an old soldier?" A one-armed beggar sat in the dust next to the stoa wall, his remaining hand clutching an empty bowl that he extended towards me.

The beggar's threadbare tunic was cinched tight around a waist that had surely been thicker in the past. The man, gaunt as he was, had a large frame and might have been strong once, but he had been betrayed by age and ill-fortune. His matted grey beard and thin hair framed a tired face with sad, clouded eyes that still retained a spark of intelligence. I squatted next to him.

"Where did you fight?" I asked.

The beggar grinned, revealing his few remaining yellow teeth. "Where didn't I fight, more like it!" he said. "Pylos! Chios! Thasos! A hundred battles!" His misted eyes flashed with pride at the memory of it.

"As a rower or hoplite?" I asked.

His eyes widened. "Do I look like a could afford my own armour?" he said with a raspy laugh. "No, I was a peltast, lad!" The lightly-armed peltasts with their javelins and hide-covered wicker shields were not much different from most of my comrades in the *peripoli*.

"And your arm?" I asked, glancing at the stump.

The beggar spat. "Got too close to a Spartan at Munychia!" he said, wiggling the stump. But he got the worst of it!" he added with a wink.

I raised an eyebrow. "You were at Munychia?"

The old man's chin rose slightly. "With Thrasybulus himself!" he declared.

The man had been my ally then, standing with the few against the many in a just struggle against the Tyrants. In my eyes, that made him better than most of those filling the agora that day. "I was there. It was a great victory," I said, not elaborating on the role I had played in that battle.

The beggar seized upon our new-found warriors' bond. "Surely you can spare a coin for a brother," he said. "Or perhaps two."

I smiled. "I can do better than that."

I pulled out the small bag of coins from the bandit camp, my share of the newly-minted tetradrachms we had found there. I poured a clinking stream of coins into the bowl, saving a few for my dinner. "Take these, old man, and don't squander it all on wine," I said, rising to my feet.

The veteran leaned forward, bringing his dimmed eyes close to the bowl. He looked up at me in disbelief at his sudden change in fortune. "May the gods protect you, stranger," the beggar said. "But what is your name?" I just waved and waded into the sea of activity that was the agora.

To the half-blind beggar, I would have been little more than a blurry form. I am taller and broader than most men, and with my long red hair and Whisper slung over my back, I was recognizable enough to those whose eyes still served them. The people in the agora knew me. I was the man who had slain the tyrant Kritias on the hill of Munychia. I had cut down the Spartan general Chairon in the streets of Piraeus. I had hunted down the remaining Tyrants and slaughtered them to a man. I had helped free Athens from slavery and taken vengeance on her enemies. But instead of the honour I was due, many resented my existence, for I, a non-citizen, had fought and won glory when they had yielded to the Tyrants' yoke. I was better than them and they knew it in their petty hearts.

Eyes fell upon me as I made my way through the jostling masses. Many stared, while others only dared furtive glances as I passed. Some whispered in hushed voices, no doubt fanning the embers of rumour kindled by my enemies. I glowered at them and they turned to evade my evil eye. At the very least, I had given them the chance to tell their wives and children how they had seen the Tyrant-slayer that day and lived to tell about it!

But not all looked upon me with resentment or fear. There were smiles and friendly greetings as well, for like the beggar, many had stood by my side when we defeated the Tyrants and the army of Sparta. Knowing nods were exchanged and some even called me by my rank of *lochagos* — captain. They knew me to be their friend and comrade.

A familiar voice shouted from the throng as I passed. "Dammo!" My mood lifted as I saw my friend Podaroes pushing his way towards me.

We embraced warmly. "What brings you here, friend?" I asked the silver-haired man with genuine affection. Podaroes was a member of the hoplite class, those with enough land to afford the arms and armour of an infantry warrior. The good-humoured warrior had been my first captain when I had gone off to fight as a young hoplite. He had saved me from my own youthful, suicidal craving for glory long enough to teach me how to fight and survive in the churning mass of flesh and metal that is a hoplite phalanx. He was wily with a nose for profit, but had a good heart.

Podaroes gave a coy smile. "Looking for the opportunity to part fools from their money, and with some success," he said, squeezing the bulging leather pouch on his belt.

"Do people ever learn?" I asked.

He shrugged. "A man's wagers are his own business." He gave my grime-covered armour and tunic an appraising look. "And you? It looks as though you've been on campaign."

"I've been chasing bandits on the border of Boeotia for nearly a month."

"Successful hunting?"

"You can ask the leader. He's hanging from a tree outside the city," I said, jerking a thumb in the general direction of the distant oak. "And he had this." I pulled out the *scytale* from a pocket in my kit-bag.

Podaroes weighed the Spartan code-stick in his hand. "Odd thing for a bandit to have," he observed.

"He was a Spartan. One of Lysander's, I reckon. Gods know he has enough of his spies in and about the city," I said. Podaroes nodded knowingly.

Lysander. Sparta was nominally ruled by its two hereditary kings, Pausanias and the younger Agesilaus. But it was the Spartan hegemon Lysander who wielded the true power in Greece. It was Lysander who had led Sparta and her allies to victory over Athens and now commanded the loyalty of most of Sparta's soldiers. Even so, Lysander was bound by tradition to obey his kings, and Pausanias, wary of his rival's growing power, had forbidden his upstart general from interfering in the affairs of the defeated Athens. Now, prevented from acting openly, Lysander sought instead to undermine Athens by more devious means, sending spies and agitators to work against leaders such as Thrasybulus and sow discord wherever possible in the hope of installing leaders loyal to him and him alone. I suspected that the bandits we had just slaughtered were one more part in Lysander's schemes to once again wield power over Athens.

Podaroes handed the *scytale* back to me and I returned it to my kitbag. We shook hands and were about to part ways when I realized my former captain might have possessed the answer to a mystery. "What madness has taken hold here?" I asked, indicating the jostling crowds of the agora. "Am I wrong, or is there a restlessness here? Has something happened?"

Podaroes creased his brow in confusion before a look of realization spread across his face. "Of course! How could you have known, being away hanging bandits and the like?" I shook my head, not understanding. "It is Sokrates! He has been condemned to death!"

My friend briefly recounted the trial of Sokrates and the jury's decision to sentence the old man to death not two days earlier. He left me with a final thought before we went our separate ways. "It is the talk of all Athens!"

I mulled over the news distractedly, pushing my way through increasingly dense crowds. The news of Sokrates' impending execution filled me with ambivalence. As long as I could remember, the ugly old man, with his bulging eyes and squashed, hog-like features, had been a familiar sight in the agora, where he would stroll about barefoot in his threadbare tunic, debating with anyone who was willing. Once, while I was a boy walking with my father in the agora, I had pointed at the odd-looking Sokrates and made fun of him, hoping to amuse my father. To my surprise, my conservative father, no great lover of sophists and philosophers, had reddened in anger and threatened to give me a thrashing if he heard me speak ill of Sokrates again. Over the years, my father's words came to mind whenever I saw Sokrates about the city. The old man seemed harmless enough.

Those who counted themselves among his followers, however, were far from harmless. The demagogue Alkibiades and the Tyrant Kritias had done more harm to Athens than all of Sparta in thirty years of wars. Other young men of influence had also come under the old man's spell and called themselves his acolytes. There was one in particular whom I despised. My mind darkened as I thought of my nemesis, but it did not matter, for I had arrived at my destination.

A knot of men was blocking the steps to the council chamber. I was not in the mood to go around them. I tapped the shoulder of the man immediately in my path to get his attention. He turned and an unwelcome face gaped back at me.

The man's name fell from my lips with disdain.

"Plato."

CHAPTER 3

"You!" Plato exclaimed.

His real name was Aristokles, Plato being a nickname from his youth. He later boasted that this name referred to his breadth of mind, but in fact it was because his ugly face was round and flat like a plate. His uncle was the Tyrant Kritias, who I had nearly cloven in two on the slopes of Munychia. Plato had been there too, but had fled like the coward he was.

The encounter drew the attention of the dozen or so agitated young men around him. One by one they fell silent as my eyes flicked across them. They had the long unkempt hair and beards that the intellectual class of Athens wore with such pride. To me they looked like nothing more than unshorn sheep. I turned my eyes back to Plato.

"Tell your flock of sheep to clear the way," I growled.

Standing a step up from me gave Plato some added height, though he was still half a head shorter than me. Perhaps this greater stature emboldened him. "You have no right to tell *citizens* what to do," he said, stiffening his back.

He was right, of course, but I did not care. I should have barged through them and been done with it. But his challenge irked me. He did not want to lose face in front of his flock. I wanted him to regret that choice.

"I understand that your master Sokrates has been sentenced to die," I said. The arrow struck deep, for Plato's look of defiance crumbled into one of pained sorrow. I loosed another barb. "It could be," I said, raising my voice so that anyone nearby could hear, "that the law-courts would be happy to see some of Sokrates' '*corrupted young men*' meet the same fate." Some bystanders started to gather about us, drawn by the possibility of an entertaining confrontation.

One of Plato's followers, a sharp-chinned young man, could not hold his tongue. "What would a *barbarian* know of a great man like Sokrates? He has taught us to think and free our minds of the restrictions of tradition!" he said loftily.

I sniffed at the air, feigning disgust. "It seems to me that all you have learned is to fart through your mouths instead of your asses," I sneered, playing to the growing crowd. The audience laughed. Plato reddened.

The young man's face pinched tight, but he was not put off. "My father spoke often of your barbaric vulgarity," he said, turning up his pointy little chin.

"And what father shat out a little turd like you?" There was a familiarity about his spade-sharp face.

"I am Myronides, son of Archinus."

I narrowed my eyes at the young man. Son of Archinus. The resemblance was plain. Now, like his father before him, Myronides chose to block my path.

Archinus, like me, had been a supporter of Thrasybulus against the Tyrants, but only, I suspect, because the Tyrants had confiscated the aristocrat's property and he wanted it back. Ally though he might have been, Archinus had also despised me, for he was a coward and it had galled him that Thrasybulus had placed so much trust and authority in me, the son of a slave. On the battlefield, Archinus was weak and a fool, something I had accused him of publicly on many occasions. But in the assembly, he was no fool. Archinus had spoken eloquently against a motion to grant me and those like me citizenship for our parts in liberating Athens from tyranny. His goal achieved, the black-livered old bastard had a seizure and died before I could ever get my hands on him. I regarded his spawn, the young Myronides, in silence.

His son must have mistaken my lack of response for awe. "And now," he said, raising his voice, "you do nothing but run errands like a dog for Thrasybulus." He was not wrong. In the past two years I had served the interests of Thrasybulus faithfully, but with little reward to show for it.

"Careful, boy," I said, though I was only a few years his elder. "It is not wise to anger the man who cut down the tyrant Kritias." It was a weak comeback, but the threat excited many of the spectators.

"My father said that Kritias was not slain by your hand," he sniffed. The claim was a misstep on his part. This was not a debate for some effete salon, but a fight to win the emotions of the crowd. I took advantage of the opening.

"How could your father have seen it? The coward Archinus was hiding in the back lines with the women and old men! Many here know it!" I said, sweeping my arm towards the mob that had gathered around us. Some shouts of support from the crowd gave support to my accusation. I stabbed a finger at the chest of Myronides. "And I do not remember seeing you there that day, boy. You must have been fighting for the Tyrants like the rest of these turd-sniffers." I looked towards Plato and the others. The frustrated shame that manifested itself on their silent faces told me that the accusation had merit.

"I was in Thebes collecting money for the war!" Myronides protested.

"Cowering behind the walls of Thebes, more like it! A coward like your father!" I taunted. More insults flew from the spectators. Myronides sputtered uselessly as the crowd turned against him. I turned on the simmering Plato. "Myronides is a poor pupil. A mere barbarian has stolen his tongue. It seems your flapping lips will need to pollute the air of the agora for some time yet!"

"You will not need to suffer us much longer," Plato said, glowering at me.

"You are going away to found your own colony of babbling idiots! The gods have blessed Athens!" I said with exaggerated reverence. The crowd, thoroughly behind me now, erupted into laughter.

Myronides piped up again. "Plato will build an academy outside the city walls where thinking men will not be bothered by the ill-bred masses!" he said triumphantly.

The boast caught me off guard. I turned back to Plato, ignoring the whelp. "An expensive proposition. Perhaps you will use the money your uncle stole from all the Athenians he murdered," I said coldly.

God of Sparta

"I have not a single drachma from my uncle," Plato said defensively.

I leaned in close so that only he could hear me. "Then whoever it is that supports you is a fool." For once Plato was speechless. I dismissed him and his gaggle of disciples with a disdainful back-handed wave and started to push my way towards the council building.

Myronides, attempting to salvage some honour, fired a parting shot at my back. "Look at him go! Fleeing to see his whore sister in her hovel!" he shouted, his voice cracking.

The words halted me like a spell. The hum of the crowd vanished as all those present strained to hear my response. I turned slowly to face Myronides. "What did you say, puppy?"

Myronides swallowed deeply, suddenly unsure of himself. He cast glances about, looking for support but none was forthcoming. If he had held his tongue then, I would have left, satisfied in revealing his cowardice. But the fool could not keep his mouth shut, just like his father. "Everyone knows what it is your sister does in her cave! She sells herself to anyone!" It was true my sister Melitta lived as a hermit in a crude dwelling in the hills outside the city. She was cursed with madness. But she was no whore, and I would suffer no one saying it was so.

It took all my willpower to restrain myself. "You have one chance," I said.

Myronides made the wrong choice. "A Thracian whore!" he spat.

In two steps I was upon him, seizing his long locks of hair and twisting savagely so that he was bent over like some aristocrat's bum-boy. He struggled to free himself but had neither the strength nor the will to do so, his weakness no doubt the result of too much time spent arguing philosophy rather than engaging in honest toil. He scrabbled and screeched as I dragged him down from the steps.

"Daimon! Release him!" Plato shouted at me. There was an imploring tone underlying the command. When I spun to look at him, I could see there was fear in his eyes — and affection? — for the young man squirming at my hip. But it was a command, one that I felt under no obligation to obey. With a growl, I continued to drag Myronides behind me.

Plato, having failed to sway me with words, lunged toward me. I caught his throat in my free hand and shoved him backwards, sending him tumbling over a bleating goat that someone had brought to the marketplace. He hit the ground hard on his shoulders and his tunic fell up around his shoulders, exposing his flapping genitals to the crowd, who roared with approval at the unexpected entertainment.

As Plato lay dazed, I dragged the babbling Myronides to a public cistern set up for livestock. I yanked him up so that we were eye-to-eye. I was half a head taller than him and he had to push himself up on his toes. "Stop your squealing, puppy!" I barked, and he did, his unblinking eyes wide with terror. "Your mouth is full of dung and needs to be cleaned."

Before he could utter another shit-smelling word, I plunged his head into the slimy water and held it there. Myronides thrashed and bucked until I jerked his head up. "Do you have something to say?" I shouted. Water spewed from his heaving chest and when his lungs were voided I thrust him under again. His struggles grew weaker but none of his philosopher friends dared risk their own necks for his because they were cowards.

Plato barged to the front of the frenzied crowd, stopping just short of my reach. He looked at me. There was desperation in his eyes. "Release him! Please! I beg you!"

My jaw clenched more tightly. But Plato's contrition satisfied my honour, so I obliged him. With a yank, I pulled Myronides's head from the fetid water. He sucked at the air like a gasping fish. The crowd laughed and jeered. He disgusted me.

And then Clotho, the Fate who spins our destinies, paused at her work as she considered how my thread should turn at that instant. She must have smiled as my actions made the pattern clear. I should have not have made her work so easy.

Myronides coughed, flecking my front with mucousy water. Disgusted, I threw the soaking young man back towards the stone steps of the council chamber. His sandal caught on a rut in the ground and he toppled backwards like a felled tree, his arms flailing uselessly. The back of his head struck the bottom stair with a crack like stone on stone, and he went limp instantly, as if his soul had been torn from him. A crimson pool began to spread from his head and drip over the edge of the step. The cacophony of the crowd suddenly dropped to a gabbling hum. I grimaced. *That* I had not meant to happen.

Plato rushed over and tried to rouse him, but the bleeding Myronides was unresponsive. Plato glared at me with hatred. We stared at each other like two dogs fighting for dominance.

"The Skythians are coming!" someone shouted and the throng strained their necks to see over their fellows.

Five brawny Skythians bulled their way through the crowd. The Skythians were public slaves who kept the peace. The club-wielding barbarians were selected for their strength rather than thoughtfulness, and they carried out their duties with ruthless zeal.

"He is there!" Plato shrieked, pointing at me. "He has killed a citizen! Strike him down!" he said, wild-eyed.

Whisper was still slung across my back. Even outnumbered, I could have cut down the Skythians with ease had I wished to do so. But I made no move towards my weapon. The Skythians were brutes but not evil, and I wished them no harm. But nor would I be beaten like a dog or flee like a coward. Not in front of Plato and his weak-livered speech-givers. I stood with clenched fists at my side.

But then the Skythians surprised me. One of them barked an order and his companions pulled up short, surrounding me but keeping their distance. "You will come with us," the leader said in that peculiar rolling accent of his people. The dark-haired Skythians brandished their clubs with assured familiarity, awaiting my response.

There was no fear in the leader's almond-shaped eyes. But there was wary respect, and I realized he knew me, if only by reputation. There was another victory to be salvaged here, if only a moral one.

I unclenched my fists. "I will come with you." The Skythian let out a breath, dipping his head slightly to acknowledge my surrender. He beckoned me to follow him. An angry murmur rolled from the mob, upset that they had been denied the entertainment of watching me take on my prospective captors.

I shouldered past Plato, leaving him to gape at my back. The remaining Skythians fell in behind me, escorting me to my new destination, for I knew where it was they led me.

I was going to prison.

CHAPTER 4

No one came for me.

Word of my detention would trickle through Athens until it reached the ears of my friends and comrades and they would see me freed one way or another. But on that first day, no one came for me.

This was not the case for the man occupying the cell beside mine. Visitors came and went like so many buzzing bees to a patch of flowers. A few of them cast wary glances in my direction as I leaned on the iron grill that filled the cell doorway and watched their comings and goings with a prisoner's bored interest. But I was a mere curiosity, whereas my fellow inmate was the most famous prisoner in Athens. Sokrates' death sentence, it seemed, had only acted to make him more popular than ever.

A familiar figure entered the prison yard. I sucked in the hot summer air between my teeth. Plato had arrived to see his master. Sensing my gaze boring into him, Plato froze mid-way across the open space and locked his eyes on mine. Finally, he came to some resolution and, visibly girding himself, strode towards me, eyes forward and head slightly bowed, his lightly balled fists held unmoving at his sides. He stopped a finger's length beyond my reach. I spat and the gob of saliva hit the dust at his feet with a splat.

"Have you come to apologize and set me free?" I said, curling my lip.

Plato lifted his chin slightly. "It is by your own actions that you find yourself in that cage," he said, looking down his nose at me.

"That logic must apply equally to your master Sokrates," I said, nodding towards the cell beside mine.

Plato winced at the jibe. "It is not the same thing," he said, his haughty composure beginning to crack."

I twisted the knife further. "He will die by poison, no?" I asked, recalling what Podaroes had told me in the agora.

It was too much for Plato. He stepped closer and lowered his voice. "Better than your end," he hissed. "You will be strapped to a post outside the city and left to choke in the hot sun! You will die worse than an animal for what you did to Myronides!"

"We will see," I said with exaggerated calm. Without warning I lunged at him through the bars and he stumbled backwards with a yelp. I grinned wolfishly at him and his face reddened. With a snarl, he turned and entered the cell beside mine as my laughter echoed through the prison courtyard.

IT WAS NOT UNTIL SUNSET that the muffled voices of Sokrates and his guests finally ceased. Plato was the last to leave, resolutely refusing to meet my stare as he strode across the courtyard with his jaw clenched. Night fell fast and the torches at the far end of tiny prison courtyard did little to illuminate the darkness of my cell. I lay down on the too-short pallet that would serve as my bed. The bare wood creaked threateningly under my weight but did not crack.

A voice spoke into my ear. "With whom do I share my accommodation this night?" the bodiless voice asked. My fellow prisoner, Sokrates, was speaking through a small gap in the stonework. I turned over on my side and ignored him. "It is Daimon, son of Nikodromos, if I am not mistaken?" he persisted. I did not respond. The old man took my silence as permission to pester me further. "I fought alongside your father once, you know," he continued. "It was in Phocis. I was in the second rank behind your father. A Megarian lodged a spearhead in your father's breastplate and he was driven down. I slew the man who thrust it," Sokrates said, recounting the memory with some relish in his tone.

I knew of what he spoke, for my father had recounted to me the tale many times when I was a child, though he had never mentioned Sokrates' part in it. I still have the breastplate, with its mended hole where the spear had done its damage. Despite my determination to ignore the old man, I found myself responding. "When the Spartans seized control of Delphi," I said.

"Yes! Yes!" Sokrates said with greater enthusiasm. "I could not have been much older than you are now! It is curious that the Fates have brought us together under such circumstances, is it not?"

"The Fates seek to punish me with your prattling, old man," I growled.

"Oh, I know how nattering words can grate upon one's ears!" Sokrates continued, brushing off my attempt to dissuade him from further disturbing my sleep. "Why, this cell has granted me refuge from the lashing tongue of my wife, Xanthippe! The gods have bestowed upon me the gift of peaceful slumber!" he said, chuckling.

"The gods have cursed me, then, with the opposite," I muttered.

Sokrates was quiet for a moment. "What harm have I done you, child?" he asked. The light-hearted tone had vanished, replaced by one of confusion. "I am a just a foolish old man awaiting death. My enemies are many, but I would not count you among them, for we have never met before."

I sighed, succumbing to the man's gentle persistence. "It is not you but those who follow you who have done me evil," I said.

"I seek no followers," Sokrates protested.

"Was the tyrant Kritias not your disciple?"

"He was not."

"But he claimed you as his teacher."

"Then I am a poor teacher, for he did not heed my words," Sokrates scoffed.

"I slew him at Munychia," I said.

"Then it was justly done. Does not the manner of a man's death say something of his deeds in life?" Sokrates asked.

I snorted. "If that is so, then it does not say much about your follower Alkibiades. He died by flame and arrow like a cornered dog."

"Alkibiades." Sokrates let the name hang in the air. Was there longing in the old man's voice? I would swear that I heard it. "Alkibiades," he said at last, "was not my follower. He was my failure."

"Your failure sent my brother Heliodoros to his death," I said.

"Alkibiades' flame burned so brightly," Sokrates said softly. "Like so many others, I too was drawn to his light. You do not know, Daimon, but for a time I was able to guide his impulses, to harness the good in him. But in the end, I failed and the power of his ambition consumed him and so many others, like your brother. It is my greatest regret. I am sorry for my role in that, young Daimon."

The apology disarmed me with its frankness. But my anger flickered anew as the cause of my present plight came to mind. "And Plato?" I asked. "Is he a failure of yours as well?"

Several heartbeats passed before Sokrates spoke. "Tell me," he said simply.

I recounted my numerous dealings with Plato, including my suspicion of his involvement in the murder of my wife. My Phaia. I finished with the incident in the agora and Plato's part in it.

Sokrates uttered not a word as I spoke. When I had finished, he considered his words carefully before responding. "I believe Aristokles to be a just man," he said, using Plato's real name. "Too clever by half at times, yes. And overconfident, too. Sometimes he is blind to what lies in the hearts of other men. But he is not an evil man."

But I knew Plato. He was sanctimonious, cunning, and a bastard. "I think it is you who are blind, old man," I said.

Sokrates sighed. "Do you think, young Daimon, that we can blame one man for the actions of another? Can you blame Aristokles for the evils committed against you by his uncle and his cousin?"

I was unmoved. "He showed his true self when he stood by their side and said nothing. He showed himself when he fought on the side of the Tyrants. He showed his weakness in the agora this day past!" In frustration, I kicked the small pitcher of water in my cell and it shattered in a spray of wet shards against the far wall.

My outburst did not quiet Sokrates. "Do you blame all those who stayed in the city when the Tyrants ruled?" he asked.

"Those who stayed until the end, yes!"

"Even those with wives and children and elders in the city?"

"They had a choice!" I said, slamming the table. "Many chose to fight and risk their families instead of submitting to the tyrants! They showed their arête, their courage, their virtue!"

Sokrates was warming to the subject. "Yes! Yes! But what is arête, Daimon?"

"It is our actions before the eyes of others. It is only by our deeds in this life that we can win *kleos* – fame – that will survive us once our souls have quit this earth!"

"Is it only before the eyes of others that our deeds gain worth? Is an act less brave or less good if it is not seen by others?"

The effort of the conversation made me rub my temples. "Gods, old man, I do not know!"

"Or does an evil deed become good when it is judged so by the many? Or is the deed itself inherently good or evil by itself?"

"I know good and evil when I see them," I said.

"Yes! Then you understand, do you not?"

My head was beginning to throb. "No, old man, I do not," I said tiredly.

"But you do, lad! You see that we recognize the inherent goodness and evil in others' actions and our own. You know, Daimon, I have a spirit that follows me and whispers in my ear — my own *daimon*, so to speak. When I am tempted to do evil or think evil of others unjustly, my *daimon* whispers of my error. My initial reaction is anger, for I do not wish to see the evil in my own heart, and I lash out at it, trying to drive it from my mind. But it is relentless. That is its nature. Only when I accept the truth of what my *daimon* is telling me do I become a better man."

"Do you have a point, old man?"

He laughed. "I do prattle, as you have said, but I hope my meandering path takes us to a destination worth arriving at! Tell me, Daimon: what would happen if you showed a man in the agora that his actions were evil so that he could not deny the truth of it? And in front of his fellows, no less?"

It sounded like a good way to start a brawl, and I told him so.

Sokrates clapped at this. "Yes! When a man sees his ugliness reflected in a pool, he is more likely to slap the water in anger and denial than to try to peer more deeply. Now our destination is finally in sight."

"These prison cells are our only destination, old man!" I said, shaking my head in the darkness.

"Daimon!" Sokrates exclaimed. "You see it then!"

"See what?" I asked, bewildered by the frantic swing of topics.

"Our similarity! That you and I are like the vessels of water in which our fellow citizens glimpse their own ugly natures, and they hate us for it. My questions undermine the false foundation of their arête, and it gnaws at their souls. The same happens when they spy you in the agora, the son of a slave who slew tyrants and Spartans while they stood by and did nothing. It is easier to lock us away in these cells than to face the truth we show them. These cells," he said, slapping the wall, "are the final destination for good men like us."

"I am not a good man," I said quietly. It was true. I had failed to protect my family, my wife, my son, my sister. They had suffered because of my actions. And I only knew one thing better than most and that was war. It was my talent, sending men to the Underworld by sword and spear. It was not the calling of a good man.

"I have heard it told otherwise, *pai*," Sokrates said. *Pai* could mean slave or child, but I knew from his gentle tone which one the old man meant.

"Then you have heard wrong, old man," I said.

"Then I can be the *daimon* that whispers in your ear," he said, dropping his voice. "Daimon's *daimon*, so to speak."

"And what wisdom would such a creature impart?" I asked with more than a hint of sarcasm.

"Look around you! A good man finds himself surrounded by other good men!" Sokrates asserted. "If you do not believe my words, then look to your comrades and companions, for the good and the innocent instinctively recognize the goodness in others. They will be drawn to the good man like moths are drawn to a flame in the night."

"I have seen many moths burn for their misplaced faith," I said.

Sokrates paused to consider this. "A good point, young Daimon! I will dwell on this further." He lapsed into a silence so long that I wondered if he had fallen asleep in his ruminations. "The Pythia!" he proclaimed suddenly. I flinched at the burst of sound.

I thought I had misheard. "The Pythia?" I asked. The Pythia was an old woman who lived in Delphi, a Parnassian town many days' journey from Athens. She is an oracle, the most famous in the world, for it is said that Apollo speaks through her. Men from all corners of Greece and the lands beyond seek an audience with her, for it is said that the answers to all questions can be found at her temple, at least by those willing to listen. And those willing to believe.

"You must ask the Pythia!" Sokrates repeated. "She will tell the truth of my words."

I had no interest in pursuing Sokrates' advice, for I have little faith in the fraudulent claims of oracles, seers, or any others who claim to speak for the gods. But the direction of the conversation had stirred unhappy memories to wakefulness. I seized the opportunity to change the subject to my more immediate predicament. "The Pythia will never hear my pleas if I am rotting on a post outside the city," I said, remembering Plato's threat.

"Bah!" Sokrates said, dismissing my concerns. "Have faith in the gods!"

I barked a laugh. "I would sooner place my faith in a Megarian claiming to be a trustworthy man!"

"Then perhaps you should trust in the wisdom of a jury of your fellow Athenians," Sokrates offered.

I scoffed. "Did the wisdom of your fellow citizens help you, old man?"

"I suppose if I am indeed guilty of the crimes of which I have been accused, then the judgment of the court is sound, and now I must face the penalty," he said, referring to his imminent execution.

"And you will let yourself die for 'corrupting the youth of Athens?'" I asked, remembering what Podaroes had said about the charges levelled against Sokrates.

"No, young Daimon. I will let myself die for staying true to my nature," he said with accepting resignation.

My antipathy towards the old philosopher dissipated in a breeze of weary sympathy. The old man's disarming lack of ego deflected my anger. "You need not die. A gold or silver key unbars all cell doors," I suggested. Escaping from prison by bribing the guards was so common as to constitute a tradition in Athens.

"I am in my seventieth year, young one. What awaits me outside this prison but decrepitude and illness? Here I choose the time and manner of my death, with what constitutes Sokrates still intact."

"And a final performance for your audience?" I ventured.

I could almost hear Sokrates wink through the stone wall. "They think that my death will silence my criticism, but in death I will become the immortal conscience of Athens."

"Its *daimon*?" I asked.

"That is for others, I think," he said, sighing. "You are kind to let an old man bend your ear with his ramblings, *pai*, but it is time for sleep, no? Let us see what the next day brings. Faith!" the strange man declared one more time before his tongue at last fell still for the night.

The old man's groans and grunts drifted through the gap in the wall as he settled down on his bed and soon there were only the rumbling snores disturbing the night. I lay down on my own hard pallet but sleep did not find me immediately, for the strange conversation left me pondering matters for a long time. I admired the old man's steadfast resolve if nothing else. In the end, I could do little more than see what pattern the Fates would weave for me. Perhaps, as Sokrates had suggested, the three sisters of destiny would do me right for a change. I let my fatigue overtake me and I entered into the familiar world of troubled dreams.

CHAPTER 5

Contrary to the optimism of Sokrates, the new day brought no respite from ill-fortune, save for the fact that Tibetos and the others had located me. Now my cell was so crowded with *peripoli* that their number rivalled the daily pilgrimage of devotees flocking to see Sokrates.

"How did you find me?" I asked Tibetos.

My friend arched an eyebrow. "It was impossible not to. The — " He paused to consider his next word. "— *incident* is the talk of Athens. They're already talking about how you ran Myronides through with your sword and then cut off his head right on the steps of the council chamber. That's not true, is it?"

"He tripped on his sandal," I said and recounted the tale for my audience.

"He said that about Meli?" Tibetos asked, his face darkening. He was very protective of my sister. "Maybe you should have cut off his head after all." The other *peripoli* murmured in agreement.

"It's my head that I'm worried about now," I said, dipping my hand into the sack of food my friends had brought me.

I munched gratefully on the fresh bread and hard cheese while my comrade Stachys apprised me of the full nature of the deep legal mire I had landed myself in.

Among the rough-mannered *peripoli*, the polished Stachys was an anomaly. Most of the fighters in our organization came from humble backgrounds. They were the sons of poor farmers or talented but landless veterans who knew no skills but those of war.

The *peripoli* provided such men with a home and a purpose. Stachys was different. An aristocrat from one of the wealthiest families in Athens, he had no need to include himself among our number. Indeed, his father had been a staunch supporter of the Tyrants and had expected his son to do the same. But Stachys had turned his back on his family and chosen instead to fight at the side of Thrasybulus. Following the restoration of the democracy, Stachys could have gone back to a semblance of his former life, yet he had chosen to aid me in my efforts in rebuilding the decimated *peripoli* to its former glory. He was, as Sokrates would say, a good man.

His educated, precise voice now held the attention of those present. "A lawsuit has been registered with the courts," Stachys said. "The trial is to take place in four days." Usually the legal process dragged on for some time before a dispute ever resulted in a trial. Four days was unusually fast.

"What's the rush?" I asked.

Stachys put his fingertips together. "Given the unique circumstances of the case, it was decided that to proceed without delay would be prudent."

"It does not seem prudent to me!" I said.

"It is better than the other possibility. As a non-citizen who has killed a citizen, you could have been executed without any trial at all."

"Why didn't they?"

"Your past service to Athens, as well as your father's, worked in your favour. Some of the magistrates, at least, argued for a trial."

"That must have upset the family of Myronides."

"No doubt," Stachys observed. "But it was not the family of Myronides who brought the accusation before the courts. That is another irregularity, one of many."

I frowned in confusion. Generally it was the family of the victim who chose or chose not to make a formal accusation against someone. "Then who was it?"

"Aristokles, son of Ariston."

I felt my anger rising. "Plato?"

"Myronides has a sister and a fourteen-year-old brother, neither of whom can register a lawsuit with the courts. He has one ancient uncle, but I've been told the old man can only babble and drool like an infant. A cousin is away in Cyprus and it is not known when he will return," Stachys finished, counting off each family member with his fingers. "With no relatives available, the courts made an exception and will allow Plato to present the case on behalf of the family."

"That was generous of them," I observed dryly.

"The magistrate himself was eager to see the trial go forward," Stachys said. That was not a surprise. The magistrates were selected from the richest class of citizens, many of whom had supported the Tyrants rather than side with Thrasybulus and his democratic faction. They had little sympathy for the likes of me.

"Am I to speak in my own defence, then?"

"The exception does not go that far," Stachys said. My knuckles cracked as I clenched my fist. As a non-citizen, I did not have the right to speak in the courts. An Athenian citizen would need to present my defence while I sat in the court like a child.

I suppressed my irritation as I considered the matter. Then the answer was obvious. "Go to Thrasybulus and tell him I request his aid," I said. "He will speak for me at the trial."

Thrasybulus was the most respected man in Athens. He had enemies among the elites, to be sure, but among the average citizens who would make up the bulk of the jury, the general's words would carry great weight. Moreover, he was the loudest man in the city. His booming voice would drown out the whiny protestations of Plato. The thought of witnessing such a humiliation made me smile.

Stachys nodded in agreement. "That would be a wise course of action. I will speak to him immediately."

When Stachys and the others had left, I lay on the wooden pallet and studied the crumbling stone ceiling as various trial scenarios played out in my mind. For the first time in days I felt a spark of optimism. Perhaps Sokrates had been correct after all.

But of course both of us were wrong to trust in the Fates.

For the gods hate me.

FOR TWO DAYS, I HAD NO VISITORS. The provisions left by Tibetos and the others kept me well fed if not entertained. Between bouts of exercise, I had little to do except observe the comings and goings about the prison.

Sokrates had been moved to a larger cell across the courtyard, for the daily stream of visitors only increased as his day of execution drew nearer. The reason for the postponement, the old man had told me, was that a ship had left Athens on a pilgrimage to the holy island of Delos the day before his trial. According to the old man, until the pilgrims had made their offerings at Apollo's temple there and had returned to the city, it would have been an offense against the god to carry out any public executions. "Apollo has been kind enough to grant me some days to put my affairs in order!" Sokrates had said cheerfully enough. Whether the ship would return in five days or fifteen he did not know. "But I am thankful for each day Apollo has seen fit to give me."

Those seeking wisdom from Sokrates or trying to persuade the old man to flee the city would stay late and the old man and I had little opportunity to speak as we had during my first nights in prison. When the sun set and shadows encroached on the world, I would fall asleep to the sounds of debate in the cell across from mine.

Plato came each day as well. My baleful gaze would follow him across the courtyard and I spat at his feet as he passed. He steadfastly avoided my stare and refused to acknowledge my presence, even when I taunted him. I was beneath his notice. It only infuriated me more and I simmered in the heat of my cell.

Two days before my trial, there appeared two figures at my cell door. One was Stachys. Beside him was Thrasybulus. Relief filled my heart, for like a caged beast I had long since grown weary of my confinement. One of the guards admitted the two of them to my cell while another warder brought stools for my guests.

I clasped hands with Stachys. His smile was forced and his words formal, something I put down to the presence of Thrasybulus. I turned my attention to my former general. "*Strategos*," I said with as much warmth as I could muster.

"Daimon," he said in a neutral tone.

Thrasybulus was fifty or so years old, but showed little of his age beyond the silver hair at his temples and in his beard. He was barrel-chested and thick of limb, and he looked more like a farmer or sailor than the first man of Athens. He was dressed in a simple robe, and only the thick gold signet ring on his right hand betrayed the fact that he was one of the wealthiest men in the city. We appraised each other for a moment, but as usual, his intelligent brown eyes revealed little of what he was thinking.

We had our disagreements, for we differed as much in our natures as earth and water. Thrasybulus was a *strategos* to the very depths of his being. He put winning wars before winning battles, much to my frustration on occasion, for where I saw opportunity, he often saw unacceptable risk. My impatience exasperated him at times, but he needed me for all that; I was his spear. He supported my efforts to rebuild the *peripoli* and made sure there were funds — never enough! — for our endeavours. I suspected part of him envied the freedom I enjoyed hunting down spies and bandits.

I sat down on the pallet, facing Thrasybulus. "*Strategos*, I apologize for putting you in this situation, but I am grateful for your aid," I said with sincere gratitude. But I had presumed too much.

Thrasybulus took a deep breath. "I cannot speak for you in the trial, Daimon."

The refusal struck me like a spear-point, its cold point digging deep into my chest. I had stood by Thrasybulus throughout Athens' darkest days and saved his life on more than one occasion. This was in addition to how I had aided him in his goal of protecting Athens from the schemes of hostile outsiders. Would he truly abandon me to whims of the lawcourts? I thought, against hope, that I had misheard him. "What did you say, *strategos*?"

The sense of betrayal must have been apparent on my face, for Thrasybulus' look of discomfort deepened. He did not address my question, instead extending a hand towards Stachys. "I have spoken to Stachys, and he has agreed to deliver your defence." The corner of Stachys' mouth twitched apologetically. My eyes bore into Thrasybulus. He raised a hand to cut off any protest. "Stachys far outstrips me in rhetorical ability and will serve you better than I ever could before the jury," he said.

Of my friend's talent, I had little doubt, but that was not the point of contention; it was Thrasybulus' standing in the city that the jury would esteem, not his flowery words. "You would abandon me, *strategos*?" I asked, biting each word.

His face tightened. "It is not as simple as you think, Daimon."

"It never is with you," I shot back.

"By the gods, Daimon!" Thrasybulus thundered. "You killed a man from a prominent family in front of hundreds of people in the agora!"

"I killed no one. The fool tripped on his sandal," I said coldly.

Thrasybulus bowed his head and pinched the bridge of his nose. "I am not as powerful as you think, Daimon. Many influential men in the assembly are in the pay of Lysander. They seek to undermine me at every turn. Were I to defend you in the trial, opinion would turn against me enough to weaken Athens even further. It would be a gift to Lysander and his efforts to seize control of the city."

I had expected this justification. What Thrasybulus said was likely true, for he knew the politics and factions of the assembly far more intimately than I ever could. I was just a soldier in a greater struggle. Yet this knowledge did little to the dull my sharp feeling of betrayal.

"You should have had them killed," I said. Thrasybulus knew of whom I spoke, for it had long been a source of disagreement between us. When the Tyrants had been defeated and democracy restored, many former collaborators remained in the city. I had advised Thrasybulus to have the worst of them executed and the others exiled. Thrasybulus had opted for reconciliation, much to my disgust. Now, not only did the traitors oppose Thrasybulus in the assembly, but they were paying bandits to kill Athenians in the countryside. In his heart he knew I was correct, though he would never admit it, even now.

"Not all problems can be solved with a sword, Daimon."

"Yet somehow it always seems to come down to our swords," I said, pointing to myself and an uncomfortable-looking Stachys, "to clean up the problems you should have taken care of long ago. That *would* have been taken care of if only you would heed the advice of others."

Thrasybulus resisted my baiting. He leaned forward. "We — you and I, Daimon — have worked to make Athens strong again. I will need you in the future as well." He rose, indicating that the visit was at an end. Stachys also stood, but I stayed seated, refusing to acknowledge him.

Before he turned at the door and granted one concession as he left. "We must let the trial proceed. I know your cause is just, Daimon, and I believe that the jury will believe it so. Should things go badly, I will use whatever means necessary to see you safe, but not before." He knew me well enough not to tell me to place my faith in the gods. The guard opened the door and Thrasybulus departed. Stachys remained with me in the cell.

For a few heartbeats, neither of us ventured to break the awkward silence. Finally, I spoke. "Stachys, I did not mean to suggest that I doubt your abilities. I apologize if it appeared so."

Stachys waved off my words. "There is nothing to apologize for. I know the worth of the *strategos*' reputation had he been willing to bring it to bear." Stachys was never one to avoid hard truths, and I valued his perspective. I know that his next words were not what he wished to say. "Perhaps you should consider leaving Athens."

Leave. It was a tactful word for 'flee.' Even for a prisoner of my notoriety, escape would not have been difficult. A quantity of silver much less than what I had given the beggar in the agora would see my cell door and that of the prison conveniently unbarred at night. I had suggested as much to Sokrates. But I would not go into exile of my own volition.

I sighed. I stood up and put my hands on my friend's shoulders. "No, we will do as Thrasybulus said. Go and write your speech for me, Stachys, and make it a good one!"

He gave me a solemn nod, but then a resigned smile forced its way to the surface. "I should not be surprised, should I? After all, you always fight. It is reliable as the sunrise." Shaking his head, he said his farewells and the cell door shut with a clang, leaving me alone to my thoughts.

Stachys' advice had been prudent. Why had I rejected it? There was always work for mercenaries of my skill and experience. I could go to Thrace, where I would be welcomed by my friend Prince Zyraxes. The Thracians would appreciate me far more than my fellow Athenians. But I would stay and fight.

In great part it was because of my pride, my hubris. Now I am old, almost ancient, and I understand the danger of pride. It leads men to folly and death more often than not. But if age has given me any measure of wisdom, I know also that it is pride drives men to greatness as well. Even now, my name is known across Greece, feared even. Would I have stood against gods and armies if it had not been for my pride? Perhaps it was that I would have felt shame at fleeing when old Sokrates in the next cell faced death with such calm. Pettiness is as great a wellspring of pride as any other.

But mostly it was for my son. Nikodromos had been born five years earlier on the same night Athens lost the war with Sparta. It was an ill omen, but not as inauspicious as being my son, for in truth I was a poor father. The boy lived in the household of my childhood tutor, Iasos. If I was not patrolling the borders of Athens with the *peripoli,* I was on some other mission for Thrasybulus. My son hardly knew me.

Niko's mother, Phaia, was dead. She had been Athenian, and from a fine family at that. Yet that counted for nothing as I was not a citizen, so by the laws of Athens, neither was Nikodromos. Thrasybulus had promised to gain me citizenship, and through me, my son. He had failed so far, but had at least convinced the assembly to grant me the right to own a house in Athens, my father's house that was usually only occupied by my servant Iollas. But were I to flee now, to go into exile, any chance of my son being granted citizenship would be lost, however remote that possibility was. all for some loudmouthed fool who fell over his own sandals. He should have known better than to insult my sister, I thought.

The drone of voices from Sokrates' cell drifted across the courtyard unabated. Sokrates' distinctive voice was clear as he questioned, argued, and parried in the verbal battle with his acolytes. Always fighting. Never backing down, I thought as sleep overcame me.

I had odd dreams that night in which the spirits of the Underworld beckoned me. It was a cold and miserable place. I know the dreams came from fear.

There are men who claim to feel no fear in combat. Perhaps it is so, though I do not believe them. But on the battlefield, at least, a man's fate depends in large part on the courage and skill he brings with him.

Yet only a fool would say they do not fear the lawcourts of Athens, where one's fortune rests on the verdict of a mob whose decision not even the Fates themselves can predict.

CHAPTER 6

"Daimon! Daimon, son of Nikodromos!" It was Sokrates. The old man stood on his dirty bare feet in the open doorway of his cell. So many visitors came to speak with him that the warders did not even bother closing the iron grate anymore, trusting Sokrates to keep his word not to flee. "Where is it you go this day?"

An escort of four guards with swords and leather armour were accompanying me to the prison's gate where Stachys awaited me. A pair of manacles chafed at my wrists. The guards, it seemed, were less willing to extend their trust to me. I stopped and raised my hands. The chain joining my two wrists clinked as I shook the manacles. "I am going to the lawcourts."

Sokrates' bushy eyebrows rose in surprise. "It has come so soon?" It usually took some months before a case ever reached the courts, but Plato had been zealous in his desire to see me prosecuted. Only seven days had passed since the unfortunate end of Myronides.

"Athens is eager to see me gone, one way or another," I replied.

Sokrates wagged a finger at me. "I told you to have more faith, young Daimon," he chided me. "When you are free," he said confidently, "you must return to report to me."

"Plato will be able to tell you the tale," I said.

The old man scrunched up his face. It made him even more pig-like than normal. "Aristokles?"

"He will know every word that is said. It is Plato who is speaking against me, after all."

A troubled look flickered across the old man's face. "Aristokles?" he repeated. "He told me of no such thing." Sokrates frowned deeply and stared at some undefined point on the ground, uncharacteristically at a loss for words.

Impatient at our dawdling, a guard pushed at my back. "No more time to talk, old man," I said, leaving Sokrates to his troubled ruminations.

I had little time to dwell on my odd encounter with Sokrates. Stachys met me outside the prison gates. "Are you ready?" he asked. He radiated refinement, with a fine yellow robe draped over a pure white tunic. I was wearing a simple dun-coloured tunic and robe that Tibetos had brought me the day before. At least they were clean.

"Let's be done with it," I said, suddenly impatient.

From the prison, the lawcourts were a short walk across the agora. The journey, however, took much longer than it should have, for a mob of gawking onlookers impeded our every step. Everywhere people pointed our way or craned their necks for a better view. Athenians thirsted for drama, for distraction

"Your trial has attracted some interest," Stachys observed dryly as our ring of guards continued to shove its way through the crowds.

"But do they want to see me freed or executed?" I said, sweeping my manacled hands towards the throngs of onlookers.

Stachys forced a grim smile. "Both."

At that moment, someone shouted over the crowd. "Death to murderers!" I peered in the direction of the voice and spotted a long-haired young man atop the altar near the stoa. He cupped his hands around his mouth and continued chanting as he tried to incite the crowd against me. But his shouts were cut off as a small forest of arms reached up and hauled him down from his perch, eliciting a scattered cheer among the spectators.

"Not everyone hates me, then," I said.

"Let's just hope that's how the jury feels," Stachys muttered as we entered the building that housed the lawcourts.

The benches on the perimeter of the court overflowed with humanity. Those who could not find seats stood in the rear or crowded the entrance to the chamber. The guards removed my manacles, and I rubbed my wrists as I scanned the faces of the men who would judge me. Elderly grey-heads predominated, but whether their age signalled wisdom or senility I was not certain. "How many jurors are there?" I asked Stachys.

"Five-hundred and one," Stachys answered. "Give or take a few. I was told that twice as many showed up for the lottery to be jurors for your trial. You are the best drama in the city today, my friend," he said. Somehow I was not reassured. Five hundred far exceeded the one or two hundred jurors that sat in judgment of normal cases. But as Stachys had said, today was no normal set of proceedings. Stachys and I sat down on the wooden bench provided for the accused.

Plato strode into the court, provoking a buzz of anticipation in the chamber. Had it not been for his broad, ugly face, I might not have recognized him. His normally unkempt philosopher's curls had been whipped into something resembling order. Gone too was the dirty robe favoured by his fart-talking philosopher ilk. Today he was garbed in a fine saffron robe more in keeping with his aristocratic background. I felt the eyes in the room shift my way to gauge my reaction to the arrival of my antagonist, and I made sure to stretch my arms out and give an exaggerated yawn, which elicited both laughter and murmurs of disapproval. Plato ignored me in kind, refusing to look my way. He approached the red-robed magistrate and shook the man's hand. The two exchanged a quick word and Plato smiled before taking his own seat on the opposite side of the floor.

"Old friends with the magistrate?" I asked cynically.

"It's bad form," Stachys said. "But it doesn't matter. The decision belongs to the jury alone. The magistrate only directs the proceedings."

"Turd-sniffer," I muttered towards the magistrate.

The magistrate frowned at me before striding to the centre of the chamber. Stachys nudged me. "Time to start," he said. He held up a finger of warning. "Don't make a scene and we might get through this."

"When have I ever caused trouble?" I asked innocently.

Before Stachys could respond, the magistrate raised his hands. The thrum of voices subsided and finally died until the only sound in the court was the muffled hum of activity from the agora outside. "This trial is to determine whether this *man*," he said pointing my way, "is culpable in the untimely death of the citizen Myronides, son of Archinus."

Man. The magistrate belittled me by rendering me nameless, like a slave. My forefathers had been citizens of Athens since the time of Achilles, longer than most who would sit in judgement of me now. I was the Tyrant-slayer. I had bested a Spartan general in single combat. I was not nameless. Stachys' warning to me was in vain, for I could not let the slight pass unchallenged. I cut the magistrate off before he could utter another word. "I am Daimon, son of the strategos Nikodromos, of the deme Skambonidai." My voice echoed through the chamber.

My outburst rekindled the swell of hushed voices from the jury benches. The magistrate scowled at my lack of decorum. Plato shook his head like a disappointed father. I raised my chin, daring the magistrate to challenge me. His eye twitched, but he turned away.

Attempting to wrest back control of the proceedings, he gestured for silence. "I will offer a prayer to Athena," he said over the drone of the spectators. "I will offer a prayer!" he repeated, raising his voice further. With reluctance, the citizens ceded the floor to the magistrate, though I suspect it more in eagerness to move on to the trial itself rather than out of respect for the city's patron goddess.

With an impatient flick of his fingers, the magistrate beckoned a waiting slave who scurried over bearing a simple white cup. The magistrate took the vessel and, tilting the cup, dribbled the wine onto the grit of the courtroom floor as he addressed Athena. Glaring at me all the while, he invoked the goddess to grant the jurors the wisdom to see justice done. His appeal done, he pointed at Plato. "I call on Aristokles, son of Ariston," he said, using Plato's true name, "to state the case for the prosecution."

Plato acknowledged the magistrate with a bow and took his place in the centre of the chamber. As he began to speak, a slave removed the wax plug from the bottom of the water-filled vessel on the table beside the magistrate. Water jetted out like a stream of baby's piss into a similarly-sized pot on the ground below. When the *klepsydra* was empty, Plato's allotted time to speak would be over.

I would not sully your ears, Athenian, by repeating in detail the long-winded catalogue of lies and slanders that spilled forth from Plato's flapping, effeminate lips. I was a foreigner, an outsider with no standing among the citizens of Athens, he said. Who was this red-haired barbarian? he asked. I had no business and no land, yet I seemed to live well. Could it not be that I was one of the bandits that plagued the rugged borders of Attica, he insinuated? With a flourish, he pulled a long object from within the folds of his saffron robe. I swore under my breath. It was the *scytale* I had taken from the Spartan bandit leader. Plato had somehow gotten hold of it.

"How is it," Plato asked, holding the code-stick aloft, "that the man you see before you comes into the possession of a Spartan *scytale*?" The jury gasped. The *scytale* had no bearing on the case of Myronides, but as a means to cast further shadow over my already dark reputation it was an effective ploy. The jurors turned their eyes my way.

"I got it from killing Spartans!" I said in a loud voice.

Plato shrugged and shared a doubtful look with the jury before continuing his assault on my character. He skilfully returned to the matter at hand. My reputation for violence was well-known, he said. It was little wonder, then, that I had, without provocation, set upon innocent citizens – Citizens! – while they went about their business in the agora. The *klepsydra* was temporarily plugged while Plato paraded a string of lying witnesses before the court to attest to my wickedness.

"Does he have everyone in the city lined up to speak against me?" I whispered. Even the jurors were shifting restlessly to restore feeling to backsides pressed too long against stone benches.

"He can call as many witnesses as he wishes," Stachys said.

"They might acquit me just to shut him up," I said, nodding towards the fidgeting jurors.

Stachys quickly crushed my optimism. "Or convict you," he replied.

At last Plato seemed to exhaust his supply of perjurers. But I was wrong. The fat-headed fool strode to the doorway of the court and returned to the centre of the chamber roughly leading a reluctant young girl by the arm. The girl was perhaps fourteen or fifteen years of age, and was clearly terrified of the public scrutiny from a thousand leering old men.

"Who's she?" I asked. Stachys' frown only deepened.

Plato launched into another long-winded speech. "This," he said, holding the trembling girl's hand aloft, "is the daughter of

Eukippos." Being a girl, she had no name worth saying, for like me she had no status. She was hardly better than a slave. An image of my sister Melitta appeared in my mind's eye. It was for her honour that I had dragged the feckless Myronides around the agora. If Plato had dared touch my sister the way he handled this girl, I had no doubt that Meli would have spilt his guts in the middle of the court. The thought brought a smile to my face.

Plato's clipped voice pulled me out of my pleasant fantasy. "She was betrothed to Myronides, before his savage death at the hands of this man," he said, pivoting and pointing at me for dramatic flair. I massaged my forehead.

Stachys knit his brow. "That's underhanded," he whispered as Plato droned on with his tirade. "She is not a proper witness. Plato is just using her to sway the jury."

"She should be thanking me for saving her from a life of misery with that scrawny bag of wind," I said, recalling the worthless Myronides. Our whispered exchange drew an annoyed stare from the magistrate. I winked at him and his face pinched up as though he had just drunk some vinegary wine. If women could be called as witnesses, I wondered, perhaps we could present my sister to the jury and then have her threaten the jurors with a curse if they convicted me.

Plato finished bemoaning the fate of the poor girl, widowed before even becoming a bride. The girl, no longer needed, was dragged out of the court like the stage prop she was. I knew her father Eukippos was a wealthy man and would no doubt be able to marry her off to another aristocratic household where she would spend her life sequestered away from the eyes of wicked men like me. The Fates were cruel to the daughters of wealthy men.

With no witnesses remaining, the plug was once more removed from the *klepsydra*, and Plato concluded his case against me. Plato reminded the jurors of the longstanding grudge I harboured against the victim's late father, one of the most selfless citizens in Athens by his telling, never mind that fool Archinus has been a cowardly piece of weasel shit. So, Plato led the jury on, was it not reasonable to conclude that I had attacked the son now that my chance for revenge against the father had been denied to me? I snorted loudly, drawing another sharp stare from the magistrate. Plato's final plea to the jury dribbled out of his mouth like an old man's piss while the last drops of the water-clock did the same. Surely, he said, Athens must do justice to its fallen citizen and be rid of a man who brought the ill-will of the gods down upon the city. Plato gave a curt bow and strode back to his bench, pointedly ignoring me as I followed him with a poisonous stare.

A murmur rippled the jury. Many shook their heads and threw disapproving looks my way. From my bench, I glowered back at them.

The magistrate rose and pointed at Stachys. "Stachys, son of Hierios, you may begin your defence of ..." The magistrate cocked an eyebrow. "The Thracian," he finished, choosing the word most likely to bias the jury against me.

Stachys leaned over to me. "A prayer to the gods would not hurt right now," he whispered.

"I hate the gods," I growled back.

"Then hope that they are otherwise occupied this day," he said, rising to his feet. The slave pulled the wax plug from the refilled water-clock, and Stachys began his attempt to save my life.

Stachys, wielding the full power of his aristocratic education, presented an eloquent defence on my behalf, and I doubt Thrasybulus could have done better. To be truthful, it was good fortune that I was not permitted to speak for myself, for I have no skill with fine words or clever arguments.

Stachys first called on Podaroes as a witness. Always the actor, Podaroes put on a good show. With great emotion he related the torrent of insults from Myronides and his fellow instigators that I had borne with equanimity. and only when Myronides had slandered my family did the need to defend my honour become necessary, as every right-thinking member of the jury would agree, he added. Podaroes concluded his account and cast a sympathetic glance my way before taking a seat at the edge of the court.

His single witness done, Stachys moved on, wisely playing down the incident itself, instead speaking of my father, the respected *strategos* who had his whole life fought for democracy. He explained how I continued that legacy, valiantly patrolling the borders of Attica with the *peripoli* and keeping the jury members and their kin safe from the predations of bandits and the enemies of Athens. Stachys regaled the transfixed jurors with the tale of how I myself had cut down the cruel tyrant Kritias and thus helped restore democracy to the city. And Stachys, dropping his voice so that the jurors had to lean forward to hear him, reminded the jury that the man now speaking against me was the tyrant's nephew and had fought alongside his uncle that day to keep Athens under the domination of Sparta. Was it any wonder, Stachys asked, shaking his head in disgust, that Plato now sought my prosecution? As his remaining time ran out of the *klepsydra*, he appealed to the jury's decency, reminding them of my long service to Athens and how Myronides, after attacking the honour of my family, had tripped over his own sandals and struck his head, surely the judgment of the gods for his hubris.

Stachys returned and took his place beside me on the bench. He let out an exhausted breath. "How did I do?" he asked. His eyes were tired, for he had spent a good portion of his soul delivering his spirited defence.

I looked upon him with new eyes, for I understood better how the courts were merely a battlefield of a different nature, one which Stachys had just bestrode like a true warrior. "It could not have been finer," I said. I was proud to call him my friend.

"I just hope they agree with you," he said, glancing at the jury.

The magistrate rose and addressed the jurors once more. "Men of Athens," he said. "It is time to render your judgment." He gestured towards the entrance and two slaves carried in the two worn vessels that would determine my fate.

One by one the men of the jury filed past two urns, depositing a flat bronze token in each with a muffled *clink-clink*. In the first vessel they cast their true vote – a hole in the token for condemnation or a solid token for acquittal – while the second vessel caught the unused token. I strained my ears and wondered if the two kinds of tokens made different sounds, but if they did I could not distinguish between them. The verdict of some jurors was clear enough in any case, for they held their tokens aloft for all to see: some sympathetic jurors showed their solid disc, while others displayed their pierced one while fixing a look of contempt on me. But most of the jurors merely shuffled past the urns before a waiting attendant handed them a third token that they would exchange for their three obols' pay for serving in the court that day. Such was the price of justice in Athens.

When the final juror had cast his vote, two slaves picked up the first urn by its ear-like handles and hauled the token-laden vessel to the magistrate's table. They overturned it and my fate came pouring out in a torrent of clinking bronze discs. The count began.

From our bench, Stachys and I watched as the slaves separated the discs into two piles, but our view was partially obscured by the people surrounding the magistrate's table. Plato, too, craned his neck in his eagerness to know the verdict. Two officials kept tally of the votes, scratching a line into a wax-covered writing board for each disc counted.

I attempted to follow the count, but soon lost track. All that was apparent was that the jury was split. Like the ebb and flow in a battle between two evenly-matched armies, the two piles of discs fought for supremacy on the tabletop, with one pile surging ahead, only for the other to surpass it in size a moment later.

"It's close," Stachys murmured, his eyes intent on the count.

The last disc was tallied. The two heaps of discs were identical in size. I glanced at Plato. He bit his lip uncertainly.

The two officials handed their tablets to the magistrate, who compared their numbers. Confirming that the numbers were the same, he nodded to the two men and lay the tablets on the table. He raised his hands, holding them aloft until complete silence settled over the chamber. I searched for any clue of the verdict, but the magistrate's face betrayed no emotion. And then he spoke.

"By the wisdom of Athena and a vote of two-hundred and forty to two-hundred and sixty-one, the jury has rendered judgment. The court finds the man Daimon –"

The magistrate paused, as though savouring the next word.

"Guilty!"

CHAPTER 7

The court erupted into a battle of competing voices.

The cheers of those who hated me crashed against the angry shouts of my ardent defenders, whose number was not insubstantial. A scuffle in the north gallery of benches began to spread like a plague until the entire court was a cesspool of shoving, yelling conflict. It was chaos. It was wonderful.

The magistrate, having lost all control, blinked amidst the whirling storm that had engulfed the chamber. At last he recovered from his shock and began gesturing madly at the Skythian guards to step in and restore order. The Skythians waded into the fray with enthusiasm.

The look of triumph on Plato's face had not waned. Our eyes met across the floor of the court and he gave a thin smile. In the pandemonium, I could have throttled him then and there and no one would have noticed. I took a step towards him and the gloating in his eyes turned to fear, for he was a coward above all things. Stachys, seeing my intent, wisely held me back.

"Don't give them a reason to kill you right here!" he shouted over the din. Still seething at the verdict, I somehow yielded to the common sense of my comrade's advice.

In the end, the persuasiveness of Skythians' dense oaken clubs overcame the animosity pervading the court. Order reasserted itself, and the jurors, many bearing fresh bruises on their persons, sat their backsides down on the benches. The magistrate glared at them like a teacher who had just scolded a class of unruly children. Lingering scores would need to be settled later. For there was still the matter of my punishment to be decided.

The Fates must have smiled as they spun my destiny on their looms, for the strangeness of that day was far from done. In principle, it was a simple matter. Both Stachys and Plato would suggest a punishment. Then, by a show of hands, the jury would choose one punishment or the other. This, in theory, would lead to a fair punishment, forcing rational men to moderate their demands for either too harsh a punishment on the part of the victor, or too lenient a proposal from the condemned. But the verdict stoked the furnace of indignity and shame in my chest. I was far from rational.

As my resentment bubbled inside me, Stachys leaned close. "I recommend we offer to pay half a talent to Myronides' heirs," he whispered.

"Half a talent!" I hissed. That was many years' earnings for most citizens, and almost all the money I had secreted in various caches around Athens.

Before Stachys had a chance to tamp down my anger, the magistrate pointed at me. "What punishment do you propose for the death of Myronides?" he commanded, barely suppressing a smile. Bastard. Across from us, Plato, his fingers twitching, gazed upon me like a wolf stares at a lost sheep.

Stachys stepped forward to answer the jury leader's request. "We feel that a payment of – "

I could contain my anger no longer. I leapt to my feet and cut off Stachys before he could utter the offer of a half-talent's compensation. I would not beggar myself for that worthless lump of dung Myronides. I would not give Plato the satisfaction of watching me haggle for my punishment. "I will pay nothing!" I shouted, pointing my finger at the magistrate. "I will pay not a drachma! Not an obol! I will pay nothing!" But I was not done. "It is I who should be compensated for what I have done for Athens! For protecting your worthless skins while you sleep or gossip like women in the agora! It is I who should be asking what you should pay me! You are not my betters!" With a roar of frustration, I sat down and glowered at the stunned faces of the jury.

Plato's eyes flashed in triumph. He could now ask for anything and it would be granted. Exile from Athens and confiscation of my property would have been generous. But Plato had promised that he would see me strapped to a wooden frame and left to die. That he would get his wish was now a real possibility because of my rashness.

The magistrate said something to the jury, but I could not hear it over the pounding of blood in my ears. Stachys spoke. "That was *not* wise," he said.

I hunched over further. "To the crows with them!" I spat, watching the magistrate prattle on.

"I heard that your fellow prisoner Sokrates said much the same thing as you at his trial. That Athens should pay him, that is."

The revelation broke through my simmering rage. "Truly?" I asked. My respect for the old man grew.

"Look what happened to him," Stachys muttered. He grasped my forearm and leaned close to my ear. "The *peripoli* are outside the courthouse. They will die before they let you be led to the execution ground," Stachys said.

My chest tightened at this declaration of loyalty from my brother. "You must tell them to stand down," I said. "They are not responsible for my rashness. Give Thrasybulus a chance to honour his word."

Stachys smiled grimly. "There is not a man there who does not owe you his life from one time or another. We will take our own counsel in this, Dammo." The resolve in his voice told me he would not be swayed by either argument or command. As I have said, he was a good man.

I let out a long breath. "Thank you, Stachys. For everything. But," I said, nodding towards a scene of some commotion at the courtroom entrance. "Do not loosen your sword quite yet." We looked on as a thin, older man insisted on being admitted with increasing irritation. He gestured at Plato, who in turn appealed to the magistrate. The magistrate barked an order to the courtroom guards to admit the man, who hurried over to Plato's side. The murmur of the jury grew to a low rumble at this breach of protocol.

"Is this your doing?" Stachys asked.

I shrugged. "I've been in prison for the past seven days," I said. "Not much I could do from there." The man took Plato aside and began to whisper in his ear. The interloper seemed familiar. "Do you know who that man is?" I asked Stachys, my eyes not leaving

Plato and the messenger as the two men's whispered exchanges grew more and more heated.

"He is Chaerephon," Stachys said. "He is a close friend of Sokrates," he added, raising an eyebrow. Now I know where I had seen the gaunt-looking man: he was one of the many visitors who had come to see the old philosopher in his cell.

Whatever the message was, it must have been important, for the man's lips moved with some urgency. Plato's eyes narrowed and then opened wide in disbelief. His face tightened in anger and he shook his head like a spoiled child. Suddenly, Plato's cry cut through the background drone of the jurors' voices. "No! I will not!" he shouted. He glanced my way, a look of desperation upon his face.

Whatever the old man said in response was masked by the noise in the courtroom. His skeletal finger jabbed Plato's chest. His mysterious ultimatum delivered, the man crossed his arms. Plato blinked hard against the burning frustration in his eyes. At last he slowly turned to the magistrate, his fists clenched as tightly as his jaw. His chest swelled and fell as he fought some internal struggle

The magistrate called for silence and the noise of the courtroom subsided and then flickered out. The jurors' expressions ranged from angry to delighted. The trial of Daimon, son of Nikodromos, had promised to be entertaining and they had not been disappointed. All were eager to see how the unexpected drama would play out, their disagreements put aside for the moment. The magistrate pointed at Plato. "What punishment do you demand?"

Yet Plato said nothing. He stood as if turned to stone, with only his furiously blinking eyes betraying any sign of life. A susurration of confused whispers began to fill the prolonged silence. Stachys and I exchanged a confused glance.

Then the miracle happened. Plato's shoulders sagged, and I knew he had lost whatever internal battle he had been waging. "I withdraw the charges," he said quietly. I inhaled sharply.

Even the jury was stunned into silence. The magistrate's eyes narrowed. "What did you say?" he asked, not quite believing what he had heard.

"The charges are withdrawn," Plato repeated. Humiliation dripped from each word.

Any semblance of order was abandoned. Some jurors shouted at Plato. Others pointed at me, screaming for justice. Not a few were cheering for the strange turn of events. The magistrate slumped back in his chair, stone-faced. Stachys grinned broadly and slapped me on the back. I had no idea what had just occurred. The Skythians, anticipating further need of their skills, leapt to their feet. The sight of the club-wielding slaves was enough to cow the jurors back to silence.

The magistrate had recovered enough to speak. "It is the accuser's right to withdraw the charges at any time," the magistrate stated, addressing the jury. He turned to Plato. "Are you certain of your decision?"

Plato looked at the ground. For a moment, I thought he might shake free whatever invisible shackles prevented him from exercising his desire to see me dead. But the bonds were too strong. "I am certain," he said. With that, my accuser pushed his chin into his chest and stalked out of the court. The crowd at the entrance parted to let him pass and he was gone.

A thrum of confused voices filled the air. "We should leave before someone changes their mind," Stachys advised me.

"There is someone I need to speak to first," I said, looking at the magistrate. Stachys regarded me sceptically. "No need for concern," I assured him. "I will behave myself." Stachys' eyebrows rose even further.

The magistrate was slumped in his chair. He made no effort to hide his disgust at my approach. I held out my hand.

He clenched his fingers and pulled his hand back to his waist as though he feared I might reach out and snatch it from him. "You have made a mockery of justice!" he growled. "You pollute this court with your presence!"

I withdrew my hand. "The whims of a mob are hardly worthy of the name 'justice,'" I said coldly. I began to turn away but paused. I narrowed my eyes at him, as though searching for a memory. "I do not remember you fighting for justice by my side at Munychia," I said. The magistrate's mouth tightened. "Perhaps you were farther down the hill, fighting with the Tyrants and the Spartans?" I ventured. Words could pierce as deeply as any blade.

The magistrate's face flushed red. It was confirmation enough. "I thought so," I said. I leaned forward. "I will not be lectured on *justice* by traitors like you," I said, twisting the knife deeper. "Be on your guard; I might come for you in the night and deliver the justice you deserve." The magistrate's face blanched. He opened his mouth, but no words came. Let him cower in his bed jumping at shadows, I thought. I left the magistrate mulling his former treachery and rejoined Stachys, who was waiting by the entrance.

We stepped outside under the late morning sun. I took a deep breath, and the smells of the agora – the dust, the spices, the cooking smoke of the sausage-sellers, the stale piss – rushed into my lungs. The aroma of freedom was sweet. I had little time to savour it, for my *peripoli* brothers materialized from the throngs in the agora and crowded around me. My comrades embraced me, their joy overflowing. The ox-like Mnasyllus gave me a playful punch in the shoulder, nearly sending me tumbling.

"I thought we would have to fight our way out of the city, Dammo!" Tibetos said, grinning ear to ear. Seeing the swords concealed discreetly in his cloak, I knew he meant it.

"Thanks to Stachys, not today," I said with a bow towards my defender.

"But we lost!" he protested.

"Without you it wouldn't even have been close," I replied.

Tibetos frowned. "You lost?" he asked.

"It's a strange story," I said.

Stachys tugged at my tunic. "I think there is someone else who wishes to speak to you," he said. I followed his gaze to where the man Chaerephon was standing patiently in the shade of a vendor's awning, his hands clasped in front of him. I begged off my comrades and left Stachys to relate the tale of what had transpired in the court to Tibetos and the others. Chaerephon raised a quizzical eyebrow at my approach.

I nodded in greeting. "It looks as though I have you to thank for my freedom. I am grateful," I said.

The corners of Chaerephon's mouth curled in an amused smile. "Your gratitude is misplaced. Thank Sokrates."

"Sokrates?" I exclaimed. Chaerephon acknowledged this with a slight bow. "What could he have done?" I asked.

Chaerephon's eyes revealed little. "Perhaps you should go ask him yourself," he suggested.

"It would be easier if you told me," I said.

Chaerephon shrugged but was not forthcoming with any more details. Our conversation was at an impasse. I thanked him and watched him head off in the direction of the prison. As I mused over the old man's words, another familiar figure caught my eye.

Thrasybulus stood by the steps of the council chamber. The loose hood of his thin cloak was pulled over his head as much to preserve his anonymity as to protect himself from the hot summer sun. He raised his hand and smiled. Apparently news of the verdict had reached his ears. Still smiling, he beckoned to me.

Thrasybulus could wait. At that moment, I had nothing to say to him. His smile faded as I turned away and returned to my waiting comrades of the *peripoli.*

THAT NIGHT, I LURKED IN THE SHADOWS near the prison. One by one, the friends and acolytes of Sokrates departed for the night, for even the great philosopher needed sleep. Plato was the last to leave. I watched him shuffle across the deserted agora. My eyes had long adapted to the darkness, and in the dim light cast by the torches around the perimeter of the market, I could see him clearly enough. My courtroom adversary moved as if in a trance, oblivious to his surroundings. It would have been no large matter to follow him and bury a knife in his ribs. But that was not my purpose that night.

The prison warder's look of surprise quickly turned to one of fear when he discovered that it was me who was pounding on the prison gate so late. Perhaps he thought I had come for revenge, but I bore no grudge against the man for carrying out his duties. During my imprisonment, he had been respectful if not courteous. His relief was palpable as I slipped him a coin and asked to see Sokrates.

Unsurprisingly, the old man was not asleep. By the light of a pair of oil lamps, we spoke. I sat on one of the many chairs in his cell and watched his restless pacing around the small room. "You should sleep," I told him.

A lively energy still flickered in his weary eyes. "How can I sleep when so little time is left?"

There was something concealed in his words. "The boat from Delos?" I asked.

Sokrates let out a resigned breath. "It arrived this morning. I will die by poison in two days' time."

"There is still time to flee," I said, though I knew how he would respond.

He waggled a finger at me. "It is better to die as Sokrates than to live on as a traitor to Sokrates' principles. No, I will stay true to myself, young Daimon, even if it only for a short time." He changed the subject. "That is not why you have come this evening?" he asked innocently.

"Chaerephon suggested I speak with you." The old man's eyes flashed with mischief, but he said nothing. "What message did you send to Plato?" I asked.

"I said that if he did not withdraw the lawsuit against you, I would refuse to see him again."

"That was all?" I asked, not quite believing what I had heard.

"That was all," Sokrates confirmed. He waited while I struggled to comprehend this, which ultimately I failed to do.

"I don't understand," I said.

"For some reason," Sokrates said, "young Aristokles holds me in high regard, misplaced as that regard may be. Above all things, he aspires to please me, to impress me, to earn my praise. For me to scorn him now, before my execution, would have been too much for him to bear."

"Would you have carried through had he refused to listen? Scorn him?" I asked.

Pain rippled across the old man's face. "Sometimes we must be cruel to those we love, for it is worse not to be honest." He gave me an appraising stare. "You two are more alike than you realize," he said.

I barked a humorless laugh. I could think of no one who differed from me more. Plato was a snake who squirmed and twisted. Even the most junior of the *peripoli* could lay him low in a heartbeat. But I took the bait Sokrates had cast before me. "How?" I asked.

"Your weapons of choice differ, no doubt, but you both never cease fighting in your own separate ways. And, if I am any judge of character," he said, giving me an affectionate but sad smile. "you are both lonely."

Of all the words Sokrates could have uttered, such a claim was what I would have expected least. I searched for a response, a rebuttal, but I found none. I rose from the chair. "For my part, I thank you for your assistance today," I said a little stiffly.

Sokrates dismissed my gratitude with an idle wave. "If you listen to your *daimon*, like I do, it is never difficult to know the right thing to do." He accompanied me to the door of his cell.

There was little more I could say. "I thank you again, O Sokrates," I said, suddenly feeling a wave of affection for the strange old man.

Sokrates smiled. I turned to leave, but the old man could not let me go without one last word. He reached up to put his hand on my shoulder. "Remember, Daimon: Be true to yourself and your path will be clear." He stopped me once more. "And promise me you will go to Delphi. The Oracle will reveal all that you wish to know." These last words he spoke with some urgency, as though something great were at stake.

"I will," I said, lying.

My false promise seemed to put the old man at ease, and his cheery demeanor reasserted itself. He saw me to the main gate of the prison. I stepped out into the sleeping city. Sokrates waved one last time before the gate swung shut and hid him from view.

I took a deep breath of the cool night air. I was grateful for the philosopher's aid in my release. But I would not heed his words. I had turned away from the gods long ago. I would never grovel before the Pythia to ask what the gods had in store for me.

I was wrong, of course. I was wrong about everything.

PART TWO
GODS ΘΕΟΙ

CHAPTER 8

"Who are we waiting for again?" Tibetos asked me.

I glanced over at my oldest friend. In the shade of the warehouse, his eastern complexion seemed darker than normal. He had been a slave in my father's household but had won his freedom fighting for Athens against Sparta and the Tyrants. His slim build and short stature were deceiving, for he was as tough a fighter as any man I knew.

"All I know is he is from Delphi," I said, touching the iron knife on my belt to ward off the evil eye. The mention of Delphi made me uneasy. It had been almost two years since Sokrates drank the executioner's poisonous draught. The old man's final words to me were a plea to consult the Oracle at Delphi, advice that I had steadfastly ignored. But now an insistent itch in the back of my mind was warning me that the gods were conspiring against me once more.

We were in Piraeus, the port of Athens, at the request of Thrasybulus. My thoughts turned to my former general and why I was languishing in the port that day. Since my trial, our interactions had been stiff and distant, despite many attempts on the part of Thrasybulus to mend the rift in our relationship. As I saw it, our continued association was one of mutual interest: Thrasybulus needed the *peripoli* to keep Athens safe, while I needed the support of Thrasybulus in the assembly to secure funds for the *peripoli*.

Our last meeting had been a strange one. He requested to meet in person rather than trust the message to a slave or soldier, as had been my preferred form of communication for some time. All light had bled away in the evening when I arrived at the council chamber. The deserted hall magnified the sound of my footsteps as I approached the lone figure sitting in the dimly-lit chamber. The cloaked figure of Thrasybulus rose to greet me.

"*Lochagos*," he said, addressing me by my formal rank. His normally resounding voice was, for him, barely a whisper.

"*Strategos*," I replied, keeping my tone flat.

Thrasybulus leaned close. "I have a mission for you," he said. In his uncharacteristically hushed tone, he explained that an ambassador was coming from Delphi and insisted that I be the one to meet him and bring him to the city.

"Surely there are other people who can greet an ambassador," I said curtly.

"The ambassador's meeting is secret and must remain so," Thrasybulus responded, matching my formality. His expression softened. "Daimon, I know — " He hesitated, searching for words. "I know that I have disappointed you." My stony expression remained unchanged. "But this matter is of gravest importance. There is no one else I would trust with this task."

"Have I ever failed *you?*" I asked. Thrasybulus' lips parted but closed quickly, smothering whatever words he wished to say. When he spoke again, it was a general giving orders. He instructed me on what I was to do in Piraeus, but he did not elaborate on the need for secrecy, only that it must be so.

Tibetos' voice brought me back to the present. "He must be important for us to be waiting around all this time," my friend said with a shrug before going back to lazily observing the organized chaos all around us.

We sat like two stones sitting idly in a river as a torrent of activity surged all about us. Ships laden with sundry types of cargo squeezed into every available space along the wharf. The only sound that could compete with the shouts of customs officials directing the unloading of freight was the cacophony of merchants bidding manically for the precious goods from every corner of the known world, and sometimes from beyond. Other trading ships lay at anchor in the harbour, waiting their turn to take a berth. Absent, however, were the great warships that had once made Athens great, as Sparta had forbidden the city from keeping a naval fleet. It seemed of little consequence, as merchants still found great profits in satisfying Athens' insatiable demand for anything that could be bought and sold.

Small skiffs darted between the anchored ships as customs officials performed preliminary inspections, calculating duties and no doubt palming bribes at every stop. I kept my eye on one customs skiff in particular and due course my patience was rewarded. After visiting a particularly weather-beaten ship, the small boat returned to shore. The customs official disembarked and hurried over to where Tibetos and I were sitting.

"He's on that ship," the official said, pointing at the boat in question.

"I'm surprised that wreck is even floating," Tibetos said, squinting to see the ship better.

The customs official shrugged. "Not my problem. As long as she sinks after she pays her fees, that is."

"How long until she docks?" I asked, surveying the small fleet of waiting ships that dotted in the harbour. We had already idled away three days waiting for the mysterious ambassador to arrive.

The official sucked his teeth. "Could be a day. Lots of others in the queue before that one."

I sighed, taking out a small purse of coins from my tunic. "Perhaps sooner than that, gods willing," I said, handing the bribe over.

The official gave the purse a tiny, jingly toss, no doubt accurately assessing the value of the coins therein down to the last obol. Apparently satisfied, he slipped the purse into a hidden pocket. "Of course, I'll see what can be done," he said. He flashed an officious smile before turning on his heel and striding away purposefully.

The customs man was at least honest in honouring the bribe. It was not long before the derelict ship weighed anchor and lumbered towards an empty berth along the wharf. "Let's go meet her," I said to Tibetos.

A throng of dock slaves, foremen, and curious merchants had already gathered to greet the new arrival. I jostled my way through the crowd with Tibetos in my wake just as the ship made its final approach. The oars were retracted in a haphazard clatter of wood and the groaning craft lurched closer. As a sailor on the front deck tossed a rope to waiting hands on shore, my eyes drifted over the men around me. It was the usual mix of resigned labourers and anxious traders who were already competing for access to whatever cargo was about to be unloaded.

I was not the only one observing the crowd rather than the ship; indeed, someone was watching me. He was leaning against one of the cranes that lined the wharf, his arms folded across his chest. I held his stare for a few heartbeats before he blinked slowly, like a cat, and then turned his gaze back to the arriving ship.

The man was dark-skinned, more so than Tibetos but not as deeply coloured as the men of Egypt. It was not this made him stand out in my eyes, however, for Piraeus abounds with men of all tribes, from Africans as black as charcoal to copper-haired Thracians to men from the far north with pale skin and eyes the colour of the sky. What caught my notice was the company he kept.

My instinct prickled at the sight of his four larger companions. Their bearing radiated a slight coarseness that suggested violent natures creeping just under their skins. No weapons were visible but they no doubt had blades or other weapons hidden about their persons. Like any port, Piraeus had its own share of gangs running protection rackets or hiring themselves out to businessmen anxious to intimidate upstart competitors. This group was most likely the same, a pack of dogs sniffing about for potential prey.

A surge in activity brought my attention back to the ship, which had finally docked. As crew-members secured the mooring lines, I glanced back towards the crane, but the dark man and his crew had already departed, apparently losing interest in whatever business they had anticipated. My interest vanished with them, for I had my own task to attend to. The leather-skinned captain stepped off the bow onto the wharf, only to be immediately set upon by all manner of touts and hagglers. I shouldered my way to the captain and grabbed his arm. "A passenger from Delphi?" I shouted over the din.

The captain jerked his head back towards the ship and got back to negotiating with the clamouring mass of people. I looked past him, finally laying eyes on the purpose of my journey to Piraeus. On the deck of the ship stood a haggard old man in a dark cloak who was clutching a leather sack to his chest like it was the most valuable thing in the world.

*

A CUP OF WINE AND A BOWL OF BARLEY STEW in a nearby tavern did much to return some colour to the old man's cheeks. "The sea does not agree with me," he said, wiping some drops of broth from his beard. "No, it does not agree with me at all!"

"You came from Corinth?" I inquired. Crossing the isthmus at Corinth and continuing the journey by sea to Piraeus would have been the shortest route from Delphi.

"Apollo be praised, yes!" the old man exclaimed. "A long sea voyage around the Peloponnese would have seen me to my tomb!"

The old man told us his name was Samolas. He was a priest from the temple at Delphi, but I wondered if there had not been any younger acolytes who would have been more up to the journey. "I have been sent by the Pythia herself to deliver a message to Thrasybulus of Athens." As he said this, his claw-like hands pulled his travel sack close to his chest.

"And as I have said, Thrasybulus has sent us to accompany you." I had shown the priest the letter marked with the seal of Thrasybulus, but the old man was still suspicious. "In any case, we should set off for Athens soon if we are to reach our destination by nightfall." The city was a seven-mile walk from Piraeus, and I was eager to avoid spending yet another night in the port. The aged priest hardly looked up to the trek, however.

A better alternative came to mind. "I can deliver the message to Thrasybulus," I suggested.

The priest shrank a little. "I was instructed to deliver this to Thrasybulus in person!"

I beckoned the tavern owner for another pitcher of wine.

"Under the protection of Apollo, I will see it safely to his hands," I said, mustering as pious a tone as possible. Tibetos raised an eyebrow at my sudden reverence for the gods.

"It is my charge," the old man said, wavering.

My younger self would have simply seized the priest's satchel and been done with it, but I suppressed the urge to do so now. "Tibetos will see that you are well taken care of, O Priest," I said.

"Tibo, that tavern beside the theatre serves fine roasted goat, does it not?"

"With the best wines in Piraeus, I reckon," Tibetos added, playing along. "They always have the finest selections from Chios,"

"Roasted goat?" said the priest, his eyes suddenly alight. "Wine from Chios?"

I felt the priest's resolve crumbling. "Eat well and rest in the *peripoli* compound in Piraeus," I prompted. "It will give you the energy to make the journey to Athens tomorrow."

The priest closed his eyes, as if searching for a thought. At last he opened them and smiled. "I sense no malice in you, my boy. Apollo has told me to place my faith in you." With that, he handed me the bag he had been guarding so jealously.

No longer burdened by his task, the priest of Apollo looked relieved. He reached out and clutched my hand with surprising strength. "May Pythius," he said, using one of the Apollo's many names, "give you swiftness of foot on your journey." He mumbled a prayer and nodded. Then his piety vanished, replaced with a look of anticipation of more earthly concerns. "Now, you said something about roasted goat?"

I LEFT THE PRIEST SAMOLAS in the trustworthy hands of Tibetos. I was relieved to be rid of the old man, for without him I would make good time. I loped past the carts, porters, and knots of travellers that tread the straight road between Piraeus and the city. In the distance the temples of the acropolis beckoned in the late afternoon sun. On both sides of the road, the scattered rubble of once formidable walls lay partially hidden by shrubs and grasses. The sight was a reminder that although Athens was an independent polis in theory, in fact her freedom only existed by the grace of her Spartan conquerors.

The shattered walls also brought unwanted memories of the murder of my wife and my comrades by the Tyrants installed by Sparta. I had avenged their deaths with the blood of their killers many times over, but that did not stop me from waking in the night, wracked by tears or rage.

By habit, I suppressed the oft-present pain, focusing on the journey, but even so something lingered, the prickling of hostile eyes. I came to an abrupt stop and scanned the road in all directions but there was only the normal traffic one would expect. A merchant leading an amphora-laden cart made the mistake of meeting my gaze and, withering under my intense stare, trundled past me while keeping his own eyes fixed on the flagstones at his feet.

I quickened my pace, wanting to reach the city before the gates were locked at sunset. My skittishness annoyed me. I groped the satchel under my arm, feeling the scroll within. Was the scroll the source of my unease? I scorned the gods but was now their messenger, of sorts. The resentment caused by this thought simmered in my gut and by the time I passed through the city gates, I was quite eager to fulfill my duty and be done with it.

The head house slave admitted me to the home of Thrasybulus. "Wait. I will fetch my master," the slave said, leaving me to gaze idly at the familiar surroundings of Thrasybulus' home.

The flagstone-covered courtyard was much like my own, though slightly larger. Limestone columns lined the perimeter, supporting an upper floor of sleeping chambers and private rooms for Thrasybulus and his family. At ground level, the open area was ringed by slave quarters, storerooms, a kitchen area, as well as a rather grand salon where Thrasybulus met in private with the most influential citizens of Athens and ambassadors from other poleis. My eyes fell on the stone altar towards the rear of the courtyard and I walked towards it. I let my finger run along the rough limestone edge of the surface. A fresh offering of fruit and figs sat atop the altar, evidence of Thrasybulus' piety. I had a sudden urge to knock the sacrifice to the ground.

A familiar, thundering voice saved me from my own temptation. "You have met the messenger from Delphi, then?" said Thrasybulus, descending the stairway. In response, I took out the leather-wrapped scroll from my satchel and extended it towards Thrasybulus. A look of relief flickered across his face and then quickly vanished as his habitual confidence reasserted itself. "And the messenger?"

"In Piraeus with Tibetos. I thought it would be best to deliver it to you as soon as possible, *strategos*," I said a little stiffly.

"A wise decision, as usual, Daimon," he said. The dialogue faltered, and we regarded each other in awkward silence.

"If there is nothing further, I will take my leave, *strategos*," I said, giving a cursory nod to Thrasybulus.

A screech and the slap of tiny feet made me turn back. "Daimon! Daimon!" Thrasybulus' daughter Thais was running across the courtyard towards me with her little brother close on her heels. They skidded to a halt before me. The girl looked up at me. She was now eight years old, much taller than the last time I had seen her. "Why do you not come to see us anymore? Why do you not stay with us as you used to?" she asked in the innocent manner of children. In the past, I had often spent time with the children when I came to report to Thrasybulus. Since the trial, my visits had been both infrequent and short.

I exchanged a quick glance with Thrasybulus before kneeling to speak to his daughter. "I have been too busy hunting monsters, little one," I said, which was true enough. "I have been keeping you and your brother safe."

"You are not angry with me?" the little girl asked anxiously.

"Never, little one," I said.

Her five-year-old brother could no longer hold back his own urgent request. "Roar for us! Roar for us!" he begged. His sister's eyes lit up, her previous worries already a memory.

"You are getting too old for childish games," I admonished them. The children's faces dropped in disappointment. I made to leave before spinning back and giving my fiercest war-shout with arms extended. The children hopped up and down and then squealed in delight as I scooped them up, one in each arm. Their father grinned at his children's happiness as they pulled at my long red hair, a source of endless fascination for them. For a moment, things seemed as they had once been.

A figure emerged from the kitchen across the courtyard. "Children! Let him be!" Thrasybulus' wife Astera smiled but could not completely mask her discomfort at my presence. She was a woman of aristocratic refinement, and an unexpected male guest would have grated against her sense of propriety in any case. Yet my size and barbarian features made her ill at ease, even though we had known each other for many years. The sight of my *rhomphaia* slung across my back did not help.

"Lady," I said with a nod. I put the children gently on the ground and they moaned in protest. "Go to your mother," I ordered. Thais pouted but knew better than to challenge me. I winked at her and she beamed, satisfied, and led her brother back to their mother.

Astera eased visibly once her children were near her. She adjusted her headscarf to cover more of her hair.

I looked up at the rapidly darkening sky. "It is late and certainly past the children's bedtime. I will be off."

Thais stuck her tongue out at me. She shared a quick glance with her father before turning to Astera. "Momma, can Daimon stay with us tonight? Like he used to? Surely the streets are not safe now that it is dark!"

Astera stiffened, but Thrasybulus, oblivious to his wife's unease, seized upon the suggestion. "It is a fine idea! Eat! Rest here tonight. In any case, it will give us time to discuss matters further." He had agreed with a suspicious amount of alacrity. I would not have put it above him to have plotted beforehand with his daughter to put me in the awkward position of refusing a host's invitation. Once again he had extended an olive branch towards me, though with more cunning than usual.

If only for Astera's sake, I was about to beg off the invitation, but the children's expectant expressions plucked at a painful chord in my heart. There was no warm welcome awaiting me at my home on the other side of the city, only a lonely meal of stale bread by the light of a smoky lamp followed by a restless night on a hard bed. My fatigue weakened my resistance to the craving for belonging that I usually managed to keep buried in my heart.

"Only if children wish it," I said, winking at the young ones.

Thais and her little brother cheered while their mother forced a strained smile.

CHAPTER 9

A warrior ever sleeps lightly.

My eyelids flicked open. I lay motionless in the darkness of the salon, my soldier's inner sense quivering. It was an instinct honed by years of war. I strained to pick up the sounds of the night. The rumbling breathing of the sleeping slaves in the next room was the only noise to disturb the house. My muscles relaxed. There was nothing.

I closed my eyes and reflected on the evening. It had not gone as badly as I had feared. Thrasybulus had executed his sacred duty as host and extended every courtesy towards me. Astera had tactfully retired to her quarters on the second level of the house, rescuing us both from any further awkward interactions. The children clambered about me while I ate and Thrasybulus droned on about sundry political goings-on in the city. Only when Astera sent a slave-girl to collect the reluctant children for bed did we look at the message from Delphi.

Thrasybulus read it by lamplight and then handed the scroll to me. His patient gaze did not leave me as I whispered my way through the letter in fits and starts. It was curiously unenlightening. It was from the Pythia, the Oracle of Apollo herself. In it she greeted Thrasybulus and showered him with praise and platitudes which meant nothing to me. Only at the end of the letter was there something of note: she invited Thrasybulus to come to Delphi at the first consultation day of the year.

I looked up. "That is only half a month away."

Thrasybulus nodded. "We must prepare to leave at once."

I bridled at his presumption that I would accompany him to Delphi, but my curiosity overcame my irritation. "Why did she not say more?" I asked. "Why the secrecy?"

"The Pythia enjoys great esteem but not freedom. She leads a sequestered existence and her actions are closely guarded by the priests there. I suspect she feared the message would be intercepted," he said, without elaborating on who might be interested in thwarting her communications and why.

"But why would she send an invitation to you?"

"I have consulted the Oracle on several occasions," he said with a hint of awe. "She is a formidable woman. There is little that happens in the world of mortals of which she is unaware. It is a foolish man who underestimates her knowledge and wisdom. Her oracles have never failed to set me, or Athens, along the right path. In gratitude, I swore an oath to her that I would do anything in my power to support Delphi. It seems that the Pythia is now taking me up on that oath."

"Such oaths should not be made lightly," I said.

"Nor should they be lightly broken," Thrasybulus said, tapping the table with each word. He pushed his chair away from the table and rose to his feet, letting out a long yawn. "We will rise early to discuss our preparations."

Though I had made no such commitment, I was too tired to argue the point. "*Strategos,*" I said with a nod.

Thrasybulus paused at the doorway of the salon and looked back at me. "The children are happy to see you again, Daimon." He left me to set up a makeshift bed in the salon as he went to the living quarters on the second level of the house. Though my sleeping arrangements were more comfortable than the rocky earth that usually served as my bed while on patrol, my rest was shallow and fitful. Perhaps this is why I now found myself awake in the dead of night, my ears playing tricks on me in the darkness. I shut my eyes once more.

A creak from across the courtyard made my body snap to taut alertness. It was not a trick of the ears. Someone was climbing the stairs, someone trying not to be heard. I sat up, my hand drifting to the reassuring length of Whisper beside me. She was well-named, for the four-foot blade now slid from her scabbard with barely a sound. I padded to the doorway of the salon, thankful for the stealth my bare feet provided me.

A hushed voice stopped me in my tracks. It had come from the second-storey landing overlooking the courtyard. At least two men already near the rooms where Thrasybulus and his family slept. I ventured a peek outside the salon and saw the source on the creaking near the top of the stairway. The light cast by the oil lamps on the family altar illuminated intruder well enough to see that he was no common cut-throat. He held his weapon with the bearing of a professional soldier.

But his attention was focused on whatever was happening upstairs. I could be upon him before he could even turn to face me. I took a deep breath in preparation for the dash across the courtyard when a bulky shadow detached itself from the darkened doorway at the base of the stairs, lamplight glinting off the blade in the man's hand. The presence of the fourth enemy left me with no option.

I sprinted towards the man at the base of the stairs and he reacted quickly, turning towards the sound of my footsteps, his eyebrows raised in surprise. As I sped past the central altar, I shouted a warning to Thrasybulus, hoping that it would be enough to save him. "*Strategos*! The enemy are here!" And with my final strides I screamed my battle-cry and fell upon my opponent.

He had hardly begun to turn before Whisper bit deep into the cleft between his neck and shoulder. I ripped the rhomphaia free and a spray of blood splattered over me.

He collapsed at my feet, his sword clattering on the ground, and I spun to face the man on the stairs. The hitherto unseen men on the landing stared down at me in surprise. The one farthest along the landing recovered first, barking a command at the man on the stairs. But I was already charging up the stairs towards the next man, still screaming at the top of my lungs.

The man's position above me actually put him at a disadvantage, for it was awkward for him to strike down at me with his short sword while defending against the long reach of my own weapon. At the same time, the staircase restricted my own ability to swing the long blade of my rhomphaia for a killing blow, so I flicked Whisper's tip towards the man's exposed calves and yanked. The man cried out as the rhomphaia's curved end severed the tendon above his ankle and he began to buckle under his suddenly useless limb. But the man was experienced. Already falling, he used his position to launch himself at me, and caught by surprise I only barely managed to evade the stab of his sword but the jarring impact knocked Whisper from my grasp. In a tangle of limbs we tumbled down to land in a crashing heap at the base of the stairs.

The man had lost his sword but he was on top of me. With a snarl, he drove his fist down at my face with enough force to shatter stone. I jerked my head to one side and the blow glanced off my cheek and into the paving stone. The man grunted in pain and I drove my knee up into his groin. With a groan he crumpled and I heaved his body off of mine. He clutched his crushed testicles, struggling to get to his feet, but his ruined ankle betrayed him and he stumbled back to his knees. Whisper lay where she had tumbled a body length away and I scrabbled towards her.

As I scooped the rhomphaia off the ground, a noise like thunder exploded above me. Thrasybulus had burst from his sleeping chamber, bellowing his challenge at the assassins on the landing. He was naked, but brandished a leaf-bladed sword. His wife Astera appeared behind him in the doorway. She screamed at the sight of the assassins. Thrasybulus whipped his sword to and fro, fending off his attackers in the narrow space of the landing, but against two opponents he would have little chance of holding out for long.

My second attacker had recovered enough to begin crawling towards his fallen sword, but flipping my weapon, I ran him through the back and he had not even collapsed before I was bounding up the stairs to even the odds for Thrasybulus on the landing.

The intruder closest to the stairs spun away from Thrasybulus to face me. His eyes widened at the sight of the wicked-looking weapon in my hands. In a few more strides I would be upon him. His death was coming and he knew it. But then something happened that made both me and my attacker freeze.

The door at the top of the stairs swung open and a small figure in a thin tunic stumbled out onto the landing between me and my opponent. Thrasybulus' daughter, Thais, blinked in confusion at the battle raging about her. The assassin and I locked eyes for an instant, each of us suddenly seized by indecision.

I moved first. "Thais!" I shouted desperately, rushing up the last few steps towards her. But I was too late, for the assassin reacted more quickly. My heart lurched as he lunged forward and roughly encircled the sleepy child with his free arm and hefted her off the ground to his chest. By now I was on the landing, Whisper held out in front of me, but I was powerless. The assassin grinned in triumph as he held his blade at Thais' throat, daring me to move.

The landing was a mass of confusion and noise. Astera, seeing her daughter's predicament, cried with a mother's fear. Thrasybulus bellowed in pain as his own opponent darted inside his defenses and stabbed his sword deep into my former general's thigh. The attacker holding Thais screamed at me to drop my weapon. But it was all just dull distraction to me, for I only focused on one thing.

Time slowed, like pine resin oozing from a tree. Every detail was clear to me. In the middle of the chaos, I looked at Thais. There was no fear in the little girl's expression as she stared back at me. Then, as if hearing my silent plea, she moved. It was not much, merely shifting her weight in her captor's arm, but it was enough to distract her would-be killer. As the assassin adjusted his grip, I reacted.

Even after all these years I shudder to think what would have happened if the stroke had missed. But it did not. Whisper flashed in an overhead arc. The rhomphaia's blade is so long that with such a strike the tip moves with the force of an axe. Now that tip hewed down through skull and brain to the bridge of my enemy's nose. Time's arrow suddenly shot forward once more, and my senses were assaulted once more. Blood sprayed over me as I ripped Whisper from the dead man's forehead and he collapsed in a misshapen heap. Thais fell to the ground with a thud and she began to scream, her previously calm demeanor suddenly vanishing. I stepped forward so that I stood astride the shrieking child like a lioness protecting its cub. I roared at the remaining intruder.

Suddenly trapped between me and the wounded Thrasybulus, the final assassin glanced in my direction and I saw his face clearly for the first time. With a growl of recognition, I realized he was not unfamiliar to me. It was the watcher from the docks.

I extended Whisper towards him, approaching cautiously. "Who sent you?" I demanded. The assassin smirked and hazarded a look towards Thrasybulus, who, though limping, was like me carefully closing the distance on his would-be killer. Then, without warning, the killer vaulted the railing into the courtyard below.

A leap from such a height should have led to injury, but it did not. Instead, I watched in disbelief as the man landed on the courtyard altar and then used the momentum to propel himself forward. Like an acrobat performing at a festival, he rolled out of his landing, coming fluidly to his feet before dashing across the remaining distance of the courtyard and out the door.

"Daimon!" Thrasybulus shouted, but I was already hurtling down the stairs in pursuit.

Bursting out the door, I looked about frantically for the fleeing killer. His shadowy form vanished around a corner far up the darkened laneway. I cursed under my breath as I sprinted in pursuit, for the fleet-footed assassin had a considerable lead on me. Soon my lungs and muscles burned. But the would-be killer's endurance began to flag as well, and the gap between us narrowed.

He suddenly spun in mid-stride and something flashed in his right hand. I dropped instinctively into a clumsy roll as a throwing dagger spun through the air where the center of my chest had been an instant earlier. I scrabbled up just in time to see the assassin's fleeing form dash around another corner.

My heart was pounding from the sprint. "Now I have you, bastard," I gasped as I launched myself in pursuit once again. I knew the streets and lanes of the Athens intimately, having spent the better part of my childhood prowling them. The assassin's choice of escape route would take him to a dead-end. There would be nowhere to hide.

My footsteps echoed off the walls of tightly-packed houses that lined the laneway, their doors shut tightly against the night. Fearing an ambush, I pulled up as I approached the final bend. I ducked my head around the corner and peered into the shadows. I frowned in confusion. In a low crouch I stepped into the dead-end, wondering if my eyes had deceived me. They had not. Except for the sound of my heaving lungs, the lane was empty.

I glanced upwards at the high surrounding walls. Could he have scaled them? It seemed improbable, yet it seemed he had done so to enter the house of Thrasybulus. The rough surface appeared unclimbable and the height along the entire alley was two storeys. Looking back the way I had come, I wondered how my prey had eluded me, there having been neither time nor opportunity to hide.

I slapped a wall in frustration. The assassin had escaped.

WHEN I RETURNED, the courtyard was crowded with people. Neighbours, woken by the clamour, had come to the assistance of Thrasybulus and his family. Clad in simple tunics and wielding whatever weapons had been at hand, the men and slaves of nearby homes now gawked at the bodies of the three assassins I had slain. The appearance of my blood-spattered figure caused a moment of tension, but Thrasybulus called them off before the misunderstanding turned violent.

A pale-looking Thrasybulus had donned a rough tunic and now leaned against the altar while his head slave bound his blood-drenched leg with linen. He winced as the slave pulled the bandage taut.

"There is a rope outside. He used that and then let the others in," Thrasybulus informed me. So the assassin did not have wings after all, I realized. But still did not understand how he had eluded me. Thrasybulus looked at me expectantly.

I shook my head. "He escaped," I said.

Thrasybulus exhaled a long breath. "It is of no matter. My family is safe, thanks to you," he said, waving towards a knot of people near the bottom of the stairs.

The general's young son was sound asleep in the arms of his nursemaid, seemingly oblivious to all that had occurred. Astera spoke in hushed tones to two house slaves, who waited obediently on her instructions. Beside Astera stood the small, silent figure of Thais, who clutched her mother's robe.

The little girl's chin was pulled into her chest, but her wide eyes were fixed firmly upon me. Under the child's gaze, I suddenly became self-conscious of the fearsome, bloody visage I must have presented, standing there in the courtyard with Whisper in my hand, my wild copper hair unbound. The tightness of drying blood pulled at the skin on my face and I looked down to see the darkening stains on my tunic. I laid my weapon down on the flagstones and approached Thais. I knelt down so that we were of a height. "You were very brave, child," I said gently.

I thought she might cower in fear, but she did not. The little girl's eyes drifted over me, taking in the gore of violence that covered my person. She reached out a tentative hand and touched my blood-stained cheek, feeling its tackiness. Finally, her eyes returned to mine. "I was not afraid," she said. "*Mou daimon eisai.*" You are my *daimon*. She launched herself forward and wrapped her arms tightly around my neck. I returned the embrace, for I loved the child as if she were my own.

After some time, we separated. Taking the little girl by the hand, I took her to the waiting Astera. "Go with your mother, child. She will clean you up," I said. Astera, disheveled and wide-eyed, grasped her daughter's hand. "Lady," I said quietly before turning away.

"Daimon," came Astera's haughty voice. I turned back, surprised, for Thrasybulus' wife had never addressed me by name. Astera stepped close and looked up at me with eyes reddened by tears and fatigue. She suddenly pushed herself up on her toes and kissed my cheek. "You have my gratitude," she said. "And I understand my husband's faith in you." It must have taken great courage for Thrasybulus' austere wife to say those words. For his own part, Thrasybulus viewed the exchange with an eyebrow raised in quizzical amusement. My voice taken from me, I watched as Astera led her daughter back up the steps to the sleeping chambers above.

I recovered from the odd encounter with renewed clarity. Assassins had tried to kill Thrasybulus. They had tried to kill me. And they had threatened the life of a child I loved. The Furies, those spirits of vengeance, whispered in my ear, and I found myself succumbing to their seductive urgings.

I approached Thrasybulus. "Tell me about Delphi," I said.

CHAPTER 10

"The Pythia wished to speak to you personally," Samolas said, somewhat peevishly, I thought. The old priest had arrived with Tibetos at the home of Thrasybulus before midday and since that time had been trying to persuade the *strategos* to accompany him back to Delphi.

"I am in no condition to make the journey," Thrasybulus repeated, wincing as he put some weight on his wounded leg. "Daimon can speak to her on my behalf and report back to me." Samolas regarded me sceptically. Thrasybulus took another tack. "Perhaps it is for the best. My presence in Delphi would only draw attention. Athens is weak and it is better that we not be seen interfering in the affairs of Delphi. Among the travellers and pilgrims, Daimon will be inconspicuous. I have utmost faith in his ability."

Samolas began to protest again. "But — "

Thrasybulus had had enough. He seized a handful of the old man's robe. Hobbling, he hauled the reluctant priest to the middle of the courtyard and pointed to unmistakable stain there. "I have little doubt," he said, "that the task at hand may be more suited to someone of Daimon's particular skills and talents. There are those who wish to prevent you from completing your mission, O Samolas, by any means necessary. The question is whether you would feel more at ease travelling to Delphi with me at your side or Daimon."

Samolast stared at the dark patch on the ground where one of the assassin's lifeblood had drained out. The priest looked at me. I returned his gaze with a dead stare. My fingers caressed the pommel of the sword on my hip. Samolas' throat bobbed as he swallowed deeply. "Upon further consideration, I am certain the Pythia will understand your decision."

Thrasybulus dipped his head. "If that is what you think is best, O Samolas," he said. He turned to me. "And when will you depart, Daimon?"

I glanced at Tibetos. "I will take some of the *peripoli*. We can leave in two days," I said. Tibetos nodded in agreement.

It was decided. Tibetos would return to Piraeus with Samolas and enlist some of the *peripoli* in our endeavour; if more assassins attempted to impede our journey, I would prefer the odds to be more balanced.

I would meet them in Piraeus the following day, after which we would negotiate passage on one of the many ships travelling to Corinth. From there we could cross the isthmus and take another ship north to Kirrha, a port a few miles away from Delphi itself.

But there were some people I needed to see first.

I POUNDED ON THE WOODEN DOOR of my first stop. There was no response. I thumped the door again. As I waited, I turned over recent developments in my mind. The more I considered the situation, the more I believed that Thrasybulus had manipulated me into making a journey to Delphi. He knew I would crave vengeance for the attack at his home. For all his moralizing and stiff virtue, the general had a cunning, subtle mind. He was ruthless in pursuit of his goal to restore a humiliated Athens to its former greatness. It was his first loyalty and I would be foolish to forget it.

The door groaned open and I put aside my thoughts. The elderly slave's only greeting was a look of boredom. His slate-grey eyes ran over me in no particular hurry, taking in my blood-stained tunic and the long blade slung over my back. Several days of beard growth scratched at my face and I was weary from the previous night's exertions.

His inspection finished, the slave's grey eyes returned their flat gaze to mine. "Your appearance has improved markedly since you last visited, *pai* " he sniffed.

"Shut up, Xanthias, and let me in. I must speak with Iasos," I said. I had known the Thracian slave since I was a boy and had never seen him express anything more than bored indifference. I had no time for his impudence.

"As you wish. Follow me," Xanthias said, turning away with a shrug. I followed him into the courtyard. "Wait here. I will fetch my master." He shuffled off towards a doorway at the back corner of the house.

The house's layout was similar to that of Thrasybulus or my own, but everywhere within was littered with the detritus of its owner's particular interests. A number of tables were laid out in the courtyard, all covered with rolls of papyrus, writing implements, and assorted models and contraptions. Even the altar had vanished under a heap of scrolls. A few larger machines in various states of completion, whose function I could only guess at, lay scattered about.

A familiar figure soon strode out from the rear room. Iasos had been my tutor as a child, but he seemed ageless, for his appearance had changed little since that time. He was as bald as an egg and must have been approaching seventy years of age but possessed the vigour of two men half his age, something he attributed to his eschewing all types of meat and subjecting himself to the myriad other forms of self-denial prescribed by his strict Pythagorean beliefs. Eccentric in his ways, perhaps, but he was just, brave, and a good man.

The wide smile that split his face faded as gaze fell on the stains of dried blood that patterned my tunic. "What has befallen you? Are you hurt, *pai*?" he asked, grasping my shoulder with one hand.

I towered over my former tutor but still felt like a child before him. "I am unharmed, Teacher," I said, not elaborating further

Iasos narrowed his eyes at me. "Trouble has a way of finding you, *pai*. Or is it the other way round?" he said, arching an eyebrow.

"Is my son safe?" I asked.

Iasos raised both eyebrows in surprise. "Of course he is! Is there some reason he should not be?"

The tension that had gripped me since the assassination attempt eased ever so little. The killers had been after Thrasybulus, of that there was no doubt, but I had become involved and fear for my own son's safety had seized hold of me. "No, the danger has passed," I said. Before Iasos could press further, I spoke again. "I need to leave the city. It might be some time before I return. I will leave some money for you," I said, fumbling for the small bag of coins in my tunic.

Iasos gently but firmly gripped my wrist. "Do you think you need to pay me, *pai*?" Iasos asked. "My home is yours, or your son's, for however long is necessary."

I nodded my thanks. In truth, my son, Nikodromos, was closer to the grandfatherly Iasos than to me, for the old man's school was where he had spent most of his childhood. I was rarely in the city myself, more often than not away hunting the bandits that infested the borders of Attica.

Niko had no mother to care for him in my absence. His mother, Phaia, was dead, murdered by the tyrants who had ruled the city after Athens had lost its decades-long war with Sparta. I had avenged her death, slaying her killers with my own hand, but vengeance had not brought me peace. Phaia had been my light and joy, my friend and saviour. I missed her.

I was not a good father. On the rare occasions when the boy and I resided in our own home, it was as though we were strangers. The easy manner I had with the children of Thrasybulus would vanish to be replaced by a brooding silence. No wonder the boy was frightened of me.

In truth, the sight of Niko provoked an overwhelming sorrow in my heart. Whenever he looked at me expectantly, starved for praise or any other gesture of affection, I saw only Phaia's wordless shade staring at me from the Underworld. She wanted to know why I had failed her. Why I had let her die. Then I would turn away from Niko to escape his anxious stare, mumbling a rebuke or saying nothing at all.

"Come with me," Iasos said. "He is studying with the other boys."

We stopped at the doorway and quietly observed the five boys within. One was daydreaming, his eyes glazed with boredom, while three others whispered and giggled, not yet having noticed the return of their teacher. Only the remaining child, a boy with raven-black hair like his mother, was focused on his task, scratching away at his wax tablet.

Iasos leaned closer to me. "He is a brilliant boy," he said in a hushed tone. "Better at his letters now than you ever were. And he has a talent for mathematics beyond his years. Yes, a most promising pupil," Iasos finished, more to himself than to me.

Niko was seven years old at that time. He paused, his brow furrowing at some mental obstacle on the tablet before him. It was an expression so reminiscent of his mother that it exhumed memories that were better left buried. My face tightened as I struggled to contain the anguish that suddenly welled up inside me.

As if sensing my presence, Niko swivelled on his stool and saw my stern, scowling face looming over him.

And he began to cry.

I LEFT NIKO IN THE CARE OF IASOS, much to my son's relief, I was certain. Niko had calmed down with some reassuring words from Iasos. I had invited the boy to sit on my knee, but my son had rebuffed me, preferring to remain by his tutor's side. My clumsy efforts to reach out to Niko had not been helped by the fact that I departed soon after arriving. But I had little choice; there was someone else I needed to see before I set out for Delphi. I going to visit my sister.

The pebbles on the winding path to Meli's cave crunched underfoot. The path was well-trodden by many visitors on secret night-time journeys to her abode, not because she was a prostitute, as Myronides had taunted me, but because she was a soothsayer of some repute. In public, many dismissed her oracles and mocked the superstitious credulity of those who sought her out. Secretly, though, they feared and respected her. They came to the mad Thracian woman in the hills and knelt before her, humbly asking to know the gods' intentions for their business ventures, political futures, but above all matters of the heart and family fortune. I came often as well, not as a suppliant but to bring my sister food, fuel, and other provisions. Today, in the daylight, I was likely the only visitor, as few would wish to be seen coming here.

Up a rise and round the last bend, the entrance to the cave became visible. Sheltered from both the scorching summer sun and driving winter rains, it was well situated. The entrance was covered by weathered leather curtains that blended in almost completely with the surrounding rock. Only a shield-sized brazier of battered bronze resting above a stone-lined fire-pit indicated that the cave might be inhabited at all. The brazier contained the charred bones of a lamb or goat, though in their blackened state they could have been mistaken for human. Whether it was a recent sacrifice or the remains of a meal, I could not tell. I stopped in front before the entrance.

"It is me, Sister!" I announced loudly. There was no response. I pushed through the leather flaps and into the chamber beyond.

A solitary lamp struggled to illuminate the confines of the cave. The breeze from my entrance caused the flame to flicker, casting eerily dancing shapes over the stone walls, the shadows fading to impenetrable darkness towards the rear of the chamber. My eyes adjusted to the gloom and I took in the familiar clutter of my sister's home.

Sundry offerings from those availing themselves of Meli's services lay all about. A small fortune in coins dotted the floor of the cave, a few gold ones glinting in the lamplight. A haphazard pile of amphorae of various sizes rose out of the ground like an enormous anthill. Assorted fine vases and cups sat here and there, the reason for their particular locations known only to my sister.

The exception to the disorder was the simple bed I had constructed for my sister. The wooden frame contained a canvas sack stuffed with straw and feathers. A pine-coloured woolen blanket from Thrace lay neatly folded at one end, its winding geometric designs faintly visible from where I stood. The bed looked as though it had not been slept in for some time.

A scuffling from the black recesses of the cave joined the sound of my own breathing. A shadow detached itself from the darkness, sharpening into a human figure as it came into the weak light.

"Hello, Meli," I said.

My sister did not reply. She approached me, each footstep deliberate, like a dance, before stopping so close that I could hear the faint sound of her breathing. She drew herself up to her full height, which was taller than most men but only reached my chin. She swayed her head slowly, her foxlike face examining me from different angles. I endured her scrutiny patiently, staring back into her green eyes and searching as I always did for a spark of the joyful, mischievous girl who I had had once known. I saw only cunning, suspicion, and the curse of madness.

Meli lived in a waking nightmare, and I wondered sometimes if death would have been a more merciful fate for her. Her lover, Lykos, my mentor and brother of Thrasybulus, had died fighting the Tyrants of Athens, but many people had suffered similar fates during those dark times. Meli's suffering had been worse. My enemy, Menekrates, had sent her to be worked to death in the lightless, airless depths of the silver mines of Laurion. She toiled there for more than a year before I found her. That she had survived so long spoke much of her fortitude and spirit. But she was not a whole person when I brought her back into this world.

"Meli! I have brought some food for you," I said, breaking the silence. I dumped the sacks on the floor. I brought provisions for my sister as often as I could. I had tried to persuade her to stay at my home in the city, but she refused. The ghosts that haunted us both were too much for her to bear, and she had retreated to her isolated haven in the hills. But she was my sister and I took care of her as best I could, though I did not doubt her ability to fend for herself should the need arise. "I am going away," I continued. "This should be enough for some time, but I have arranged for more to be brought here if I am gone longer than expected." I said nothing of my mission.

My sister narrowed her eyes suspiciously at me. She said nothing, yet nor had I expected her to. She had not uttered a word to me for more than a year.

"Tibo is coming with me," I said.

At the mention of my friend, Meli's expression softened for an instant. Tibetos often accompanied me to the cave and I was aware that he sometimes made the journey on his own, though I pretended not to know. My friend had grown into a fierce fighter in his own right, but his soul was kind-hearted and gentle, and his love for my sister was not less than my own.

"I will return as soon as I can," I said. I held out my arms, inviting my sister into my embrace. The ephemeral warmth in my sister's eyes vanished and she turned away. It had been a vain hope to expect her to come to my arms as she had done when she was a child, but her rejection still pained me.

I lowered my arms. "May Bendis protect you, Melitta," I said, invoking the Thracian goddess to whom my sister prayed. I bobbed my head in a perfunctory bow and turned away. Pushing aside the leather covering, I stooped low to exit my sister's refuge, but I was stopped by a voice at my back. At first I thought it had been my imagination, so long had it been since I had heard my sister speak. I let the leather flap drop back, turning to face my sister in the gloom.

"What did you say?" I ask, not trusting my own ears.

"You are going to Delphi," Meli said.

A chill passed through me. "How could you know that?"

She smiled cryptically. "The goddess tells me many things." The gods had shared my sister's dream-world since she was a child, whispering omens to her as she slept. Their messages, though deceptive and ambiguous, were ignored at one's peril.

"What else did they tell you?" I asked.

Her vulpine eyes narrowed. "That I should go with you."

CHAPTER 11

The creaking of the wooden dock under my weight was a welcome sound. I did not take well to sea travel, but given the urgency of our mission, it was the fastest way to reach Delphi.

A powerful grip seized my arm from behind. "Steady, Dammo! You're walking like a man who's had three too many cups of wine!"

I closed my eyes and took a deep breath. "I'm fine, Mnasyllus," I said, patting my friend's massive hand. Mnasyllus looked unconvinced.

Mnasyllus was one of my oldest comrades. Along with Tibetos, we had come up together through the ranks of the *peripoli*. A farmer's son, Mnasyllus was shorter than me but half my weight again. At peace, he was soft-spoken and gentle, but when roused to anger in battle there were fewer more fearsome. This was especially true when he wielded the enormous *kopis* sword now strapped across his back, a weapon that few men could even lift let alone swing.

While I leaned on Mnasyllus, a small, wiry figure slipped past us. "Pardon me, Master," the man said as he hauled an enormous load of gear from the ship. Iollas was a former helot, a Spartan slave. I had helped free him from his bondage many years earlier, since which time the Messenian had insisted on serving me with maddeningly stubborn devotion. I wished no man to serve me, but the loyalty of Iollas could not be shaken. He was no warrior but had the constitution of a mule and was fast enough with a dagger when the need arose. He darted past us again as I stumbled towards the shore.

By the time my feet reached solid ground, my sense of balance had reasserted itself. I sucked in the cool spring air, sweeping an appraising look over the rest of our band. It was an odd assortment. The bull-like Mnasyllus chatted with Sabas, who was as stringy and taut as a hare. The Cretan shared that animal's coiled energy as well as a fearlessness that bordered on madness. In one hand he held what looked like a thin staff but was in fact his great Phrygian bow, which was as tall as a man and strong enough to put an arrow through a bronze breastplate at one hundred paces.

Beside Sabas and Mnasyllus stood Telekles, who was taking in the scene with a characteristic look of bemusement. The good-humored Telekles was more than ten years my senior but wore his experience lightly. In our bandit-hunting patrols around Attica, he let me lead the expeditions but quietly offered wise words of advice whenever difficult decisions needed to be made. Telekles winked at me and leaned over to say a word to Stachys, who laughed at whatever was said. Like Stachys, Telekles came from a wealthy background, though he rarely spoke of it. Both of Telekles and Stachys preferred our rangers' itinerant way of life, much to the distress of both of their families. I was glad they had come.

Tibetos was there, of course. He came over to me and raised an appraising eyebrow. "You are a much paler shade of green now," he joked sympathetically. Though we had both grown up in the city and never learned to swim as children, Tibetos had taken to the sea as though he had been born to it. In the water he was like a dolphin and on ships he moved about like a veteran sailor. I, on the other hand, could hardly look at a ship without a cold sweat breaking out on my back.

"I'd rather fight a hundred Spartans than get back on that boat," I agreed. Tibetos nodded but said no more. I knew that there was something else on his mind. "What is it, Tibo?"

He glanced over at my sister, who stood apart from the rest of our band. "I'm worried about Meli," he said in a low voice.

"She has left her cave, Tibo. That's something," I said.

Tibetos was unconvinced. "Even so, she's become more closed off than usual." I knew that Meli sometimes spoke to Tibetos when he visited her at the cave, something she never did for me.

Sometimes, Tibetos told me, she would even laugh, a sound I longed to hear but which was denied to me.

As if sensing our attention, my sister turned her deep, green eyes on us. Meli stood out not only as the only woman in our group but for her quiet intensity. Amidst the frenetic activity of the port, she was like a dark, still pool. After uttering her first words to me in years at her cave, she had resumed her silent ways for our journey. The others remembered how Meli had once been in former days. They respected her wishes to be left alone, but like Tibetos and me, any one of them would have died to protect her. The sailors on the ship felt otherwise, muttering prayers or making signs against the evil eye whenever they crossed paths with her. Now they were visibly relieved to have her off the ship.

Before I could go speak to Meli, the shabby black-cloaked figure of the Delphic priest Samolas stepped into my path. "We are fortunate. The consultation day is tomorrow. We must set out for Krissa soon if you are to present yourself at the temple for your consultation," he said. The village of Krissa lay a few hours' walk up the valley from the port. From there we would ascend the mountain paths to the lofty sanctuary of Delphi itself.

I was confused. "Consultation?" I asked. This was the first mention of making a formal consultation in the sanctuary.

When I told Samolas this, he shook his head. "The Pythia was quite insistent that Thrasybulus present himself at the temple. Since he is not here, the same command applies to you. There is no time to tarry here."

"Not even for supper?" I asked innocently.

The priest gave a pained expression. Throughout the journey old man had consumed copious quantities of food and wine at every possible opportunity. "Perhaps a small bite," he conceded, casting a hungry glance towards a row of food vendors who were doing good business selling to the many visitors crowding the port.

There were a few hours before sunset. I reckoned we could make it to Krissa in that time, but it would be dark when we reached Delphi itself. I assented to the priest's advice with a grunt and turned to find Meli's impenetrable stare still locked on me. I matched her gaze with my own as I spoke.

"*Peripoli*," I announced. "Gather your kit and buy some food. We set off for Delphi immediatcly."

Meli's eyelids twitched. I thought I saw a trace of a smile as she turned away, but it may have only been my imagination.

"WATCH IT!" THE MAN GROWLED. In the torchlight I had not seen him lying on the path. Before I could respond he had burrowed back under his blanket, once again becoming just another bump in the shadows.

It was nearly midnight. Samolas, Meli, and I were picking our way through a ring of temporary campsites just outside the town of Delphi proper. Small cooking fires and tents dotted the slopes. Also scattered about was a small army of sleeping bodies like that of the man whom I had just disturbed.

"It is always like this before a consultation day," Samolas explained as he stepped over another dark lump in the pathway. "Especially for the first consultation day of the year." The priest's vigour seemed to grow as we ascended the slopes towards Delphi.

The town itself was hardly the size of a single district in Athens, for it was limited in size by the surrounding steep terrain of the mountains. Nine times a year, however, the population of local Parnassians swelled with not only with those who came to consult the Oracle, but also their parties of slaves, friends, and any other family members who had chosen to accompany them. For this reason, the slopes outside the town were packed with anyone unable to find accommodation in the town, which was almost everyone.

Only Meli and I had accompanied Samolas to Delphi. The rest of our group had remained in the valley below where another temporary village had sprung up. Enterprising locals, quite accustomed to the periodic influx of visitors, were selling food and other necessities at lofty prices that would have left even the most extortionate of Athenian merchants with their mouths agape.

The path crested one last ridge and we found ourselves among the houses at the edge of the village. "We are almost there," Samolas said

The priest zigzagged through the shadowy warren of houses and walled compounds, leading us to a destination known only to him. Meli dogged his heels with almost noiseless footsteps and I brought up the rear. The unfamiliar laneways were rife with ambush points and my soldier's instincts thrummed. Unconsciously I reached to unsling Whisper from my back only to find empty space. I had reluctantly left the *rhomphaia* with Tibetos and the others, for Samolas had said that weapons were strictly forbidden and I had no wish to see my blade confiscated by some overzealous Delphian guard. The small dagger concealed under my cloak would have to do.

Samolas stopped abruptly in front of a moderately-sized house. "We are here!" the priest announced. He rapped the iron doorknocker three times and stepped back.

In a moment soft firelight from within the home spilled out onto the laneway as the door opened. A young man holding a lamp appeared. "Samolas! You have returned!" he said with a grin. The man ushered us into the building, strangely unsurprised by the appearance of the Delphic priest and two strangers in the middle of the night.

Meli and I stood aside as the young man greeted the older priest and inquired about his journey. A brazier in the centre of the small courtyard burned gently, giving me the chance to study him more clearly. The man was of average height with an athletic build. He wore several layers of robes to combat the chill of the early spring night. His clothes were plain but had the texture and cut of fine material. Having finished addressing Samolas, the young man turned towards me and my sister. Black curls of hair framed a handsome, welcoming face. He extended a hand.

"I am Agasias," he said. "And you are not Thrasybulus, I see!"

"I speak for him," I said. "My name is Daimon, son of Nikodromos, and this is my sister, Meli."

The young man's eyes narrowed. "The Tyrant-Slayer?" he asked. I nodded. "And his sister, the Thracian soothsayer?" Under her hood, Meli's hard, green eyes were unreadable. Agasias clapped his hands together "Wonderful! The hero of Munychia in my own home! You must tell me about the battle on the Munychia Hill before you return to Athens."

"You know of me?" I asked, surprised a young man in Delphi had recognized my name.

"Some people collect gold, but we at Delphi collect information, which is sometimes the more valuable of the two!" he said, winking at me. He leaned in close and lowered his voice. "To be honest, I'm glad it is you who came instead of Thrasybulus. A bit of a stuffy bore, or so I've heard." I liked the young priest even more.

Before I could confirm or deny this assertion, the priest Samolas interjected. "That is quite enough, Agasias!"

The young man gave a chastened bow. "I apologize, O Samolas," he said with unconvincing humility

The old priest turned to me. "You must excuse Agasias," he said. "He is empty-headed at times, but has a good heart. In any case, he will be your guide in Delphi."

"My guide?"

"Tomorrow will be quite chaotic. I have my own duties to attend to, so Agasias will accompany you into the temple sanctuary where the Pythia will see you."

"Can we not see her now?" I asked.

"Impossible!" the old priest said. "The Pythia is deep in preparation for tomorrow's consultations. She must be pure before the god or Apollo will not accept her as his vessel."

"Can we not wait until the following day?"

"The Pythia instructed that Thrasybulus or his ambassador consult her at the temple with the other suppliants. Unless she says otherwise, we will adhere to her instructions. Now," Samolas said, "I must report to Zelarchus, the head priest. I leave you in the care of Agasias."

Agasias showed the old priest out. "He is probably just looking for something to eat," he joked knowingly. "But," he said, becoming more serious. "You must both be tired from your journey. My slaves will prepare some food and bedding for you." He called out and two sleepy-looking youths appeared. Unlike the well-wrapped Agasias, the slaves only had simple tunics between their skin and the chill night air. Agasias assigned them their tasks and they hurried off to do his bidding. "You must forgive my humble home. It must be less than you are used to in Athens," he said.

In fact, it was a fine house from what I could see in the firelight and I told him so. Agasias seemed pleased at the praise. I had one more question for him. "Samolas said, *'if* the consultations go ahead.' What did he mean?"

"Ah," Agasias said. "A sheep will be sacrificed at dawn and its entrails examined. Only if the omens are good will the Priestess go to the sacred spring to purify herself one final time," he explained.

"Are the omens ever bad?" I asked.

"Not in my lifetime," Agasias said. "Apollo always seems to make the steaming pile of stinking guts that spill out acceptable to everyone. There's too much business riding on the outcome, even for Apollo," he added coyly. He turned his smile on Meli. My sister returned his gesture with a stony, unblinking stare and Agasias' smile faltered. For the first time since we had arrived a twitch of uncertainty cracked the young man's amiable self-assuredness.

The return of his slaves relieved him of dealing with the awkward silence. "The room is ready," the nameless youth said.

"Good!" Agasias said, his confidence reasserting itself. "Please follow me."

The room was little more than a storeroom with two cloth sacks stuffed with straw and some blankets. On a short table sat a lamp, an ewer, and two cups for whatever the ewer contained. An ancient chamber-pot was tucked discreetly just inside the door. It was simple but more comfortable than anything the pilgrims sleeping on the rocky slopes outside the town could enjoy.

"We thank you for your trouble, Agasias," I said.

Agasias beamed. "It is my honour to have such renowned guests in my home," the young priest said with a bow. "You should rest while you can. I will come for you at dawn and accompany you to the temple."

I thanked him once more and settled down on my mattress. Meli had curled up on her bed with her back to me. Soon her breaths became deeper and more regular. I got up and pulled the blanket over her sleeping form. Meli was mysterious and sometimes frightening, but was still my little sister for all that.

I extinguished the lamp and lay back down on the straw bedding, feeling it crunch under my weight. I closed my eyes and pondered what new burdens the coming day would inflict on me. Before I could get caught in my worries, I fell asleep.

Had I known what Apollo had in store for me, I would have returned to Athens that very night.

CHAPTER 12

The hordes of pilgrims and their retinues rose with the sun.

The young priest Agasias looked over his shoulder to make sure that Meli and I were still with him. He spotted us a short way's behind him and waved. "This way!" he shouted before pushing forward only to be swallowed by the crowd once more.

"This is worse than Athens!" I muttered, shoving through the throngs in pursuit of the priest. I felt Meli's presence at my back, sticking to me like a shadow.

We caught up to Agasias, who was standing beside a high stone wall. "Watch out!" he said. All three of us pressed up against the wall as a line of fully-laden donkeys trudged past us on the narrow road.

"Is it always this way?" I asked. The narrow paths and laneways that served as the roads of Delphi teemed with life and commerce. The accents of a hundred poleis filled my ears as well as voices speaking odd foreign tongues. Dark-skinned Africans dotted the crowds as did fairer Thracians and Makedonians and others whose dress I did not recognize. The world had converged on Delphi, making it like the bustling port of Piraeus rather than the small mountain village I had expected.

"Only on consultation days," the priest said. "The Oracle only speaks on nine days every year, so it is the only chance people have to hear the god's counsel. And today is the first consultation day of the year, so it is even worse." He shrugged. "Everyone wants to see the priestess, but there is only one of her."

"And when it's not a consultation day?" I asked.

"Then it's just a peaceful village," Agasias said. "You'll see. In two days, there will be no one here but a few hundred locals cleaning up the mess."

"With their pockets heavy with the gold and silver from their grateful guests, no doubt," I said. It seemed as though every man, woman, and child in the village was out hawking their wares, from grilled snacks to a miscellany of small statues and charms that visitors could take back to their homes as a reminder of their close encounter with Apollo.

Agasias smiled innocently. "Apollo blesses the people of Delphi."

"Chickens not so much," I said, pointing towards a vendor selling fine black hens. A customer handed the vendor a coin and received a squawking bird in return. I had noticed an abundance of such stalls as we had wended our way up through the village towards the temple complex.

"Every consultant must offer a bird as a sacrifice before entering the temple," the priest explained.

"And how much does a sacred chicken cost?" I asked.

"Two drachmas," the priest answered.

"Two drachmas!" I said. It would take two or three days of hard labour for a man to earn that much. "And at the end of the day the people of Delphi enjoy a feast of chickens on behalf of Apollo," I said. It was a good trick, getting other people to pay for your dinner and pocketing some silver at the same time.

"Apollo blesses those who serve him," Agasias said with a grin. I laughed. I liked the priest's honesty if nothing else. Agasias changed the topic. "Let's proceed to the temple. I have duties to perform after all," he said, lifting a corner of his yellow robe. "Unless you need a moment more to rest," he added, glancing uncertainly at Meli. My sister, concealed under the hood of her oversized cloak, remained silent.

"We are ready," I said, speaking for both of us.

"Then follow me," Agasias said.

The early-morning sun was eclipsed by a blushing rock face that reached towards the sky just beyond the temple complex as the priest led us eastwards along the wall. "The wall encloses the entire sanctuary," Agasias explained as we passed the throngs of pilgrims and locals. "The entrance is at the south-east corner." This accounted for the growing density of the crowd as we proceeded. The staff Agasias bore gave him some authority and the throngs parted to let him through.

A line of armed Dephians blocked the entrance to the sanctuary. "Wait here," Agasias told us. "And keep your hood up," he advised my sister. "Women are not normally permitted into the sanctuary, though the Pythia has made an exception in your case." The priest left us to speak to one of the guards, who cast a suspicious look towards me and my sister. The guard nodded and moved aside to let us pass, much to the chagrin of those suppliants still waiting to be admitted.

Only when we had crossed into the complex did the full chaotic grandeur of the sanctuary become apparent. It was though a rain of small temples had fallen from the heavens to land on the slopes surrounding the grand temple of Apollo, which dominated the heights above. "These are the treasuries," Agasias said, sensing my curiosity. "They house the offerings the poleis and kingdoms beyond Greece have given to Apollo in gratitude for his divine favour."

"And how much treasure do they hold?" I asked.

"After hundreds of years? Beyond reckoning," the priest said as he led us upwards.

Though the sanctuary had not yet filled with those seeking the Oracle's counsel, the complex felt far from empty, for every space not occupied by a treasury was filled with statues of men, women, gods, and all nature of beasts from horses to sphinxes, all offerings to Apollo from hundreds of years of grateful suppliants. Pedestalled figures stood in rows several ranks deep in many places, their looming, frozen visages mutely witnessing our progress. Had the assembled mass of stone and bronze suddenly become flesh, it would have been a formidable army indeed.

A final turn took us to the wide ramp of packed earth leading up to the temple of Apollo itself. As we ascended the incline, the temple, hitherto only glimpsed between other buildings and statues, revealed itself in its full glory.

"Here we are!" Agasias said proudly, sweeping his arm across the view before us. Even Meli let out a small gasp at the sight of it.

The temple itself, though smaller than the Parthenon that crowned the Acropolis in Athens, was no less grand. A central stone ramp sloped upward through the columns to two great gold-plated doors, beyond which the dark interior of the temple lay hidden. More statues and monuments adorned the grounds around the temple, though in a more orderly fashion than in the rest of the sanctuary.

If there was any doubt as to whose temple it was, this was immediately dispelled by the enormous figure of Apollo standing in front of it. The god was as tall as the temple itself, looking down on those who had come to seek his counsel. Just then the sun at last crested the mountain to the east and the sun god brightened in his own radiant light. My own gaze rose to meet that of the illuminated god and the power of it transfixed me. It was only with great effort that I wrested myself away, only to be brought up short by the sight that greeted me.

Across from the sun god, on the other side of the temple, was another impressive statue. The body was perhaps twice the height of a normal man, but nonetheless did not stand much lower than the statue of Apollo, for a high, ornately-carved pedestal raised the figure so that he was almost eye-level with the sun god. The figure was that of a Spartan, his lambda-emblazoned shield resting at his feet. One arm raised a golden sword in a salute of victory. But it was not just any Spartan. I knew him. The Spartan challenged the god opposite him with a sword-sharp stare. The artist had done a fine job capturing the menace-laced authority of the man's features. Beside me, Meli let out a low hiss.

"Lysander," I said in a low growl.

"You recognize him, then?" Agasias asked. I had forgotten that the priest was still standing at my side.

"We've met," I said. I had met the Spartan general twice. When I was not yet twenty, I had been one of the heralds who had gone to ask Lysander for permission to collect our army's dead from the field of battle after the black-eyed general had smashed our force outside the walls of Ephesus. The second time had been in a tent outside Piraeus after Thrasybulus had defeated the Thirty Tyrants installed by Lysander to rule Athens after the great war. In the negotiations, the Spartan king Pausanias had undermined his upstart rival by taking away Lysander's influence in the city and by granting Athens a measure of autonomy. Lysander had not been pleased.

Agasias and I stared up at the statue for some moments before the young priest broke the silence. "Lysander commissioned the statue to give thanks to Apollo for Sparta's victory over Athens at Aegospotami," he said, his eyes not leaving the image of Lysander towering over us. At Aegospotami, Lysander had captured the entire Athenian fleet of triremes, forcing the city's complete surrender and ending thirty years of war in a day. He had also executed thousands of Athenian prisoners. "He brought in the finest sculptors in the world to make it," Agasias continued. "It is said that it is one of the largest marble statues ever built. It was only finished just recently."

"And you priests let him erect it here in front of the temple?" I asked.

Agasias shrugged. "I had no say in it," he said. "Anyway, how could they refuse him? He is the most powerful man in Greece." He turned towards me suddenly. "Did you know that the Samians have declared Lysander to be a god?" he asked.

"I did not."

"Oh! It's true!" Agasias said, warming to the subject. "Oh yes! Sacrifices, prayers, offerings… All the normal rituals! But that won't happen here," he said, jerking his head towards the statue of Apollo. "It's not Lysander's house, after all."

"Lysander might disagree," I said.

"We'll find out soon, won't we?" Agasias said.

I frowned. "What do you mean.

Agasias' eyebrows rose in surprise. "Did you not know? Lysander is here in Delphi."

Lysander is in Delphi. The sense of irritated anticipation that I had been feeling all morning evaporated with that utterance. Suspicion and hostility welled up to fill the void. Surely the Spartan hegemon's presence in Delphi could not be a coincidence. "When did he arrive?"

"A few days ago. He and his bodyguards have taken over the home of Eurylochus," Agasias said, as though I should recognize the name.

"Eurylochus?"

"The wealthiest man in Delphi," Agasias added.

"He must be the chicken merchant," I said flatly.

"Ha! I see! No! But he has a hand in almost every other business in the town and down in Kirrha," Agasias said, waving a hand in the general direction of the port. "What could the old bandit do except graciously offer the god from Sparta use of his home. He sees it as a chance to get in good with Lysander, no doubt."

I frowned, still pondering the implications of Lysander's visit. "And why has Lysander come to Delphi?"

"To consult the Oracle, of course!" Agasias replied, his tone suggesting he was surprised anyone would even need to ask the question. "He has been granted the right of *promanteia.*" *Promanteia* was the right to speak to the Oracle first, an honour of great prestige.

"Then he will be arriving soon?" I asked. As we had been speaking, more of the day's hopeful pilgrims had been admitted to the sanctuary and were beginning to arrive in front of the temple proper.

"Oh yes! I expect so."

Another question occurred to me. "When will the Oracle call for me?" I asked.

Agasias knitted his brow as he considered the matter. "The Oracle grants her audiences in order of importance, though there is some political calculation," he confided in a lower voice. "After *promanteia* the people of Delphi usually go first, followed by the more powerful suppliants such as tyrants or representatives of foreign kings and the like. Then we get the aristocrats and wealthy merchants worried about politics and business. By the end of the day it gets down to a few dirty bumpkins asking about who they should marry their daughter off to or other petty concerns," he finished disdainfully. "So, I don't know where you fit in. It is up to the Oracle."

"So I might be here a long time if the Oracle deems the visit unimportant?"

Agasias gave another unhelpful shrug. "Watch for me at the temple entrance. I'll come get you when it's your turn. But now I have completed my task of accompanying you here, I must go attend to my other duties." He flashed a smile and walked away, disappearing into the dark interior of the temple.

Meli had wandered away and was now at the foot of the statue of Apollo. She stared up at the god. Her hood had fallen back almost completely, revealing not only her face but her flaming tangle of hair.

"Be careful!" I said, pulling her hood up. "Women are not officially permitted in here, remember?" From within the shadow of her cloak, my sister eyed me with silent scorn. I sighed. "At least we have some good seats for the show," I said. Before Meli could protest, I heaved her up onto the low pedestal so that she sat beside Apollo's right foot. I hopped up after her and sat down. Meli narrowed her eyes at me, but I stared down her challenge. She gave an angry sniff and turned away but did not flee, so I counted it as a small victory. Seeing Meli's red hair reminded me that my own copper hair was hardly indistinct. I drew up the hood of my own cloak and settled back to watch the proceedings.

The temple grounds were filling up quickly. Temple attendants in yellow robes like those of Agasias attempted to maintain order by shepherding the pilgrims to certain areas, but they soon gave up as the crowds grew too unwieldy. I scanned the increasingly raucous mass of people and was surprised to pick out more than one woman among their number. Many of the men or their servants clutched their sacred black chickens, most of which seemed quietly resigned to their approaching doom. The pedestal on which Meli and I sat was soon packed with other spectators. A festival atmosphere pervaded the place.

The buzz of voices suddenly grew in intensity and there was a mass shuffling of sandaled feet as the assembled crowd collectively turned towards the ramp that ascended into the temple forecourt. The trill of Spartan flutes started up as if in response to the waiting spectators' anticipation.

Lysander, the hegemon of all Greece, had arrived.

CHAPTER 13

With some effort, the crowd parted to make way for the Spartan general's party. Those farther away craned their necks to catch a glimpse of the great man. From my perch on the pedestal I had an enviable view but was also more conspicuous. I sank further into the shadow of my cloak.

A pair of flute players led the delegation. The two garlanded youths swayed in unison as their fingers danced over their double-piped instruments. Behind them came Lysander, flanked by an honour-guard of spear-wielding Spartan soldiers marching on each side of their leader, their burnished bronze breastplates glinting under their heavy scarlet cloaks. The hegemon himself was draped in a pure-white cloak that parted as he raised his arms in acknowledgement of those gathered in front of the temple. He was unarmoured, unless one counted the wide golden collar-piece that covered his chest. Two slaves leading a massive snow-white ram brought up the rear.

From within my hood, I watched with a curled lip as Lysander's entourage made its way through the gawping onlookers to the front of the temple where a trio of Delphic priests awaited them. Many would remember this occasion as the day when they consulted the god Apollo through his oracle, but surely just as many would return to their cities and villages to tell the tale of how the great Lysander himself had passed close enough for them to have reached out and touched him, though it would have been a most foolhardy thing to do.

As though reminding those present of this fact, upon reaching the front of the temple, the Spartan guards formed a line in front of the temple steps, facing outward towards the crowd. The two slaves leading the ram handed the beast's rope to Lysander, who led the animal up the central ramp-way to the waiting priests. At the top of the steps, Lysander gave up the ram and turned to the assembled spectators. He raised his hands and a hush fell over the crowd.

"I have come here today," he began, "to humbly consult the great Apollo, Protector of the Shrine at Delphi, Slayer of the Python, He Who Strikes From Afar. As a token of my humility and respect, I offer this ram as a sacrifice to Him," he said, bowing towards the statue of the god where I now sat. An appreciative murmur rippled through the crowd. Beside me Meli scoffed loudly enough to draw glances from those nearby. Lysander accepted a dagger from one of the priests. The ram, possibly sensing its imminent fate, began bleating loudly. Its protests were cut short as Lysander seized one of its massive horns and drew the blade across the creature's throat, spilling the beast's lifeblood over the stone. The ram fought to stay standing but its strength rapidly diminished. It dropped to the ground, rolled over, gave a few spasmodic kicks and was still. Lysander returned the dagger to the priest, the Spartan general's white cloak somehow unstained by the sacrifice. The hum of the crowd reasserted itself.

But Lysander was not finished. He raised his hands and the crowd fell silent once more. "And," Lysander said, his voice rising, "I pledge that Sparta, the liberator of Greece, guarantees the freedom and independence of Delphi and her Oracle for all time. Should anyone seek to impose himself on her, then they will answer to the spears of Sparta!" he ended triumphantly. The crowd, made up in large part by citizens of Delphi, erupted in a roar of approval.

I frowned. It was true that Delphi craved autonomy. Because of its importance, other cities always sought to control it for the prestige and wealth that it brought. But, I thought, the Dephians were fools if they believed that Lysander would truly grant them freedom. Many cities had acccpted similar pledges from Sparta only to find themselves oppressed under the burden of the Spartan yoke. Let the Delphians do as they would, I thought. It was not my home. Let the Oracle give me her message and I could return to Athens and be done with it.

Lysander acknowledged his audience with one more wave before following a tall, long-bearded priest into the gloom of the temple. In his absence, the drone of voices began anew as those assembled speculated on what question Lysander might put forth to the Oracle and what advice the god Apollo might give in response. The murmurs of anticipation only grew as time passed.

I nudged the young man sitting next to me. "Does it usually take this long?" I asked.

The man scratched his thin beard. "No, but who knows?" he said in a local Parnassian accent. "Lysander is probably getting special treatment."

At last Lysander appeared at the top of the stairs and there was a small cheer from the crowd. But the Spartan's previous mien of benevolent protector was no more. From my vantage point, the scowl on his face was clear. For the first time that day I felt a smile emerging. Whatever response the Oracle had given him, it had not been what he had wished to hear.

Descending the temple steps, Lysander barked an order to his bodyguards. With practiced discipline, the soldiers formed a circle around the Spartan leader. The Spartans began to advance through the crowd. Those not quick enough to move were shoved roughly aside by the Spartan soldiers, producing a tremor of anger in the air. Lysander stared straight ahead, oblivious and unconcerned. People craned their necks to watch as the Spartan delegation marched out of the sanctuary and out of sight.

WHATEVER EXCITEMENT LYSANDER HAD CAUSED, the business of the day soon retook its proper place. After all, hopeful suppliants had travelled from far and wide to put their questions to the Oracle. It would be another month before they could do so again, which for most meant that today was the only chance they had.

The priests and attendants managed the affair with the business-like efficiency of customs officers at the docks of Piraeus. Names were called, two-drachma black chickens were duly sacrificed, and nervous-looking pilgrims were led into the temple one after another. My long-dead friend and mentor, Meges, had believed that men used the gods to frighten or cajole the gullible into giving up their silver. He would have been sneering with justifiable delight at the proceedings at the temple that day. When it came to the effectiveness of sacrifice and prayer, he had passed much of his suspicious nature on to me. I missed him.

As for those consulting the Oracle themselves, the outcome of their encounter with Apollo was written on their faces. Most re-emerged into the light of day with a look of relieved awe. Many left the sanctuary with their brows knitted in contemplation of the cryptic replies of the Pythia. Some grinned, others were in tears, and a few appeared with an expression of pale shock. But no one left unmoved by their experience.

Those entering the temple had something else in common: I was not one of them. Throughout the morning the consultations continued apace with nary a sign of Agasias. As the sun rose high in the sky, many sought the shade on the north side of the temple. The warmth of the spring was, for me, welcome after the months of winter damp, and I kept to my perch beside Apollo's stone feet. Meli would go off on her own, sniffing and prowling about the temple grounds like the curious vixen she was.

The morning crowds dwindled with the daylight. The rich and powerful had long since asked their questions and left. Now it was down to common folk to pester the god with their queries about business, proper marriages, or whether to undertake some long journey or other. The long wait was irritating; it was not I who had requested a meeting with the Oracle but the contrary. I joined my sister in her explorations to stretch my legs and fight the tedium. In the last hour of the day, I took to pacing the forecourt like a wolf trapped in a pit, taking the time to mutter a curse at the lofty statue of the victorious Lysander whenever my gaze fell upon it.

I looked about in the waning light of dusk. Besides a few stragglers and temple attendants, my sister and I were the only ones remaining. Agasias, I recalled, had noted that the last suppliants of the day were of the least import. My jaw clenched more tightly.

Thus, a stew of impatience, hunger, and slighted pride was simmering in my gut when Agasias finally appeared at the top of the temple ramp. The priest waved for me, but I refused to acknowledge him. With Meli at my side I stood unmoving like one more statue in the sanctuary, my arms folded across my chest. Agasias was forced to come to us.

Fatigue from the long day showed on the young priest's face, but his eyes still flashed with mischievous intelligence. "The Pythia," he said in a slightly exasperated tone, "will see you now."

Agasias led us up the ramp past the blood-spattered altar. We passed through the towering gilded doors into the temple. Despite the numerous braziers lining the main aisle and suspended from the ceiling, the interior of the temple was so dim that it took a moment for my eyes to adjust. A gaggle of priests awaited us near the rear of the building. I recognized the long-bearded priest who had greeted Lysander. He scowled at me and my sister, his eyes ablaze with hostility. "With me!" he barked. Without waiting for a response, he pivoted and vanished down a narrow stairway that disappeared into a square black hole in the temple floor. Agasias shrugged and shot a look at the hole, indicating that we should follow the scowling priest into the shadowy vault below our feet. Meli and I descended into the gloom.

After ten steps the stairs reached a small platform and reversed direction. A faint but clinging odor reached my nostrils. It was not like any incense I had ever known. "What is that smell, priest?" I asked.

The head priest flashed me an irritated scowl. "It is the *pneuma*. The breath of Apollo," he snapped, offering no other explanation. "Now come!" He continued to descend further into the depth of the earth.

Another ten steps brought us down further into the bowels of the temple and we entered a square chamber a little more than a spear-length to a side. The air was close with humidity. The faint but pervasive "Breath of Apollo" scratched more insistently at my lungs and eyes. I could only blink away the acrid fumes and suppress a sudden tremor of fear that tickled at my guts. My eyes adjusted to the dim light of the small space. My gaze fell first on the dour bearded priest, who hovered at the base of the stairs. When I turned, I finally saw the reason for my journey to Delphi.

The Pythia sat on a high bronze stool flanked by oil lamps hanging from the ceiling of the vault. The old woman was not the grand figure I had expected. A simple robe cascaded over the priestess's knees all the way past her feet so that at first glance she appeared to float above the tiled floor. She was unadorned with any jewelry, despite the prestige of her station. Her thick grey hair was unbound and flowed over her shoulders in great undisciplined waves. Kohl-lined eyes brimming with wisdom and power peered at the visitors who had intruded her sanctum. Her stature was diminutive, yet the hair on the nape of my neck prickled. The thinnest of smiles creased the old woman's lips.

"The God welcomes you to his house, Daimon of Athens."

CHAPTER 14

The force of the Pythia's stare hit me like a crashing wave. I wished to evade those burning eyes, but my pride was stronger, and I returned her gaze with equal intensity. As if sensing my challenge, the Pythia let the corners of her mouth curl slightly upwards in tolerant bemusement. She blinked slowly, like a cat, before tilting her head towards the head priest. "Zelarchus, leave us," the Pythia said. There was a core of iron authority in that old woman's voice.

The head priest's eyes widened. His mouth opened, but no words came. "O Oracle! I must protest!" he finally managed to sputter.

"Your protest is noted, Zelarchus. Now heed my command," the Pythia said in a tone that would brook no argument.

"It is not permitted for the Oracle to be left alone," the head priest said, his voice rising. He glanced at my sister before leaning towards the Pythia. "And with a woman!" he added with a hiss.

The Pythia barked a humourless laugh. "Am I, Apollo's voice on Earth, not a woman? I will keep His counsel, not yours, Priest! Now be gone, Zelarchus!" With great effort, the head priest swallowed any further objections. His mouth tight, he gave a perfunctory bow and ascended the steps out of the chamber, but not before shooting a curse-filled look towards me and my sister. The sound of the priest's footsteps receded above us and my sister and we found ourselves alone with the Oracle of Delphi.

The Pythia addressed my sister first. "Melitta, daughter of Erta, approach. The God would speak to you, servant of Bendis, beloved sister of Apollo." Upon hearing my mother's name spoken thus, I felt my chest tighten. My father was prominent enough so that his name might be known by others, even here in Delphi, but how the priestess came to utter the name of my mother, a Thracian slave, was a mystery. It unnerved me.

Meli glanced at me and I saw a crack in her cold confidence. But my sister cowered before neither god nor mortal. She walked across the chamber with her typical insouciant grace and stopped directly in front of the Oracle.

The Pythia reached out with her right hand, gently cupping my sister's cheek. She leaned forward and began to whisper in Meli's ear. Meli began to shake her head gently and while mumbling a response. Meli shook her head more vigorously but the Pythia continued to deliver her message in a murmuring whisper.

Meli looked back over her shoulder towards me and a trickle of tears on her cheek glistened in lamp-light. "No!" she said suddenly, the sound of it cleaving the calm that had heretofore filled the audience chamber.

But the Pythia had finished. The Oracle sat erect on her tripod. "Heed Apollo's word, Child," she said. "Now leave us. I must speak with your brother."

My sister glanced my way once more, but the dim light hid whatever her intense eyes might reveal to me. Before I could reach out to her, she had spun away and scurried up the stairs back to the world above.

I was alone in the chamber with the Oracle of Delphi.

"What did you say to my sister?" I asked.

"That is between her and the God. She has her own journey to take, though she will need you in the end, just as you shall need her. Now," the Pythia said firmly, "come and stand before me, Daimon, son of Nikodromos, Killer of Tyrants, Enemy of the Gods." Each word cut the air like honed iron. I did not move. Her kohl-lined eyes peered into me. I felt my will wavering.

"You know of me," I said, breaking the silence.

The Pythia's nodded with a slow blink of her eyes. "Whispers and rumours from a thousand cities converge on this place. Would it not be strange if I had not heard of the Tyrant-Slayer of Athens?"

"I find it more strange that I have waited from dawn in the hot sun to stand here before you now, though it was you who requested this audience," I countered.

The Pythia's eyes widened and I thought I had offended her, but I was wrong. She laughed in delight, and in that laugh I heard echoes of my mother's voice from long ago. "Good!" the Pythia said with a clap of her hands. "Good! You are proud and impudent, even in Apollo's own house! He has chosen well! And," she said, leaning forward, "do not think that being the last to enter this chamber is a reflection of your insignificance, for now there is no need for haste. On the contrary, those who come last shall find themselves first in the god's eyes, young Daimon."

"I thought that honour belonged to Lysander," I said, thinking of the Spartan hegemon's being given the *promanteia* privilege of being the first person to see the Pythia that morning.

"Often things are not as they seem, *pai*," the Pythia said.

The familiarity with which the Pythia regarded me unsettled me. "Lysander did not seem pleased when he left the temple," I observed.

"The God did not give Lysander the answer he wished to hear," she said vaguely.

"And Lysander. His presence here. Is that why you contacted Thrasybulus?" I ventured.

The Pythia bowed her head in acknowledgement. "It is."

"What message should I take back to Thrasybulus?" I asked.

Her eyes narrowed. "You believe that to be your mission? To be a mere courier for your *strategos*?"

"That is the task entrusted to me," I responded.

The Pythia fixed her cat-like gaze on me as though I were a mouse. At last she spoke. "Then my message is this: Lysander seeks to usurp the power of Delphi."

It was a bold claim. The temple of Delphi, in theory at least, was above the constant squabbling and wars among the poleis of Greece. The independence of the Oracle was sacrosanct. Such was her pre-eminence that one hundred years earlier even the invading Persians had dared not violate the holy temple while they were ravaging the rest of Greece. "He wishes Delphi to serve Sparta?" I asked.

The Pythia shook her head. "More than that, *pai*. He wishes Delphi to serve *him*."

I frowned slightly. "To what end? He already rules the entirety of Greece in all but name," I said.

"And now he wishes to rule in name, as well," she said.

The Pythia's meaning began to push into my awareness. The old woman watched me expressionlessly like a teacher watching a dull-witted student stumble and struggle towards a conclusion. "He wishes to become King of Sparta?" I asked, incredulous.

"That is correct," the Pythia acknowledged with a nod.

I tried to understand. Sparta was ruled by two kings from two separate bloodlines. Each king could veto other's decisions so as to prevent one man from accumulating too much power. I had met one of the kings – Pausanias – after Thrasybulus had battled the Spartans to a stalemate that compelled them to negotiate a truce with Athens. Pausanias had no love for the upstart Lysander, to be sure, and it was he who had tacitly approved Athens' limited independence as a counterweight to Lysander's growing power.

Of the other Spartan king, Agesilaus, I knew less. The king was said to be stunted and lame, and only his royal birth had saved him from the death that awaited other malformed infants in Sparta. There were other rumours as well that Agesilaus was under Lysander's control and did nothing without the Spartan general's consent. The notion that Lysander desired more power for himself held no surprise for me. But my powers of perception had reached their limits.

"But how could Delphi help him achieve this?" I asked. The Oracle had great influence, it was true, but I could not see how Delphi would convince the conservative Spartans to abandon their traditional kings in favour of Lysander.

The Pythia took a deep breath. "The Spartan lines of kings are failing. Pausanias is weak, and Agesilaus is not his own man. Lysander already commands the loyalty of many Spartiates. But only Delphi can grant him legitimacy if he decides to claim the throne of Sparta for himself."

"He has requested this of you?" I asked.

"He has."

"And he was not pleased with your answer," I stated, remembering the look of rage on Lysander's face as he exited the temple that morning.

"He was not."

"Then he has failed," I said. Yet I knew it unwise to underestimate the cunning of the Spartan hegemon.

"Lysander does not need my blessing to succeed," the Pythia said.

"But surely it is your word that matters," I said.

The Pythia sighed. "I am the focus of this temple, its reason for being. But I am not all-powerful. There are factions here, as in your own city. Priests are human, and some crave power more than they honour the laws of the temple, and some seek to undermine me." I recalled the anger with which the head priest Zelarchus had spoken to the Oracle.

"But how?" I asked.

"Lysander forgets who I am. I am like a spider at the centre of the great web that is the world. Every matter of importance sets a thread quivering and I feel it, whether it is from a great city or a village on the edge of nowhere. And one such vibration has told me of Lysander's plan."

I felt the Fates smile as they changed the direction of my destiny. I felt their hands on my back compelling me forward. I could not resist. "Tell me."

"Now that I have denied him, Lysander will put his contingency plan into motion. I am the voice of the God, but I serve at the pleasure of the priests of the temple. If Lysander can show them that Apollo himself supports his claim to the kingship of Sparta, my protests will matter little."

"Apollo?" I asked.

The old woman smiled at my confusion. "Not the true god, child, but someone that could convince enough people to support Lysander's bid to usurp the kingship of Sparta."

"Who?" I asked.

The priestess's next words were filled with queenly scorn. "The son of Apollo!"

CHAPTER 15

I thought I had misheard. I shook my head in an effort to rid myself of the lightheaded feeling brought on the stuffy, biting air. My head cleared somewhat, and I peered at the old woman, searching for signs of madness. She bore my scrutiny patiently. "Son of Apollo? You speak nonsense, Oracle," I said at last, scowling. "I will return to Thrasybulus and report that age has turned the Pythia's brain to barley porridge." I turned towards the stairs out of the pit.

"Wait!" the Pythia called. I stopped but did not look back. The Pythia spoke again. "Let me tell you a tale and then you may judge how much porridge my aged head contains."

I sighed and with reluctance returned to my place before the Oracle's tripod. "You are fortunate my mother taught me to respect the aged," I said.

The Pythia gave a conciliatory dip of her head. "A wise woman she must have been, then." The old woman straightened her back and began the promised tale. And what a mad tale it was. "A few years ago," she started, "The whispers of a rumour reached my ears: a maiden far in the north of Thrace claimed to have given birth to Apollo's child."

I scoffed. "Gave birth to the local chief's bastard, more likely."

The Pythia held up a challenging finger. "In this, you surely speak the truth, young Daimon, but the miraculous nature of the story does not end with the child's birth. It is said that the boy, Silenus by name, grew to manhood in a single year. Those who have seen him say that this young man of Thrace is so beautiful to behold that there is little doubt that he is the god's son."

"Thrace is a long way from Delphi," I said. "What does this son of Apollo have to do with Lysander?"

The old woman smirked with satisfaction, knowing she had hooked my curiosity. "I am not the only spider in this world. Lysander, too, has a web of spies, through which he learned of this young man. Word quietly spread to the slavers that there would a great reward for anyone who brought this Silenus south." Thrace was a great source of slaves, mostly captured and sold by their fellow Thracians. My mother had been one such slave.

"And I gather that Lysander is now in possession of this Silenus?" I asked.

"His agents have found him and hold him in Thrace."

"Where?" I asked, for Thrace was an immense land filled with warring clans and tribes.

"The young man was discovered far to the north, almost in the lands of the Skythians. Now he has been brought to a village in the south. Soon Lysander will travel there with priests from Delos and Delphi to bring this false prophet back to the temple. He will make a great spectacle of it, parading the impostor through all of Greece on the journey back to Delphi."

"And where is this village?" I pressed again.

The Pythia gave a cryptic smile. "Lysander keeps his secrets close, but there is little that can remain hidden from me, for Apollo himself is my eyes and ears! Even Zelarchus, who knows so much, does not know the name of the village. But I know!" She laughed to herself but did not reveal the name of the Thracian village to me.

Let the old woman play her games, I thought, shaking my head. Yet I was intrigued. "But for what purpose does Lysander make these efforts?" I asked, trying to conceal my interest.

The Pythia leaned forward. "The man Silenus is but one half of Lysander's scheme. Delphi is the other."

"In what way?"

"The wolf Lysander has scented an opportunity."

"Opportunity?"

The old woman leaned back. "So you do wish to hear more?" she asked, narrowing her eyes.

I gave a small, defeated wave. "Since I have travelled to Delphi to do so, tell me the other half."

The Pythia composed herself for the next part of her tale. "One of our elder priests discovered some scrolls deep in archives of the temple. It is said they record the oracles of one of my predecessors from many generations ago. Oracles that concern the leadership of Sparta." The Pythia's voice dripped with disdain.

"What do the oracles say?"

"I know nothing except that they will be favorable towards Lysander."

"You believe the records to be false?" I ascertained.

The Oracle barked a laugh. "Ha! They were planted there by one of Lysander's agents."

"One of the priests?" I asked.

"Most of the priests are good men dedicated to serving Apollo, but some are mortals of lesser character who can be swayed by gold and power. Lysander has servants among them who do his bidding."

"Do you not know them?"

"Just as you cannot see the end of your own nose, some things are obscured even to me," she said, tapping the tip of her nose.

I grunted, taking her point, for Lysander's plan was still hidden from me. "But how do these two halves — the false son of Apollo and the false oracles — fit together? Why does he wish to bring Silenus to Delphi?" I asked.

"This Silenus will be brought to the temple to be questioned by the priests on the summer solstice, Apollo's day. When they determine that this impostor is a true son of Apollo — and they will! — the false prophet will read the forged oracle for all to hear and all will know that Apollo and Delphi wish Lysander to take the throne of Sparta."

I shook my head in disbelief, for the scheme sounded ludicrous. "I think you overestimate the influence of a few priests and dusty scrolls!"

"Lysander will make a great show of the proceedings. He will bring Apollo's priests from Delos and other temples. He will invite the leaders of cities friendly to him. All will bear witness as the contents of the oracle are revealed in Apollo's own temple!"

I shrugged away a growing unease tickling my skin. "To what end? Words will not give Lysander the throne."

"Belief is a strange beast, *pai*," the Pythia said, her shoulders sinking. "More often than not, it is people's faith that leads to the realisation of a prophecy, and not the other way round. No, not everyone needs to believe, only enough for Lysander to achieve his goal. You, a child of Athens, should know only a majority is needed to win the day in the assembly!" she admonished me. She pointed a finger at my chest. "No, *pai*. News of the prophecy will spread to all corners of Greece, including the mess halls of Sparta. Those dissatisfied with the rule of the two kings will find new reason to throw their lot in with Lysander. With the legitimacy of Delphi behind him," the Pythia continued, "Lysander will move openly and depose the two current kings and become the sole ruler of Sparta."

The audacity of Lysander's plan amazed me, but I quickly realized that it was not as far-fetched as it appeared. Even kings and tyrants deferred to the authority of Delphi, and the Spartans were superstitious to a fault. If Lysander usurped the throne, it would strengthen rather than undermine the veracity of the prophecy, false or otherwise.

"If Lysander becomes king of Sparta, he will rule Athens as well," I said. The last time Lysander had exercised power over Athens, he had imposed a cruel tyranny upon the city, a tyranny that had led to the deaths of my wife and countless others. I would expect even worse if Lysander had absolute authority.

"You do not understand, *pai*. Athens is only the beginning of Lysander's ambitions," the Pythia said. "Persia is weak and divided. With the wealth of Delphi, Lysander can raise an army to topple the Great King." Her words called to mind the treasuries on the temple grounds that were bursting with sacred offerings of gold and silver. How many talents were there? I thought. Enough to outfit a thousand ships, at least. The Pythia leaned forward. "And now, this man Silenus, this supposed son of Apollo, this *blasphemy*," she almost hissed, "will aid Lysander to achieve this!"

I pondered her words. "Can you not just burn the scroll with the oracle?"

The Pythia dismissed my simplistic plan. "Another scroll would be produced before the ashes had even cooled." She peered at me, waiting for my response.

I knew where she was guiding me. "And this son of Apollo? This Silenus?" I asked.

She nodded her head with deliberate slowness, like my childhood tutor Iasos had done whenever I finally grasped the elusive point he had been trying to force through my skull. The Pythia's lips cracked open, revealing a sharp-toothed smile. "A son of Apollo is not so easily replaced," she said. The old woman's eyes seemed to burn. "You must kill Silenus, Daimon of Athens."

I looked at the priestess of Delphi in disbelief. "What madness is this?"

From her perch upon the tripod, the Pythia stared down at me. "The God has chosen you, Daimon of Athens. That is why Apollo has brought you here," she declared.

I was in no mood for such foolishness. "If Apollo is so powerful, why does he not smite Lysander himself?" I sneered. "Let Apollo use his silver bow to inflict sickness on Lysander and be done with it!"

The Pythia ignored my impiety. "The gods work through mortals to see their will done. You are the instrument with which Apollo will crush the ambitions of Lysander. I have foreseen it." She spoke as if it were a command.

I asserted my freedom from the god's machinations. "You are wrong," I said, stabbing a finger at her. "I am the slave of neither god nor man. I follow my own counsel." I regained a measure of control, remembering my mission. "But I will deliver your message to Thrasybulus. It is up to him to decide what to do with it." I gave a stiff bow. "Pythia," I said and then turned away. My movement brought on a wave of dizziness and the darkness seemed to ripple before my eyes. Suddenly I wished nothing more but to leave the Pythia's poisonous underworld lair and return to the fresh air of the world above.

The Pythia's called out. "Stop!" she said sharply. The command pulled at me but I pushed through its power. I resumed my ascent out of the Pythia's lair. "Please," the Pythia said more gently. Where authority had failed, a soft tone made me yield. "Come. Stand before me," the priestess of Apollo said. Gone was the sternness in her voice, a voice that was accustomed to speaking on behalf of a god. What remained was warmth. I sighed and returned to the centre of the chamber. The Pythia stepped off her tripod. She was surprisingly small. I towered above her.

The Oracle of Apollo lifted her chin to peer at me. For some time we regarded each other in silence. At last she seemed to come to a decision. "It has been a long day, *pai*, one that has exhausted me for many reasons. I have neither the will nor the power to force you onto the path Apollo has laid before you. I will give you a message to deliver to Thrasybulus, if that is what you wish."

"It is, O Oracle," I said cautiously, caught off-guard by the Pythia's sudden abandonment of her demand that I go to Thrace.

But the Pythia was not finished. "It is no small thing to disobey a god. You frighten me, Tyrant-slayer," she said. "'*Theomachos*' they call you — '*God-fighter.*' You think yourself free of the gods, but you are not. Even if you do not serve Apollo, you are the servant of other beings."

"I serve myself," I responded.

The old woman smiled sadly. She shifted to one side and peered past me to an inky dark corner of the chamber. "Tell that to *them*," she said. The skin on my neck prickled with those words, for in my heart I knew the dark spirits of which she spoke. "You bring great evil with you, Daimon of Athens; Even now, the Furies are here, in the shadows, watching you, waiting. I see them!" A chill enveloped me and the Pythia seemed to shimmer before me. I swallowed the fear that was suddenly welling up inside me. A waft of air made the lamps ripple and I knew it was not the breath of Apollo I felt on my neck. I dared not turn to see if the snake-haired spirits of vengeance were indeed at my back, coiled with poison-dripping fangs ready to bite.

The Pythia returned her gaze to me. "They are drawn to you, the Furies, for you are their instrument in this world. Through you they exact justice on the wicked and cruel. Their aura infuses your being. Others sense this but do not understand; that is why so many fear you." She extended one hand towards my cheek. I flinched slightly, as though her touch might, burn me. But her hand was soft. "Do not fear. They have no power here, not in the house of Apollo." The chill at my back receded and the lamplight grew stable once more. "But know this: you are as much the Furies' victim as their instrument, for they taint you with their essence. There is so much anger in you, Child. So much pain. So much sadness," she said. In her eyes, I saw the Pythia's true power. More than cunning, more than guile or wisdom, she used another weapon to tear down the walls that hid what lay in men's hearts. It was kindness.

I found myself responding, almost against my will. "They bind me," I whispered. "The anger. The pain. They torment me."

"You are wrong, child," the Pythia said, letting her hand fall. "It is not they that hold you, but you who will not let go of them. Your family. Your comrades. Your wife. Their souls seek the peace of death and forgetting, but you will not let them rest. You must let them go."

The pounding of my heart filled my ears. "I cannot," I said, the words catching in my throat. "I have tried, but I cannot."

Again, I tried to leave that dark chamber, if only to hide my sorrow from the old woman's gaze, but once again the Oracle's voice held me fast. "Daimon," the Pythia said gently.

I looked back at the Pythia. The Oracle sat once more high atop her bronze seat. "Do you have yet more burdens for me to bear, Priestess?" I asked.

The Pythia turned her palms upward. "You have forgotten where you now find yourself. Would you leave so hastily? Countless men from the ends of the earth to this place. They dream of having an audience with the priestess of Apollo. Many find their way here to Delphi in hope of seeing me, but only a few are given the privilege of hearing the God's words from my own lips. Do you cast aside so easily that which kings and tyrants covet? The God awaits your question, should you wish to ask it."

I was about to dismiss her words, but the Pythia's stare stopped me. That terrible gaze cut through my flesh to lay bare the question that I hid in my heart. The question that burned in me when I awoke in the dead of night drenched in sweat, the screaming faces of the men I had slain still seared into my mind's eye. The question that made me doubt myself when people in the agora made the sign to ward off the evil eye at the sight of me. The question that filled me with shame whenever my son looked up at me in fear. The question I dared not utter aloud. Until now.

"Am I a good man?" I asked softly.

The Oracle's mouth stretched into a thin, unknowable smile. Her eyes closed. A pure silence settled over the chamber. The lamps burned more brightly, and the foul taint of the Furies was driven from the shadows. The air became pure and I knew that the God was present. I was afraid.

The Pythia's head began to roll languorously, as if she were listening to a gently strumming lyre that only she could hear. Then came soft, inflected humming, almost inaudible, like that made by a person caught between the world of dreams and the waking world. At last her movements ceased and she let out a deep, extended sigh. Her eyes snapped open and a new, unworldly gaze fixed upon me. And then, in a voice not her own, she spoke:

"With arete, the Demon will vanquish evil,
With strength, he will forgo temptation,
With mercy, he will gift the world with wisdom,
With scorn, the world will remember his name."

The reply given, the Pythia seemed to shrink as the God's power left her. The old woman blinked at me with mortal eyes once more. "Did you find the answer you were seeking, Daimon of Athens?" she asked.

"I do not know," I said.

It was true.

CHAPTER 16

The Pythia shifted on her tripod and winced. "We have been down here a long time. Zelarchus and the other priests will be jealous of your time with me. It is time to leave." The old woman slid off her stand and I held out my arm for her to steady herself. Grasping my arm, she looked up at me. "I will retire to my residence in the town to rest. You will come to me later tonight. I will have more information to give you. All will become clear."

The Oracle's exhaustion was palpable as I accompanied her from the vault. We had not reached the first platform when a silhouetted form blocked our path.

"Oh!" exclaimed the shadow. It was Agasias, who met us ascending from the Pythia's vault. How long he had been skulking in the stairway I did not know. As if anticipating my suspicion, the young priest explained his presence. "Zelarchus just sent me to fetch you. He was worried that some evil had befallen the priestess," he said with a quick bow to the Pythia. "Though I would think the Oracle could be no safer than at your side, Tyrant-slayer," he added, a touch ingratiatingly. "Follow me, before the head priest collapses in a fit of apoplexy," Agasias said, leading the way back up to the temple proper.

When we emerged into the relative brightness of the main hall, more than the light I welcomed the fresh air. Each breath purged my lungs and mind of the cloying vapours from the pit below. An anxious-looking Zelarchus was waiting along with a small crowd of temple functionaries and servants.

The head priest glanced down at the Pythia's hand on my arm. Noting the impropriety of it, he frowned with disgust but visibly restrained himself from seizing her from me. Behind Zelarchus stood Agasias. The young priest was clearly enjoying the displeasure my presence was causing his superior.

"Agasias! Take the Oracle to her residence," Zelarchus ordered, biting each word.

Agasias snapped to attention. "Immediately, O Zelarchus," he said. He raised his eyebrows at me before gesturing to two of the servants to relieve me of my duty assisting the Pythia.

The Pythia squeezed my arm before allowing herself to be escorted from the temple. As she passed near Zelarchus, she stopped, beckoning the head priest to her side. Zelarchus, who shared my height if not my bulk, leaned down to receive his instructions from the diminutive priestess. He shot a glare in my direction before bowing towards the Oracle. From our respective positions, Zelarchus and I watched the Pythia and her retinue exit the temple into the failing light of the evening.

We were alone in the temple. Zelarchus turned my way and cleared his throat. He waited for me to approach, but I crossed my arms. Irritated, the head priest opened his mouth, most likely to bark an order at me, but then thought better of it. He strode towards me, mumbling into his beard the whole way, coming to a stop before me. I said nothing.

The long-bearded priest's officious tone failed to mask his disdain. "The Pythia has made the highly irregular request to speak with you in private at her residence, something I strongly disagree with. Nevertheless, I shall obey her command. The day has been long and strenuous. The Pythia needs some time to rest and refresh herself. I will have the town guards ring their bells when she is ready to see you." He told me where to find the Pythia's private sanctuary in the town outside the temple complex.

The head priest accompanied me in resentful silence out of the temple and under the towering gaze of Lysander's stone tribute to himself. The complex was empty, save for a few sentries, the bustle of the day's events already a vanishing memory. Only the barest remnants of day clung to the sky over the mountains in the west, and the brightest stars had begun to break through the curtain of night. We meandered down the pilgrims' path to the entrance, the army of statues looming in the shadows to either side of us the entire journey.

No sooner had I stepped through the main gate than the heavy door thudded closed behind me, leaving me standing alone on the road outside the temple precinct. Here, too, the throngs from the morning had dissipated, leaving only a few stragglers roaming about in the quickly darkening streets. I cast a glance about in search of Meli, but she was nowhere to be seen. I was not overly concerned. My sister knew how to take care of herself.

A rumble in my gut reminded me that I had eaten nothing since the morning. I recalled seeing a tavern near the edge of the town where vendors had been slinging food for crowds of hungry travellers. I headed in the general direction of the inn, hoping that it would still be open.

My mind was still unsettled by the events in the temple, but not so much as to overwhelm my warrior's instinct. A silent warning rang in my mind, and my senses stretched out, seeking the enemy I could not see. I continued walking. Every so often I would turn randomly, cutting right or left into smaller lane-ways and even doubling back on myself. Sometimes I would wait, stepping back into deep shadow. It was an old habit from my childhood when I had roamed the streets of Athens while engaging in all manner of mischief. If anyone were following me, I would see them.

But there was no one. The sound of voices and laughter nearby told me that the tavern was still open. As I turned the final corner, the aroma of something warm and edible wafted invitingly onto the street. I scanned the roadway but could find nothing untoward. I frowned. The encounter with the Pythia had unnerved me and now I was jumping at shadows. I took a deep breath and pushed through the leather flap covering the doorway.

The front part of the building was an open courtyard filled with tables, half of which were now occupied. A dozen pairs of eyes glanced my way, but I was evidently not a threat and the assorted customers went back to their conversations. By the look and sound of them, the majority of the patrons were local Delphians gladly spending money fleeced from the travellers who had come to consult the Oracle. A few other hard-to-place accents floated in the air, but it was of no matter. I wended my way to an empty table in the rear corner of the courtyard and sat down on a stool with my back to the wall.

A stout man wearing a time-beaten leather apron appeared from a back room. Spying me, the iron-haired man ambled to my table with a proprietor's smile. "What can I get you, friend?" he asked. His thick arms and neck told me he had little trouble keeping the peace in his establishment.

"Wine, bread, figs, and sausage, if you have any," I said.

The owner pulled on the thick hoop of gold dangling from his right ear, looking doubtful. "Well, if you'd come earlier I might have had more to offer, but on Oracle days, it's like a swarm of locusts descends on our town. I've got some onion stew and bread left but no sausage and no wine."

"A bowl of that, then," I said, keeping on eye on the front door. I gave him a few obols for the food.

"It'll do you right," he promised. As the owner walked away, he signalled to a wiry youth hidden in a doorway leading to the rear part of the building. The owner flicked his chin in my direction and the boy scurried away, appearing a moment a later with an ancient ewer full of water and a cracked cup. He dropped them heavily on the table and turned to leave, bumping into me as he did so.

My hand shot out and grabbed the boy's arm. "Hey!" I said. The boy tried to twist away. His corded muscles strained against my grip. There was strength there. "I think you have something of mine," I said. My free hand moved down to the boy's fist, relieving him of the small leather satchel clutched there. The familiar metallic heft of my coin purse settled in my palm.

My hold still firm on the boy's arm, I examined him. He was perhaps thirteen or fourteen years old, give or take a year. His dirty blonde hair betrayed his northern ancestry. Some Makedonians had his colours, as did some traders who came from the tribes of the Euxine Sea beyond the Hellespont. The boy was likely a slave, taken from his village when he was young, like my mother or Tibetos had been when they were enslaved. The boy's blue eyes glared at me defiantly, almost but not completely hiding his fear.

"Your bump was too strong," I said to him quietly. "Too deliberate. You need to work on that." I had once been a child-thief like him, lifting purses and whatever else I could from the careless in the agora.

"Eat shit, turd-sniffer!" the boy hissed back at me. I felt a grin breaking out despite myself. He was a boy after my own heart.

"Look in your hand," I said. The boy narrowed his eyes at me but did as he was bidden. He glanced down at his palm and his feral anger transformed into a look of stunned incomprehension as he stared at the drachma coin resting in his palm. "*That* is the soft touch you need to master," I said.

I slowly released the boy from my grip. He looked unsure now, as if waiting for a trap to spring. When the realization of his freedom dawned on him, he spun and darted away like a frightened hare, nearly colliding with the owner, who was returning with the promised food.

"The lad giving you trouble? He'll get a thrashing, I promise you," the owner said.

"No, no," I said. "I was wondering where he was from, but he didn't know."

"What does it matter?" the owner said. "Thracians, Skythians, Kolchians... They're little better than animals." His eyes moved up to my copper-red hair. "Present company excepted, of course," he added hastily.

I smiled thinly and the owner took it as his cue to depart. In any case, the aroma of the stew distracted me from my thoughts. I had eaten nothing since my meagre breakfast that morning and my belly now rumbled in anticipation as I dug in. It was simple fare but hearty and filling. I slurped it down greedily.

Over the rim of the bowl I saw the leather flap over the doorway push inwards, admitting two cloaked men into the courtyard. I made as if I were occupied with my food but kept them in my field of vision. They were no farmers. They moved like fighting men. Former soldiers, then. Or mercenaries. They scanned the fire-lit room, pausing when their eyes fell on me. One of them whispered something to his partner but was interrupted by the arrival of the tavern owner.

The brawny proprietor greeted his newest customers. I strained to hear the men as I wiped up the last of the stew with the bread but could not catch their low response. I chewed on the final crust of stew-softened bread, watching as they pushed past the owner and strode towards me. They came to a stop on either side of my table.

"Stand up," the one on the right ordered. His flat, crooked nose and a partial left ear attested to a familiarity with violence. Under his scars, there was a familiarity to his features, but I had little time to reflect on this hazy sense of recognition. "You're coming with us." The thick accent was unmistakably Spartan. I ignored the Spartan, finding interest in something at the bottom of my bowl. A growl came from the man's throat. "I said," he said, reaching out to grab the bowl, "you're –"

I launched myself from the stool, snatching the ewer of water as I rose and slamming it into the Spartan's temple in a wet explosion of ceramic fragments. His partner reacted like a professional soldier, looping a fist towards my cheek, but I dropped low and was already moving towards him. His forearm deflected off my scalp. I threw my head upwards and my crown caught him hard under the chin, sending him reeling. I spun back towards the first assailant, who was trying to rise from his hands and knees with little success. My foot drove hard under his ribs and he collapsed into a ball as he heaved for breath.

Both the men were down. The few other patrons of the tavern were rising to their feet, unsure whether to flee or join the fight. I shot a look towards the door. Two more men appeared in the doorway. The short swords in their fists made clear their intent. I was trapped.

"Hey!" someone shouted. I pivoted towards the voice, anticipating another attacker. But I was wrong. The straw-haired slave stood in a shadowy doorway at the back of the shop. "This way!" he said, indicating I should follow him. I did not hesitate. As I plunged after the boy, I heard the commotion of more attackers pushing through tables and patrons in pursuit.

The owner appeared in front of me. "What's going on?" he yelled. The slave-boy darted past him, but in the narrow confines of the passage I had no such luxury. I barrelled into the proprietor's shoulder, the impact of my body sending him sprawling to the ground. I leapt over him in pursuit of the boy, emerging into a dimly-lit storeroom with a few sacks in the corner and lines of onions suspended from the ceiling. I cursed, thinking I had been led to a dead-end.

"Here!" the boy said, pointing at a barred door. I had missed it in the gloom, but my eyes were rapidly adapting to the dark. The boy hefted the bar, grunting with the effort. I jerked the door open to an even darker street outside. Wary footsteps were drawing closer to the storeroom. My pursuers' caution had given me just enough time to escape.

"Out!" I said. The boy needed no encouragement and fled into the night. I was right behind him but ducked to one side of the doorway, hugging the shadows of the wall. I had hardly concealed myself when two more pursuers burst out of the doorway, grinding to a halt right in front of me.

There was no time to draw my dagger. I stepped from the shadows and kicked the closest man's knee with the bottom of my foot as though I was breaking a timber. I felt the joint crack and the man collapsed with a howl. The other was fast, launching himself at me, but I was ready. I caught him chest to chest and flung him to the ground and I felt his hot breath in my face as the wind was knocked out of him. In an instant I was up, straddling his waist, my dagger already drawn and raised to dispatch him. But before the killing blow fell, my world disappeared in a flash of blinding light as something hard and dense connected with the back of my head.

I was faintly aware of my dagger skittering away across the stony ground. I tottered to my feet with my fists raised, swaying like a punch-drunk boxer. The man with the broken leg was still moaning somewhere to my right. I was surrounded by blurry figures. Iron blades glinted in their hands. I was a dead man.

But the end did not come. Instead of a sword in the back, there came a voice from behind me. "You see, lads? This one is a cagey bird. Didn't I tell you he wouldn't come nicely?" The rough voice had the guttural accent of the island of Andros. Even in my addled state, I recognized it instantly. A surge of rage coursed through my body, evaporating my dizziness like a raging fire consuming a drop of water.

"Orchus!" I spat. I spun towards the voice. The Andrian mercenary was my sworn enemy. He had participated in the murder of my parents and my wife. But the wily veteran had always eluded my blade. Even when I had slain his masters, the Tyrant Kritias and his vile son Menekrates, Orchus had managed to slip away. I tensed, getting ready to get at least one attack in before I died.

But a sword tip flicked up to my throat. "Uh uh uh.." Orchus said mockingly. "I would love to open your gullet, my Thracian whoreson, and I will if I have to. A corpse don't bite, after all, eh lad? But I have instructions to accompany you to my master."

"Accompany me?" I said through gritted teeth.

"Of course, lad!" Orchus laughed. "You've received a very special invitation! You are to have an audience with a god!"

CHAPTER 17

My captor and host spread his arms. "Welcome, Daimon of Athens!"

Lysander leaned back in the handsome chair, property he had usurped from Eurylochus, the wealthiest man in Delphi and in whose home I now stood. Warm light filled the central courtyard, for every pillar bore a hissing torch. Yet the cold glare of my Spartan escorts was frosty enough to negate the heat in the air.

I brushed aside Lysander's greeting. "Why have you brought me here?"

The hegemon of all Greece shrugged. "My captain," he said, glancing at Orchus, "noticed you lurking in the crowd. He reported your presence here in Delphi to me. I requested that he find you and invite you to my temporary home here so that we could speak." Orchus, standing at his employer's side, grinned wolfishly. I wanted to smash his yellowed teeth down his throat.

"Having your men accost me is hardly an invitation," I said, curling my lip at the Spartan whose face I had smashed with the ewer. His right eye was almost buried by the swelling of his cheek, but his left eye glared at me.

Lysander stroked his beard. "Perhaps I should not have sent Drakontios," he said. "The man has a history with you."

I turned to face the swollen-faced Spartan. Once again, I was struck with the sense that we had met before, but I could not place him. "Do I know you?" I asked him.

"You killed my brother," the man Drakontios snarled.

I scratched at my nose. "I've killed many Spartans. You'll have to be more specific."

"You hanged him like a dog!" Drakontios growled through his clenched jaw. Reaching for his sword, he took a step towards me but his murderous intent was checked by Lysander's raised hand. I narrowed my eyes to consider the Spartan's features more carefully and it came to me. Now I knew why the man's face tugged at my memory. Beneath his swollen face and twisted nose, the man bore a striking resemblance to the Spartan bandit leader I had left swinging from an oak tree more than a year earlier.

"Hanging was better than he deserved," I said coldly.

Lysander interceded once more before the purple-faced Spartan could reply. "Drakontios, you are dismissed. Leave us." Only the man's Spartan discipline prevented him from attacking me, such was the look of murder in his eyes. I watched him stamp off and disappear into the rear section of the home.

I looked back at Lysander. "The man's brother was one of your agitators," I said.

Lysander did not deny the charge. "Soldiers know the risks of their trade. But you must understand that Drakontios and his brother Pasion were very close. They were twins, like Castor and Pollux. It is no wonder he wishes to see you dead. I, on the other hand, see you more as an old friend."

"Friend is not the word I would have chosen," I said. The last time I had spoken to Lysander was at a peace negotiation after a bitter series of battles. Lysander had demanded my death, for I had slain a Spartan general. In return I had threatened to gut him with a dagger.

"As fellow soldiers, then," he conceded. "Sons of Ares who found themselves on opposite battle-lines through no fault of their own."

The façade of civility irked me. I could not help provoking him. "I thought I was brought here as a sacrifice," I sneered.

"Sacrifice?"

"It is said that you are a god now," I said.

Lysander laughed. "Foolish excesses of those grateful for the freedom granted by Sparta!"

"Your statue in front of Delphi's temple is godly enough," I responded.

"Merely a humble offering to show my gratitude to Apollo," Lysander said.

"It is passable," I prodded. "The head seemed a bit small. You should have hired Athenian sculptors. Their workmanship is the best in Greece." Lysander's genteel mask slipped for an instant as a cold, predatory anger flashed in his eyes. I walked to a nearby table and poured myself a bowl of wine, draining it in one gulp. I flung the empty bowl away and it shattered on the paving stones.

Lysander regained his composure, shaking his head. "You see? That is why I like you, Daimon! You fear neither gods nor men, perhaps to the point of foolishness." It was not an inaccurate observation. "That is why you are a valuable servant to Thrasybulus."

"I am a free man. I serve no one," I said carefully.

"Oh? Then why has Thrasybulus sent you here? Why do you come to Delphi, Daimon of Athens?"

"I come to consult the Oracle," I said flatly. "Like you."

The corner of Lysander's mouth twitched upwards. "And did the old woman give you the wisdom you sought?"

"She speaks nonsense," I said.

Lysander clapped his hands. "So she does! So she does! And what will you report to Thrasybulus, the saviour of Athens, upon your return?" he persisted.

"I do not think he would care to hear an old woman's ramblings," I said.

Lysander eyed me keenly and then bowed in a gesture of defeat. "So be it! Keep your own counsel! But worry not, Daimon. I care not for the petty intrigues of smaller men. Let Thrasybulus play at his plots and schemes. It is of no concern to me."

"Then I am free to leave?"

"You are my guest, not my prisoner. But I thought that it must have been the gods who caused our paths to cross here in Delphi," Lysander said, glancing skywards. "I only wish to discuss a certain matter with you. As equals."

"If we are equals," I said, "How is it I stand here before you like a servant while you remain seated?"

Lysander's smile never wavered, but his eyes belied his irritation. He gestured to a dark-skinned slave, who scurried off to fetch a chair for me. Lysander and I regarded each other in feigned civility as we awaited the slave's return. Beside Lysander, Orchus let his grin widen further, no doubt anticipating the potential for violence to break out.

The slave appeared carrying a proper chair, not the splintery stool I had been expecting. He set it behind me and I sat down, easing into a pose of casual disrespect. For some time, neither Lysander or I uttered a word, both of us as still as statues.

Lysander's sword-sharp eyes cut deeply. I could feel them. Seeking. Probing under the expressionless silence that was my armour. At last, he leaned back and exhaled with an air of disappointment. "Why do you serve Thrasybulus, Daimon?" he asked. "Why do you come at his call, like a faithful hound, to lick his hand and chase after whatever stick he throws for you? You lay on his threshold, guarding his home, but you are dependent on whatever scrap of meat he throws for you. You are valuable to him, but what reward does it earn you?"

I rankled at his phrasing, which no doubt had been his aim. Where the Pythia had found my sorrow, Lysander attacked my soul's long-buried resentments, carving them out and throwing them back at me. I remained impassive. "The *strategos* respects me," I said a touch too firmly. But it sounded weak, even to my ears.

Lysander barked a laugh. "He *uses* you," he said, leaning forward. "You are but a tool to him, someone to command. You, Daimon, are the one who does what must be done, while Thrasybulus reaps the reward, his own shining reputation unsullied by the mud and shit and blood that splatters all over you and your name."

I stared at him impassively but made no attempt to contradict him.

Lysander attacked again at the gap he had opened. "Even when you were accused of murder, Thrasybulus would not speak in your defence, so worried was he that any association with you would stain his own eminence. Or so I have have heard," he added. He sipped at his wine, regarding me over his cup's rim.

His words opened old wounds. "You are well informed," I said.

Lysander smiled. "My spies know what interests me. And *you* interest me, Daimon."

"As a tool to be used?" I retorted.

The god let out a very human sigh. "The world is changing, Daimon. No longer is a man's success dictated by his birth. It depends on his abilities, his will to achieve greatness. The old aristocrats know this and fear it, for now even the son of a slave," he said, pointing at me, "can rise to great heights if he is a man of talent."

I was not proud that my mother had been a slave, but nor was I ashamed. She had given the gift of my Thracian ferocity, something I had come to embrace. "I feel no shame about my mother," I said, my blood rising.

"Then you are better than me!" Lysander snorted. "Look at me, Daimon. All of Greece bows to me and I bow only to Sparta's two kings, Pausanias and Agesilaus. Yet I am not so different from you. My father was a Spartan warrior, descended from Herakles himself, just as your own father was a *strategos* of Athens. But did you know my mother was a slave, like yours?" I remained silent. I had heard such rumours but had dismissed them as impossible. It was well known that Spartans were even more zealous about maintaining pure lines of descent than Athenians. "Not just any slave," Lysander continued, "But a *helot*. The lowest form of man that exists."

"She still lives?" I asked, my curiosity getting the better of me.

The Spartan hegemon shrugged. "It matters not to me. I despised her. The day I went to the *agoge* to train with the other boys was the greatest day of my life, for it meant I never had to lay eyes on the bitch again," he said, his words suddenly dripping with venom. Taking a deep breath, Lysander regained control of himself. "In the *agoge*, I was the best, the strongest, the one with the most cunning, but I was still less than them because I was a helot half-breed. You know of what I speak, Daimon, for you have lived much the same life in the shadow of your fellow Athenians, have you not?"

I did not deny it. "I have."

"Then you also know," Lysander said, his voice dropping, "what saved me from a life of obscurity. What allowed me achieve greatness. My truest parent." He leaned back in his grand chair, awaiting my response like a teacher testing a student.

But I knew the answer, for I was as much its child as Lysander. "The war," I said.

Lysander clapped his hands. "Yes! The father of us all!" He leaned forward. "They were losing, Daimon. Sparta was losing the war to Athens. They were desperate. Desperate enough to let excellence come before birth. And as you see," he said, spreading his arms. "I have taken advantage of the opportunity the Fates have afforded me."

"The Fates do not bless me so," I said.

Lysander's eyes flashed. "But they do. They bring you opportunity now."

"I do not understand."

And then he revealed his purpose to me, what all his talk had been leading towards. "You no longer need to skulk in the shadow of Thrasybulus, Daimon. It is time for you to come into the light. I will help you become the leader of men you are meant to be. A *strategos* of Athens, like your father. Return with me to Sparta and I will see it done."

I wished to reply, but my tongue betrayed me. I could find no words. I did not doubt he had the power to make his boast a reality.

Lysander seized on my hesitation. "I see much of myself in you, Daimon. I need men like you. Men of ability. The Persians meddle in the affairs of Ionia. The Syracusans grow ever bolder in the west. They need to be reminded that it is Sparta that now rules Greece. But I need generals to lead my armies. Men like you, Daimon of Athens."

"You wish me to abandon Athens?"

"I will let you choose your men," Lysander continued, ignoring me. "Spartans, Corinthians, Athenians… They will all obey you."

My eyes slid over to Orchus, who still stood to the side of Lysander. "Including him?" I asked. The smug expression that usually graced the Andrian mercenary's scarred face suddenly vanished, replaced by one of uncertainty.

Lysander gave me the wicked grin of a fellow conspirator. "He shall be your first recruit, should you wish it!"

"By Ares' hairy balls, I won't!" Orchus growled.

Lysander turned viciously on him. "You will not speak!" he snapped. Orchus tensed with anger but held his tongue. He glared at me.

It tempted me greatly. The Andrian and I had crossed paths many times, but the wily veteran always managed to slip away and delay a final reckoning. "What else?" I asked.

"Lead my armies! Bring me victories against the Persians! Do this for me and I shall make you *harmost* of a city in Asia." A *harmost* was one of the military governors the Spartans appointed to kept watch over their conquered city. To be appointed a *harmost* was to be given the opportunity to enrich oneself almost beyond measure.

"It is a generous offer," I conceded.

Lysander's eyes narrowed. "I could make you *harmost* of Athens," he said. "Then it would be Thrasybulus and the rest of his ilk running about doing *your* bidding."

It was a step too far. My credulity, already strained by the weight of Lysander's promises, began to crack. "Even you could not make this so," I said.

Lysander laughed, the only genuine laugh I ever heard pass his lips. "Not now, no. But soon. You said it yourself: I am a god."

"Not yet," I said quietly.

Lysander's friendly tone vanished. "You doubt my word?"

"Only your ability," I said. I rose from my chair. "I am free to leave?"

"You are my guest not my prisoner," Lysander repeated. "But it would be best to be my friend."

"I will remember that." I turned my back and walked away. The two Spartans in front of the door parted to let me pass.

As I stepped out onto the narrow street, Lysander called out one last time. "Come back when you are ready. My door is open to you, Daimon of Athens."

But I did not look back.

CHAPTER 18

I wended my way through the dark laneways of Delphi, soon emerging at the south edge of the town. I still had not heard the watchman's bell signalling that the Pythia was ready to see me. I sat down on a boulder and looked out over the valley below. The swathe of darkness was dotted with a few lonely campfires. A denser patch of light marked the village of Krissa and farther to the west was the even greater glow of the port of Kirrha where we had docked a day earlier. Against the charcoal-black silhouette of the mountains on the far side of the valley, the deep blue moonless sky was radiant with stars. The back of my head still throbbed from the clout Orchus had given me, and with a groan I rubbed the soreness out while I mulled over my encounter with Lysander.

If Lysander had wanted me dead, my cooling corpse would be lying outside the tavern being gnawed at by dogs. Instead, he had sought to win me over to his cause, offering me the chance for glory and honour that had been so long denied me.

I confess to you, Athenian, that as I sat alone under the night sky of Delphi, I was tempted by Lysander's offer. Thrasybulus had promised me better prospects for years, but what had come of it? The promised gift of citizenship had never materialized. I was still little better than a mercenary, barely tolerated by those I protected. I had helped liberate Athens from the oppression of Sparta and her Tyrants after the war. With Tibetos and the other *peripoli*, I kept the roads and passes of Attica free of bandits and foreign incursions. Lysander had twisted the nature of the relationship between me and

Thrasybulus, but there was truth in the hegemon's words nevertheless.

The Pythia's warning about Lysander's ambitions echoed in my mind. He was a man who had been successful in all his endeavours. There was no sign that his growing power would cease its ascent anytime soon. If he became king of Sparta, as the Pythia claimed he was plotting to do, then it would be wiser to be with him than against him.

Of course I did not trust Lysander. As my father had taught me, the company a man keeps is a reflection of his character, and I did not care for the men Lysander inevitably drew into his circle. And if I were to reach out to take the hand of welcome that Lysander was proffering, I would just as likely find it coated with poison, for the man was as cunning as a serpent and not one to forgive past grudges. Like me, I thought. But the desire for my suspicions to be wrong was not insubstantial.

Yet there was a simpler truth that drowned out Lysander's whispers, and it was this: Thrasybulus was a good man. His sanctimony grated against me and his unfulfilled promises tested my loyalty at times, but in the end I had a grudging admiration for him. I did not want to disappoint him. I did not want to fail his children.

I sighed. I was sure I was choosing the harder path, turning down the fame and wealth offered by Lysander for continued hardship and resentment in Athens. I cursed my lack of resolve but inside felt curiously at peace, for I was still Daimon of Athens. I thought of my conversations with Sokrates. The old man had advised me to be true to myself. He was right.

The sound of the watchman's bell pulled me out of my ruminations. I stood up, brushing the dust off my cloak. Lysander could go to Hades. I would hear out the Pythia and take her pleas back to Thrasybulus. With any luck I would be back in Athens in four or five days.

I was a fool to believe the gods would let me escape so easily.

THE PYTHIA'S RESIDENCE WAS EASY ENOUGH TO FIND. I approached the door.

"You must wait here," the guard said, taking a step forward and holding his hand out to block me.

"I am expected," I said.

"You must wait here," the guard repeated without emotion.

I grunted impatiently and took a step back. The guard settled back into his accustomed place in front of the grand door. The door itself was not wood but a great gate composed of bronze rods twice as thick as a man's thumb. There was space enough between adjacent bars to put a fist but no more than that. I reckoned there was enough metal there to outfit half a dozen hoplites. Fluted pillars twice my height framed the bronze gate and supported a triangular relief showing a scene of Apollo grappling with the great snake that was said to have dwelt in Delphi in ages past. The coils of the serpent rippled in the lambent torchlight in its futile struggle to free itself from the Apollo's muscular arms, a reminder that it was no simple task to escape from a god.

I glanced back at the guard. The hiss of the torches on either side of the entrance filled the silence as we sized each other up. I could hardly blame the man for doing his duty. In any case, it gave me the chance to take a closer look at the Pythia's residence. I strolled along the length of the front wall and back again. The guard, his bronze helmet glinting in the torchlight, kept a wary eye on me.

The residence was located outside the sanctuary on the eastern edge of the disordered mess of the town. It was not large, perhaps the size of my home in Athens, but was more like a temple or treasury. For one thing, the high walls were cut stone, not the plaster-covered mud-brick walls of typical houses. I peeked around the corner. The smooth wall continued to the back of the door without any other entrance, which was surprising, for a residence this size would normally have doors for servants and deliveries. It was unlikely that there was a door at the rear, for there was a steep slope rising towards the sacred mountains to the north. I turned around. Some activity at the gate greeted me as I strolled back to the entrance. A familiar face appeared.

"Daimon," Agasias said warmly. "The Pythia bids me to welcome you. Come inside." Holding a lamp, he stepped aside to let me pass. I stepped over the threshold, being careful not to tread on it lest I offend Apollo. I do not pray to the gods but I respect their power enough that I avoid provoking them needlessly. With a few more steps I emerged into the courtyard of the Pythia's home.

As was the case with the exterior, the interior of the building had much in common with my own home in size and layout but was overlaid with the clean austerity of a temple. Well-fitted square stone tiles covered the ground of the courtyard and around the edge evenly-spaced hanging lamps burned brightly in their metal holders. Like most homes there was an altar at the rear of the space, but with the unusual feature of a bronze statue of Apollo towering behind it, his palms turned outward in a gesture of benevolence.

Agasias smiled at me. "You found something to eat, I hope?" The young priest did not look worse for wear despite the long day at the temple.

I ignored his question. "Does only the Pythia live here?" I asked.

My rude manner did not put him off. "The upper rooms are hers alone and normally only her female attendants are permitted there," Agasias said. "The head priest Zelarchus is there," Agasias said, nodding towards the central door on the right. "This day has been too much for the old man," the young priest said, a hint of contempt creeping into his voice. "I think you offended him into an exhausted stupor."

I made no reply. The two of us stood in awkward silence for some time before my patience could no longer bear the delay. "I waited in the sun for a day. I waited an evening to be here. Am I to be made to wait further?" I growled with more ferocity than I had intended.

The menace in my tone seemed to unsettle the heretofore cheerful Agasias. "I'm sure the Pythia will see you soon," he said through a nervous, placating smile.

I was about to curse the young man when a muffled thud from the upper level of the residence caused me to hold back on my insult. I cocked my head to one side, focusing my ears like a hunting dog that has heard the faint rustling of potential quarry. I stood as still as a statue. For a few heartbeats there was nothing. Then a faint but unmistakable sound. I heard a muffled scream.

I bounded up the stairs, leaving a stunned Agasias stammering in feeble protest. A pair of ornately-carved wooden doors marked the entrance to the Pythia's chambers. I pounded on the ancient wood. "Pythia!" I shouted. There was no response. Footsteps behind me signalled the belated arrival of Agasias. I shot a look at the startled priest and then, taking a deep breath, slammed my foot into the doors. They flew open to reveal the scene within. I was too late.

The Pythia lay curled on the floor, struggling feebly. Even in the lamplight I could see the darkness that stained her robes and hands. Movement at the back of the room drew my gaze. A row of three identical windows was cut into the rear wall of the chamber, black rectangles looking out into the night. In the centre opening crouched the killer, ready to make a leap into the night that had spawned him. He gave one more glance over his shoulder.

"You!" I gasped in recognition. The dark-skinned assassin I had chased through the streets of Athens shot an icy grin at me and vanished into the night.

I spun towards Agasias. He was staring wide-eyed at the prone form of the Pythia. "Tell the guards to raise the alarm!" I shouted, but Agasias was paralyzed. "Do it!" I yelled. The young priest nodded dumbly at me before stumbling off to alert the guards.

I dashed over to where the gasping Pythia lay. I knelt on the ground and placed one hand under her head and the other on the wet, red stain that soaked her robes. There was too much blood. She was going to die. Her rapidly blinking eyes locked on mine and her hands moved to clutch my own.

"Pythia! Do not move!" I said. Her lips were moving. I leaned closer to hear her final whispered words.

"Siragellis!" she said. It meant nothing to me. "Siragellis!" she repeated.

"What is Siragellis?" I asked, leaning closer.

"A village!" The old woman's face knotted in pain. She forced her eyes open again. "The false prophet is there! He must not be allowed to live!"

"In Thrace," I said.

"Do not tell anyone!" she urged. She coughed and a trickle of blood dribbled from the corner of her mouth. Then, by the gods, the old woman smiled, showing me her bloody teeth. "Apollo has chosen you," she said. Her eyes pinched tight as her smile turned to a grimace. "It hurts! More than I expected!" she said through gritted teeth.

I nodded at the strange words, for there was little I could do and I had no wish to argue with her in her last moments. "Do not move, Pythia," I said gently.

Her breathing became erratic. She freed her hand from mine and raised her trembling, bloody palm to my cheek. "So much pain, *pai.*

Free yourself." Suddenly my tears were mingling with the blood on my cheek. The Pythia's face relaxed into a calm smile. "Let go, *pai*. Let go." Her eyes closed and her spirit left her.

With care I laid the Pythia's body on the floor. I rose to my feet and wiped my bloody hands on my tunic. The dagger that killed her was lying a pace away from her. With a sickening feeling of recognition, I picked up the blade. It was the dagger I had lost fighting off Lysander's men earlier in the evening. The Furies must have cackled in delight as a growing rage began to eclipse my grief for the murdered Oracle. I knew that Lysander was behind this. And I would kill him for it.

Just then Agasias reappeared in the doorway of the Pythia's private chamber, the residence's guards beside him. The unfortunate priest became a target at which I could unleash my anger. "Not here, you fool!" I shouted at him. "Raise the alarm!" I looked down once more at the Pythia's corpse. Hearing no sound from Agasias, I glanced back toward the doorway of the chamber. Agasias and the guards had not moved. "Did you not hear me, fool? Go!"

And our eyes met. And I saw something I had missed before, blinded as I was by the young man's flippant charm. The spark of mischief was gone, displaced by the cold glint of ambition. And I realized I had erred in my judgment of him. The Pythia would not be Lysander's only victim this night.

Agasias shot his arm out and pointed at me. "The Athenian has murdered the Pythia!" he yelled. "Kill him!"

CHAPTER 19

The three guards advanced on me, their swords drawn. I crouched down, the bloody dagger held out before me. My opponents were no farmers who only held a spear once a year; they moved with the practiced caution of experienced fighters. I prepared to defend myself, knowing I would die in the attempt.

A new voice shook the room. "Stop!" The authority of the command stopped the guards in their tracks. Zelarchus shoved his way into the room past the stunned Agasias. The head priest's black eyes stabbed at me from across the room.

Agasias snapped a glance at the head priest before pointing at me once more. "He has slain the Pythia. Avenge her now!" The guards hesitated but regained their resolve and began edging closer.

"No!" Zelarchus shouted, countermanding the young priest. "In the name of Apollo, this blasphemer's blood must not defile the sacred residence of the Pythia! Seize him!"

Agasias, seeing the guards' uncertainty, did not give up. "Kill him!" he insisted, a note of desperation creeping into his voice.

"He will be executed for his crime, but Apollo will punish those who deny Him the justice that is His alone!" Zelarchus' voice thundered. The head priest's baleful glare never left me.

A hard realization came over me. There was only one reprieve from death, even if it was to be only fleeting. It was something that all my instincts were screaming against. My next action did not come easily to me.

The dagger tumbled from my fingertips and clattered on the floor. I raised my empty hands. "I surrender."

THE PRISON OF DELPHI WAS HARDLY MORE THAN a storage hut at the edge of the village. But the walls were stone and the solid wooden door was bolted, so it served its function well enough.

The chains of my manacled hands clinked in the darkness as I touched the tender area under my eye. Zelarchus had ordered guards to take me prisoner, but that had not prevented them from handling me roughly. Sitting on the rough floor, I leaned back against the wall and shut my eyes. A soldier's ability to sleep anywhere had not abandoned me, at least.

Voices outside the door brought me back into the waking world from my dozing slumber. How much time had passed I was not certain. The rasping of sliding metal was followed by a heavy clunk as the bolt was drawn. I shuffled to my feet as the cell door swung inward. The sudden illumination of the torchlight from outside stung my eyes. Two silhouetted figures stepped forward, filling the doorway and throwing the cell into shadow once again.

My eyes adjusted quickly. I recognized my visitors well enough. "Agasias," I growled. I lunged towards the young priest. Agasias instinctively retreated, but I was held fast by my chains.

The other man did not flinch. "Looks like the cagey bird has finally been caught in a cage he can't escape from," he said in his rough Andrian accent.

"Orchus," I said. A rotten-toothed grin split the mercenary's face.

Agasias had recollected himself. "I have come to inform you of your fate." His former friendly manner was gone, replaced by an officious air that did not quite suit his youthful features.

"When I am free, I will cut your head off," I said flatly.

His mouth twitched. "Unlikely," he said, raising his chin. "Unless you survive your own execution."

"I will cut your head off," I repeated.

Agasias ignored the threat. "Tomorrow at dawn you will be thrown from the Hyampeia Rock as punishment for your crimes."

"The murder of the Pythia is on your hands, Parnassian, not mine," I said bitterly.

The corner of the priest's mouth curled upwards. "Murder of the Pythia? No, nothing so grand, I'm afraid. You will die as a common thief. It will be said that you were caught trying to steal some sacred objects from the temple. You have something of a disreputable past. The story will be believed easily enough."

Orchus barked a laugh. "We're going to see if the cagey bird can fly," he said, flapping his hands by his shoulders like tiny wings. I strained against my chains and he laughed even louder. I stopped fighting.

"The Pythia's death will not go unnoticed," I said.

"If you believe that, then you don't know how the sanctuary works. Pythias come and Pythias go," Agasias said dismissively. "When one Pythia dies, a new Oracle takes her place. This is a matter for the guardians of the temple. The rest of the world neither knows nor cares, as long as there is an Oracle to answer their petty questions. Should anyone ask, they will be told she died in her sleep. She was an old woman, after all. That will be the official story, of course, by unofficially, the rumour will be that Thrasybulus had the Oracle assassinated by his head mercenary Daimon the Thracian. How long do you think it will take to spread to the ears of Thrasybulus' allies? They might reconsider their loyalty to someone so ruthless and impious as to murder the Pythia."

The full scope of Lysander's plot became clear. The Pythia was removed not only as an obstacle to his attempt to become king, but also to undermine the nascent alliance being formed by Thrasybulus among those poleis chafing under the heavy-handed rule of Sparta.

"And the new Oracle will no doubt be more tractable," I surmised. "Someone whose messages from Apollo are more likely to support Lysander's claim for kingship."

Agasias gave a thin smile. "As it happens, we have a young girl who would make a fine Pythia. She is a bit simple, but all she needs to do is babble some nonsense for the priests to interpret. I expect she will serve for many years."

"The temple or Lysander?"

"Apollo has always shown favour to those who honour his temple, and Lysander has been a most generous benefactor," Agasias conceded.

"And what do you get out of this?" I asked.

The young priest's voice took on a tone of humility. "The world is changing," he said, echoing Lysander's words to me. "The sanctuary is in need of new blood and new ideas. Lysander rewards those who are loyal to him and wishes the temple to be led by someone who shares his vision."

I scoffed. "You are a fool if you trust his word. Lysander wants the wealth of Delphi for himself. He wants to invade the lands of the Persians."

Agasias shrugged. "He is welcome to it, as long as he leaves a little for the rest of us. There is always more every year. Now I bid you farewell," he said. "Come, Orchus."

"I will come for your head," I promised once more as Agasias turned to leave the cell.

"Hardly frightening words from someone who will never see another sunset," the priest said over his shoulder as he disappeared.

Orchus paused. "I'll enjoy watching you fly, boy."

"I will kill you, Orchus."

"Only if you land on me, boy!" the veteran laughed.

"Tell Lysander I will come for him, too."

Orchus winked at me. "A corpse don't bite, my Thracian whoreson. A corpse don't bite." He spat a gob of phlegm at my feet before following Agasias out of the cell. The door thudded shut and the iron bolt ground back into place. Once more I was alone in the darkness.

Waiting for dawn.

And my execution.

CHAPTER 20

Fear is the enemy.

On the battlefield, *Phobos* whispers in your ear and tells you to flee. What is the point of dying for a lost cause? the god asks you. It is a very compelling argument, one that many take to heart.

Phobos is there on the execution ground, too, trying to persuade you to struggle against your captors, to cry, to beg them to spare your life, to say anything for a few more moments of existence. Many listen and obey the voice of the god of fear, but it gains them nothing.

If a man claims not to feel fear, then he is a liar. Many who have served with me or have faced me in battle would swear that I am fearless, but this is not true; *Phobos* has haunted me as much as any man. It is just that there are other voices more powerful than that of Fear.

The loudest among them is *timos* — honour —, which is merely another kind of fear. For some, the dread of dishonour is stronger than the fear of death and the grey, meaningless eternity in the Underworld that follows. Honour is the fear of being regarded as a coward, to be remembered as someone who fled the enemy and then perished from wounds to his back. Honour drives foolish men into a sea of enemy spears to meet inglorious deaths on forgotten battlefields. I have always been a fool, if nothing else.

Hope is another voice, small and quiet, but with strength in its persistence. It tells you that there is a path to victory, perhaps an obscure and daunting one, but a path nevertheless. Often Hope is a liar, but it does not let you surrender to despair, even when the gods themselves oppose you. On that night, however, hope had deserted me.

Meli had vanished after hearing the Pythia's words. Even if she knew of my plight, she could do little to save me. Tibetos and the other *peripoli* might have fared better, for they had the skills and audacity to seize me from my captors. In the darkness, the assorted rescue scenarios in my mind made me smile. But my companions were down in the valley below. I would be a shattered pulp at the base of the Hyampeia Rock before they ever learned of my peril.

In the darkness other memories fought for my attention. My mother's strong face was there, as was that of my father, his expression stern but fair as it always had been in life. My childhood arms-master, Neleus, stood with them. Lykos, the brother of Thrasybulus and the man to whose excellence I aspired to every day, seemed to nod at me, just as when as a youth I had done well enough to meet his high and uncompromising standard. Behind him were the other *peripoli* who had perished for Athens, my brothers. They awaited me.

But all of these ghosts – friends, family, comrades-in-arms – dissipated like fog in the morning sun when the brilliant light of Phaia appeared in my mind's eye. My wife had believed that not all of us are doomed to the endless misery of the Underworld. For those who had been initiated into the Mysteries of Eleusis, she had told me, there waits a realm of light and happiness. I wondered then, as I imagined her there before me, whether she had indeed found that place.

Her mysterious smile waned and her features shifted into those of my son. I closed my eyes against the sight, for I knew I had failed the boy and Phaia. I suddenly wanted nothing more than to see the boy again, to tell him of his mother, who had been the greatest love in my life. But he would never know that, instead knowing only that his father had been executed as a common criminal. The whispers of *Phobos* grew more insistent and my resolve faltered.

I slipped into half-sleep and Phaia reappeared in my dream, her radiance forcing the god of fear to retreat into the corners of my soul. She smiled her enigmatic smile and reached out towards me. I extended one hand to touch her fingers, but she began to fade like the evening light and was gone.

I awoke from my dream. The blackness inside the cell had slid into a shadowy world of deep slate greys and blues, as though Phaia's spirit had imbued the walls and floors of my prison with a trace of residual light. I looked up towards the ceiling. The first inkling of the brightening dawn was creeping through the seams in the boards above me. Apollo's chariot of the sun was coming soon and with it my doom.

Muffled footsteps approached the door of my cell. There was some shuffling and the sound of low voices. The grating sound of metal against metal echoed in the cell as the iron bolt was drawn back. The door swung inward and the predawn light was blocked by the silhouettes of two cloaked figures. A hooded form stepped towards me. I wondered if Lysander had decided to simply have me murdered in my cell.

"Hold out your hands," a familiar voice ordered me from under the hood. It was Zelarchus, the head priest. If he had come to kill me, then it would have been odd to free me from my bonds. I extended my hands. The other figure stepped forward and withdrew the pins from my manacles. The iron circles fell to the ground with a clatter.

"Quiet!" Zelarchus hissed. "Stay here and make noise if you want to die. Come with us if you want to live!"

I gave a grunt of acknowledgement and followed the priest and his companion from the tiny prison. A body lay slumped just outside the door, presumably that of the guard Agasias had left to watch over me. There was little time to consider the dead man's misfortune as my rescuers were in a hurry to put some distance between us and the town.

We picked our way down a path through the olive groves towards the valley below. We moved carefully, for though the boulders and bumps were more apparent in the twilight, a misplaced step would have led to a twisted joint or worse. It was not long before Zelarchus halted our descent.

"I must leave you here. Arexion will accompany you the rest of the way," he said, indicating the hard-faced man who had freed me from my manacles.

It was the first chance I had had to speak. "Why have you freed me?" I asked. "I am grateful for your aid, but I do not understand. You know that I did not murder the Pythia?"

Zelarchus studied me, his flint-black eyes staring hard. "It takes great effort to disbelieve what I saw with my own eyes, but no, I do not think you killed the Oracle," he said. His intervention at the Pythia's residence now made more sense. But ally though he appeared to be, the hostility in his voice was undiminished.

"But why have you risked saving me? Guilty or not, my death would surely have meant little to you."

"The Pythia compelled me," the head priest replied, his distaste evident.

"The Pythia?"

Zelarchus grimaced. "I do not like you. Death follows you like a shadow. But I am loyal to the Pythia. I am loyal to Delphi. After your audience in the temple, the Pythia made me swear an oath to Apollo to aid you no matter what happened. I am keeping my oath."

"I thank you for your aid. I will return to Athens and report to Thrasybulus."

"No!" Zelarchus said. It was an order, not a protest. "No, you will not. You will go north. You will kill the false prophet Silenus. You will stop Lysander. The Pythia had foreseen it."

"It is not my battle to fight, priest," I said. "If Thrasybulus can help you, he will. But it is not my concern." I turned and started heading down the kill. The rasping hiss of a sword being drawn made me stop. I looked back. The stone-faced Arexion held his weapon loosely but ready. "You will carry out the executioner's task after all?" I asked.

"You defy the will of Apollo!" Zelarchus shot back.

I wondered if there was something more to the priest's urgency besides his misguided belief in the Pythia's prophecy. Then I remembered something. "You do not know where this Silenus is, do you?" I asked. The deepening of the priest's scowl told me I was correct. Siragellis. The Pythia had told me the village's name with her dying breath, but apparently she had not shared the information with her head priest. I laughed. "Kill me and you will never know, priest." I resumed my march back down the mountain. "When I am safely returned to Athens, I will tell you where your prophet is, priest!" I called out over my shoulder.

"Nikodromos!" Zelarchus said. I froze. "Nikodromos!" the priest repeated. "Is that not your son's name? Does he not reside in the home of Iasos, your childhood teacher?"

I faced back up the slope. His meaning was clear. "You threaten my son, priest?" My voice was ice.

"The life of the false prophet for the life of your son. It is a simple exchange. You cannot fail," Zelarchus said. "We use the weapons available to us, Athenian, and at Delphi our weapon is information. There is little we do not know."

"Except where to find your prophet," I said coldly.

"It is true," the priest conceded. "But *you* know, and you are the instrument of Apollo. There is no time to return to Athens. Even now Lysander prepares for his journey to Thrace. You must kill the prophet before Lysander is able to claim him."

At that moment, the cosmos hesitated. The gods paused, turning their eyes to that dark mountainside of Delphi, anticipating my response. The hands of the Fates quivered over the cloth that records the lives of men and gods alike, waiting, unsure which direction my thread would take. The Furies writhed in anticipation of a feast of blood and vengeance.

I looked northwards back up the slope towards Delphi. I cared little for the Delphians' lucrative monopoly on access to Apollo and his oracles. The god and his devotees could go to the crows. To the east, a few days hard travel away, lay Athens, where Thrasybulus awaited my return from the sanctuary. South was the port of Kirrha, where Lysander would board a ship this day or the next to journey to Thrace and collect his prophet in Siragellis, wherever it may have been.

Zelarchus had threatened my son unless I participated in his mad scheme to murder Lysander's son of Apollo. I doubted neither the priest's zeal to serve his god nor his ruthless practicality. I had little choice but to aid him. But when I was done, I would come back and kill the long-bearded priest and place his head next to that of Agasias. I did not take threats to my family lightly.

But the truth, Athenian, is that deep in my heart there was something more. The Furies had awoken from their stupor and whispered what I already knew to be true. I wanted to hurt Lysander. His assassin had murdered the Pythia, an old woman, in her home. I had respected her. The black-eyed Spartan bastard had set me up for the crime and left me to be executed. Now there was an opportunity to harm my enemy, to stick a dagger in the belly of his ambition and twist it in his guts.

I was not the instrument of Apollo.

I was the weapon of the Furies.

And Lysander would know it.

CHAPTER 21

Apollo's instrument. That is what the Pythia and Zelarchus had called me. I scoffed aloud, drawing a hard look from the soldier Arexion.

"Why do you laugh, Athenian?" Arexion asked in his flat voice. The dour soldier Zelarchus had assigned to accompany me was thickly muscled, like a lion. Traces of scars on his arms and face indicated he was no stranger to a fighting life. His expression revealed little, but his watchful eyes suggested there was more to the man than brute strength.

I shot my minder a scornful glance. "I was wondering how much I can trust a man who just drew a sword on me, Parnassian."

He stopped. "I serve Apollo." A hint of zeal rippled under his words. "As do you, Athenian," he said, tapping his finger on my chest. "Only our service for Delphi matters. Remember that and you have little need to fear any consequences," he said with deliberate slowness.

The reminder of the implied threat to my son stoked my anger. "Touch me again, Parnassian, and I'll cut off your finger and feed it to you."

A humourless grin spread across the Delphian soldier's face. "I'd like to see you try, Athenian."

With a frustrated growl, I turned away and continued down the mountain, Arexion tramping a few paces behind me. As little as I trusted the Parnassian warrior, I needed him if I had any hope of succeeding in finding the mad prophet. It was not Arexion's sword I required but the substantial pouch of gold and silver coins that Zelarchus had provided him

The immediate danger of capture diminished with each step down the mountain, but in my mind the enormity of the task ahead only grew. I did not know how my companions would react. Tibetos and the others had come willingly to Delphi but might be less enthusiastic about accompanying me all the way to Thrace and beyond on a fool's errand. There was also the matter of my sister. I had not seen her since her meeting with the Pythia. I had no lack of faith in her resourcefulness, but her absence concerned me.

Had I not been so distracted by these matters, I might have noticed our pursuer earlier. Out of long-practiced habit, I glanced over my shoulder to ensure we were not being followed. A flash of movement on the edge of my vision made me pull up. Arexion, alerted by my sudden wariness, came to a halt and followed my line of sight to a mess of brush about thirty paces back up the hill.

I signalled to Arexion to approach the clump of scrub from the right side while I took the left. He nodded, our enmity temporarily put aside while we dealt with the current threat. When we were both five paces from the brush, I raised my hand and Arexion halted, his sword pointed towards where our quarry had gone to ground.

The cluster of juniper bushes was hardly large enough to conceal a grown man. But I suspected that it was no man who lay hidden within.

"Melitta," I said. "Reveal yourself before the Parnassian skewers you." The juniper branches rustled and became still. I was losing my patience. "Meli, this no time for games!" In a few steps I was at the bush and thrust my arm in. My hand found a thin arm and I yanked its struggling owner from the vegetation in an explosion of twigs and leaves.

I had been correct in my assumption that our pursuer was not a man. But my other conclusion had been wrong. It was not Meli whose arm I grasped.

My young captive glared at me with fear-tinged defiance. "Let go of me, turd-sniffer!" the boy spat. He had straw-coloured hair and blue eyes.

It was the young slave from the food-seller's shop.

The boy was still following us when we neared Krissa, scampering behind us like a dog.

"I want to go with you," the boy declared. I ignored him. He had to trot to keep up with our pace. The slave-boy sped up so that he was at my side. "I helped you escape," he added for the hundredth time.

"Helped me escape into another ambush," I said, breaking my silence. I swatted at his head and the boy danced nimbly out of reach. It was not fair to blame the boy, for it was not his fault that Orchus had been smarter than me. But I had more pressing concerns.

"I can't go back. Palus will beat me," the boy said, keeping just beyond the range of my hands.

I kept walking. An escaped slave would find little sympathy from strangers. He could survive by foraging and thieving for a while, but the nights were still cold. Some escaped slaves managed to find their way back to their homelands, but it was rare. In any case I doubted the boy knew any home but Delphi. For most escaped slaves, there was only one fate, and that was to be recaptured. Such slaves, no longer being worthy of trust, were more often than not worked to death in mines, quarries, or any other essential but ultimately fatal forms of labour. The boy would have to go back and take his punishment. Better a thrashing from his master now than what awaited him should he not return.

The boy was more wary of Arexion, but the Delphian paid the slave little attention. The boy still bit at our heels like a street cur begging for scraps. It was of no matter. Once we had horses, dog or not, he would be left behind. When we reached the others at their campsite outside of Krissa, the boy was suddenly nowhere to be seen, though Arexion stayed close.

My *peripoli* companions were seated around a fire watching a bubbling pot of barley porridge with the intensity of hungry men. Tibetos saw me first and waved. He stood up and approached, his relieved smile fading when he saw my battered, rough appearance. His eyes flicked to the austere Arexion and back to me. "What happened to you?" he asked.

"Old friends," I said grimly.

The others also sensed the tension Arexion brought to the camp. They abandoned their breakfast and ambled our way, forming a perimeter around us.

Telekles stared at Arexion. My friend's hand rested lightly on the pommel of his sword at his belt. "Any trouble, Dammo?" Arexion appraised the men around him with casual indifference.

"More than you know," I said, eliciting a smirk from Arexion. The Parnassian's gaze drifted past me and his smug expression vanished. His hand moved towards his sword but he only touched the iron hilt, protection against the evil eye. I turned and saw the thin, red-haired figure of my sister step out from one of the tents.

Tibetos saw my relief. "She came back last night," he said. "She told us you would be back this morning." My sister's predictions were usually right, though, in the manner of oracles and soothsayers, often not in the way that one expected.

"And who is that?" Tibetos asked, pointing. The boy had reappeared at the edge of the camp and was pacing warily with alert, cautious eyes, like a fox scavenging near a wolf's kill.

"A dog from the streets of Delphi," I said loud enough for the boy to hear. His pale skin reddened in shame but he kept his silence.

"You still haven't explained this one," Telekles said, jerking his head towards Arexion.

I looked towards the pot of porridge cooking over the fire and my stomach rumbled. "Give me some breakfast and I'll explain everything."

AND I DID. I described what the Pythia had asked of me but not her oracle to me or the other words that had passed between us. My companions listened attentively, reacting with little more than the occasional raised eyebrow or a hardening of faces as I related my encounter with Lysander, the Pythia's murder, and my subsequent imprisonment and escape, omitting only Zelarchus' threat against my son, for I feared they would kill Arexion then and there. I told them of my intention to travel to Thrace with Arexion to stop the false prophet from ever reaching Delphi.

The men of the *peripoli* were not easily put off. Tibetos at once declared that he would accompany me. Identically fierce pronouncements from the others followed that of my friend. "After all," said Telekles. "Look at what happened when we left you on your own for just one night! And there is no excitement to be had in Athens," he added, a statement met with nods of agreement from the others.

Another voice, sharp and clear, cut through the morning air. "I too will go with you." The men parted to let my sister come forward. Her sea-green eyes dared me to contradict her.

"It will be a long journey, sister," I said.

"What is such a journey to me, one who has travelled to the Underworld and back?" Meli said. "Worry not for me, brother." It was the longest conversation we had had in many years.

A hesitant cough snapped the tenuous thread connecting me and my sister. Sabas the Cretan addressed Meli. "What do the gods say, O Seer? Do they favour us in our quest? Are the omens propitious?" he asked humbly. Like all of the former *peripoli*, Sabas regarded my sister with equal parts awe, dread, and protective love.

"Apollo is silent," she said, looking at Arexion. The Parnassian's face tightened. "But the whispers of Bendis," she said, invoking the name of the Thracian goddess, "tell me to go north with my brother." That seemed to satisfy Sabas and the other men, who bobbed their heads with approval.

"Whispers or not," I said, drawing a sharp stare from Meli, "We must leave at once if we are to reach Thrace before Lysander."

The men needed no further prompting. With practiced efficiency, we dismantled the camp so that little trace of it remained. Horses were easy enough to locate, for Krissa was awash with traders from the port of Kirrha. The Persian coins that Arexion drew from his pouch were very persuasive, each gold daric being enough to purchase two serviceable animals. The Krissians' eyes danced with greed and they no doubt wished to extract even more gold from the Arexion's purse, but the sight of a glowering Mnasyllus with his Cyclopean *kopis* sword convinced them to settle for their already healthy profits on the day.

The horses were bridled and loaded with what little gear we had. Even the freed helot Iollas had his own mount, though he was regarding his pony with some suspicion. I was more worried about my sister. I had asked her to ride with me, but she shrugged off my offer with irritation. Instead she insisted on her own mount. To my surprise, she sprang to her horse's back as though she had been born to it. My nickname for Meli as a child had been Amazon. The comparison to the mounted female warriors had always made her smile, a smile that I had not seen for many years. I pushed the insistent memory to the back of my mind as I mounted my own horse.

Throughout the morning, the slave boy had dogged us, keeping to the edge of our group. He had been darting about and aiding the others as we prepared the horses, all the while casting furtive looks my way. I focused on my own thoughts and ignored him. Now, as it became clear that he would be left behind, a desperate realization of his plight began to dawn on him. He dashed to my side, seizing one of the reins in his dirty hand.

The boy's self-assurance abandoned him. "Take me with you!" he pleaded.

I liked the boy, despite myself. Headstrong and not lacking in audacity, he had the makings of a fine *peripoli*. But that was a thread that the Fates would never weave. I took the rein from him. "Go back to Delphi, boy," I said.

"Palus will beat me," he protested again.

"Better than what you will encounter where we are headed," I said. I kicked my heels into my horse's flanks, leaving the crestfallen slave-boy staring at my back.

A sharp whistle to my rear made me pull up. I wheeled my horse around, expecting to see the boy running after me. But I was wrong. It was Meli who had whistled, and not to me. Her gaze fixed on the boy, she gave a small jerk of her head to indicate he should approach her. The boy cast an uncertain glance in my direction before making his decision. He ran to where my sister sat astride her horse. She reached down and pulled him up so that he was sitting in front of her.

Meli turned her piercing gaze my way. The others in our party watched me, awaiting my response to my sister's defiance but knowing better than to get involved.

A warrior knows when to fight and when to retreat. This was a battle that was not worth waging. To the crows with them, I thought. To the crows with both of them.

"Let's move!" I shouted.

And we set out. Racing against time. Racing against a god.

CHAPTER 22

With luck, we would reach the town of Kynos on the Locrian coast in two days. As far as I knew, Lysander would sail from Delphi to Corinth before crossing the isthmus and continuing to Thrace. Even if he went directly to Thrace, we would be stealing a lead of several days from him by cutting directly north instead of sailing the long way round. It was the only advantage we enjoyed in this mad quest, for I only had the vaguest of notions where we were headed.

We maintained a hard but steady pace, not wishing to blow out the horses, but the journey was taxing for bodies not accustomed to riding. I am a fair horseman, having learned the skill in Thrace during my years soldiering there at the side of Thrasybulus. The other *peripoli,* too, managed their beasts with competence. The freed slave Iollas was clearly terrified of his animal but bore his fate in resolute silence as was his nature.

My sister was the true source of my quiet astonishment. She handled her mount as though she had been born with the riding skill of her Thracian forebears. Even with the extra rider, she guided the horse with ease, often leaning forward to whisper some secret or other in the animal's ear. At the end of the first day, she alighted from the horse no worse for wear from the journey. I was waiting for her as she dismounted.

"Why did you bring the boy, Meli?" I demanded. The boy stayed behind her, watching me with nervous intensity. Meli fixed me with a gorgon-like stare before attempting to move past me. I stepped into her path and repeated her question. Most men I know would have withered under her glaring gaze, but I was one of the few on whom it had no effect.

Her lip twitched. "Bendis told me he is necessary," she said. She stepped past me once more and I made no attempt to hinder her. I rubbed the fatigue out of my eyes. Since she was a child, Meli had claimed to hear the words of the gods. That she was touched by the second sight, there was no doubt, but it was a convenient excuse to justify any action she wished. It also undermined any argument one could find to challenge her opinion.

The boy, sensing my distraction, began to edge away to make good his escape. My angry expression fixed him to the ground as though I had pinned his foot to the earth with a spear.

"What is your name, boy?" I asked.

"Sosias," he said, holding my stare despite the quaver in his voice.

"No. That is not your name," I said. "Your name is *Kuon* because that is what you are: a scrawny little dog following us about and begging for scraps. So what is your name, boy?" He clenched his jaw tightly. I leaned in. "What is your name, boy?" I repeated, biting each word.

"Kuon," he said through gritted teeth.

"What?"

"Kuon!" he repeated, glowering at me. Good, I thought. It was better if he started hating me. Perhaps he would just sneak off in the night and be done with us.

"Kuon, do you think we are your parents?" I asked?

"No," he said.

"Does that man look like your mother?" I asked, pointing at the hulking Mnasyllus. The big man grinned.

"No."

"I don't want you here. Do you understand?" I said, jabbing a finger in the boy's chest. His silence was answer enough. "But my sister wishes you to be here, so I accept her wishes *for now*," I emphasized, shooting a look my sister's way. "Do you understand?"

"Yes," he said, turning his eyes downward.

"Look at me!" I ordered him. He raised his eyes. "Understand this. While you are a member of our party, you will do as I command. You will not question me. You will obey the others as if they were me. You will carry our gear. You will clean our camp. You will see to the horses. You will work so hard that you will wish that you were back in Delphi serving drunks and being beaten by your master. Do you understand?"

"Yes," he said.

"You will address me as *lochagos*," I said.

"Yes, *lochagos*."

I regarded him coolly. "Why are you still looking at me?" I asked. "Unload the horses and help Iollas set up the camp!" I barked.

"Yes, *lochagos*!" the boy barked back before spinning on his heel and hurrying off to do his duties.

THE BOY WORKED HARD. I would give him that. Just at the edge of the firelight, his exhausted form lay asleep outside Meli's small tent. The blanket that covered his body rose and fell with his deep, regular breaths. My heart hardened as my eyes moved to the dark shape that was the sleeping form of Arexion. The soldier from Delphi had wisely kept himself apart from the rest of our party and retired early. My gaze returned to the sputtering campfire in front of me.

Like the flickering flames, thoughts danced and leapt in my mind, burning at what little confidence I had managed to muster during the day. So unlikely was success, I reckoned, that Herakles himself would have wisely admitted defeat had he been burdened with such an impossible task.

Most of all I thought about Silenus, the false prophet. I have met many seers and soothsayers in my time. They are, almost without exception, clever tricksters who play on the hopes and fears of superstitious fools, just as skilled orators could manipulate crowds with honeyed speeches. This false son of Apollo to whom Lysander had tied his fortunes and whom it was my mission to kill was likely just another false *mantis*. Yet doubt gnawed at me. I had killed many men in my time on the battlefield and in defence of my city, my comrades, my family. But I was no assassin like the man who had murdered the Pythia. I let out a long, slow breath.

Tibetos looked over at me, sensing the source of my grim silence. "That turd-sniffer Lysander will get what he deserves, Dammo." The others, pulled from their own thoughts, grunted in agreement.

Their loyalty moved me but prompted me to speak of another problem that had been consuming my waking hours.

I rose to my feet and addressed the men. "Fellow *peripoli*," I said. "I am a fool on a fool's errand. I can't ask you to risk your lives for what is likely a lost cause."

It was Telekles who answered. "Lost cause or not, we will follow you, Daimon." The pledge brought about another round of nods and grunts.

I raised an eyebrow. "I always thought you the wisest among us, old friend, but perhaps I was wrong."

The veteran considered his response, giving me a moment to look at him. In the firelight, I could see the silver in his hair and beard where only a few years earlier there had only been youthful black. His handsome face was creased with more than forty years of sun and dust and experience. Age was catching up to him. I was in my prime as a warrior, but Telekles reminded me that youth is fleeting.

"I ask myself," Telekles began, "what Lykos would do." There were knowing nods from the others at the mention of the *peripoli* captain who had been the best of us. He had been my teacher and friend as well as my sister's lover. He had died in front of me and I had avenged him.

"It seems to me," Telekles continued, "that Lykos would not abandon a fellow *peripoli* were he here, even one as rash and pig-headed as you," he said, prompting chuckles from around the fire. He smiled gently "So I would be ashamed to meet him in the Underworld were I to let you continue on your mission alone, let alone allow your sister to head into danger while I could do something about it. How many times over the years have you stood at my side in battle, Daimon? We are brothers."

"Lykos held you in the highest esteem, Brother" I said. "Your deeds have earned you a place at his side a hundred times over."

Telekles shrugged doubtfully. "You honour me too much. But there is more. We are *peripoli*. We swore oaths to each other, as I have said. But have we not also sworn an oath to protect Athens? If Lysander succeeds in becoming king of Sparta, how long will Athens survive? He will install loyal tyrants just as he did before," he said. "They will rule with cruelty and greed. We cannot let this happen. The *peripoli* have always protected the borders of Athens, and we will do so again, even if we must journey into barbarian lands to do so." The other *peripoli,* roused by their comrade's declaration, let out a hearty cheer.

Telekles looked into the flames. "And there is another reason," he said more softly, "It shames me to say it, but the truth is I miss the war. More and more I have found myself longing for the days when the *peripoli* patrolled the hills and took the fight to the enemy. When we were feared by every Spartan who set foot on Athenian soil. My hair is greying and my teeth loosen with each passing month. But in the last few days, by Zeus, I have felt my vigour return as once again my life has purpose. And I tell you my friends, it is sweeter than the finest Samian wine," he finished.

"My friend," I said. "Feel no shame at your words, for you have only given voice to what every man feels. I, for one, welcome your fast sword and wise counsel at my side. Let us swear now," I said, rising to my feet, "to remind that Spartan shit-eater Lysander that he should fear the *peripoli*. Let us give our oath to Lykos and all our brothers in Hades' realm that we shall succeed in our task or die in the attempt!"

As one the men leapt up and swore the same oath. Cups were drained and backs slapped. Telekles and I embraced each other. When we separated, he put a hand on my shoulder. "Lykos would be proud," he said earnestly, and suddenly I missed my old friend even more.

Exhaustion began to take its toll. One by one the others went off to sleep on the hard ground under the stars as they had done so many times in their lives. I was left alone contemplating the smoldering embers of the dying fire, wondering how I would keep my oath and defeat Lysander.

CHAPTER 23

On the third morning we reached Kynos. The port could not compete with Piraeus in scale, but there were a healthy number of trading vessels loading and unloading cargo. A squadron of five Spartan triremes had also found berths along the wharf.

"Ten years ago it would have been our ships," Stachys said bitterly. I kept my silence. Once Athenian ships had controlled the seas, extorting tribute from reluctant allies. Many poleis like Kynos had once thought Athens' defeat would mean their freedom, but they were sadly mistaken. One master had replaced another, and now it was Spartan ships that sailed the Aegean, extracting tribute with as heavy a hand as Athens ever had. Now I cast a wary eye over the warships. There was nothing to mark them as out of the ordinary, but I could not help wondering what the purpose of their mission might be.

"Do you think they're Lysander's?" Tibetos asked, echoing my concern. If Lysander was already at Kynos, then our mission had failed before it had even started. The triremes were in fair condition but not new. Lysander's squadron would have been a grander affair with more support ships in tow. "Too small a number," I said. "Looks like a routine patrol." I hoped I was correct.

Our initial inquiries among the captains for passage north met with failure. Most were headed south to the lucrative markets of Athens, Corinth, and beyond, while others would cross the sea east to Ionia. At last one ship yielded more promising results.

"I'm bound for Thrace as soon as we're loaded," the captain informed us. Members of his crew were eyeing the rhomphaia hilt peeping out over my shoulder. "But I don't take passengers," he said, reading the situation correctly. An apologetic smile multiplied the creases on his leathery, sun-worn face. Once again, the appearance of a few Persian darics from Arexion's pouch proved persuasive. The coins vanished into his tunic. "There might be some room, if you don't mind sleeping on deck with the cargo."

"That is acceptable," I said.

He extended his hand. "Xenius, captain of the Delphinus." We shook on the agreement. "You're fortunate. Half a moon ago it would have been impossible, but the spring winds have come early this year. A good chance to get to Thrace while other traders are still stuck in Egypt!"

Captain Xenius and I watched as his men hurried up and down the gangplank, nimbly dodging one another on the narrow ramp. A sharp-eyed harbour official scrutinized the comings and goings from his stool beside the ship, dropping various small coloured tiles into an urn. Beside me, Xenius muttered bitterly to himself with each chit that plopped into the container. "By Poseidon's cock, the duties cost me more every year! Hard for an honest trader to keep a drachma for himself."

The boy Sosias had worked his way into the rotation, hauling up our own gear one load at a time as I had ordered him to. Xenius nodded admiringly. "Your slave works hard. Is he for sale?"

"No."

"Pity," the captain replied.

Xenius's interest in Sosias was not without reason. The boy had been less than no trouble since my ultimatum, carrying out any task I assigned him efficiently and without complaint. When he was not working, he watched the others intently. Telekles, in particular, had taken a shine to the boy. "He reminds me of you when you joined the *peripoli*," he had told me by the fire the previous night.

Arexion returned from having sold our horses, no doubt for a fraction of what he had paid for them. Since nearly coming to blows during my escape from the Delphi, the Parnassian had done little to provoke me. The dour soldier of Delphi had kept to himself for the most part, communicating when necessary but otherwise content to let others do the talking. He stood away from the others, who had claimed an idle crane as their spot, except for Meli, whose hooded form could be seen wandering farther up the wharf.

Captain Xenius followed my gaze to our party. "They're an odd lot, if you don't mind me saying. Something of a mixed stew, if you know what I mean. You've got a couple of Athenians, a giant with a sword to match, a Parnassian, a Mede, a shifty-looking Cretan, and a couple of slaves. All you need is a Spartan or two to round it out," he said with a chuckle. His eyes glanced over towards Meli, who had turned around and was heading our way. The captain became serious. "And I don't know if I like the looks of that one, by Poseidon," he said under his breath. His hand slid down to touch the iron of the sailor's knife on his belt to ward off the evil eye.

"She's my sister," I said. There was an edge of warning in my voice.

"No offense," Xenius said hurriedly. "It's just that she has an ill-omened aura about her, you must admit. My men are nervous about having her on the ship."

"She's touched by the gods," I said. "Your ship will be under their protection."

"If you say so," the captain said, clearly unconvinced. "And then there's you," he said, changing the subject.

"Me?"

"Returning to Thrace, are you? With your sister, I mean? Can hardly hear it in your accent."

"I'm Athenian."

"Really?" the captain said, raising a bushy eyebrow. "Never would have thought it. You look every inch a Thracian, especially with that blade on your back."

"My mother was Thracian," I said.

This seemed to satisfy him. "Oh, I see. Common up there in the north, you know. Greeks and Thracians marrying. Thracian girls a bit on the wild side, you see. Better than Hellene girls, in my experience. There are some whorehouses in Abdera where..." He left the sentence unfinished, suddenly remembering who he was talking to. "Thracians are alright by me is all I'm saying."

"Do you do much business in Thrace?" I asked. The change of topic appeared to relieve the captain.

"Enough. There are Thracian traders I deal with in the Greek towns."

"What do they want?"

"Wine is an easy sell, even this vile Locrian stuff," he said, jerking a thumb towards amphorae the ship. "Sometimes bronze if I have it."

"And what do they offer in exchange?"

"Silver. I swear by Zeus's shining balls that the place is made of silver. And I can spend silver anywhere. It's either that or slaves," he said with a sniff.

My heart began to chill towards the amiable seaman. "Slaves?"

Xenius did not notice the frost that had crept into my voice. "Silver and slaves. That is what comes out of Thrace. Mind you, a small trader like me will take girls and children; easier to control."

"And where do you take them?" I asked coldly.

"The islands, mostly. They fetch higher prices in Athens and Corinth, but I find it's better to offload them as soon as possible," he explained.

With difficulty I suppressed the anger rising inside me. The captain had done me no harm and was friendly enough, but suddenly I saw him as something else. It was likely that as a young girl my mother had been torn from her Thracian village and carried to Athens in a ship much like the one before me. Sosias had shared a similar fate. The boy, sensing my eyes on him, flashed a smile as he was picking up another load to carry onto the boat. The smile evaporated when he saw the stern expression on my face brought on by the captain's words on slave-trading. Sosias turned his gaze downwards to escape my stare.

Beside me, Captain Xenius carried on, unaware that my thoughts had wandered elsewhere. Then something he said pulled me back to the present. "What did you just say?" I asked, turning towards him.

"I said that with the situation in Thrace, I expect the supply of slaves to pick up," he repeated.

"What do you mean?"

"The king," he said, scratching at his beard as he tried to remember the name. "Malikos? Methikos?"

"Medokos," I said.

"Yes! That's it! Medokos is dying, from what I've been able to gather. Now every Thracian chief is itching to break free and scratch out his own little kingdom. Rebellions are springing up everywhere. It's no surprise, is it? Thracians aren't happy unless they're slaughtering each other. It's not my affair, but more fighting means more slaves."

I pondered his words. I had met the king when I was a young warrior fighting alongside Thrasybulus in Thrace. Medokos had been an impressive man in both stature and ability. He had managed the near impossible by bringing most of the Thracian tribes under his rule, though not without the aid of Thrasybulus and his Athenian army. I had been there as well, fighting alongside Medokos and his son Zyraxes on more than one occasion. The prince was my friend and more than talented enough to take over for his father.

"Does Medokos' son not rule in his place?" I asked.

Xenius scoffed. "When your ship is sinking, one man bailing water with a bucket is not enough. Medokos might be dying, but he is no fool. From what I've heard, his son rules in the west only. The king has sent one of his generals to retake control in the east. Seuthes, I think his name is."

"It is dangerous to split his kingdom," I said.

Xenius shrugged. "Better half a kingdom than no kingdom at all. Anyway, it's no business of mine, especially if it's good for business if you know what I mean," he said with a wink. The loading of the ship was almost complete, and Xenius wished to oversee the final preparations. "Tell your men – and your charming sister – to be ready to board."

As the captain attended his duties, our team boarded the ship, finding nooks and gaps among the sacks and amphorae on deck. Telekles had not been wrong. Freed from the shackles of routine life in Athens, the *peripoli* were in their element. Banter and smiles floated in the air, temporarily overcoming any doubts that overshadowed the mission. Even the freed slave Iollas was enjoying the adventure, revealing his jagged teeth in a lighthearted grin.

My sister and I were the exceptions. Nervous glances passed between the sailors and hands moved to touch iron as her hooded form ascended the gangplank. I came last, finding myself reluctantly entering the sea god's realm once more. I leaned against the reassuring solidity of the mast.

Xenius bellowed an order and the sailors cast off the hawsers. The ship's oars chopped the dark salt water into foam as the crew manoeuvred the portly vessel out of the harbour and into the open sea. With keening gulls overhead, the captain ordered the sail unfurled. The westerly breeze off the coast filled the square canvas, relieving the sailors of their rowing duties.

The coast receded behind the ship. I was returning to Thrace, just as I had promised Prince Zyraxes more than ten years earlier. But the anticipation I might have felt was diminished by something else. In my mind was the faint echo of callous laughter.

The laughter of the gods.

CHAPTER 24

Poseidon was merciful. Any grudges he held against me for my past blasphemies did not manifest themselves as storms or squalls during the voyage. Even Xenius was impressed by our steady progress across the sea.

"If the winds hold," he kept reminding me. He looked up with constant doubt, as if the billowing sail would suddenly go limp at any moment. But it never did. The sky remained clear as the wind pushed us across a coruscated sea. "Perhaps you were right about your sister being touched by the gods!" he confided. This attitude seemed to be one shared by the superstitious sailors. Their previous skittishness about having Meli aboard turned to curious glances at the cloaked, motionless figure seated at the prow of the ship.

In contrast to my sister's brooding dignity, the boy Sosias was a storm of restlessness. His unending movement about the deck was not born of agitation or boredom, but of delight from the vista before him. His usual insolent wariness evaporated, revealing the child within. "I have never been on a ship!" he told me breathlessly, his sense of wonder temporarily overcoming his fear of upsetting me. The appearance of a pod of leaping dolphins beside their namesake, the Delphinus, brought about shouts of joy that spread to the other *peripoli*, the lot of them cheering the animals on until the creatures lost interest and veered away to the south for reasons known only to them. The boy's enthusiasm was a pleasant distraction from the task looming before us.

The heavily-laden ship lumbered through the night. I slept fitfully, certain that the sea-god was only biding his time before he rose up to smite our vessel. But no storms or monsters hindered our progress and it was with tired relief that I greeted the sunrise over a flat sea. On the second evening, Xenius brought the ship into the sheltered cove of a small island. "I often stop here for water," Xenius explained. "We can spend the night here." The locals sent out small boats to greet us and ferried our party ashore. They knew the captain well and provided a market for us to buy fresh food and other provisions. A makeshift camp sprang up as darkness fell. Knots of sailors and *peripoli* clustered round fires scattered along the beach. The muted murmur of voices grew softer as one by one people lay down to sleep, and soon the lapping of waves on the shore was the only sound to be heard.

At the farthest edge of the bivouac were Tibetos and I, the last people awake on the beach, or so I thought. I threw another piece of driftwood onto the fire, watching it succumb to the insistent flames. The quiet gave me time to think. Tibetos was lost in his own thoughts, perhaps not so different from my own. Soft footsteps approaching through the stony shingle made both of us look up. A cloaked figure became visible at the edge of the firelight. It was my sister.

Meli sat down on the ground opposite me. She pulled back her hood and stared at me from across the fire. Her green eyes seem so dark as to be almost black, like opals. I had seen brave men wither under such a gaze but to me Meli was not a witch to be feared. She was my blood. My only remaining kin besides my son. I held her stare, waiting.

"You let him die," she said at last. Her voice was soft but sharp with blame, like a dagger slipping between my ribs. I knew she was speaking of Lykos, brother of Thrasybulus. Her love. And I knew that our unspoken battle, so long delayed, was finally playing itself out.

"Lykos let himself be killed. He thought you were dead. He did not want to go on without you," I said, rebutting her accusation. Memories of that terrible night came back to me. While Lykos and I were away, the Tyrants attacked the *peripoli* compound. We returned to a burning pyre of death. Most of the *peripoli* and those who lived within had been slain. Rage and grief overcame my friend. Lykos launched himself at the giant Syracusan warrior Akras in a reckless attack. I saw him impaled on the mighty *kopis* now wielded by Mnasyllus. I escaped from Akras and the flames carrying the corpse of my wife, Phaia. In my mind I carried her still.

"You let him die," Meli repeated, her trembling voice rising slightly. Between us sat Tibetos, like the sole jury member at a trial. He peered into the fire, withholding his judgment while my sister and I battled across the flames.

But I cast a spear of my own back at my sister. "You knew," I said bitterly. "Your dreams told you death was coming, but you said nothing! Lykos. The *peripoli*. Phaia, You knew they would die."

Meli shook her head, deflecting my charge in turn. "I knew no such thing!"

But now neither of us could stop. Deeply-buried resentments burst out, like stinking pus from wounds that have festered untreated for too long. "You let him take me. You let him send me to the mines," Meli hissed. She was talking about Menekrates, the vile son of the Tyrant Kritias. He had murdered our parents. He had murdered my wife. I had avenged them all. Meli was crying now. "I waited in the darkness for you to get me, but you did not come!" she sobbed, stabbing a finger at me. "You left me in the darkness with the dead and the dying."

"Did I? Then why are you here now, Meli? Who found you? Who brought you to the surface? Who gave you your vengeance?" I said, biting each word. "Who has brought you food and fuel and provisions for the past years? Who, Meli?"

She ignored me. "You promised to protect me. When we were children. You promised," she said, rising to her feet. Tears streamed down her face.

A soft voice cut through the space between us. "You are both wrong." It was Tibetos. Still seated, he prodded idly at some embers. "You are both wrong," he repeated, looking at neither of us. He let out a long breath. "It was evil men like Menekrates and his father who harmed you and those you loved. Not the gods or Meli's dreams," he said, looking my way. He smiled sadly. He turned to Meli. "And your brother loves you more than any other. After he learned that you were alive, there was not a day he did not search for you. I know, for I was there with him." Tibetos was steadfast and brave, but at the core of his being he was gentle and kind. And now his sincere words disarmed us. Meli and I both stood stiffly, blinking at him.

"There is only one thing to do with evil men like Menekrates and Kritias and Lysander" he continued. "And that is to stop from them doing evil. To avenge those they have harmed. To send the bastards to Tartarus. That is what Lykos believed. He loved you both, like I do. But he would be saddened to see what has become of you." Having said his piece, my friend fell silent.

I stared at him, unable to speak or move. Then the sound of weeping unlocked my paralysis and I turned towards my sister, whose face was buried in her hands. Meli's shoulders heaved. I went to her and pulled her close to me. She sobbed into my chest. She had never wept since I rescued her from the mines. Now the years of pain came out in a torrent of grief. I do not know how long I held her before she spoke.

"It was what the Pythia told me," she said, looking up at me tear-reddened eyes.

"What?" I asked.

"She said that I would have a living death forever unless I killed the one I loved."

"I don't understand," I said, recalling my sister's outburst in the temple at Delphi.

"She meant that I must let Lykos go. To let his shade rest in the underworld. She was right." Meli stepped away and wiped the tears from her face. She smiled at me for the first time in many years and my heart broke, for I had not known how much I had missed it.

My sister turned towards Tibetos, who had risen to his feet but stood apart from us. "Tibetos, you sweet man," she said. Tibetos dropped his head in embarrassment. "There is no finer soul than yours." She approached him and kissed him on his crown.

When he raised his head there were tears in his eyes. "It is good to see you whole again, Meli. Your brother and I have missed you."

"You are our brother, too, Tibo," I said.

"We three orphans," Meli added.

"Forever," Tibetos finished, and we embraced each other with laughter and tears of joy.

In time, we took our places around the smouldering embers. In their warm glow, we began, hesitantly at first, like strangers meeting for the first time, to talk. Soon the words were flowing like a spring stream, as of old, and we were one family again.

There, under the stars beside the sea, for a short time at least, we began to heal.

IT WAS LATE BEFORE WE FINALLY SUCCUMBED TO SLEEP. My rest was deep and dreamless. When I awoke, the goddess Nyx was surrendering the night to her daughter Hemera, who came as a creeping and ever-brightening glow to the east. Meli and Tibetos slept soundly on either side of the charred remains of our fire. Let them rest, I thought, picking up Whisper and a water skin.

Our dispersed camp was stirring to life. Tents and bedrolls were being folded and nearly-dead embers coaxed back to life to cook the morning meal. Sabas already had some fish grilling and he waved to me as I passed by. I walked until the end of the beach, aware that I had picked up a companion.

"Go help Sabas," I said without looking back.

"Where are you going?" the boy Sosias asked at my back.

"'Where are you going, *lochagos*,'" I corrected him.

"Where are you going, *lochagos*?" he repeated.

The previous day I might have growled at him for not obeying my order, but my mood was still elevated from my reconciliation with Meli. In response to the boy's question, I freed Whisper from her scabbard and snapped the blade smartly away from me, holding the rhomphaia motionless parallel to the ground and pointing to a boulder. "Sit over there," I said, "and be quiet." Sosias obeyed this time, clambering up the rock and sitting himself down with his knees pulled up to his chest.

Once I was certain Sosias would not move, I pivoted slowly towards the east, bringing Whisper around so that I grasped her long hilt in a low, two-handed grip, her gently hooked tip bending down towards the crystal sea.

The Thracians believe that weapons have spirits the same way rivers are inhabited by naiads or certain trees are the homes of tree nymphs. This is why they name their weapons. My old friend Meges would have sneered at this, considering it to be superstitious nonsense. But on that morning, such superstitions could not be easily dismissed, for Whisper seemed to thrum with restless energy. With eagerness even.

The rhomphaia is an awkward weapon for those untrained in its use because of its length, easily twice that of a Greek xiphos sword. But in the hands of someone who knew how to wield it, the gently arcing blade is a wickedly fearsome tool, combining the reach of a spear, the manoeuvrability of a sword, the pure power of an axe. And I knew how to wield it.

Then, as I did most mornings, I went through my exercises. I began slowly at first, going through basic cuts and thrusts. Soon the attacks and parries grew more forceful as my imaginary enemies crystallized in my mind's eye. And then I set Whisper free.

She danced in my hands, her adamantine blade becoming a swirling, metallic blur. From atop his boulder, Sosias looked on with rapt attention. My breathing deepened and a sheen of sweat soon covered my body. The rhythm guided my movements until I was outside myself. Cuts and parries flowed into rolls and leaps as I fought invisible adversaries on all sides. With a final lunge I snapped the blade forward and impaled the last of my ghostly foes.

For some moments I stood there, my arm fully extended. My shoulder protested against the dead weight of the iron blade. When my muscles screamed for release, I held the position for ten more heartbeats before finally lowering the weapon. I walked over to where I had left the scabbard and returned Whisper to her protective sheath.

On his rock, Sosias, his eyes wide, quivered with excitement. Unable to restrain himself any longer, he slid down from his perch and ran up to me. "Where did you learn, *lochagos*?" he asked in a hushed voice.

"I was taught by a Thracian prince," I said, indulging his curiosity.

"Did it take a long time?"

"It took many years to master and I still practice almost every day," I said.

"Why?"

"In a fight, there is no time to think. You must kill your enemy quickly. There are few vulnerable areas on a well-armoured opponent, and those are small and moving. If you miss, your enemy will not repay the favour," I said.

"*Lochagos,* can you teach me?" Sosias blurted out.

I smiled, as much at the boy's sincerity as the absurdity of his request. Rather than responding, I extended the rhomphaia's forearm-length hilt in his direction. He looked at me uncertainly, but I nodded my permission. When his small hands grasped the handle, I let go.

I laughed as the tip of the sheathed weapon defied the slave-boy's will and dropped to the stony shingle of the beach. "How can you use it when you can't even lift it, Kuon?" I asked.

With effort, Sosias wrestled the rhomphaia into a vertical position. "I can lift it, *lochagos*," he said defiantly.

I took Whisper back from him. "Without strength, even the finest weapon in the world will not help you. When I was your age, a former hoplite named Neleus trained me. He made me stand under the sun holding a spear above my head all afternoon. Sometimes he made me pull a loaded cart to the agora and back. That was if I had been good!" I said with a tinge of nostalgia.

"Then make me strong, *lochagos*. Please," he added.

It would have been easy to refuse him. He was just an escaped slave. Tibetos had been a slave once as well but was no less a person for it. I sighed. "I make no promises, Kuon," I said finally.

Satisfied that he had wrung a small concession from me, Sosias grinned. "Thank you, *lochagos*!"

I waved him off. "Now go help Sabas with breakfast."

"Yes, *lochagos*!"

As the boy rushed off, I could not help shaking my head in amusement at how fate could turn and how people could change their minds, even myself. Despite my initial reluctance in having the escaped slave as part of our expedition, I was beginning to like the boy.

THE FAVOURABLE CONDITIONS HELD for the next part of our journey. Captain Xenius could not stop commenting on his good fortune. "Poseidon must have accepted my offering of wine," he offered by way of explanation. The only wine I had seen was the copious amount the captain had poured down his throat the previous evening. More likely we had just had a lucky run of it. Of more concern to me was Lysander. If the Spartan hegemon had indeed set out from the south, his sleek triremes would be enjoying the same steady winds as our rotund trading ship, no doubt gaining on us with each passing moment.

But for the time being, my world was limited to the deck of the Delphinus. With nothing to do, I decided to grant Sosias his wish, much to the amusement of the other *peripoli*. The boy's task was simple enough: to hold a fishing gaff above his head for as long as possible.

When the pole dropped, I thrashed him across the shoulder blades with the flat of a sheathed sword. "I thought you wanted to be a warrior, Kuon!" I shouted.

"I do, *lochagos,*" he shouted back. It was a harsh first lesson, but as a boy I had been treated no worse by my father's captain, Neleus, for whose strict instruction I was grateful. And though Sosias would not have guessed it, I was quietly impressed by his willpower. Few Athenian boys training at the *gymnasia* would have done half as well.

Soon the bored *peripoli* were wagering on how long the boy could hold out before receiving another thrashing. With hoots of laughter, the men jeered and encouraged the boy in equal measure, depending on which way they had bet. Even Meli was smiling, a change that did not go unnoticed among the *peripoli*. Mnasyllus tentatively brought her a cup of water and when she took it from him with a gentle touch on his thick forearm, the ox-like warrior beamed like a child receiving praise from his mother. Tibetos gave me a knowing nod from where he sat at the ship's bow.

The almost imperceptible line along the northern horizon grew into a thin ridge as the voyage continued. By the late afternoon, it had resolved into the rugged coastline of Thrace. The faint outline of the hills and mountains that lay beyond the coastal plains became visible. In the air the scent of dust and the pine resin mingled with that of the salty tang of the sea. It was familiar to me, though it had been many years since I last set foot in the land of my mother's ancestors.

Meli and I stood side by side, contemplating the view before us. I took my sister's hand in mine, a gesture that would not have been possible even a day before. Her gaze was fixed on the ever-nearing land of Thrace. "How do you feel?" I asked her.

She squeezed my hand and looked up at me, a smile on her face.

"Like I'm coming home."

CHAPTER 25

Another two days' sailing east along the coast took us to the city of Ainos. The bustling port sat at the mouth of a large river, the Hebros, which Captain Xenius told us penetrated deep into Thracian territory. "The farther north you go," he said, "the wilder it gets," he added.

The wharves swarmed with activity. "It's the location," the captain explained as the Delphinus waited for a berth. "Greeks from the south and west, Thracians from the north, barbarians from the east," he said, pointing out various styles of ships and traders on the shore. "Silver, slaves, timber, horses, wool," he said, counting off the commodities on his fingers. "Ainos is the place for them."

"And what about those?" I asked, indicating a row of five triremes. The warships were moored at the far end of the harbour. To my eye they looked similar to the ones we had seen in Kynos, but I could not be sure.

Xenius shrugged. "Who knows? Hardly a port out there without a trireme or two."

"Whose are they?" I asked.

The captain squinted. "Spartan," he concluded.

"How can you tell?"

"No decoration. Those humourless bastards don't waste any effort on making their ships look pretty. But I could be wrong."

Doubt gnawed at me. Lysander had demonstrated a fondness for ostentation, something that these ships lacked. But the very presence of Spartan ships put me on edge. At last the Delphinus was permitted to dock. We disembarked, our odd group hardly drawing a curious glimpse among the din of Greek, Thracian, and barbarian voices that filled the air. It was as good a place as any to remain anonymous.

Captain Xenius saw us off. "You're welcome to be my passengers anytime! This trip has been profitable and I haven't even done any business yet!" He said with a broad grin, patting the heavy coin pouch tucked inside his tunic. He waved one last time before turning to bark orders at his crew.

"What now?" Tibetos asked.

"Food and supplies first," I said. "And information."

We hefted our gear and headed past the warehouses into the warren of shops and homes beyond. There was a market atmosphere as inns, food vendors, and brothels all competed for the itinerant business of the hungry, concupiscent sailors wandering the streets. At one tavern, the sound of raucous Thracian voices spilled out onto the street. "Let's try here," I said.

Our entrance drew some curious glances but that was all. From behind a counter at the far end of the room, the proprietor watched us file in, no doubt trying to gauge the wealth of his latest customers. We exchanged nods across the room and I made my own assessment of the tavern.

The atmosphere was amiable and the aroma was encouraging. The customers were mostly Thracian by the look of them, but there was a scattering of Greeks and barbarians and even a dark-skinned Egyptian. A harried-looking girl with a long braid of copper hair coiled around her neck rushed to and fro slinging steaming bowls of stew on the tables and clearing away empty dishes. She gave us one look and jerked her thumb towards some rough-hewn tables at the back of the tavern.

No sooner had we sat down than the girl returned with loaves of coarse bread and an ewer of watered-down wine, quickly followed by bowls of stew. The wine hardly deserved the name, but the bread was fresh and the mutton stew hearty and filling. There was little talk as we filled our bellies. At the end of the table, the slave-boy Sosias shovelled down his food as though he had never eaten so well, which as a slave might well have been true.

I let my gaze wander over my other companions. I suddenly noticed that we were short one member. "Where is Arexion?" I asked. The Parnassian was nowhere to be seen.

"He said he was going to start inquiring about horses and that he would be back soon," Sabas reported between mouthfuls of stew. I frowned. It irritated me that the Arexion had not seen it necessary to notify me before wandering off on his own.

Still annoyed by the Delphian soldier's disappearance, I stood up and walked to the counter. "How much?" I asked in Thracian.

"Two drachmae," he said. It was a fair price.

I gave him the coins from my pouch. "Where can I get horses?" I asked.

"Travelling, then?" he inquired. "Well, my brother Stallos has horses, if you can afford them. There's a lot of demand for horses right now."

"That is not a problem," I said.

The tavern owner laughed. "I should have charged you more for the food!"

"Why the demand for horses?" I asked.

The owner raised a quizzical eyebrow. "You've been away for a while, I gather."

"Been fighting down south for a few years," I said vaguely.

"Mercenaries. I'd assumed so," the owner said, not questioning my story. It was no wonder, for *misthioi* – mercenaries – were Thrace's most sought-after commodity after slaves and silver. The warriors were mostly used as skirmishers and scouts, and were prized for a fearlessness that bordered on recklessness. They were also feared for their merciless brutality.

The merchant held out his hand. "Kadvast," he said, introducing himself.

I shook his hand. "Ardomir," I said, giving a common Thracian name that would be easily forgotten.

"Looks like you've done well for yourself, Ardomir," Kadvast said. "Must have, to own a weapon like that," he added with a nod towards the rhomphaia slung across my back.

"Well enough."

"Maybe you should have stayed down south a little longer," the owner said.

"What do you mean?"

"You're not Kikone, are you?" he asked, lowering his voice. The Kikones were a Thracian tribe whose ancestral lands lay to the west of Ainos.

"No, Thyran," I said, giving the name of a distant northern tribe.

"You don't sound like a Kikone, but just checking," he said. "The Kikones have revolted and refuse to acknowledge Medokos as their king. Both the king's forces and the Kikones have been rounding up all the horses they can find. If this weren't a Greek city, no doubt my brother's horses would have already been claimed by one side or the other." A Kikone revolt was hardly surprising. The powerful tribe had long resented paying tribute to Medokos, the warlord king of Thrace. That Thrace was in a state of upheaval did not bode well for our quest. The tavern owner continued. "The Kikones don't have a hope, if you ask me. In fact, I just heard yesterday that the King's son is gathering an army a day or two's ride north-west of here."

"Prince Zyraxes?" I exclaimed, unable to contain my surprise.

"That's the one. You know of him, then?"

"Only by reputation," I said, lying. In fact, I knew Zyraxes very well. He had befriended me during Thrasybulus' campaigns in the region. The Thracian prince had trained me in the Thracian fighting style and gifted me with Whisper and my horse-hoof corselet. More than that, he had adopted me as a sworn brother. If Zyraxes was nearby, he might be able to help me find the town of Siragellis and Lysander's prophet more easily.

News of Zyraxes' proximity was heartening, but there was another matter that concerned me. "There were five triremes in the harbour," I said.

"The Spartans," the tavern owner said without hesitation, confirming captain Xenius's conclusion. My heart sank.

"How long have they been in Ainos?" I asked.

"Arrived yesterday. A lot of soldiers with them, but isn't that always the case with Spartans?" he said disgustedly. "Arrogant bastards. Always looking down their noses at us and refusing to pay fair prices for what they take."

"Any idea who they are?" I asked.

"Some general or other, I expect," the owner said with a sniff. "They've kept to themselves and hopefully they'll soon be on their way." A little of my optimism returned. If the ships belonged to Lysander, some rumour of it surely would have spread. Perhaps the Spartans' presence in Ainos was merely a coincidence as Captain Xenius had suggested. In any case, I would not feel at ease until there was plenty of distance between us and the Spartan ships. The tavern owner gave me directions to his brother's stables and I thanked him for the information, sliding him another coin for his trouble.

Arexion was waiting for us outside. "Did you locate any horses for sale?" I asked.

"Not even a cursed nag," he replied. "We'll steal some if necessary. We must find the false prophet before Lysander."

"We have a lead on where to get some," I said.

The Delphian grunted. "Best we be off, then. Lead the way." For someone who had just claimed to have conducted an exhaustive search for horses, he was strangely unsurprised.

Kadvast's detailed directions proved accurate. The man Stallos greeted us. "My brother sent you? In that case I'm sure we can reach an agreement." After much haggling, we acquired horses as well as the services of one of Stallos' sons, who would guide us to Zyraxes, if the Thracian prince was indeed where Kadvast had said he was. The horse trader, having extracted a healthy profit of Persian darics from Arexion's purse, nevertheless insisted that he had come off worse in the deal. "I could have sold them for twice as much," he said, but his broad smile suggested otherwise.

Soon the town lay behind us as we headed north. The marshy land around the mouth of the river meant for a slow start, but soon we were onto the coastal plain with the mountains visible in the distance. Stallos' son told us we would reach the Thracian village the next morning if we kept up a good pace. Only then would we know if my Thracian brother, Prince Zyraxes, awaited us.

CHAPTER 26

Prince Zyraxes, son of Medokos, King of Thrace, emerged from the chieftain's lodge at the centre of the village accompanied by a dozen warriors of his retinue. Upon seeing our party, he strode towards us, his arms spread wide.

"Daimon, son of Nikodromos!" Zyraxes said in faintly accented Greek, a joyous grin splitting his face. We embraced each other warmly. "You have returned to your home at last!" he said in Thracian when we separated.

"Did I not promise I would do so?" I replied in Thracian.

"You did, my brother. You did! Yet that does not diminish my wonder at the sight of you, by Pleystor!" he said, invoking the Thracian god of war.

He had called me his brother, which could have easily seemed true to an outsider, for we were much of a size and appearance. The prince was perhaps six or seven years older than me, but looking at him at that moment, I would have guessed him to be older had I not known better. His still-handsome face was creased by deep lines and his current happiness could not conceal the underlying weariness I saw there.

For the moment though, he was happy to play the gracious and generous host. He reached out and touched my corselet. "And what have you done to my gift? It is most insulting to treat the object of a prince's generosity so poorly!" he said with a mischievous spark in his eyes.

The prince had given me the armour when I had last departed Thrace. The light, flexible corselet allowed me to move faster than my opponents and had saved my life many times when I did not move quite fast enough. Its horse-hoof scales had once shone like the skin of an enormous jet-black serpent, but had suffered from years of battle and exposure to the elements. Numerous repairs had left it functional but faded and with more than one missing scale filled in with a bronze replacement.

This I told Zyraxes, who assumed a serious expression. "We will look into repairing it properly while you are here," he said with a wink. "Now, brother, introduce me to your companions,"

I did so, giving the names of each man as I did so. Zyraxes greeted Arexion with an official air. "We have great respect for the Oracle of Delphi. I speak for my father, King Medokos, when I say that we will assist you in any way we are able," Zyraxes said. The grim warrior thanked the prince stiffly and Zyraxes moved on to the rest of our party.

Zyraxes warmed to the *peripoli*, and they to him, for I had told them many tales of the prince's skill as a warrior and as a military leader. The second-to-last in line was Tibetos, who had been with me during Thrasybulus' campaign in the region many years before.

"Tibetos," Zyraxes said, grasping my friend's hand between his own. "It brings me joy to see you once again."

"Thank you, Prince Zyraxes," Tibetos said with a slight bow. "I am honoured that you remember me."

"Are you not also my brother?" Zyraxes said generously. "And I thank you for keeping your promise to rescue Daimon when he inevitably got himself into trouble?"

"More than once!" Tibetos said and they both laughed like old friends. I raised an eyebrow at Tibetos, who shrugged, for I had been unaware that such words had passed between them.

At last Zyraxes came to Meli. The lighthearted banter he had shared with the others gave way to a tone of solemnity. "We have never met, but I know you by sight. You are Melitta, daughter of Erta," the prince stated, switching to Thracian. "Daimon told me of you with great love. He is my brother, and I would be honoured to call you sister, should you permit me to do so." He bowed to her as though she were a queen.

"You have no need to ask for that which has already been given," Meli said, touching Zyraxes lightly on the arm. "Daimon has told me so many tales of you that I have long considered you our elder brother."

Zyraxes beamed at the compliment. "I welcome you home, Sister! I welcome you home!" He then addressed us all in Greek. "You are all welcome to enjoy our hospitality as long as you wish," he said, casting an appraising eye over our motley group, "though I suspect that you have other plans. But first you must eat and drink after such a long journey!"

By now, the village square had filled with common folk and warriors, all curious about the visitors who their prince was greeting with such enthusiasm. Zyraxes gave orders for an impromptu banquet to be prepared and for accommodation to be found for us among the dwellings in the village.

The crowd began to disperse. While Zyraxes made arrangements and the others were led away to various huts in the settlement, my sister and I took a seat by the lodge. As we watched the activity of the village, my warrior's sense tingled. Scanning the village square, my eyes fell across another familiar face, one that I had never hoped to see again.

Her name was Zia. She was a Thracian soothsayer, a witch, and I feared her. The gnarled hag was much as I remembered. An ornately patterned cloak covered her diminutive frame, but I knew her aged appearance was deceptive, for her wizened body was spry and hale. On many occasions I had seen her gleefully execute captives as sacrifices to her bloodthirsty Thracian gods. She was an evil woman.

As she gazed towards us now, the swirling blue tattoos covering her face and neck only served to draw attention to malevolence radiating from her deep-set emerald eyes. Then I realized that the witch was not looking at me but my sister, who had locked eyes with the soothsayer. My fear of the old woman was eclipsed by a sudden rush of anger.

"Wait here," I told Meli. I strode across the square to confront the witch. I stopped in front of Zia, blocking her view of my sister.

Zia looked up at me in amusement. "So, the One-Who-Walks-Alone has returned. But not so alone this time, yes? What gift have you brought me, young Daimon?" she said. Her lips parted in a vicious grin of yellowed teeth, like a wolf baring its fangs.

"I do not like the way you look at my sister, witch."

"She has power, that one," Zia declared. "But it is wild, untamed. The gods have brought her here for me. My end draws near. She will be my heir."

I loved my sister and she had only just escaped from the madness that had imprisoned her for so long. To let her go down a road that would turn her into a witch like the cruel, spiteful Zia would be but another form of prison. That Zia laid claim to her stabbed at something deep inside my soul.

"You will stay away from my sister," I snarled.

"Do you think I fear you, pup?" she said. "Your sister's path is not your own! Her fate is already spun and it belongs to me. Now be gone!" She sneered, waving a dismissive hand. My own hand snapped out and seized her narrow wrist. She spun and pulled to free herself like a snared fox. I tightened my grip. Gods, she was strong! Her expression changed from shock to barely contained rage. "What are you doing, boy?" she hissed.

"Do not infect my sister with your foulness, crone, or we will see if your gods are strong enough to stop my blade across your throat."

"Then you will be cursed! The gods will curse anyone who harms their servants!" she spat.

I yanked her close to me and squeezed harder, causing a twitch of pain in her face. "You forget, hag, that I am already cursed," I said through clenched teeth.

The old woman's self-assurance was betrayed by a ripple of fear in her eyes. She tried another tack. "I am protected by Prince Zyraxes. You have no power here!"

I grinned coldly. "The prince is my sworn brother. Perhaps you are right and he would punish me for your death. But perhaps you overestimate your worth to him. Perhaps," I said, looking over my shoulder at my sister, who watched us from across the square. "You can be replaced." I released Zia from my grip, pushing her away from me.

The witch glared at me. Then her hands flew about in a series of complex figures while she spat arcane curses at me. And I laughed in her face, which infuriated her even further. "Bah!" she snarled.

She cast one last obscene gesture my way before scuttling off, muttering to herself. I had made an enemy.

The battle won if not the war, I took a deep breath and walked back to my sister, who rose to meet me. "You need to be careful of her, Brother. I could sense her power from here."

"She is strong," I conceded.

"I helped you."

I looked at Meli, whose face revealed little. I shrugged. "You should stay away from her," I said. My sister did not reply.

Before I could say anything more, Zyraxes returned, accompanied by two women. The women's dress differed little from that of the male warriors and they moved with graceful strength. Both had short, hooked *sica* swords on their hips.

Zyraxes addressed my sister. "These are Thruna and Ullana. They will take care of you, Sister." The two women gave a small bow.

Meli's face brightened and I smiled, for I knew the source of her joy. As a child, my sister had always wanted to be an Amazon, one of the female warriors of ancient times. She would listen with delight as my mother told tales of the Amazons' bravery and martial prowess. Now my sister was standing in front of their descendants. The matter of the witch Zia was temporarily forgotten. "Thank you, Brother," Meli replied to Zyraxes with genuine delight. "And thank you, Thruna and Ullana!" The two women bowed again before leading my sister away to her accommodation in the village.

Zyraxes and I watched them go. "I remembered what you said about her wanting to be a warrior," he said. The Thracian prince put his arm around my shoulder. "It is good to see you, Brother. Once you have eaten and rested, you will tell me what has passed since we last met and what brings you here now. There will be much to discuss."

"I, too, would have news of you and your father, the king," I said.

The prince's shoulders fell slightly and a weary sadness filled his eyes. "Much has changed since you were last here, my friend.

"And not for the better."

CHAPTER 27

Xenia.

The sacred obligation of a host to provide his guests with shelter, food, and gifts. By all measures, Zyraxes fulfilled his duty of *xenia* in the chieftain's lodge that night. The feast was a welcome change from the dull travellers' fare of our journey so far. Savoury mutton and goat meat, charred and dripping with juices, sated appetites that had gone unsatisfied for many days, and both wine and *rappa* flowed freely. Tibetos was familiar with the Thracian drink, but to the other Greeks the tangy, cloudy liquid made from fermented barley was a revelation. Mnasyllus declared it superior to wine, winning him the eternal friendship of our Thracian hosts. The wine and *rappa* loosened tongues and many tales were exchanged.

Zyraxes and his finest warriors listened with rapt attention to my description of the defeat that had brought Athens to its knees. I omitted nothing. I spoke of how the Tyrants installed by Lysander had ravaged the city to satisfy their own lust for wealth and power. The Thracians voiced their anger as I described the noble last stand of the *peripoli* against the soldiers of the Tyrants. They wept unashamedly when I told of how Lykos fell battling the Syracusan giant Akras. Meli wept, too, for she had never heard a detailed account of her lover's death, and Zyraxes ran to comfort her, the weeping pair consoling each other like long lost siblings.

A hush descended as I recounted the murder of my own wife. It was a story whose details I had never even shared with Tibetos, let alone the other *peripoli*. By the end of it, there was neither Greek nor Thracian whose face was not wet with tears.

But the tale had not finished. Tears turned to gasps and then to cheers when I told of how Thrasybulus had raised an army and fought to overthrow the Tyrants and their Spartan masters. There were knowing nods among Zyraxes and some of the older Thracian warriors, for many of them knew of Thrasybulus and his skills as a general from his time in Thrace many years earlier.

With pride, I described the deeds of each of the *peripoli* in the war against the Tyrants, and my companions' esteem in the eyes of the Thracians rose with each passing moment. Tibetos showed them the sling that had slain the mighty Akras, and the Thracians marvelled at the giant's massive *kopis* sword with which I had cut down the tyrant Kritias and then given to Mnasyllus, the only man I knew strong enough to wield it with ease.

The combination of food, drink, and emotional storytelling began to take its toll. One by one the men retired to their billets in the village and Meli disappeared with her escort of the female warriors Thruna and Ullana. Soon, along with the watchful Tibetos, only Zyraxes and one of his veteran captains, an old friend named Basti, remained with me around the central hearth of the chieftain's hall.

The prince, having done his duty of *xenia*, turned to the host's right to question those who accepted his hospitality. "Tell me, Brother," Zyraxes said, his intelligent eyes no less sharp for the long evening of feasting. "What brings you back to Thrace?" I explained what had happened in Delphi and our mission to prevent Lysander from bringing his false prophet back to the sanctuary. "And like a madman, you ran up to Thrace without a plan," he said with a familiar smile.

"I'm working on it," I said.

"And what will happen if this plot succeeds?" he asked.

"With the legitimacy of Delphi behind him, Lysander will seize power from the hereditary kings of Sparta and become the sole ruler in their place," I said.

Zyraxes seemed troubled by this. "Since Athens lost the war, Sparta has been making her power felt all over the Aegean. They are no friends of Thrace, that is for certain. By Pleystor, you Athenians are hard-nosed bastards, but you were fair in your way. We could deal with Thrasybulus. But those arrogant Spartan bastards treat us like subjects. Every year they demand more and more tribute from our people while offering less and less in return." He slapped the table in frustration. "Damn them to Hades!"

"Can you help us?" I asked.

Zyraxes gave a small shrug. "Perhaps. Where is this so-called prophet?"

"The Pythia told me he is in a Thracian town called Siragellis."

"Ah," Zyarxes said, exchanging a knowing look with the veteran Basti. "That makes things more difficult, my friend."

"Is it far?"

"Not very," he said. "Three days west of here on horseback."

This was in fact good news, for I had feared that we would have to travel much farther north towards the Euxine Sea. "Then what is it that makes you hesitate?" I asked.

Zyraxes sighed. "Things have become much more complicated since you were last here, my friend."

I recalled that Captain Xenius had implied as much. "Does your father not rule all of Thrace?" I asked.

"In name, perhaps, but not in fact.' Zyraxes took a long pull of *rappa* before continuing. "The Spartans do not want Thracian tribes united under one leader. They remember the close relationship between Thrasybulus and my father, and so they send their agents to foment rebellion among the chieftains. That is why you happen to find me here: The Kikones are claiming to be an independent kingdom, and we are showing them the truth is otherwise."

The Kikones were a troublesome tribe whose territories lay just to the east of us. As a twenty-year-old squadron leader, I had been present when their chief had been slain in battle and the tribe capitulated to the combined armies of Thrasybulus and Medokos, the present king of Thrace. The news that the Kikones and other tribes were rebelling surprised me, for the King Medokos I knew had been an able commander and a shrewd politician. "Where is your father now?" I asked.

A pained expression crossed Zyraxes' face. "My father is not well. Illness has weakened him. This has not helped his cause, for the tribes know that he is not fit to campaign. This only stokes the fires of rebellion even more," he said. I reckoned that the king would be around sixty years of age. He had been an imposing giant of a figure when I met him ten years earlier. But the years defeat even the mightiest warriors and reduce them to shadows of their former glory. As I look now at my aged, gaunt hands, I know the truth of it.

"Does the king's mind still fare well?" I asked. Beside Zyraxes, the Thracian warrior Basti looked down at his drinking horn uncomfortably.

"My father's judgment is… compromised at times," Zyraxes said, choosing his words carefully.

"You disagree with his decisions?" I asked.

Zyraxes sighed. "With some. But he is still the king. I must respect his wishes. But his decisions will have a direct impact on your mission and my ability to aid you."

"In what way?"

"Siragellis is a village west of the Hebros River. The king's name has little influence there these days, and mine even less so. Even if I had men to spare, if I were to lead a large force across the river, it would likely provoke a war between eastern and western Thrace, a war from which my father is unlikely to emerge victorious."

"Have the rebel tribes been so successful in the west?"

Zyraxes scoffed. "On the contrary. Most of the tribes have been brought to heel, save for those in the north, but they were only ever subjects in name only."

"Then why do you say you are unwelcome in the west?" I asked, confused.

The prince took a deep breath. "Thrace is too large a territory and there are many rebellious chiefs to be dealt with. To this end, my father decided to divide his kingdom into two separate regions, each under the control of a different general. I am responsible for the territory west of the Hebros River and another general is responsible for maintaining order to the east of the river."

"And you object to this?" I asked.

Zyraxes consider the matter before responding. "The decision itself is sound enough. It is my father's choice of leader that is more questionable." Basti spat on the ground in disgust.

"Who leads in the east?" I asked.

"A general named Seuthes," Zyraxes said, his face tightening. Basti spat again.

"What is wrong with this Seuthes?"

"He is a competent enough general," Zyraxes conceded. "But he's a slippery bastard who uses honeyed words as much as force to achieve his ambitions. He is more interested in consolidating his own power than remaining loyal to my father. I have said as much to my father, but Seuthes always manages to convince him of his loyalty," Zyraxes said bitterly. "There are even rumours that he wishes to become king of the territories he now — " Zyraxes searched for an appropriate Thracian word, but finding none switched to Greek. "— a*dministers* for my father."

A grim silence settled over the table. The situation was even more perilous than I had feared. I considered my options. "Will Seuthes object to us crossing his territory?" I asked.

"I am sure of it."

"Where is Seuthes now?"

Zyraxes scratched at his beard. "My spies tell me that he was at his fortress at Zorlanae. It is on the way to Siragellis. He has spent much gold and silver on a fine hall there. He enjoys the trappings of wealth, so it is likely that he is still there, though I cannot say for certain. However, if you stay clear of heavily-travelled routes, it should be possible to slip in and out of his territory without being discovered."

"How many men and horses could you spare?" I asked.

Zyraxes considered the request. "A dozen warriors, plus horses for you and your men. Basti could be your guide. He is familiar with the area and was heading in that direction in any case." Basti nodded his consent.

"We must leave tomorrow," I said, thinking back to the Spartan warships we had seen moored at Ainos. "Lysander cannot be far behind."

"It will be done," Zyraxes declared.

It was not much, but better than I could have hoped for when we had set out from Delphi. With horses we could be at Siragellis in a matter of days. Lysander would be denied his prize, if the false prophet was in fact at Siragellis as the Pythia had claimed. If the Oracle's information was wrong, however, our journey would have been for naught. Part of me hoped that this would be the case, for the prospect of murder weighed heavy on my mind.

I was rescued from my bout of conscience by Zyraxes, who raised his drinking horn in a toast. "May the gods protect you," he said. We downed the tangy *rappa* in a single gulp.

The gods had other plans.

CHAPTER 28

The copious amounts of *rappa* consumed the previous evening left the Thracians no worse for wear. Mnasyllus, however, fared less well, much to the amusement of his new Thracian comrades.

"It feels like quarrymen hammering in my head!" the big man said, massaging his temples.

"Makes sense," Telekles said. "I've always said you had a head of stone!" The men laughed at the jibe, but Mnasyllus just groaned and leaned against the side of his horse.

The preparations were underway. With luck we would set off before mid-day. Finding volunteers had not been an issue, for Thracians will rarely pass up an opportunity to raid their neighbours and earn some reputation as warriors.

"Basti will be your guide," Zyraxes said. "He will take you on the fastest route to Siragellis." He looked disapprovingly at the *peripoli*. "Your men are not dressed for a long journey on horseback," he observed. He was correct of course, for our chafed legs had hardly recovered from the two days on horseback from Delphi to Kynos. The prospect of once again having our skin rubbed raw by horse hides was hardly appealing. "You'll freeze to death if the weather turns, and your southern dress will only draw attention. Better to dress in the Thracian manner," the prince concluded. Before I could say anything, Zyraxes had barked a command to one of his slave attendants to fetch Thracian garb for me and my men.

The other *peripoli* watched with amused expressions as I donned a pair of woolen Thracian leggings and one of the long, patterned wool cloaks. I spread my arms wide for my audience. "See?" I said.

The barbarian breeches drew the most scepticism. "How are you supposed to take a piss in those things?" Sabas asked.

"There's a cord around the waist," I said, hiking up my tunic to show them.

"Must be hard to untie in the middle of the night," Stachys observed.

"At least all your noisy fumbling will give your favourite bumboy time to hide!" Telekles exclaimed with a thrust of his hips, and more laughter ensued.

"They're more comfortable than you think," I said. I pointed at the pile of clothing brought by Zyraxes' slaves. "Now find some that fit and get dressed. You're in Thrace now!"

The new clothing brought much-needed distraction from the gravity of the task before us. Soon the *peripoli* were laughing and marching about with exaggerated strides and striking heroic poses as they tried out the unfamiliar breeches, causing much hilarity among the Thracians.

Zyraxes smiled as he looked upon his newest subjects. "I have one more thing for you, Brother," he said. The prince turned and beckoned a slave boy, who hurried up to us bearing a familiar-looking item. "You might need this," Zyraxes said, taking a polished horse-hoof corselet from the boy and presenting it to me.

It was typical of his generosity. "This is your armour," I said. "I cannot take this." The black scales had the bewitching lustre of snake skin.

Zyraxes waved my protest off. "Then it is not a gift. As a prince of Thrace, I command you to accept it," he said.

I put the corselet on. The tough underlying leather was supple enough that I could still move with the ease and flexibility of the serpent the armour called to mind. "Thank you, Brother," I said.

"Try to keep better care of it this time," Zyraxes said with a smile before going to talk with Basti.

Once the novelty of the new costumes had worn off, we set about preparing our kit for the journey ahead. We would travel light, taking only weapons and enough rations for five days, with only our thick Thracian cloaks for shelter from the changeable northern spring weather. Even Arexion had seen the wisdom of the cloaks, though he had refused to don Thracian leggings like the others.

I surveyed the scene. The *peripoli* packed up their gear with practiced efficiency, as did the dozen Thracian warriors Zyraxes had selected to join us. Except for Basti, the Thracians were young, hardly past their twentieth year for the most part, but they moved with confidence and had the hungry look of young warriors eager for glory and reputation. Two of their number were women, but they were as hard-looking as the men. It did not stop the curious stares of the *peripoli,* who were unaccustomed to such things. Basti vouched for their skill. "They are blooded warriors. I would not have them with me if I did not trust my life to their abilities," he said proudly of the female warriors.

Mnasyllus, his beloved hoplite shield slung across his back, shuffled uncomfortably. "Do they not fear, um, the unwanted attentions of the men?" the shy farmer asked in a whisper with as much tact as he could muster.

"You mean a spear attack in the night?" Sabas asked loudly. Mnasyllus turned red.

Basti turned and poked Sabas in the chest. "Any man who dared to put his 'spear' in the wrong place would soon find it sliced in two by their *sica* swords," he warned with a challenging smile. Sabas regarded the short, curved swords at the women's waists with new respect.

As the others continued to discuss their new Thracian comrades, my eyes fell on Sosias, who had flung a pack bag over the neck of a small horse. I strode over to him. "What do you think you're doing, *Kuon*?" I asked, frowning.

"I'm preparing my pack for the journey," the boy said. He continued to busy himself with his kit, pretending not to see my disapproving stare. Armies almost always travelled with a train of slaves, servants, women, and even children. But we were to be a raiding party, not an army. There was no place for the boy.

"You will not be coming," I said sternly. "You will stay here."

Sosias stood up and faced me. "I can be of use," he said, looking at me squarely. It was brave of him. But I was having none of it.

"You will stay here!" I said loudly enough to draw glances from the others. They knew better than to interfere and went back to preparing their gear.

Sosias was crestfallen. "But you will need a servant!" he protested. "Someone to take care of the camp!"

"Iollas will be sufficient," I said, gesturing at the former slave. "Where we are headed is no place for a boy," I said.

"But I want to be a warrior like you and the *peripoli*!" he said, revealing his true motive. Knowing he had said too much, his mouth tightened.

At his age I had been much the same, eager for war and battle but ignorant of the horror that waited there. I understood his desire but also the foolhardiness of his wish. There would be no compromise. "Challenge me one more time, boy," I said coldly.

For a moment, I thought he would dare to defy me. But his resolve failed him and he blinked back tears. He turned and scurried off before I could see his shame. I let out a long breath. My sympathy for the boy's disappointment quickly vanished behind a roiling cloud of suspicion as my eyes fell on another figure on the periphery of the village. The witch Zia watched me from afar. And she was not alone.

My temper rose as I strode towards Zia and my sister. The witch had not heeded my warning to stay away from Meli. Now I would show her the folly of that decision. Meli stepped in front of Zia, preventing me from throttling the old woman. "Stop!" she said, thrusting a hand forward. I glared at the sneering Zia, who wisely stayed out of my reach behind my sister.

My gaze snapped towards Meli. "Why are you not preparing with the others?" I demanded.

"I cannot come with you. My destiny lies here with Zia. She will teach me the mysteries of the gods of our ancestors." Beside her, Zia's eyes flared in triumph. I wanted to skewer the old woman.

"She is nothing but cruelty and spite," I said, speaking as though the aged Thracian priestess were not there. "I do not wish you to become like this shrivelled piece of fox dung," I said, an edge of pleading creeping into my voice. Zia bared her craggy teeth at me.

"I do not need your protection anymore," Meli said firmly. Her tone softened and she touched my arm. "Nor do I need your permission, Dammo." She was right, of course. What could I do? Bind her hands and feet and throw her over a horse?

My shoulders sank. "It was ever true, Sister," I said.

Zia's thin lips parted in a malevolent grin. But I was not done with her. My hand shot out and seized the witch by the neck. She clawed at my arm. My fingers squeezed her scrawny throat and she ceased her scrabbling. Under Meli's passive gaze, I pulled the hag close. "Remember my promise, crone. Harm my sister and not even the gods will be able to protect you from me." I pushed the witch away. She made to hurl a curse at me but I lunged at her like an animal and she ran away with an undignified squeak.

"I do not trust her," I repeated.

Meli gave a thin, enigmatic smile. "I can protect myself."

I exhaled in defeat. There was nothing more for it. We embraced each other. "We depart soon," I said simply. I turned to leave.

Meli stopped me. "There is one more thing," Meli said.

"What?" I said.

"It is Sosias. You must take him with you." Her tone was that of a command.

I snorted. "*Kuon?*" My sister's stare did not waver. I suppressed an urge to laugh. "I grow fond of the boy," I conceded. "But the pup will just get underfoot at best. There is danger where we are headed; I cannot guarantee his safety."

But Meli insisted. "Without him the mission will fail and Lysander will become king. I have foreseen it."

"How?" I demanded, not being able to imagine how the boy could be of any importance.

As usual, my sister's omens were frustratingly lacking in detail. "I do not know," she said. "Just that he needs to be at your side. I told you so in Delphi," reminding me of what she had said at the beginning of this mad journey. It seemed to have happened an age ago.

My plan, poor and makeshift as it was, was fraying to the point of snapping before we had even departed. First it was my sister's refusal to join us and now her demand that I take Sosias. I turned my face skyward as though salvation might suddenly crash to the earth to save me from the burden that Fate and the Pythia had loaded on my shoulders. The overcast Thracian sky mocked me with its silence. The meaning of my sister's premonitions was always obscured, like a precious stone hidden in folded cloth. One by one the layers would peel back until the gem of truth within revealed itself. More often than not the cloth also concealed a scorpion whose sting was the price of knowledge. Yet I had also learned that one ignored her words at their peril.

"*Kuon!*" I bellowed, still looking at my sister. Her expression revealed little. The sound of rapid, approaching footfalls followed by that of a skidding stop in the grit behind me told me that Sosias had heard my summons.

"Yes, *lochagos*?" the boy managed between gasps.

"We will leave soon. If you are not ready, you will stay here and feed the villagers' pigs."

The words had scarcely left my lips when Sosias answered. "Yes, *lochagos*! Thank you, *lochagos*!" he said brightly, sprinting off before I could change my mind.

"Thank you for believing me, Dammo," Meli said.

"Have I ever not?" I asked.

In response she stepped forward and hugged me as she had as a child. She let me go. "Goodbye, Brother."

"I will return, Meli."

"Dammo," she said. Her voice dropped. "The gods are watching you, Brother. Apollo. Bendis. The Hero," she said, invoking the name of the Thracian's most revered god. "They have converged on this place," she whispered.

And with those words a chill ran through my soul.

For when events drew the interest of the gods, death was sure to follow.

PART THREE
FURIES ΕΡΙΝΥΕΣ

CHAPTER 29

Sosias rode with me. If nothing else, it would keep him out of trouble. The boy's excitement manifested itself in endless questions and observations until I silenced him with a low, rumbling growl. With the boy's tongue now stilled, I could observe the land around us with a more focused eye.

Half a day's ride had already taken us far away from Zyraxes and my sister. Once out of the village, we had soon descended from the foothills onto the broad coastal plain. The land was flat and fertile, suitable for the many isolated farms that dotted the greening fields. Patches of forest persisted, mostly pine, but with occasional stands of taller oaks and beeches visible far before we came close to them. Cool spring air fought the sun's rays with remarkable obstinacy, a reminder that winter in Thrace yielded with much more reluctance than in the south. Already the cold was regaining its sharp edge as the sun grew ever lower in the sky.

I kicked my horse into a canter and caught up with Basti. "How far will we travel today?" I asked the Thracian.

"We will soon reach the fortress at Krashabek," he said. "We can rest there tonight."

"Fortress?" I asked. Thracian villages often had palisades or crude defenses of ditches, but in my previous time in the area, I had not seen purely military fortifications.

"Well, fortress might be generous," he conceded.

The truth of his words became apparent as a bump became visible on the eastern horizon. The nub grew only slightly in stature as we neared it, its existence marked more by rising tendrils of smoke than the impact it made on the landscape. I began to resolve a stone wall atop a raised mound. The mound itself was neither tall nor broad, being perhaps the height of a man and thirty or so paces across. Yet even such a small rise still made the mound the highest object for miles around, offering a commanding view of the plain to anyone posted atop the wall.

Our approach had surely been noticed but had caused little concern among the fort's occupants, at least the human ones. A dozen or so horses corralled north of the mound had turned their attention on us, their tails flicking with alert curiosity but no man was to be seen. At last a figure appeared atop the wall. Basti raised his hand and the figure waved back. "Why has no one challenged us?" I asked.

"They recognize me. Dotos is there," he said. Dotos was another one of Zyraxes' trusted captains, as tough and reliable as the man beside me. "Besides," Basti continued, "it's people coming from the east they're more concerned with."

"Seuthes?" I asked.

Basti spat at the mention of the rebellious Thracian general. "Bastard sends raiding parties across the river," he said, referring to the Hebros, the river that divided Thrace and flowed south down to Ainos. "He denies it, of course, but a lying piece of weasel dung like him would, wouldn't he? Prince Zyraxes thought it best to have some outposts like this one to discourage them. And to give us warning just in case Seuthes gets it in his head to invade with a larger force."

Now I could see the fort clearly. The stone walls were hardly twice the height of a man. The individual stones were irregular in shape and size, but had been fitted with such skill so as to present a flush, vertical surface. Eager spring plants and shrubs had found purchase in the nooks and crevices, giving the fortifications an air of age and neglect. "Did Thracians erect the fort?" I asked Basti, for to my eyes the construction looked neither Thracian nor Greek.

"The Great King built it," he said, waving a hand in the general direction of distant Persia.

"Which one?"

Basti shrugged. "One of them."

I remembered the tales my father had told me when I was a boy about how the Great King Xerxes had led his multitudes from Asia, demanding gifts of earth and water from every territory he crossed. The Thracian chieftains along the Great King's route had had little choice but to submit and had remained under Persian control long after Xerxes had fled from Greece like a whipped dog. The fort before us was but one example of the conquerors' occupation that lay scattered throughout the land.

The generally poor state of the outpost became more apparent as we circled around to the gate on the eastern side of the fort. Material eroded from the mound had tumbled into the encircling ditch, reducing the obstacle to a mere dip. One section of the wall on the south side had collapsed into a ramp-like pile of rubble. A palisade of mature logs filled the gap, though how old the timber was I could only guess. A number of round tents lay scattered outside the walls, and a few women could be seen tending cooking pots over campfires. Men interrupted their meals or games to watch our arrival with seasoned wariness but not hostility. It felt more like a small village than a fort.

A half dozen warriors awaited us outside the gate on the east side of the defences. A familiar face stepped forward. "Basti!" Dotos called as we dismounted. "I recognized your fat body from five miles away!" The warriors behind Thracian captain laughed.

"And I smelled your stink ten miles away!" Basti retorted. "Been lying with horses again, eh? It is lonely out here."

"Perhaps you will find your wife has not missed you as much as you thought!" Dotos replied with a sly grin. The men laughed even harder. Insults duly traded, the two old friends embraced.

Our Thracian garb did not fool Dotos for long. "What is this rabble of *alabakan* you've brought us?" Dotos said, casting a critical eye over his unexpected guests. Thracians call all outlanders *alabakan* just as we Greeks call all foreigners barbarians.

I stepped from behind my horse so that Dotos could see me clearly. "Not all *alabakan*, Dotos," I said.

Dotos squinted at me for a moment before his eyes widened in recognition. "Daimon? Daimon the Athenian?" he exclaimed. Before I could answer he had already lunged forward to crush me in a rib-crushing hug. "Daimon!" he said when we had separated. "By the Hero, you have grown! You've become a man!" he said, looking up at me. He turned to his comrades. "The last time I saw this one, his balls had hardly dropped down!" he explained. The gathered warriors chuckled.

I introduced Tibetos and the others in Thracian and Dotos gave the names of the warriors who had come out with him. "But come! You must be hungry after your journey. There will be plenty of time for talk later!"

Once our horses had been seen to, Dotos led us into the fort. Whatever the original Persian layout of the fort had been, it had long vanished, replaced with the rustic structures of its more recent occupants. Two mules stood tethered in a makeshift stable in one corner of the enclosure. There were a few permanent huts of the Thracian type, with low entrances leading to even lower, dug-out interiors, but most of the accommodations were like the tents we had seen outside.

Beside me, Sosias gaped at the lounging, tattooed warriors as they chatted or sharpened their weapons. "Are they good warriors?" he asked me in a hushed voice. "As good as you?"

"Better," I said. "But stand tall. They respect confidence." Sosias pulled himself up and put some swagger into his step.

Tibetos snorted. "Reminds me of you at his age," he said.

Before I could reply, Dotos called me over to meet yet another Thracian. In this way, our progress to the large central hut was hindered by the need to stop every few steps to go through another round of introductions. When at last we reached the main hut, Basti hesitated. He leaned over to Dotos. "How is she?"

Dotos' face took on a grim air. "You've been gone for more than a moon. It might have been better for you to have stayed with Zyraxes."

Before Basti could respond, a ruddy-cheeked woman appeared at the hut's entrance, her black almond-shaped eyes scanning us with undisguised hostility. Her hair was a mess of coiled black braids which, when mixed with her inimical stare, gave her a fearsome aspect. Her eyes fixed on Basti. She barked a stream of unintelligible abuse and the Thracian captain winced. The woman scrunched up her face, spun on her heels, and ducked through the low hut door.

"Nimahe says she will prepare some food for you," Basti said. I doubted that this was an accurate translation of the woman's words.

"Nimahe?" I asked.

"My wife," he said. "She's a Skythian. I bought her from a slave-dealer from the north. Terrible slave. She was always trying to kill me. If I hadn't married her, she would have cut my throat in my sleep eventually," he explained, a note of pride in his voice. "Rides a horse like she was born to it. Shoots a bow even better. We'd better go in. She doesn't like to be kept waiting," he added hastily.

The hut's interior was illuminated by a central hearth, over which hung a large copper cauldron. The reluctant host Nimahe stirred the bubbling contents, which filled the tent with the aroma of meat and garlic.

Basti took a deep sniff of the air and let out an appreciative sigh. "Wild boar," he said. "Fill your bellies with hot stew and *rappa*, and then tell Dotos what brings you back to your motherland."

There was none of the princely fare we had enjoyed with Zyraxes, but the simple stew, as promised, was as delicious as any I have ever tasted. Nimahe's demeanour softened under the lavish praise from her guests. She grew more impressed as I introduced Tibetos and the others, relating their deeds to her in the expected dramatic fashion. She was particularly taken with Sabas, his being a fellow archer. The two of them had settled down across from me and were examining each other's bows. Nimahe's short, recurved Skythian bow was a sharp contrast to Sabas' Phrygian longbow, a source of much comment by the two. The lack of a common language did not prevent Cretan and Skythian from discussing the bowman's art, it seemed.

The day's journey and the rich food and drink conspired against us, and one by one my companions retired to their own patch of straw-lined floor. Mnasyllus, felled by a few cups of *rappa*, punctuated dim interior of the hut with his rumbling snores. Beside the big man, the sleeping Sosias lay curled dead to the world beneath a patterned Thracian cloak. Tibetos and I remained awake, discussing matters with Dotos and Basti. Arexion stayed as well. As he had for most of the evening, the dour Parnassian warrior said little and his flat, emotionless features revealed even less of what he was thinking. I was aware of his intense stare, but I doubted that he could speak Thracian.

"How many warriors does Zyraxes post here?" I asked, accepting a cupful of *rappa* from Dotos.

"Thirty or so at most times, and half that number of horses," Dotos said. "It is more of a way-station where warriors can stock up on weapons and supplies."

"Does the fort discourage Seuthes' men from raiding?" I asked.

"Not especially, but once in a while we catch a few of them. We can launch raids into his territory as well. It gives the young warriors some valuable experience," he explained before letting out a satisfied belch.

"Will Seuthes' warriors mistake us for raiders if we enter his territory?" Tibetos asked.

"If they find you, yes, but that's unlikely," Dotos said. "Basti knows how to stay hidden. Besides, word is that Seuthes is far away on the other side of the Hellespont dealing with a rebellion. He'll have taken a lot of his warriors with him. But what madness makes you wish to go there at all?"

As I explained our mission to stop Lysander from taking the prophet back to Delphi and declaring himself king of Sparta, Dotos' face showed growing signs of incredulity. It was difficult to blame him.

"So," he said, ticking doubts off his fingers one by one, "you are blindly going to Siragellis on the word of a dead Oracle to kill a prophet who you have never seen, who might not even be in Siragellis, or who may have already been retrieved by Lysander anyway."

Hearing the absurdity of it, my face fell. "That is about it," I said.

Dotos contemplated the fire for a moment before looking at me with a grin. "It is the maddest thing I have ever heard." My heart sank further. "But," he added. "who am I to question the gods? And if this false prophet is in Siragellis, Basti will lead you there and by the Hero," he said, invoking the name of the greatest Thracian god, "you will succeed in your quest."

His words left me feeling less the fool than I had a moment earlier, but not by much. Yet, as sleep and exhaustion took me, I could not throw off the feeling that once again I was not in control of my own destiny.

OUR PARTY SET OUT FROM THE FORT soon after dawn. Our number had grown by one, as Basti had soon yielded to his wife's demand that she accompany us. I have heard it said that the Skythian women are equals to their menfolk in all things, battle skills being no exception, and seeing Nimahe, I could well have believed it. Horse and rider moved as one, and though small in stature, the Skythian woman was a formidable sight, for she was clad in all her warrior's finery. The top of her smallish bow and the fletching of two dozen arrows protruded from a leather case hanging from her left hip. The bow was not her only weapon. Two daggers were attached to a baldric that crossed her chest, and tucked into her silver-plated belt was a long-handled war axe, its wicked blade balanced on the opposite side by a heavy, armour-piercing spike. The *peripoli*, already growing accustomed to the female Thracian warriors, wisely did not even question the Skythian woman's prowess.

A sheet of dark clouds obscured the rising sun. The aid we had received from Zyraxes was invaluable, but I fretted over the day we had squandered in seeking him out. I was eager to make up for lost time. Throughout the morning, we kept our pace at a healthy canter. That we were once again headed towards our ostensible goal buoyed my mood somewhat, but the knowledge that we were riding blind eroded this fragile optimism. I had only the dying words of the Pythia to guide us and Lysander's whereabouts were unknown to me. For all I knew, Lysander was already on his way back to Delphi and I was leading my men into the hostile territory of Seuthes for nothing. This thought still haunted me when we finally stopped mid-morning, our path forward blocked by the obstacle before us.

Under the overcast sky, the inky water of the Hebros cut through the land, its surface like the glazed black ceramics made by the potters in Athens. It was not the mightiest of rivers but imposing enough, especially compared with the dribbling streams that passed for rivers in the dry lands around Athens. The dark water, swollen by melting snows to the north, marched southward faster than a man walked, its current marked by a silent procession of branches and other floating detritus. A heroic javelin throw would have barely reached the opposite bank. Yet even if the river had been half as broad, it would have been just as impassable to us.

"Is there a ford?" I asked, peering northward. Any narrowing of the river would be quite a distance away. The thought of further delay vexed me. "Or a barge?" I could see no settlements in either direction that would indicate the existence of such a thing.

Basti grinned at me. "Even better," he said. "There's a bridge."

CHAPTER 30

The bridge spanning the Hebros did not inspire confidence.

"Will it support the horses?" Stachys asked sceptically, giving voice to my own doubts.

Basti's response was not reassuring. "I haven't fallen through yet."

The bridge had three sections. The first segment angled upwards from the bank to a fine stone pier a third of the way across the river. A flat central segment connected to the first pier's twin before a final ramp slanted down to the far bank. The path across was wide enough to accommodate perhaps four men walking abreast or an oxen cart. I bent over to inspect the construction more carefully.

"Who built it?" I asked, peering at the bridge's underside.

"The Great King," Basti said, being unable to provide further information on yet another abandoned legacy from the Persian invasion generations earlier.

The original Persian structure, no doubt sturdy and well constructed, was long gone. The decidedly makeshift span that I examined now was not reassuring. The wooden spans themselves consisted of two layers. A mismatched trio of broad, flat beams made up the underlayer of each section, but whether the wood had been salvaged from ships or buildings I could not tell. These beams were overlaid by an assortment of boards that at least provided a solid, if irregular, surface over which to cross. The entire construction was haphazardly lashed together by a few loops of fraying rope. I straightened up.

"It looks as though a good wind might blow it down," I said.

"A storm destroyed the previous bridge not three winters past," Basti confirmed. "The locals rebuilt it."

I scanned the area around the bridge. The land on both sides of the river was clear, the trees no doubt felled long before and floated down the river to Ainos to be traded to Athens and other poleis for ship-building and other construction. Half a mile away the forest began to reassert itself, but there were no signs of habitation to be seen except for a few wisps of smoke far on the horizon. "What locals?" I asked.

"It's dangerous to live near the bridge. Too tempting a target for raiders on both sides," Basti explained. "But there's still a lot of trade back and forth across the river. Most people nearby belong to the same clans and tribes, river be damned, and they're more loyal to each other than to either King Medokos or that weasel-shit Seuthes. So the local chiefs make sure the bridge is usable."

Nymphs and other spirits inhabit rivers and springs, and it is best not to incur their enmity. Basti wisely made a prayer to the river god before pulling out a small knife and tossing it into the river. Despite his invocation, the horses showed admirable common sense and were reluctant to tread on the bridge. With some coaxing we managed to lead them across without incident, the planking of the bridge clacking and groaning under their hooves. Halfway across the creaking, wobbling span, I too dropped a coin into the black water to appease whatever ancient deity dwelt in the river's depths. We were permitted to pass without incident.

Only when my feet touched the solid ground of the east bank did I let my tension out with a long breath. "Where to now?" I asked.

"Safer to swing south a-ways. There's more forest down there for cover and we'll stay well clear of Kypsela and Zorlanae," Basti said, waving a hand towards the east.

"Kypsela?" I said, feeling the name with my tongue. "It sounds Greek."

"It is. Basically a fortified trading post. A gathering place for mercenaries, too."

"Are there Spartan soldiers there?"

Basti shrugged. "Could be. Or not. Either way, I reckon you don't want to find out." That was true enough.

"And Zorlanae?"

"Seuthes' local seat of power when he's not in Phrygia, which is not often. Still, better to give it a wide berth if you ask me."

"Will swinging south delay our arrival in Siragellis?" I asked.

"Not much. It'll take a day and a half either way if we push hard. In any case, if we run into one of Seuthes' raiding parties coming the other way, we might not get there at all," Basti said.

"Then south it is," I said.

AS BASTI HAD SAID, the open plain became increasingly wooded and hilly. We steered clear of farmsteads and villages and only saw a few distant foraging parties that quickly vanished as soon as they spotted us approaching. We pushed the horses as hard as we dared and the miles passed quickly beneath us.

The first night was spent in the forest under overcast skies without a fire, the scent of spring pines thick in the air around us. Neither our wool cloaks nor our meal of hard bread and salted fish did much to fend off the chill of night. We woke to a layer of frost that quickly dissipated under the steady rhythm of our horses' hooves and the day's growing warmth. As dawn claimed the sky with rising confidence, our own wariness grew as we picked our way through forest and copse. In the early afternoon, Basti called for a halt. He pointed to a rise a few miles in the distance. "Siragellis is beyond that ridge."

I suppressed the urge to forego caution and simply ride into the village to find Lysander's prophet, if he was there at all. Instead our progress slowed even further as we picked our way forward until we found a well-hidden grove that would serve as our base.

"It's about a mile further on," Basti said in a low voice.

"I need you to show it to me," I said. I enlisted the stealthy Sabas to accompany us. Sosias wanted to come.

"I am quiet!" he had insisted when I denied his request.

"You will stay with Tibetos and the others, *Kuon*," I said. My stern look quelled further dissent and the boy trudged away in a brooding state.

As we moved to depart, Arexion rose to his feet to join us. I doubted the Parnassian would be put off as easily as Sosias. "The larger our party, the more likely we are to be detected," I said.

Arexion brushed off the comment. "I'm coming with you," he said, adjusting the sword on his belt.

"You move through the woods like a mad boar, Parnassian. You will stay here if you want this mission to succeed at all," I said.

Arexion regarded me with stony eyes. "This is a mission for Delphi. My mission. You do not lead here, Athenian," he said.

While Arexion and I locked horns, the *peripoli* had quietly formed a loose ring around the Delphian soldier. Basti's Thracians, sensing the tension, let their hands slip to their weapons and crowded closer. I gave Arexion a thin smile. "You speak very bravely for a man on his own in the wilds of Thrace."

The Parnassian countered my threat with his own. "Should I not return to Delphi with news of our success, there will be a price on your head and others'" he said, alluding to the threat against my son.

I almost killed him then but restrained myself. "Which is why you needn't worry about staying here. You are a soldier but not like the Thracians or the *peripoli*. Let us do what we are trained for, lest you jeopardize the mission for Delphi with your pigheadedness."

Arexion did not respond. His eyes narrowed as he considered my words. Finally he spoke. "Do not fail, Athenian," he said, sitting back down on a fallen tree. He pulled out his sword and began to hone the edge with a whetstone with rapt concentration.

As I set out with Sabas and Basti, I pulled Telekles aside. "Keep an eye on him," I said in a low voice. "If he tries to follow us, kill him." Part of me hoped that Arexion would be foolish enough to try.

Leaving the confrontation with Arexion behind us, Basti, Sabas, and I padded through the forest like a trio of wolves on the hunt. Our senses reached out, straining to hear the faintest sound or glimpse the tiniest flash of movement. We went to ground more than once at the sound of distant voices, but besides startling a stag drinking at a stream, we remained undetected.

The ground began to slope downward. Basti signalled that the village was near. Indeed, the faint staccato of voices and industry could be heard ahead of us. The light grew as the trees thinned out and soon we could see the forest's boundary. We crept forward. From a concealed vantage point, we surveyed the clearing in which the village was situated.

My heart sank. The village was there, its ditches and wooden palisade plain to see. The huts within were hidden from our view, save for the wisps of smoke that rose from the villagers' hearths. The peaked roof of the chieftain's hall in the central keep was visible, as was the activity at the front gate where two warriors stood guard, watching idly as a villager brought in a small herd of sheep from the day's grazing. The settlement itself was not the source of my apprehension, for there was little to distinguish it from those found all over Thrace and beyond. It was what lay outside the settlement that threatened to extinguish the flickering, mad hope for success that I had nurtured in my breast since Dephi.

For beside the Thracian palisade another village of sorts had established itself. The deliberate, considered layout of the dozens of dun-coloured tents is what set the Spartan military camp apart from those of other armies. I could see where the soldiers had carefully arranged their shields and spears into trophy-like structures outside their tents so that they could be taken up instantly in the event of an attack. The Spartans espoused a code of egalitarianism among their ranks, but the grand pavilion rising up in centre of their camp gave lie to that fading tradition.

At that moment, a familiar white-cloaked figure emerged from the ostentatious shelter, confirming what I already knew.

Lysander had arrived in Siragellis before us.

CHAPTER 31

Three hundred Spartans.

That was my estimate of the number of soldiers in Lysander's retinue. An almost equal number of slaves and workers went about their duties in and around the camp.

"There are likely another hundred Thracian warriors in the village," Basti added unhelpfully. The three of us — Basti, Sabas, and myself — lay on our bellies amid the scrub at the forest's edge, spying on the happenings below. What we observed did not inspire confidence.

"And what of this 'prophet'?" Sabas said in a low voice. "Where is he being kept?" Silence was my only response, for I did not know. We had seen no sign of anyone who stood out from the soldiers and slaves.

"Should we return to the others?" Basti asked.

I shook my head, for I did not want to leave without more information. But the sun was already beginning its downward journey across the sky. "We wait," I said. Basti shrugged and we continued our reconnaissance.

The camp was roughly circular in shape, with Lysander's large central tent surrounded by a daunting assembly of smaller ones. The soldiers' tents were marked by the shields and spears arranged beside their fire-pits. On the far side of the camp, a bustling multitude of helot slaves tended cooking fires, mended tools and equipment, and saw to the cavalry horses and supply carts that had accompanied Lysander from the coast. I grimaced.

"Maybe Iollas could infiltrate the camp?" Sabas offered. In speech and manner the freed helot would certainly be able to blend in. As for Iollas' courage and loyalty there was no question, but his acting ability left more room for doubt.

"Even if we had time, there's too much chance of his being discovered," I said, rejecting Sabas' idea. But there was perspicacity in the Cretan's instinct that the camp slaves were a vulnerability. I focused on a slave who was walking away from the camp with an axe. "There's our spy," I said, pointing at the slave as he entered the forest several hundred feet from where we were concealed. Sabas grinned, immediately grasping my meaning.

We stalked through the forest, giving the camp a wide berth. The late afternoon sun poked through gaps in the canopy, breaking up the shadows and dappling the forest floor with shards of light. The steady rhythm of the slave's axe grew ever louder.

Sabas, signalling for us to stop, spotted him first. The slave was pursuing his task with steady effort if not enthusiasm as he chopped through the trunk of a fallen pine tree. After every few blows of the axe, he paused to adjust the sweaty leather strap holding his lanky black hair back before resuming his attack on the stubborn tree. Sabas motioned that he would loop around to block the slave's path back to the camp should he attempt to flee.

In the end it was not necessary. The slave, his attention dulled by the monotony of his labour, was not aware of any danger until I clasped my hand over his mouth and put my dagger to his throat. "Do not make a sound," I whispered. The slave stood paralyzed, his eyes wide with fear as Basti and Sabas emerged from the undergrowth. "Good," I said.

We bound the slave's hands and led him away. Sabas scouted ahead, looking out for locals out foraging or hunting, and for once fortune was on our side and we encountered no one. Still, the need for stealth and our bound captive slowed our journey and it was not until after sunset that we arrived at our bivouac in the forest. Only then did we interrogate the helot.

The slave was clearly terrified. Ringed by his captors, his eyes darted from one grimacing visage to the next, desperately seeking a friendly face. He found one in Iollas, who greeted the slave in his thick Messenian accent. "They will not hurt you," Iollas assured the helot, who did not seem completely convinced. But his terror was quelled enough to tell us that his name was Klabo.

I sat down on a boulder opposite the fretting slave. "Do slaves ever run away from the Spartans?" I asked. I was worried that the missing helot would raise suspicion in the camp.

"Sometimes, Master," Klabo said. He shrank a little. "But they are always caught. They are always punished," he added fearfully.

"You are safe," Iollas interjected. Klabo appeared doubtful.

"We will not send you back there," I said. I could only hope that the urgency of Lysander's mission would blunt the Spartans' desire to go in pursuit of an escaped slave. I continued my interrogation. "When did Lysander arrive in Siragellis?" I asked him. Klabo looked at me blankly. "The Thracian town where your camp is?" I explained.

Klabo's eyes brightened. "Yesterday, Master," he said, bobbing his head obsequiously.

"How long will you stay?"

"We are to return to the coast tomorrow," Klabo said more eagerly. "The ships await us there."

"At Ainos?" I asked, realizing that my suspicions about the Spartan ships belonging to Lysander had been correct.

Klabo once again blinked at me. "Ainos, Master?" he asked nervously.

Perhaps the helot did not know the name of the port. It was unlikely that his masters kept their slaves apprised of such information. "Ainos," I repeated. "The port where Lysander left his ships."

Klabo frowned. "I do not know a port named Ainos," he said. "We landed at a place called Kardia."

"Kardia?" Now it was my turn to be confused. Kardia was a coastal city at least a day's sailing farther west from Ainos.

"Yes, Master," Klabo confirmed. Perhaps Lysander's ships had stopped in Ainos for provisions? I described the port to Klabo, but the helot shook his head. "No, Master. I'm sorry, Master. But I do not know this place. We arrived in Kardia from Imbros."

I scratched my crown as I considered this. The island of Imbros was a stepping stone for ships sailing to the Hellespont and beyond. The slave's words made sense. It seemed that the Spartan warships we had seen in Ainos had been there for their own reasons, just as

Captain Xenius had suggested. Whatever their purpose had been, it was not my concern now. I only need to find the prophet. "Did the Thracians in Siragellis give Lysander the prophet?" I asked.

"*'Prophet?'*" Klabo said slowly, repeating the unfamiliar word.

I rephrased the question. "Did the Thracians give a *neaniav* to Lysander?" I said, using the common word for 'young man.'

"Oh, yes!" Klabo said, lifting his hands. "The beautiful one!"

My heart rose as the burden of the greatest unknown question suddenly vanished; until the captive helot uttered those words, I had had little confidence that we would ever find the object of our mad quest. The sudden elation suddenly vanished as I remembered that the price of my own son's life was that of the young man concealed in Lysander's tent. "You have seen him? The prophet?" I confirmed.

"Yes, Master!"

"Where is he?" I pressed.

"In the tent of the *Basileus*, Master," Klabo said more enthusiastically, evidently pleased that he had the information I sought.

"The '*Basileus*?'" I asked, frowning. *Basileus* means king. "You mean Lysander?"

Klabo, seeing my disapproval, winced slightly. "Yes, Master."

"Who calls him that?" I asked.

"Everyone, Master," Klabo said.

"Even the soldiers?"

"Yes, Master."

I leaned back, mulling over what the slave had said. Lysander must have been confident indeed if he allowed himself to be addressed as *king*. To be so close to his goal, it was no wonder he kept the prophet so close to him. "Are you certain the prophet is in Lysander's tent?" I asked Klabo.

"Yes, Master," the helot said, nodding vigorously. "He is there."

Then there would be one chance to complete the mission for which we had travelled so far. The false prophet would have to die that night.

"BENDIS PROTECT YOU," Basti said from atop his horse, calling on the Thracian goddess. In whispered voices, the other six Thracian horsemen echoed their captain's invocation. The smaller shape that was Nimahe stayed silent.

Even though my eyes had long grown accustomed to the darkness, Basti and the Thracians were but silhouettes against the even blacker background of the forest. Clouds had come from the north after sunset and the overcast sky blocked out the light of the stars. The clouds brought with them a cold wind, a reminder that winter had not yet surrendered its dominion over the great Skythian plains far to the north. Yet I was glad for the wind and the darkness, for they would aid me in the daunting task that I had set for myself.

I left Basti and his men at the forest's edge and began my cautious trek towards the fires of the Spartan camp. After some negotiation, it had been agreed that a smaller party would be best. I had argued for my going alone, but Basti had insisted on accompanying me and in the end I had acceded to the stubborn Thracian's demands. In truth, I would have welcomed the company of the wily hunter Sabas, but an extra body would have only added more risk. And so, Sabas and the others had remained at our base, ready to leave once Basti and I returned. *If* we returned.

Like a fox in the night, I approached my quarry. The wind masked the faint crunching beneath my tall Thracian boots. My ash-blackened face was the only part of me visible beneath my dark green cloak. Beneath the cloak I wore no armour and bore no weapon, save for the long dagger at my belt. I felt Whisper's absence like a missing limb. My fingers moved to the dagger's iron pommel and its cold weight bolstered my confidence.

A hundred paces from the camp I stopped and observed. The Spartan soldiers were encamped in groups of three or four, with each tent separated by perhaps twenty paces. Though it was past midnight, there were not a few Spartans still sitting outside their tents around their campfires. The faint tang of woodsmoke and the sound of low, guttural Spartan conversation drifted on the breeze to where I crouched, like a shadow creature from the Underworld intruding into the world of the living.

Two fires near the south side of the camp burned less brightly than the rest. I moved towards them. At twenty paces I lowered myself to the ground. I crawled on my belly like a snake and as slowly as a tortoise. In the gap between the campfires I lay exposed, but to rush was to invite disaster. In such situations, patience is the greatest weapon, or so I had been taught by my long-dead mentor in stealth, an ill-humoured *peripoli* named Meges. It was said Meges could steal a Spartan's sword right out of its sheath with the owner none the wiser. An exaggeration, perhaps, but many times I had applied the skill passed on to me to infiltrate enemy camps in the darkness and I still lived. Yet it only took one moment of carelessness or bad luck to end up on the wrong end of an enemy's spear.

In a small dip in the ground, I paused to gather my wits. The nearest tent was a stone's toss away. The mumbling of low voices came from various directions, but nowhere close to me. I welcomed the murmur of activity, for it helped mask any tiny sounds that might have betrayed my presence. I shifted my weight to continue my advance. Just as I had begun to move, a figure emerged from the tent. I froze. The shadow came in my direction, the crunching of grit and trampled grass growing louder as he approached. I pressed myself into the hollow. The footsteps stopped no more than a spear length from where I lay. I did not breathe. There was the rustle of cloth followed by the pattering of piss on the ground as the Spartan relieved himself. The stream ended in a final few splashes before the man dropped his tunic and returned to the tent.

I waited for what seemed like an age until I moved. Only when I had reached the shelter of the first tent did I rise into a crouch. I peered into the centre of the camp. Lysander's prominent tent was there. A softly rippling torch illuminated two guards standing outside the front flap of the god-man's tent. I took a deep breath and left my temporary hiding spot.

From tent to tent I crept, drawing ever closer to the heart of the camp. At every deep shadow I paused, listening, but no one appeared to hinder my movements. With a last, cat-like dash, I found myself at the back of Lysander's tent.

The canvas glowed dimly, lit from within by a lamp or low-burning fire. I cocked my head and strained my ears, but there was not even a shuffle to indicate any movement within. I unsheathed my dagger and drew its finely-honed edge downward, opening a portal to the chamber within. I peeked through the slit and saw my way was unimpeded. Then, like a thief in the night, I pushed my way through.

Embers in a central brazier filled the tent with a ruddy light that brightened for a heartbeat as the breath of outside air passed over them. The radiant heat of the smouldering embers felt like the summer sun against my chilled skin. I stood as if my flesh were stone, scanning the interior.

I spied Lysander's shadowy form on the far side of the tent. The Spartan hegemon lay on his back on a mound of furs. Even gods had to sleep. My heart thudded in my ears so loudly that I thought it must surely wake the sleeping Lysander. Close to me was another figure, hidden from my view by a blanket. Unlike Lysander, the second sleeping occupant of the tent had only simple straw-filled sacking for bedding. The prophet, son of Apollo or not, did not warrant any luxury, it seemed.

The ground had been covered in rugs that dampened my footsteps as I approached the second figure, my dagger drawn. I mustered my resolve for the distasteful task. A stroke and Lysander would be thwarted. I looked down and involuntarily I sucked in a sharp breath.

A glance told me that this was the prophet Silenus of whom the Pythia had spoken. As she had said, the prophet was beautiful to behold, a vision of Apollo himself made flesh. Rings of overlapping golden curls framed a face whose perfection would have left the finest sculptors in Athens ashamed and tearful at the inadequacy of their work. When I gazed at the sleeping form before me, I heard the gods laughing, for as soon as my eyes fell on him, I knew that I could not slay him, false prophet of not.

In my mind, the Pythia's gentle laugh mocked me from the Underworld, and I knew that she had deceived me. For the Lysander's prophet was not a young man as she had led me to believe. No, the prophet was not a young man: the prophet was a child.

The boy was perhaps twelve or thirteen years old, his features suspended between the innocence of childhood and the handsome, rugged beauty of a young man in his prime.

But the Pythia's laughter faded to silence, snuffed out by the flood of relief that filled my soul. They had sought to play their games with me, the gods and the Fates both. But their trap was a gift. The need to thwart Lysander's ambitions had not vanished, but I would not murder a child to do it. But it did not matter. I had no such qualms about assassinating Lysander himself, an idea that had been coalescing in my mind since I had spoken to the slave Klabo. I turned towards the slumbering hegemon.

Then, for some reason, I paused. Even now, so many years later, I wonder why I did so. It was like a voice was calling me. But I stopped and looked one more time at the sleeping boy, unable to resist the urge to look upon his unnatural beauty.

The boy's eyes flicked open. Even in the dim light, I could see they were blue, like the sky. We looked at each other, unmoving, frozen by each other's gaze. The fate of the world teetered precariously on that point in time. But the gods were not done with me. With invisible breath they blew and my fate slipped out my control once again, throwing the world into the chaos the gods and Fates loved so much.

The son of Apollo opened his mouth and screamed.

CHAPTER 32

The boy's scream shattered the peace of night. The luxurious trappings of power had not dulled Lysander's martial instinct, for the Spartan hegemon leapt from his comfortable bed of furs and fleece, a sword already in his hand. Almost as swiftly, I had swept up the golden-haired Silenus, whose wailing dropped to frightened whimpering when my dagger touched his throat. The outside guards burst into the tent with their swords drawn and put themselves between me and the master of Greece.

For a few heartbeats, both sides were frozen in indecision. I tightened my grip on the squirming boy. The Spartan soldiers crouched low as they assessed the situation. Behind them, Lysander furiously blinked away the sleep until his sword-sharp gaze locked on mine. His eyes grew round in recognition. "You!" he said in a tone of utter disbelief.

The word freed me from my paralysis. My eyes not leaving the Spartans, I edged back towards the hole in the tent and pushed my way back outside. My only hope was to drag the boy away while the Spartans were still in disarray. I turned to flee towards the protection of Basti and his Thracians at the forest's edge, but I was too late.

If it had been Athenians or Megarians or a camp of horse-stinking Thebans, escape might have been possible, but Spartans were another matter. Alerted by the boy's screams, the Spartans had shown their training and roused themselves with impressive swiftness. Most were naked or clad only in tunics but had seized shields and weapons before rushing to Lysander's tent. There was no way past them. Like wolves converging on a vulnerable stag, the Spartans tightened the circle around me.

"Hold!" a voice shouted. The Spartans stopped as one, though their predatory gazes and ready weapons remained fixed on me and my hostage. I slowly turned towards the voice, the squirming boy clutched to my chest. Lysander approached, flanked by two men holding torches. One of them was the Spartan Drakontios, who seethed with barely controlled rage at the sight of his brother's killer. The other was Orchus, whose expression was a familiar mixture of malice and bemusement.

I rotated the dagger. "Come any closer and your false prophet dies," I said loudly enough for all present to hear. "*Basileus*," I added with a sneer. My mind raced, but all I could do was keep talking.

Lysander flicked away the taunt with a curl of his lip. His jet-black eyes narrowed. "Then why haven't you done it?" he replied. "That is your mission, is it not? Why else would Thrasybulus have sent you to this barbarian dung-heap?"

"You murdered the Pythia and tried to have me killed. I came to avenge her," I retorted. It was not a complete lie.

Lysander shook his head with mock regret. "An unfortunate necessity. But the past cannot be changed. We can only adapt to the present," he said. "I ask you, Daimon: what will you gain by killing the boy?"

"It will hurt you," I said, my eyes darting from Spartan to Spartan. "That is enough."

Lysander made another tilt of his head. "I cannot deny the truth of it. But it would be a setback only."

"But *they* would see your failure," I said, glancing at the Spartans surrounding me. "They would *know* that their *basileus* was mortal after all. Word would spread and you would be diminished in the eyes of many." It was a weak, desperate play for time, but the flash of anger in Lysander's eyes told me that my blindly cast words had struck a vulnerable point.

Lysander changed tactics. The hint of irritation vanished behind a conciliatory smile. "I respect you, Daimon," he said. "Most Athenians would sell out their countrymen for the right price, but I have tried to buy you and failed. Like me, you are motivated by higher principles: honour, courage, success."

"As is Thrasybulus," I said, knowing the barb would further irritate Lysander.

"Thrasybulus is a long-winded fool," Lysander snapped. Beside him Orchus grinned. The Andrian mercenary thrived on chaos. Lysander spread his arms. "You have won, Daimon. I admit defeat. Let us strike a bargain."

"I have your prophet," I said, lifting the boy's chin with my dagger. "You have little to bargain with."

The Spartan hegemon dismissed my threat with a small wave. "This is my offer: kill the boy now and I will let you leave unharmed." The surprise must have shown on my face, for Lysander smiled. "Yes. Kill the boy. Accomplish your mission. Prove to me that your reputation for ruthlessness is true and you may disappear back into the night."

"I will just leave with the boy," I countered.

"If you do, I will order my men to cut you down," Lysander replied.

"But the boy will die either way," I said, trapped.

Lysander's lips parted in a cold grin. "But he won't, will he? I know you too well, Daimon of Athens. I know that it is not in your heart to slay a child. I know that you are a *'good man'*" he said, drawing out the last words in a mocking tone, and I knew then that that weasel-shit priest Agasias had been listening when I asked my question to the Pythia.

And Lysander was right: I would not kill the golden-haired boy. I had come all the way to the wilds of Thrace only to have the Spartan hegemon see through me. I had wagered everything on one throw of the dice. And I had lost. I dropped my dagger from the boy's throat.

Lysander signalled towards his men. "Kill him. Do not harm the boy." The Spartans began to advance.

Standing beside his employer, Orchus leered, preparing to enjoy the spectacle of my death. "Nowhere to fly this time, cagey bird!" he called out, his hand resting on the pommel of the sword strapped to his belt. His torch fluttered in the increasingly gusty wind. "A corpse don't bite!" he added for good measure.

The nearest Spartan drew back his spear. His muscles tensed as he prepared to lunge. Suddenly he grunted in surprise. His spear clattered to the ground as he clutched at the bloody javelin point protruding from his chest.

Orchus was the first to react, dropping his torch and drawing his sword. "We're under attack!" he cried. Drakontios raised his shield and stepped in front of the unprotected Lysander just in time to stop another iron-tipped javelin from impaling the god of Sparta. The scattered Spartans pivoted to face the new threat. Another shaft flew from the darkness to skewer an unarmoured Spartan to my right, while the man to my left dropped his sword to scrabble at the feathered arrow that suddenly decorated his throat. Another soldier roared in pain as he collapsed in a writhing heap, both his thighs run through by a single javelin.

"Get the boy!" Lysander shouted, pointing at me. "The boy!"

But it was too late. In a wave of crashing hooves, Basti and his Thracian horsemen lanced through the Spartan camp like a swarm of centaurs. Their howling war-cries filled the night as they cut down any Spartan within reach.

Like a monster of the night, a piebald horse loomed out of the darkness directly in front of me. The beast's massive chest churned as it pounded towards me and I feared that I would be trampled in the chaos. But its rider, a young Thracian warrior, leaned out with his arm extended. In a smooth, swift motion he swept up the struggling son of Apollo from my grasp and pinned the boy belly down in front of him as a hunter might carry a deer carcass. The horse punched through a knot of hard-pressed Spartans and was gone.

"Daimon!" a voice cried. I spun to see Basti charging towards me on his black stallion. An instant before running me down, the beast wheeled around. "Up!" Basti shouted and I seized his outstretched arm. The Thracian captain's iron fingers clasped my wrist. He yanked hard as I leapt and I was on the stallion's broad back. I threw my arms around Basti's chest just as he spurred the horse forward.

A brave but foolhardy Spartan tried to block the stallion's path, but he might as well have been trying to stop a trireme. The horse's black-sheened shoulder clipped the soldier as we powered past, the impact throwing his bulky frame in the air as though he weighed no more than a child.

I turned for one last look at the chaos and carnage left by Basti and his Thracians. Lysander stood in the middle of it all, his face filled with rage and disbelief. Our eyes met and in the madness of the moment I laughed, which must have pierced him more deeply than any arrow.

The most powerful man in Greece pointed his sword at us and shouted at his soldiers in a vain attempt to muster a pursuit. But even the god-man was powerless as Basti and Thracian raiders carried off his prize and vanished into the night.

IN THE DARKNESS, we had to lead the horses through the forest on foot. I gripped the boy's hand tightly in mine, for I had no desire to crash about the trees in the dark trying to catch him should he attempt to flee. He had shown no inclination to do so, allowing us to take him farther and farther away from Lysander's camp, but we were tied together with a length of rope just in case.

The hiss of wind blowing through the leaves was joined the patter of raindrops dripping from the canopy above. Soon even the treetops were no shield against the heavy rain that started to batter us.

"It's a blessing from Zibelthurdos!" Basti said, leaning close so that I could hear him through the lashing rain. Basti's faith in the Thracian storm god was rewarded by a flash of lightning and a crash of thunder an instant later.

"It will hide our tracks," I shouted through the deluge.

"I was more worried about hunting dogs," Basti yelled back. "But there will be no trace of us once this is done!" Pursuing hounds or not, the storm slowed our progress for most of the journey. Then, as suddenly as it had started, the rain and wind let up. By the time we reached Tibetos and the others, only the sodden forest remained to testify to the storm's passing.

In the predawn light, Tibetos embraced me. "Did you find the prophet?" he asked, stepping back. He left the hard question unasked. In response, I moved to one side, revealing the child standing behind me. Tibetos peered at the shadowy form. "Who is *that*?"

"The son of Apollo," I said flatly.

Telekles and the other *peripoli* joined us. "You seem to have a talent for collecting stray children," Telekles added unhelpfully.

"There was a change of plan," I growled irritably. "Lysander will be coming for him," I said, untying the rope from my waist and handing the boy off to Telekles. "We have to put as much distance between us as possible."

"The horses are packed and ready," Stachys said.

I grunted approvingly as I pulled my cloak off. The cold air pricked through my rain-soaked tunic. I needed my gear. I looked about for Sosias. "Boy!" I called out. He was always underfoot when he was not wanted, but never present when I needed him.

Sosias appeared promptly, his arms loaded with my gear. "Your weapons and armour, *lochagos*," he said, holding out my equipment.

In the dim light, he couldn't see my eyebrow arch in surprise as I took the proffered gear. The boy was learning. "And my horse is ready?" I asked.

"Yes, *lochagos*!"

"Check again," I snapped, and he scurried off without any argument. I shrugged on my horse-hoof corselet, reassured by its familiar weight. I slung Whisper under my arm and pulled on my cloak before going to see if Sosias had indeed prepared my mount.

Arexion blocked my way, his hand on my chest. "Athenian! I must speak with you!" he said. His gaze drifted over my shoulder to where the captive boy stood among the *peripoli*. "About him, the false prophet!" he said, lowering his voice to an urgent whisper.

I pushed the Delphian warrior's hand aside. "Out of my way, Parnassian."

"Your mission was to kill him!" Arexion hissed.

"I do not murder children," I said. "Lysander has failed. Let him go back to Sparta with his tail between his legs. That is enough."

"But it is not safe!" he said.

"We will keep the boy hidden until the solstice has passed. Delphi will be safe and your mission successful, though not in the way you had hoped. Be satisfied with that, Parnassian."

Arexion bared his teeth. "Have you forgotten — " His threat was cut short and his look of anger turned to one of pain as I clutched his genitals and squeezed.

"I tire of your threats, Parnassian," I said, twisting my hand under the skirt of his tunic. Arexion's face contorted in pain. I leaned close to him. "I offer a threat of my own: if my son comes to harm, I will come to Delphi with my men in the night and slaughter every last priest before I set the temple ablaze. This I swear to the Furies. You have succeeded in thwarting Lysander. Be satisfied with that," I repeated. Arexion, blinking his watery eyes, nodded in concession. I released my grip and he let out a gasp of relief, his hands moving to clasp his injured balls. "Now prepare your horse, Parnassian. I can't imagine it will be a comfortable ride for you today," I added, leaving him.

I had shown mercy.

That was only my first poor decision of the young day.

CHAPTER 33

The sun returned from the world's end, and in the growing light of dawn the others got their first good look at the boy for whom we had gone to so much trouble. The boy Silenus was perhaps a year younger than Sosias, though with a lighter build. The boy's golden hair was matted down with rain and dirty streaks covered his cheeks, but his beauty was apparent to all. Telekles brought his horse up beside mine to examine the boy more closely. "He could actually be Apollo's son. Lysander isn't completely mad after all," he commented before falling back again to ride beside Stachys.

Telekles was not the only one to note the boy's appearance. Curious glances from both Thracians and Greeks continued unabated as we rode west towards the Hebros River. Nimahe in particular regarded our captive with fascination. The Skythian stared at the boy for long spans of time, occasionally tilting her head like a bird to observe him from a different angle. When she was not studying him, she was deep in whispered conversation with her husband, Basti. The only one not drawn to Silenus was Arexion. Since our encounter, the dour warrior from Delphi had studiously avoided laying eyes on our young captive.

The boy, for his part, bore the scrutiny with an almost unsettling equanimity, meeting the looks of the others with unblinking calm and a warm smile. Since his abduction he had neither struggled nor cried nor shown any distress at all. For most of the morning we had pushed the horses at a steady canter and the boy, sitting in front of me, had not uttered a word for the entire journey.

By mid-morning the horses needed a rest and our band slowed to a walking pace. A cool wind had pushed the dark morning clouds south to reveal a clear sky, and the sunlight worked hard to dry out our rain-soaked kit. The change in weather brought about a shift in mood as well, loosening tongues and coaxing tentative smiles as an unspoken confidence in the success of our audacious mission grew with each passing hoofbeat. My own optimism was tempered by the fact we were still a day's journey from the Hebros. Only when we had crossed the river would I feel that we had passed beyond the reach of Lysander's forces. For now, all I could do was try to talk to our silent hostage.

"You do not need to fear me, Silenus," I said in Thracian.

"That is not my name," he responded in a voice as pure as his face.

"What is your name, then, boy?" I asked.

He twisted his head around and fixed his sky-blue eyes on me. "Adaz," he said. There was no fear in his tone, nor the defiance that so often accompanied the words of Sosias.

"Do you speak Greek, Adaz?" I asked in that language.

"Yes," he said.

I dug into one of the saddlebags hanging over the horse's flank and dug out a small loaf of bread. "Are you hungry, Adaz?" I asked. The boy smiled and took the hard bread from me. He gnawed on the stale loaf while we crossed a shallow ravine.

"Where did you learn Greek?" I asked, curious to know how a Thracian boy from the north had come to learn the language.

"My teachers taught me," he said, as though it should be obvious. He pinched up his face in distaste. He slipped back into Thracian. "It was all I did every day. It was better than working like I did before, though."

"What kind of work did you do? Did you help your family?"

He shook his head. "I am a *doulos*," he said, using the Greek word. *Doulos*. A slave. That explained his appearance, for fair hair and blue eyes such as his was rare among the Thracians and even less so among the Greeks in the south, but sometimes in Athens one could see such features among traders or slaves from the north coast of the Euxine Sea.

"Where did you come from?"

The boy Adaz shrugged. "My master called me a 'northern pig', so from the north? I don't know where my parents' village is."

"What happened to your mother?" I asked, remembering the tale the Pythia had told me of his miraculous birth and upbringing. "Who is your father?"

He looked back at me. "They died," he said.

No miracle, then, but a common story. A neighbouring tribe attacked a village and killed all the men. Women and children who survived became commodities on the slave market, sold from slaver to slaver until they ended up dispersed across the world. Such a fate had befallen my own mother, a Thracian from the far north. I told Adaz my mother's story. "But you are no longer a slave," I said. "You are free."

Adaz thought about this. "Where will I go?" he asked.

It was a fair question, one whose very existence I had not even had to grapple with until that moment. "I don't know," I said. I wondered if Athens would be safe, for Lysander's informers were everywhere. Wherever the boy's fate lay, it was a matter for another time. I changed the topic. "Did the man in the tent where I –" I stumbled on my words. "—found you, the man Lysander. Did he say anything of his plans for you?"

The boy's face darkened. "I don't like him. He is not a good man."

I nodded slowly in agreement. "Aye. That is true. But you do not need to be afraid. We will not harm you. These are good men," I said, extending an arm out towards the rest of our party. Telekles saw me pointing at him and smiled broadly at us.

Adaz's expression brightened once more. "I know," he said and turned his focus back on the hard bread that I had given him. The strange conversation had left me confused. I had sought to reassure the boy, but instead he had ended up reassuring me.

I was still pondering this when Nimahe brought her horse up alongside mine. The Skythian glanced at Adaz before looking at me. She opened her mouth to speak but hesitated. I raised an eyebrow, and she took a breath. "I would like the boy to ride with me, with your permission," she said in her oddly-accented Thracian. She lowered her chin and gave me the look of a bull preparing to charge. I know that there was something about Adaz that fascinated her, but there seemed to be no harm in her request. On the contrary, the boy would be safer with her, as Nimahe was perhaps the strongest rider in our party.

I nodded my assent. "If the boy wishes it," I added. Adaz was happy to ride with Nimahe, and the Skythian gave a broad smile, the first time I had ever seen her do so.

Once Adaz had transferred to Nimahe's mount, we kicked the horses into a canter once again. Adaz clung to the mane in front of him, his golden hair even more radiant in the sunlight. Nimahe leaned forward, speaking in the boy's ear as they rode, her control of the horse as natural as most people control their own legs.

Sosias rode with Iollas. The freed slave, a poor rider, was all too happy to cede control his mount to the boy. Sosias handled his own small beast well, I noticed. The boy had a certain reckless confidence to him, I admitted. Many years earlier Zyraxes had taught me to ride when I first came to Thrace, but it had taken a month for me to attain the proficiency that Sosias now demonstrated.

At mid-day we came to a stream. "The animals need water," Basti said. "Better to let them drink now than to have them collapse under you a little later, no?" he said, seeing my reluctance to stop. The stream passed through a wooded area a little farther up the valley that would hide us from anyone in the area. I could not argue with him. "Besides," he added. "There is something I wish to ask you."

While the horses drank, Adaz was the centre of attention. The *peripoli* and Thracians introduced themselves to the strange boy, as did Sosias, who was now chatting excitedly with our captive. It was odd to see the two boys standing side by side. Sosias was larger, but not by much. His blonde hair was much darker than that of Adaz, and straight where the younger boy had curls, but it would not have been unreasonable to believe they were siblings or cousins. Sosias made a rude gesture and the younger boy laughed. I sighed. Already the impish Sosias was corrupting the younger generation more than Sokrates had done in Athens.

My gaze left the scene to see Basti approaching me. The Thracian looked sheepish. "Daimon, son of Nikodromos," he said formally. "I have a request to make of you." My eyebrows shot up in surprise at the seriousness of his tone. Basti took a deep breath. "The boy, Adaz. I wish to adopt him as my son."

My eyebrows climbed up even further, for Basti's request had caught me off guard. Why did the Thracian feel such attachment to a boy we had known for less than a day? I sensed other eyes on me and saw Nimahe standing with some of the horses farther up the stream. Her hard stare suggested she was the true origin of Basti's appeal. "Nimahe wishes this?" I asked.

The Thracian shuffled uncomfortably. "The gods have not blessed us with children," he explained. "But Nimahe has had dreams for many years that the gods would one day grant us a child – " He leaned forward and whispered in my ear, " – a child of gold!" He straightened his back and looked me in the eye. "She believes that Adaz is the child she dreamed of, and I would see her dream fulfilled." The resolution in his voice dared me to defy him.

My gaze flicked back to Nimahe, whose eyes burned with intensity. Her desire to claim the boy as her own was unexpected but not unwelcome. Adaz would be much safer from the machinations of Lysander and Delphi in the backwaters of Thrace than he would be in Athens. I put my hands on the old warrior's shoulders. "I can think of no better place for the boy!" I said, smiling through my weariness.

Basti beamed. "By Bendis, you are a good man!" he said. "A great man!" Before I could react, he lunged forward and wrapped his arms around me, crushing me like an olive in the press. Over his shoulder, I spied Nimahe, who herself gifted me with another rare smile. Air raced back into my lungs as Basti released me. "May Bendis bless you!" he said before hurrying to share the news with his wife.

I joined the knot of *peripoli* and Thracians who still surrounded Adaz. There was a gentle hand on my shoulder. It was the veteran Telekles. "Better to have an extra pair of eyes on that one," he said, looking over my shoulder across the glade. I turned and saw Arexion glowering at us as he adjusted the bridle of his horse.

"And another pair on the boy Adaz," I said. Arexion turned away under our hard stare.

"I have not liked the look of that one since I set eyes on him," Telekles said. There was a hardness in his voice, a glimpse of the dangerous man that lurked beneath his usually genial nature.

I gave a grunt of agreement. "You have always been a better judge of character than me, old friend."

The killer in Telekles vanished as a mischievous glint appeared in his eye. "Aye. That is why you always find me on the side of the best men!" he said with a wink. "But time to go, I think. No?"

I manoeuvred through the men to loom over our involuntary guest. Adaz showed no fear, instead giving me a smile as luminous as his golden curls. The smile morphed into a yawn. "Can we not rest awhile?" the boy asked me.

"When we reach the other side of the Hebros, there will be time for sleep. But until then we must press on." There was a resigned murmuring as the rest of our party shuffled off to prepare their mounts. I led Adaz to where Nimahe and Basti awaited us. "You will ride with Nimahe," I told him. The boy gave a slight bow to the Skythian and her eyes lit up with emotion

"Up!" I said, helping Adaz onto Nimahe's horse. The nape of my neck tingled and I glanced across the glade towards Arexion. The Delphian looked away, but I knew he had been watching us.

Adaz bent down from his perch atop Nimahe's horse. "He is not a good man," Adaz whispered, his face deadly serious.

"Stay close to Nimahe," I told him. I had no doubt that the Skythian would be as deadly as a Spartan should the need to protect the boy arise. "She is a good person."

"I know," Adaz said in a tone that suggested that I had just stated the obvious. Nimahe leapt up behind the boy with leopard-like nimbleness. Giving me one last nod, she nickered at her horse and the beast snorted in response before pivoting and trotting away.

Our party headed west through the wood, each step taking us closer to the Hebros and the sanctuary of the dilapidated Persian fort beyond. But an instinctive unease persisted in scratching at the edge of my perception. I cast a wary eye towards Arexion, but the sullen Delphian kept well away from Adaz and Nimahe, absorbed in his own thoughts, his eyes fixed forward. I brought my horse up beside that of Basti.

"It is an easy journey from here," the Thracian said cheerfully. "If we ride until dark and start out again at dawn, we'll reach the bridge sometime tomorrow morning." He slapped my back and steered his horse back to join Nimahe and Adaz.

My hand moved to the iron dagger at my waist to ward off the evil eye. But with his confident words, I knew Basti had challenged the gods. I do not trust the gods or the Fates, for they are ever eager to thwart the designs of mortals for their own amusement. My faith in their cruelty was quickly rewarded.

For as we emerged from the wood, a line of fifty or more horsemen awaited us. I cursed and began to wheel my horse around. "Back in the forest!" I called. But I saw there was no escape there, for many more horsemen were crashing through the trees to our rear. We were surrounded.

The riders were Thracian in appearance, indistinguishable from Basti's warriors. The horsemen levelled their spears at us but made no move to attack. A warrior with a fox-skin headdress kicked his grey stallion forward. He cast a disdainful eye over our ragged band. "Who are you and what brings you to these lands? Bandits, no doubt! Worthless raiders who should be cut down and left to feed the crows!" His followers shook their spears and rained insults down upon us.

When the surge of curses had subsided, Basti spurred his own mount forward. "We are no bandits, whelp!" he shouted, matching the Thracian warrior in scorn. "We serve Medokos, your king!" Basti said. "Let us pass!" The horde of Thracians broke out in mirthless laughter. Basti reddened. "Did you not hear me? By order of King Medokos, let us pass and be gone!"

The fox-skin-capped leader sneered. "Medokos does not rule here, thief! You are in the lands of King Seuthes now!"

Basti spat. "Seuthes is no king! He governs at the pleasure of King Medokos!"

The Thracian horseman bared his teeth in a feral grin. "Then you can tell him yourself!" He pointed his spear at us. "Seize them!"

CHAPTER 34

Seuthes was an impressive man.

If Mnasyllus could be likened to an ox, then the Thracian general was a bear, for his appearance evoked that animal's brute strength, natural intelligence, and latent ferocity that threatened to erupt at the slightest provocation. His beast-like aspect was enhanced by an impenetrable beard that spread from his face in great coppery waves and poured down to cover most of his fine bronze breastplate. Cunning grey eyes peered out from under similarly thick eyebrows, giving away nothing as he regarded the captives before him.

Outnumbered and with exhausted horses, we had no choice but to surrender to Seuthes' Thracian horsemen; to have fought would have been to invite inglorious slaughter, children and all. But we were not so weak that the Thracians could have destroyed us without significant losses on their part. After a tense standoff, our captors had allowed us to keep our weapons as they escorted us north to Seuthes' fortified stronghold. "Zorlane," Basti said as the stout stone walls came into view. "The strongest fortress in this region." Only when Seuthes had sworn an oath of protection did we give up our weapons. Now we stood before Seuthes himself and awaited the Thracian general's judgment.

The aroma of new wood scented the air of the grand hall in which we found ourselves. Wooden pillars as thick as the columns of Athena's temple in Athens held up a great roof that towered above us. King Medokos himself might have envied as fine a hall as this. Medokos was not master here, however. Seuthes, with my rhomphaia Whisper laying across his legs, sat upon a wooden throne that matched the hall in splendour. Gilded reliefs of horses and heroes battled on the thick posts that made up the frame, almost ready to leap out from the wood that bound them. If the Thracian general was not a king, then judging by his throne, he was doing little to counter the rumour. The wood creaked as he leaned forward.

"You are a mystery to me" he said in a low, sonorous voice. "Thracians, a Greek, Greeks in Thracian dress, a Skythian horsewoman, slaves, and children," he said, pointing at each group in turn. His finger stopped at me. "And you, who look like a Thracian but are not, I think. You are an Achaean, no?" he asked, using the ancient word for 'Greek" favoured by the Thracians.

"I am Lykos of Athens," I said, giving a false name. "And we are peaceful travellers, detained unjustly by your men."

Seuthes' eyes flashed. "For peaceful travellers you are certainly well armed!"

I did not deny the charge. "We are *misthioi*," mercenaries, "returning from Persia. It has been a long time since we have seen our homes." For many years the scent of profit had been luring mercenaries to the east where some great unrest among the Persians was playing out. Few had returned, but those who had trickled back to the west spoke of battles in the desert on a scale hardly to be believed, with a hundred thousand men in each army. That we were some of those returning mercenaries was not an implausible explanation for our appearance.

"And tell me, Lykos," Suethes said, switching to Greek. "How did you fare in your expedition?"

"We survived," I said without elaboration.

Seuthes nodded sagely. "Then you are more fortunate than most," he said, humouring my lie. "Those boys," he said with a glance towards Adaz and Sosias, "are no mercenaries. How did you come by them?"

"I purchased the pair in Sinope for a gold daric," I said, spinning another falsehood.

"A high price for slaves, even pretty ones like that one," Seuthes said, waving a finger at Adaz.

"There is always demand in Athens for northern boys. The golden-haired one in particular will earn me what I paid for him many times over to prance about naked in some rich man's salon," I boasted.

Seuthes chuckled warmly but his grey eyes remained as cold as stone. "I have heard of such tastes among the Greeks. They are almost as bad as those perfumed Persians when it comes to indulging their lusts!" he said, drawing a laugh from some of his men.

Seuthes picked up Whisper from his lap and drew the rhomphaia from her scabbard with exaggerated slowness, admiring the play of light across the smoky ripples on the blade's surface. He lifted his arm and pointed the weapon at me so that both formed an unbroken horizontal line from his shoulder. With one eye shut, he peered along the line of the sword, searching for some warp or flaw but finding none. "Your weapon is fit for a prince," Seuthes said, returning Whisper respectfully to her sheath. "And distinctive. I know of only one other blade of such fine craftsmanship." He smiled thinly. "It belongs to a man name Zyraxes."

Seuthes had baited the trap. To deny any connection to Zyraxes would have been foolish, so I could only spin my tale further. I had learned at a young age that a liar's greatest shield is confidence. I smiled warmly. "My cousin," I said. "He bestowed the weapon on me as a parting gift before we set out to the east. He said it would keep me from getting killed, and he was right!"

Seuthes' eyes narrowed. "I spent many years in Medokos' court. I do not recall your face."

I shrugged. "I was not there most of my life. I was born in Athens. My father was a mercenary in the south and fought for the Athenians during the great war."

"And your mother?" Seuthes inquired.

"An Athenian whore," I said, my voice hardening. "Though should any man say so, he shall soon be finding his way to stand before Hades."

Seuthes chuckled. "I do not judge a man by his parents. A whore may birth a king, and a king a whore. But," he continued, probing. "How did you come to know Zyraxes?"

"When it was clear that the gods favoured the Spartans, my father sent me north and beseeched Medokos to take me in and teach me the ways of my ancestors. Zyraxes pitied me and took it upon himself to make a proper Thracian of me." It was the first honest phrase I had uttered.

"And did he succeed? In making you one of us?"

"When I am in Thrace, men call me an Athenian, but in Athens, I am called a Thracian." This was also the truth.

Seuthes leaned back in his throne-like chair and ran his hand down his coppery beard as he considered my tale. Finally he spoke. "Whatever you are, you and your men will be my guests. Fear not and know that you are under the protection of *xenia"* he said, drawing out the Greek word. "You must be tired from your journey, Lykos," Seuthes said, stressing my name. He spread his hands. "Rest! Gather your strength! Feast with us this evening! Let it not be said that Seuthes is a poor host."

I bowed. "You are gracious, O Seuthes, and I thank you." Seuthes did not offer to return our weapons.

The Thracian general barked a laugh. "You have an Athenian's oily tongue, that is for certain. Now rest. My slaves will see to you and your men." He dismissed me with an idle wave of his hand.

I dipped my head. Turning to leave, I paused. It has ever been my nature to poke a stick into the eye of Fate when wiser men would tread softly. "O Seuthes," I said. "Your men called you 'King Seuthes.' Should I address you as such while I am your guest?"

A ripple in his beard betrayed a twitch in Seuthes' lip below. Then the beard parted to reveal the Thracian's yellowed teeth. "My men are loyal and sometimes address me so as a jest," he said, lying through his smile. "In truth I am the general of King Medokos and have never claimed to be anything more than that. Now be off, Athenian, before I change my mind about you," he added.

"Of course, O Seuthes," I said. The Thracian general's suspicious stare burned into my back as I left the hall. That we were hostages rather than guests, there was little doubt. My mind was already racing with ways to escape the latest prison in which I had found myself.

CHAPTER 35

The hall had been transformed since our audience with Seuthes. Under the warm light of torches and lamps suspended from the high ceiling, dozens of wooden tables now ringed a great stone-lined firepit. A score of glowering Thracian warriors occupied the stools on the opposite side of the chamber with Seuthes at their centre, well-ensconced in his ornate chair. Upon seeing us enter, the Thracian general rose to his feet.

"Welcome!" Seuthes boomed. "Sit! Eat! Drink! Let me share my hospitality with you, my wandering guests!" His cordial greeting was not echoed by his warriors, who pointedly remained seated, sipping from drinking horns and sharing comments in low voices.

"We are honoured by your generosity, O Seuthes," I replied with feigned warmth, while those in our own party matched Seuthes' Thracians glare for silent glare.

While the others took their seats, Seuthes came and draped his thickly-muscled arm over my shoulder. His other arm swept across the grandeur of his newly-constructed hall. "Look at it! Even the king of Persia would be impressed, no? A fortune of gold and silver went into its construction," the Thracian general boasted with evident pride.

"And blood," I added. I wondered how many slaves had been sold to pay for Seuthes' comfort.

The general gave me a hungry smile. "You understand the ways of the world, Lykos," he said with a wink. "Now join your friends and replenish your spirit!" He gestured to the tables where the *peripoli* and Basti's Thracians sat and then headed for his own grand table.

I took my place beside Tibetos. "He has us trapped in here like sheep in a pen," my friend muttered.

"Eat and gather your strength," I said before forcing another smile towards our host.

Tibetos was correct in his assessment, but there was little to do but bide our time. Following the interrogation, Seuthes had permitted us the use of his stables to see to our horses. His men had discreetly but visibly kept us under guard while we were tending to the animals. Despite his declaration of *xenia*, it was clear that we were prisoners as much as guests until Seuthes decided what to do with us. Until the cover of night offered us some chance of escape, we could take advantage of our circumstances and fill our empty bellies with our host's food.

The animosity filling the hall had little time to fester, for Seuthes' slaves appeared almost immediately bearing wooden platters piled high with hot bread and skewers of oily meat. Drinking horns filled to the brim with wine promptly followed the steaming food. In the air hung an awkward tension as thick as the aroma of the grilled meat, for no one touched their portions. Seuthes, pretending not to notice, set to with gusto, tearing his bread into chunks and quickly reducing a mutton rib to bare bone. One by one Seuthes' men followed suit and began to eat.

From two tables away, Mnasyllus leaned forward and cast an inquiring look in my direction. I shrugged and the big farmer took it as his cue to fall upon the tempting fare before him. The rest of us joined him, though with less enthusiasm. "Better than the stale bread we've been eating," Tibetos conceded as he wiped up the meat's juices from his platter with a crust of bread. He tipped back his gilded drinking horn and washed the food down with a mouthful of wine. "This isn't bad either," he added, squinting at the delicately carved horn.

"Don't overindulge," I warned from behind my own raised horn. "We'll need our wits about us later."

"A shame, though," Tibetos said before taking a wistful, measured sip of his wine.

I sympathized with my friend. That the wine was of excellent quality was obvious even to a poor judge of such things as me. In the finely spiced meat, too, Seuthes showed off his wealth. It was not a poor man who could have such luxuries on hand in the backwaters of Thrace. For this, at least, I was thankful, for the nourishing fare infused my body with a vigour that had been sapped by the journey.

Seuthes, sensing my eyes on him, glanced my way and raised his drinking horn. After draining the horn's contents, he set the vessel down and gave three sharp claps. "Musicians!" he bellowed.

The musicians' rousing performance did little to lift the subdued mood among the feast's guests. Sosias and Adaz, conscripted into service along with Seuthes' own slaves, hurried to keep the Thracians' drinking horns full and to clear the tables of animal bones picked clean of meat. Among our number the wine was only topped up, for no one drank more than was necessary to wash down their food.

Sosias followed my orders and played the part of slave. Only once did his gaze meet mine and I could see the simmering resentment burning behind his intelligent eyes. With the barest shake of my head, I dissuaded him from committing whatever rash act he was planning. His mouth tightened and he went about his tasks.

Sosias, a slave in a tavern his whole life, moved about as a well-trained slave should. He was almost invisible as he scurried from table to table, skilfully refilling drinking horns from the amphora on his shoulder without a precious drop of the fine wine spilled. Adaz was another matter. Slave though he might have been, the golden-haired boy struggled with the heavy amphora, splashing more wine on the table than in the drinking horns of those he served. Seuthes' Thracians, deeper and deeper in their cups as the evening progressed, paid no heed to Adaz's clumsiness.

This was not true of Seuthes, however. The general's serpent gaze followed Adaz as the boy stumbled about from table to table. Nimahe, in turn, glared at Seuthes whenever the warlord's eyes fell on her adopted son, a fact surely noted by the wily Thracian. The Skythian warrior's fierce sense of protectiveness towards Adaz was admirable, but I feared that it only acted to further arouse our host's suspicions.

Seuthes' gaze shifted from Adaz, his attention drawn elsewhere. I followed his gaze to the hall's entrance, where a Thracian warrior had just come in. The man had evidently just arrived from a journey, for he still wore his peaked cap and his patterned cloak was spattered with mud. Catching the eye of Seuthes, the man strode with purpose to his general, but not before turning his tight-lipped face and casting a hard look in my direction.

"That was the evil eye if I've ever seen it," Tibetos muttered as we watched the Thracian arrive at Seuthes' side.

The Thracian bent over and whispered in Seuthes' ear. The Thracian general sipped from his drinking horn and nodded as the man spoke, but his cunning eyes stayed fixed on me through the rippling air above the fire-pit.

"This is not good, Dammo," Tibetos said more urgently.

Before I could answer Tibetos, Seuthes rose to his feet and raised his arms. The musical performance petered to a halt. "My friends," the Thracian general said, his great voice filling the hall. The murmur of voice died away. "I have just received an intriguing report," he said. The whispers of danger in my mind grew to a screaming gale. My hand drifted down in search of my dagger only to find an empty sheath, for Seuthes' men had been thorough in seeing us disarmed.

Seuthes tipped a finger at Adaz and a nearby warrior wrapped his arm around the golden-haired boy and pulled him close. Adaz struggled to free himself, but the man's forearm might as well have been an iron bar. As one our party leapt to our feet, overturning many of the tables and their contents in a clatter. At the same time there was a flash of metal as swords appeared in the hands of Seuthes' Thracians. No one moved. Unarmed as we were, our new enemies would have made short work of us. My only weapon was words.

"What is the meaning of this? You are violating your oath of *xenia*!" I said.

Basti spat on the ground. "This piece of dung knows no honour!"

Seuthes laughed. "Before gods and men, I tell you I have violated no oath, for it was given to a man named Lykos. However," Seuthes continued, "I gave no such oath to Daimon the Athenian, son of Nikodromos."

My gut clenched, for I knew for certain then what intelligence the messenger had brought him. "Lysander!" I hissed.

Seuthes bared his teeth in a cold grin. "It seems that many Greeks are crossing *my* lands these days," he said dryly. "Without my permission," he added, his tone hardening.

"Lysander is no friend of Thrace," I said.

Seuthes turned his palms upwards in a gesture of resignation. "That may be so, but that is a matter for another time. All I know now is that he had offered me five talents of silver for the safe return of the boy," he said, indicating Adaz. "And an equal amount for those who took him." Ten talents was equivalent to what many cities had paid Athens in annual tribute before she lost her empire. "And if that is his first offer, I suspect that he can be made to pay much more when he arrives tomorrow morning," Seuthes said shrewdly. "His silver will be very useful to me."

"To attack Medokos in the west?" I ventured.

Seuthes could not help lifting his chin. "Why should I attack with my men when I can pay the Makedonians to do it for me?" he said, his grin growing into a wolf's smile.

"Lysander cares only about power," I said. "He seeks to become king of all of Greece."

"If he succeeds, he will remember those who aided him," Seuthes countered.

I laughed bitterly. "Then you are a fool. If Lysander succeeds, he will turn and invade Thrace." Seuthes scoffed, but I pressed on. "I have heard so from his own lips. By thwarting me, Seuthes, you are inviting your own doom."

"Bah!" Seuthes barked. His eyes burned with rage. "You dare call me a fool in my own hall?" he snarled. "When it is *you* who finds himself at the wrong end of my mens' blades? If I am a fool, then it is a lesser one than you!" His men laughed at this, and Seuthes reined in his temper. "And, *Daimon, the Athenian*," he said stressing each word of my name, "Lysander showed me due respect by addressing me as '*King* Seuthes,' something which you would do well to consider this night." He waved a hand and his warriors closed in on us.

For the third time in recent memory, I became a prisoner.

CHAPTER 36

Our prison was not one of stone and iron like the one in Athens, but it was no less effective for all that. An axe would have made short work of the lattice of saplings, but absent one the young wood was surprisingly resilient. Seuthes and his men erupted into laughter as Mnasyllus tried to force the wood apart only to have the flexible strips snap back into place when the farmer's endurance gave out.

"Save your strength," I said. Mnasyllus' taut neck muscles bulged as he gave one last groaning pull at the stubborn cage before turning away with a growl.

Every Thracian settlement greater than a certain size contains slave pens. Just as rivers travel to the coast, so too do the streams of men, women, and children flow to the south coast of Thrace, all destined for the slave markets of Greece and beyond. They come from the interior, from small, miserable villages too small to defend against the seasonal raids of their countrymen from the south. My mother had been from one of those hovels far in the north, captured in her ninth or tenth year. Before ending her journey in Athens, she must have spent many long days in cages much like the one we now found ourselves in.

Adaz was not with us. The boy was no doubt being kept under close guard until Seuthes could extort a sufficient price from Lysander. Sosias, too, was not among our number. I had not seen him since our capture, but whether he had managed to slip away in the chaos or had been forced to join Seuthes' small army of slaves I did not know.

Seuthes and his men regarded us with a mixture of disdain and wine-fuelled jubilation. Adaz was the main source of the Thracians' happiness, for Seuthes was sure he would receive a vast sum from Lysander for the boy's return. "You, not so much I reckon," Seuthes had taunted through the slats of the pen. "But perhaps I am mistaken."

"Then free my comrades after Lysander has gone," I said. "Neither you nor Lysander have any quarrel with them."

Seuthes laughed. "You should ask me to throw my silver in the ocean! The Persians will offer me a good price for this lot, especially for the Skythian woman and the large one," he said, casting an appraising eye towards Mnasyllus. "He looks like he would do well in the boxing contests."

Basti lunged forward. "Zyraxes will have your head!" A guard's spear darted forward through the pen's wall and only with an undignified leap was Basti just able to avoid being run through.

Seuthes scowled at the Thracian prince's name. "I will have *his* head if he dares cross the river. But I almost hope he is so foolish, for I desire the opportunity to blood my newest blade," he said, holding my rhomphaia. Gazing at me all the while, Seuthes pulled Whisper from her scabbard in a slow, drawn-out motion. "Once again, I thank you for your gift, Daimon of Athens," he said with a mocking smile.

"You are a fool to trust Lysander. He will betray you, Seuthes" I said.

Seuthes' grin vanished. "I do not need lessons in negotiations from you, Athenian!" he snapped. "I have dealt with kings and Persian satraps and deceitful Greeks and I am still here, while you are my prisoner. It is you who should worry about what you will say to Lysander when you are begging him to spare your miserable life!" With a dismissive wave, Seuthes turned away, leading his retinue of warriors back to his hall to celebrate their good fortune. The two young warriors left to guard us watched with envy as their fellows abandoned them to their nighttime vigil. Resigned to their fate, the two wandered back towards the pen to mock the captives within.

"If you are Zyraxes' best fighters, Seuthes will soon be king of all Thrace!" one of the pair sneered.

One of Basti's young warriors, a man named Rhoglus, stepped forward. "You should talk! Only the shit warriors like you get stuck sitting in the cold guarding the livestock!" he retorted, setting off a round of laughter among his comrades.

"We have this to keep us warm!" the other guard said, revealing an amphora he had been holding beneath his thick cloak. He raised the vessel to his lips and took a deep swig. Wiping away the trickle of wine from his chin, the guard chuckled. "Remember that when you are a slave chained to an oar on some Persian's galley!" His companion slapped his back, and the two of them, laughing at our fate, retreated to sit down on some boulders across from the slave pens. Basti's young Thracians hurled abuse, but the guards ignored them, content to enjoy the contents of the amphora with exaggerated gusto. Basti's young warriors gave up their taunting and huddled in groups, speaking to each other in low voices.

I leaned against the cage wall and surveyed the pen for any weaknesses, but there were none. Telekles moved about the confined space, methodically testing the lattice. If anyone could break out of the pen, it was Telekles, but the structure defeated the veteran *peripoli,* who looked at me and shook his head. I scanned the enclosure again. My eyes fell on Arexion.

The Delphian warrior glared at me. "I told you to kill the boy!" he said in his thick Parnassian accent, the mist of his breath curling like smoke. "Now Lysander will be king because you were too *weak* to do what was necessary.

Before I could respond, Telekles took a step towards Arexion. "Do you want me to kill him?" he offered.

"Try me, Athenian," Arexion growled, rising to his feet only to face a wall of glowering *peripoli*.

Basti joined Telekles in my defence. He stabbed a finger at the Arexion. "I like you less and less, Parnassian." Nimahe and his young Thracians loomed behind him.

With a shrug, Arexion backed down. "Your wrath is misplaced, Thracian. We will all be slaves because of him," Arexion said, pointing at me. He slumped back down on the ground. "I only speak the truth," he muttered.

And in my heart, I did not disagree with him.

THE DISTANT REVELRY FROM SEUTHES' EXULTANT FOLLOWERS grew fainter with the deepening night. Now, only the drunken snores emanating from one of our guards disturbed the darkness. The man had lost his battle with the potent uncut wine and now lay sleeping against a boulder. The other guard huddled close to a small fire as he fought the effects of the wine and drowsiness, casting only the occasional bored glance our way.

In the slave pens, no one slept. Each prisoner fought back the dread of death or enslavement that would come with the dawn. Basti and Nimahe huddled close together. The abducted helot Klabo wept to himself, muttering pitifully of the fate that awaited him when the Spartans arrived the next day. Among the *peripoli* and the Thracians, whispered conversations sprang up and died, absorbed by the chill night-time air, leaving each person to grapple with their fears and regrets alone. But salvation came in a voice in the darkness. The Fates, if nothing else, have a sense of humour.

"*Lochagos!*" The murmurs of the prisoners ceased at the sound of the new voice. Dangerous hope sparked in my chest.

"*Lochagos!*" The whispered voice hissed again. It came from a shadow crouching just outside the pen. The others were savvy enough not to show any reaction. I edged towards the dark figure. My heart surged. It was Sosias.

Without a word, Sosias reached through the pen's grating. The distant torchlight glinted off the iron dagger in his hand. My grateful fingers wrapped around the hilt, which was warm from his grip.

"Can you open the gate?" I whispered.

"Yes, *lochagos*," the shadow replied. He crept away, circling to the front of the pen. Like shades emerging from their tombs, the others rose in anticipation of their chance to cheat the Lord of the Underworld of his prize.

Sosias reappeared at the gate and began working at the locking bolts on the pen's door. The locking mechanism was simple yet effective. The series of bolts and pins was unreachable from anyone inside the pen, but Sosias' clever hands made short work of them, guided by the breathless gaze of all of us within.

Too late, the young guard spotted the intruder. With a startled grunt he stumbled to his feet and scrabbled at his weapon. Had he been wise he would have called out to his sleeping comrade or sounded the alarm. As it was, any good sense he had was dulled by wine and *rappa*.

Reacting without thinking, the guard dashed towards Sosias just as the last pin fell on the ground. In a few bounding steps, the Thracian was there, slashing at Sosias, but the wine-addled warrior was no match for the agile boy, who dodged the clumsy attack with ease. My hand shot through a hole in the lattice and my fingers entwined themselves in the Thracian's long hair. I yanked him towards me and the waiting dagger, driving the blade up through the bottom of the man's chin. The wide-eyed guard jerked and quivered as his spirit protested against his death but then went limp, crumpling to the ground when I released his greasy hair from my grasp.

"Quickly!" I said. Mnasyllus and Tibetos joined me in pushing against the door, which was blocked by the guard's corpse. The dead weight of the man's body put up more resistance than he had in life, but soon the gap was great enough for me to slip through. I was free.

Like a hound freed from its lead, I loped towards the second Thracian, who had not stirred from his slumber. My hand pressed over his mouth as the dagger slashed through his throat. The drunken Thracian's eyes sprang open in surprise, but his lids slackened as his lifeblood left him. It was a foolish death for a young warrior, his future feats of valour stolen from him by a blade in the night. But he should not have fallen asleep. I wiped the blade clean on his cloak.

Behind me, Sabas the Cretan echoed my thoughts. "Too young to pay the ferryman," he muttered under his breath.

"Help me prop him up," I said. We put the dead warrior in a sitting position. Seeing what we were doing, Telekles and Tibetos dragged the body of the other guard over and did the same. The ruse would not stand up to scrutiny but might be enough to fool someone at a distance. We trotted back to the darkness beyond the pen.

I spotted the smaller form of Sosias among the shadows "By the gods, boy! Where did you go?"

"I was by the door when they captured you. I ran away and hid in a storage room." There was a trace of shame in his voice.

"Where did you get the dagger?" I asked, holding up the blade

Sosias pointed towards Seuthes' hall. "I stole it from a sleeping Thracian."

"How many are awake now?" I asked.

"No one."

"No one?" I asked in disbelief.

"Maybe some of the slaves. But the warriors are passed out in the hall," Sosias confirmed.

I should not have been surprised. The Thracians were fierce fighters, but too often they were seduced by plunder and the celebrations of victory. "Where is Seuthes? Is he there?" I asked.

Sosias shook his head. "He has his own sleeping chamber at the back of the hall."

"And Adaz?" I asked. Basti and Nimahe leaned in closer.

"I don't know," Sosias said. "I didn't see him." A feline growl built up in Nimahe's throat. I considered the possibilities. It seemed certain that Seuthes would have kept the boy Adaz close.

Sosias interrupted my thoughts. "Did I do well, *lochagos*?"

I gripped his shoulder. "The god of thieves himself could not have done better!" I whispered. The other *peripoli* murmured their agreement. My sister had insisted I bring the boy, and by the gods, at that moment I was grateful I had given in to her wishes.

Basti stepped forward. "Daimon! We must attack them while we have the advantage!" he said in Thracian.

I held up my hand. "There are too many of them and we do not have weapons," I said. "If the alarm is raised, we are done for."

"Do you suggest we flee, Athenian?" Nimahe challenged me, bristling. "Without our son? We must attack!"

"No," I said, motioning to Tibetos and Telekles. "I have a better idea."

CHAPTER 37

The sharp odour of stale *rappa* and the rumbling of Seuthes' snoring filled the warm air of his chamber in equal measure. The soft light from a trio of suspended oil lamps was enough to reveal the opulence of the Thracian general's private quarters. Reflections of the flickering flames danced over the surfaces of gold and silver vessels that sat on fine tables of carved wood. Intricately patterned carpets worthy of a Persian satrap covered the floor, dampening our steps as we penetrated deeper into their owner's lair. The life-sized figures of Dionysus and Ares gazed upon us with god-like indifference, but were as silent as the guard who now lay dead outside the doorway.

The self-proclaimed king of Thrace lay sprawled on his broad bed, a blanket barely hiding his nakedness. His deep chest rose and fell with each groaning breath. I could have killed him then. But I needed him alive.

A scuffling betrayed the presence of someone else in the darkest recesses of the bedchamber. Telekles pointed his sword towards the source of the noise. I took a lamp and held it out, revealing what I already knew to be there.

Adaz blinked at the flame. The boy sat on the ground, tied fast to the leg of a heavy wooden table. His eyes became round discs and his mouth opened to call out, but I pressed my finger to my lips and the boy's jaw clamped tightly in understanding. I motioned to Tibetos, who set to freeing Adaz from the ropes that bound him.

I put the lamp down and returned to the bed. Telekles had taken up a position on the opposite side, his sword ready. I approached the sleeping Seuthes with my own dagger and saw something else. Adaz had not been the only prize stolen from us by the Thracian general. Whisper was leaning against the far bed-post, patiently awaiting the return of her owner. I sheathed my dagger and with more gratefulness than I should have felt, I took the rhomphaia and drew her from her scabbard, her heft and balance as familiar as an old friend. I extended my arm and lay the tip where Seuthes' great beard hid his throat.

"O *Basileus*," I hissed through clenched teeth. Seuthes' eyes flickered beneath his lids as his soul returned from the dreamworld. "Move and you are dead, O King," I said.

Seuthes' eyes opened and rolled about, seeking the source of the voice. He blinked in confusion as his gaze fell upon me. His eyes widened in recognition. "You!" he sputtered. He made to rise, but the pressure of Whisper's tip under his chin dissuaded him of that notion.

"Get up," I ordered. "Slowly."

Seuthes slid off the bed and got to his feet. "I will have you flayed for this, Athenian!"

"A threat I would take more seriously from a man in a tunic," I said. I gestured to Telekles, who circled around behind the naked Seuthes.

"Here," Tibetos said, handing Telekles the rope that had secured Adaz. The boy now stood beside me, rubbing his wrists. In a moment, Seuthes' own hands were bound behind him.

"Time to leave," I said. Telekles pricked our captor-turned-captive in the back.

We passed the body of the slain sentry and entered the main hall. The Thracians still lay like the dead. If Seuthes had expected his men to save him, he must have been disappointed. The Thracian general suddenly cried out. "To me! To me!" he shouted. I punched him hard in the gut and he doubled over.

With a startled groan, the warriors rose, scrabbling for their weapons and looking for an enemy. Their eyes fell on us. The Thracians hovered in the shadows at the edge of the hall like wraiths in the Underworld. By the dim light of the smouldering central fire-pit, they could see my hostage plainly enough.

"Drop your weapons or he dies," I said. They did not move. I placed the tip of my rhomphaia beneath Seuthes' exposed manhood and the general froze.

"Do it!" Seuthes rasped, still recovering from the blow I had dealt him. I feared that some ambitious warrior would spy an opportunity to be rid of Seuthes and seize Adaz for himself, but evidently the wily Thracian general had been careful to winnow out anyone who might challenge him. The wine and *rappa* had also taken a toll on the Thracians' spirits. The first weapon dropped with a clang and was soon followed by clattering of falling swords, axes, and spears.

I jerked my head towards one side of the hall. "There," I said. The warriors shuffled over to gather near the wall. I shot a look at Tibetos, who took my meaning and hurried out of the hall to fetch the rest of our party. The shame-faced Thracians glowered at us in impotent silence.

One of the warriors stepped forward and interrupted the wordless standoff. I recognized him as the captain who had captured us. "Do you mean to kill us?" he asked.

"We could have cut your throats while you slept," I said flatly. "But we did not."

The man ran his hand down his face. "The way my head feels that might have been preferable." I fought the urge to smile despite myself. I could see that in other circumstances I might have liked this man.

"Don't make me change my mind," I said and the captain stepped back with his fellows. The return of Tibetos and the others ended any further conversation. The *peripoli* and Basti's Thracians seized weapons from the ground and pointed them at the unarmed warriors on the far side of the hall. Seuthes' men stepped back.

"Do they share your sense of mercy?" Seuthes' captain asked, his voice wary.

The spirits of chaos whispered in men's ears, pleading for just one man in the hall to act rashly. Peace balanced on a sword-edge. "As long as they have reason to," I said.

"And the *basileus*?" the captain asked.

"For breaking the laws of *xenia,* he deserves no less than death. But if he attempts no further harm, then you have my oath that no one in my party will do him injury," I said, carefully avoiding any mention of what might befall Seuthes once he was in Zyraxes' hands.

The captain acceded. "May the gods hold you to that oath."

"Where are our weapons?" I demanded.

"Piled behind the throne," the captain said. "We were going to fight over them in the morning." Seuthes' men watched helplessly as their former prisoners rooted through the heap of spoils and reclaimed their stolen weapons. Mnasyllus, finding his massive *kopis*, sighed as though he had been reunited with a long-lost love.

"And our other gear?"

"Still where you left it with your horses," the captain said.

"Now go outside," I ordered Seuthes' men. We herded our enemies back to the slave pens. "Go into the cage," I ordered.

The Thracian captain balked. "You dishonour us," he protested.

"It is that or slaughter," I said.

The captain's mouth tightened, but he waved his men towards the pens. The defeated warriors shuffled into the pens where they had imprisoned us so recently. Once they were inside, Telekles and Stachys set the locks with a satisfying click.

Basti and his warriors went to get our horses and our gear. In a low voice I gave instruction to Tibetos and Sabas, and they set off for their own special task. Seuthes' men stared out at the rest of us in shame and rage.

"You are a dead man," Seuthes threatened while we waited for the others to return.

"If you avoid punishment from Zyraxes, you can come and find me, O King," I replied. Soon Basti appeared out of the darkness. "Are the horses ready?" I asked.

"Almost," Basti said. "We took his best," he added, spitting at the feet of Seuthes.

"And the remaining horses?"

"Scattered. It will take days for this lot to round them all up again." I heard the smile in his voice. He was right to smile, for thanks to Sosias we had slipped the bonds of slavery and denied Lysander, Seuthes, and the gods themselves the pleasure of our defeat. Before I could respond, the sound of hooves heralded the arrival of Basti's warriors with our mounts.

"It is time to leave, O King" I said, pulling Seuthes back towards the waiting animals. Basti had stolen for me the fine grey stallion that Seuthes' captain had ridden earlier. Mnasyllus heaved the naked Seuthes up so that the bound Thracian general lay belly down over the horse's back. I leapt up behind the supine general and turned back to the captain in the slave pen. "If I even see a rider on the horizon, your *basileus* will be in need of a new head," I warned, and the captain nodded his agreement. I knew someone would come from the village and free them soon enough. In case Seuthes' warriors suddenly rediscovered their loyalty for their general and considered pursuing us, I left them with something more pressing to deal with.

From the direction of the great hall, Tibetos and Sabas came trotting towards me. Tibetos gave a crisp nod and I knew that their task was done. "O King," I said, lifting my gaze to the hall behind the throng of warriors, "For the hospitality of *xenia* you have shown us, I return the gift in kind."

Crisp cracking sounds like dry twigs snapping underfoot began to reach our ears. Seuthes let out a low, painful groan, and his warriors turned towards the intensifying glow that was beginning to envelop Seuthes' prized hall. The hungry flames breached the roof timbers and soon were reaching for the heavens.

"Gold and silver can buy a fine fire," I said.

Seuthes strained to look at me. "I will kill you, Athenian," he rasped.

I laughed. "Perhaps one day, O King," I said, digging my heels into the stallion's flanks. "But not today."

CHAPTER 38

Even from many miles away, the conflagration's glow appeared to fill the sky. We kept the horses to a walk, for to have gone faster would have risked injury. I do not know how well horses can see in the dark, but the beasts seemed comfortable enough at the modest pace we were setting.

Adaz rode with Basti. The Thracian captain was already explaining the basics of horsemanship to his adopted son. Sosias was with Telekles. The two of them spoke in soft voices, but their words were hidden from me by the never-ending stream of threats of promised suffering from Seuthes. A suggestion that I might cut out his tongue silenced him but for a short time before captive general's muttering began anew.

Someone called from my left side. "Athenian!" It was Arexion. "Let us stop and get our bearings!"

"We keep going," I responded.

The Parnassian soldier persisted. "At least for a piss, then."

I was about to deny him, but Basti spoke first. "It would not be unwelcome," he said. "At least for the boys."

Even the greatest warrior was a slave to hunger, thirst, fatigue, and the pressure of a full bladder. "We halt just for as long as it takes to piss," I conceded.

"What about me?" Seuthes asked.

"Whatever you need to do, you'll do it from where you are now," I said.

People found their own space to relieve themselves and stretch their cramped bodies. In the starlight, each person was but a shadow, distinguishable only by their shape and bearing. The purposeful gait of Arexion made him easy to recognize as he strode towards me.

"We should head south to Ainos," he said bluntly. "We can be there just after dawn."

"We will return to Zyraxes," I said, dismissing the idea curtly.

But Arexion would not let the matter drop. "There will be ships in Ainos. If you insist on keeping the boy alive, then Ainos is the fastest way to escape the reach of Lysander," he insisted.

"You no longer wish the boy dead?" I asked, suspicious of his apparent change of heart.

"I have thought on it. As you said, once the solstice has passed, he is no longer of use," Arexion said a little too agreeably. "Ainos is the nearest port and the best way to guarantee the boy's safety, if that is what you wish."

I sucked my teeth. "The boy will be safe with Prince Zyraxes," I said. "There will too many curious eyes in Ainos. Perhaps they have already been warned to be on the lookout for us. And there is the matter of Seuthes," I said, jerking a thumb towards the Thracian general, who was still slung naked over my horse's back like a sack of grain.

Arexion's reasonable demeanor began to crack. "Kill the Thracian, then!" Arexion said. Too loudly, I thought. "Only our mission for Delphi matters, Athenian!" A stillness settled over our party as the others stopped what they were doing to listen to our exchange.

"Seuthes' fate," I said, barely restraining my rising anger, "is for Zyraxes and Medokos to determine. As for you, if you wish to go to Ainos, I give you permission to do so. You are no longer needed here."

"I do not need your permission, Athenian!" Arexion growled.

My patience was at an end. "Then it is not permission, but an order, Parnassian. Leave now or it is you who will end up feeding the crows. Go back to Delphi and tell the priest your mission was a success. Inform him that Lysander's prophet is dead, if you wish. The boy will disappear into Thrace. Be satisfied with that."

Arexion stood still, silent but for his furious breathing. Outnumbered as he was, there was little else he could do. "You are making a mistake, Athenian," he said before turning to return to his horse. Why Arexion was so eager for us to go to Ainos, I could not fathom. but it was obvious that we should stay away from the port and whatever danger lay hidden there.

"Time to leave!" I called out, watching Arexion check his horse's harness. I wandered back to where I had left Seuthes under the watchful eye of two Thracians. I dismissed them and looked at the would-be king of Thrace. "Zyraxes awaits you, *O Basileus*," I said.

"I'll be eating your guts in a stew tonight, Athenian!" Seuthes spat.

"A fearsome threat from someone slung naked over the back of a horse," I responded. Seuthes answered with a stream of curses and promises of the painful, drawn-out death that awaited me.

"If the Fates will it," I said when he had exhausted himself. I glanced back at Arexion just as the soldier of Delphi turned away from his horse. Even in the darkness I could see the sword in his hand. He began to trot towards a smaller figure who stood at the edge of the group. My heart lurched.

"Adaz! Move!" I cried, drawing my dagger. But I was too far away from the boy to help. Arexion lunged forward, stabbing at the Lysander's prophet. Adaz would surely be impaled, I saw.

But I was wrong. A dark shape dove between Arexion and Adaz and shoved the boy away from the deadly blow an instant before it struck. It was Telekles. The veteran *peripoli* rolled to his feet and ended up in low crouch between the Delphian warrior and his prey. Arexion roared in frustration and charged, chopping down at the *peripoli*'s shoulder. The clang of iron against iron spawned a bright spark that flashed into brief existence as Telekles blocked the blow. There was a feral cry of pain from the shadow that was Arexion, and his weapon fell to the ground. But the Delphian was an experienced warrior and kicked Telekles hard before the *peripoli* could follow up with a killing stroke.

Telekles stumbled back from the impact. The others, caught off guard by Arexion's attack, were now converging on him. Arexion, his last opportunity to be rid of Adaz squandered, spun and began to run for his life. He had a good head start. The forest would swallow him before we could run him down.

"I have him." It was Sabas. The Cretan archer bent down to string his bow. His eyes never left the shadowy form of the fleeing Arexion and only a hint of strain in his breath revealed the effort needed to string the great Phrygian weapon. In one smooth motion, Sabas nocked, drew, and loosed an arrow with a snapping thrum. Perhaps Apollo was protecting Arexion, for no sooner had the shaft sprung from the bowstring than the Parnassian stumbled and pitched forward, and the arrow only pierced the empty space where his back had been. Arexion scrambled to his feet and disappeared into the forest's shadows.

I ran to Telekles, who was doubled over. Too slowly he pulled himself up. He was clutching his side. "Is the boy safe?" he asked. The other *peripoli* were now crowded around us.

"He is with Basti and Nimahe," I said. Nimahe stood in front of Adaz, her Skythian axe drawn. "Are you wounded?"

Telekles looked at his hand. Even in the night I could see it glistened with dark blood. "I've had worse," he said, suppressing the wince in his voice. "I told you the Parnassian was trouble."

"Can you ride?" I asked.

Telekles pressed his side and drew in a tender breath. "It's either that or lie down here and wait for Seuthes' horde of screaming Thracians to find me. I'd rather risk the former. Just help me get on the horse."

Basti strode over to our knot of *peripoli* and stood before Telekles. "I am in your debt, Athenian," he said.

Telekles waved him off. "Consider it repayment for saving this hotheaded fool so many times," he said, putting a hand on my shoulder.

Before Basti could respond, a cry of alarm from one of the young Thracian warriors cut off the Thracian captain's next words. I glanced back at my horse and cursed. Seuthes was gone. The wily general had used the distraction of Arexion's failed attack to flee. I strained my ears but could hear nothing. Either he was too far away or more likely had gone to ground like a frightened hare. There was no time to stumble around in the dark of the Thracian wilderness in hapless pursuit of our hostage.

"It is no matter," I said, unconvinced by my own words. "Seuthes has served his purpose. We will be on the other side of the Hebros before anyone even finds him. Mount up!"

I boosted Telekles onto his horse and the *peripoli* grunted with pain. I leaned in close. "You are able to ride alone, Telekles?" I asked him quietly.

"All the way to Athens if I have to," he assured me, failing to completely mask the strain in his voice. I was worried, but there was nothing to be done.

Wounded, betrayed, and absent our hostage, we continued west. Seuthes' escape grated on me, but Arexion's attack disturbed me more. The Parnassian had been compliant enough until I refused his urging to return to Ainos. There was something I was missing and it bothered me. I dismissed my fears and focused on reaching the bridge. Once over the Hebros, we would be safe, I thought.

I was wrong.

CHAPTER 39

Lysander found us.

The sharp-eyed warrior Rhoglos spotted the hegemon's scout on a distant ridge to the east. There was little doubt that the red-cloaked rider had seen us, for he immediately turned his horse and vanished behind the faraway rise.

"It won't be long before the scout reports back to Lysander," Stachys said.

"He would have known that we were headed for the bridge anyway," I said. Once Lysander had learned of the bridge over the Hebros, it would not have been difficult for him to reason that it would be our most likely destination.

Basti made an unmistakable rude gesture in the direction where we had seen the scout. "Let them ride as hard as they can!" he scoffed. "They will never reach the bridge before us!"

I remained silent. We would reach the bridge before Lysander, but not by much. Telekles was wounded, and the boys and other inexperienced riders would slow us down enough for us to lose the lead we currently enjoyed. And after we crossed? Dotos and the refuge of the Thracian fort were still a hard ride away, plenty of time for Lysander's cavalry to run us down in the flat plain between the river and the fort. Even if we made it to the fort in time, Lysander would be able to trap us there. The old, poorly-manned fort was in no condition to withstand any kind of siege. No, fleeing across the bridge was only to delay defeat and failure.

I turned my eyes westward. The bridge was still some distance away. The misty shape of an idea began to coalesce in my mind's eye. I played through the scenario. There were a hundred ways the scheme could go wrong. Still uncertain, I explained my plan to the others. Their eyes widened as they understood what it was I was proposing.

"By the gods, you're a mad bastard, Dammo," Tibetos said.

"If it does not work, Lysander will win," I said.

Telekles gave a wan smile. "He will not win." He was pale, but the wound in his side had stopped bleeding.

It was decided. We would not flee like frightened sheep. We would stand and fight.

Because there was a chance to defeat a god.

THE THRACIAN RHOGLOS SPURRED HIS HORSE DOWN THE HILL, shouting his warning. "They're here!" he yelled, pointing towards the small rise to his rear. His eyes flashed with breathless excitement. Sure enough, the first riders of Lysander's force were appearing at the edge of the forest a mile or so away. More and more Spartan cavalry poured out from the distant tree-line. In their centre was the distinctive white cloak of Lysander.

"Time to go!" I shouted. "But not too fast!"

The Spartan vanguard galloped towards us, hoping to catch us before we could cross to the western side of the river. Sabas and Tibetos were first to the bridge, hurrying Sosias and Adaz in front of them. Halfway across, Sosias tripped and fell, almost ending up in the river. Tibetos yanked the boy to his feet and at last they found the safety of the opposite bank. Basti bellowed at his Thracians, who scurried about in a panicked fashion as they tried to lead their reluctant horses across the bridge. One mare reared wildly, kicking her forehooves at her handler. Rather than continuing the struggle, the Thracian abandoned the animal and sprinted to the other side of the river to save his skin. All the while I was desperately screaming at the men to stand firm and face our pursuers. The chaos of our disorderly retreat encouraged the Spartans bearing down on us, and they bayed at the prospect of an easy victory and the reclamation of their lost honour.

But it was not chaos. It was only as real as a play in a theatre.

The Spartans could not see the suppressed smiles of the Thracians as they tried their hand at acting. Nor could the Spartans see the mischievous grin Sosias flashed my way after he had stumbled on the bridge. It was all just a ruse to make the Spartans think that they had caught us off-guard, and the actors were playing their parts as well as I could have hoped.

Almost all the others had reached the far bank. Mnasyllus and Stachys were the last to stand with me on the eastern side of the river. "Let's go," I said. The two *peripoli* nodded grimly, for we three had the most dangerous of the tasks ahead.

We did not cross all the way. Instead, we stopped at the centre of the narrow bridge. We turned back to face the ever-increasing number of Spartans on the eastern bank, our line of three warriors the only remaining obstacle between Lysander and his prize. Stachys wielded a spear and a light Thracian shield. The brawny Mnasyllus raised his beloved hoplite shield and brandished his oversized *kopis*. In my own hands Whisper quivered with anticipation.

A dense mass of Spartans had assembled on the eastern bank. The white-cloaked god-man Lysander dismounted. His sword-sharp gaze fell on me and then flicked to something on the opposite bank. As I had hoped, he had spied Adaz, the boy's golden hair radiant in the afternoon sun. The hegemon's eyes returned to me. He spoke to the armoured man next to him.

My old enemy Orchus nodded at whatever Lysander had said and grinned at me in anticipation of what was to come. By now nearly a hundred armoured Spartans had assembled at the eastern abutment of the bridge. Their apparent hesitation to simply storm the dilapidated bridge was understandable. Without room to manoeuvre, numbers counted for less than on an open battlefield. Even so, the three of us blocking the bridge were no great threat, but the javelin-wielding Thracians arrayed on the opposite bank had given them pause. On the narrow confines of the bridge, the Spartans would be easy targets. While they mulled the problem, I took the initiative away from them.

"Are you ready?" I asked, keeping my eyes facing ahead.

"Let's kill the bastards," Stachys said. "I make it thirty for each of us."

"Fifty for me," Mnasyllus growled.

"Be ready to run if this doesn't work," I said, stepping out in front of them. If the gods' eyes were upon us, as my sister had claimed, then they would witness the height of my hubris. If it were to be my downfall, so be it. There was no turning back.

"I am Daimon of Athens!" I shouted. I let the Spartans hear my name, for many among them knew of me. I spread my arms. "I am the Tyrant-killer! I am the slayer of the Spartan general Chairon! The blood of your fellow Spartans still stains the streets of Piraeus where I cut them down!" I boasted. I pointed my blade back at Adaz. "I stole your prize from you while you humped each other in your tents! I fear Spartan women more than I fear you!" On the western side of the river, my comrades jeered. "Is there a man among you brave enough to face me? Or will you hide behind your shields like cowards?" I goaded.

From the murmuring crowd of angry Spartans, one man came forward. He said something to Lysander and the hegemon nodded. The armoured figure stepped onto the bridge, testing the stability of the structure. Finding it solid, he advanced towards me. There were always a few hotheads wishing to demonstrate their prowess and win glory. But this was not one of them. This one sought vengeance.

"You wish to keep your brother's shade company?" I sneered at the familiar face.

Drakontios swung his round hoplite shield, checking his grip. "Today you die, bastard," he called, adjusting his hold on his spear.

"That is the same thing your brother said," I said. "Then I hanged him."

"I will enjoy keeping your head to remind me of this day," the Spartan said.

"My collection of Spartan heads is so large that I don't think I will have room for yours," I laughed.

Hoping to catch me off-guard. Drakontios let out a roar and charged me like an enraged boar, his shield held out in front of him. It was a sound plan. The shield was wide and heavy, and the bridge offered little room to dodge as he bore down on me.

The only problem was that I had expected him to do it. So I did the unexpected. As soon as he began to move, I sprinted towards him. At the last moment I threw my body into a low sideways roll. My back smashed into the charging warrior's shins and the Spartan sailed in the air, crashing in a sprawling heap on the wooden timbers of the bridge.

The Thracians cheered as I scrambled to my feet, my back throbbing from the impact of the Spartan's legs. I raised Whisper above me ready to attack. Drakontios had recovered quickly and was already up. He blinked at me over the edge of his shield, uncertainty beginning to eat away at his confidence. His spear had clattered over the edge of the bridge and into the river, and now he tugged madly to free his sword from its scabbard.

I twirled Whisper in a lazy pattern. "You've lasted longer than your useless brother," I taunted him.

Drakontios growled and began to advance, but cautiously this time. His *kopis* sword was kept low and out of sight behind the shield, ready to strike. I let him come to me. Whisper was loose in my hands and thirsty for blood. Drakontios closed the distance between us. Silence hung over the river as each group of spectators willed their man to victory.

The Spartan lunged, trying to bash me with his shield. His sword stabbed out at my shoulder. It was a fast strike, but I danced away and before he could follow up I flicked Whisper's tip at his exposed sword arm. The rhomphaia was in and out like a serpent's bite, leaving a shallow gash on his forearm. He pulled his sword back, concealing it behind his shield. Drops of blood spattered at his feet. I grinned wolfishly at him.

Words find gaps in armour that iron cannot reach. My barbed words flew now. "Your brother's shit dribbled down his leg as he swung from the rope," I goaded. "Like an infant. Like an incontinent old man." Drakontios stabbed but I parried easily, forcing him back with a counter-lunge. "The crows were already pecking at his eyes when I left him," I taunted him. "The great Spartan warrior: now he is nothing but the shit of crows and foxes."

With a roar, he attacked again, this time in a mad flurry of criss-crossing, hacking slashes. The blows came in a wild onslaught but the Spartan's bulky shield hindered his movement and Whisper's adamantine blade easily absorbed the powerful strokes. We had shifted so that we faced each other across the narrow axis of the bridge, both our backs to the water. Drakontios made a desperate bull charge forward in an attempt to knock me into the water and I had to leap sideways to avoid him, once again letting Whisper flick out across the Spartan's forehead as I did so.

He spun to face me. We had returned to our original positions on the bridge, me with my back towards the Thracians and his towards Lysander's Spartans. Head wounds bleed furiously and now Drakontios' face was a crimson mess. He was panting heavily. Behind his bloody mask, his eyes betrayed the first flickers of fear.

"My head is still here, Spartan," I said.

The fear in his eyes turned to rage and he charged, screaming for my blood. For an instant my mind flashed back to the mountains of Attica more than two years earlier. His brother had attacked me in exactly the same manner. Fate has a cruel sense of humour. This time I was not taking prisoners.

I lunged forward to meet him. The open mouth of Drakontios was a small target, but one I imagined when I went through my training every day. Whisper's tip plunged into the Spartan's gaping maw and punched out the back of his neck. I kept pushing forward, driving the blade in all the way to the hilt. Our faces were separated by less than a hand's breadth. Drakontios' eyes were wide with surprise. His sword dropped to the bridge with a dull clunk and his shield slid from his arm. His body twitched in a final spasm of stubborn, clinging life and then his shade left him.

There was a moan of anger and defeat from the Spartans. The Thracians and *peripoli* whooped and hollered. I held Drakontios' corpse there, suspended on the rhomphaia as though he was still standing of his own accord. Let them see, I thought.

The arrogant display of victory took all my strength and my muscles began to burn. I ripped Whisper free and Drakontios' lifeless body crumpled in a heap. Staring at Lysander, I snapped Whisper downwards, flicking the blood off her blade with disdain before picking up the fallen shield. I turned and walked back to the centre of the bridge where Mnasyllus and Stachys still stood. I half expected a Spartan javelin in the back, but none came. With grateful relief, I stepped behind the cover of my friends' shields.

"Gods, Dammo," Stachys said, letting out a long breath. "If we survive this day, I will never forget that as long as I live."

"'If,'" I replied, slipping my arm through the leather strap of Drakontios' shield. I crouched low and blocked the centre of the bridge with the wide hoplite shield. Stachys and Mnasyllus stood behind me, their weapons ready.

Then the hotheads came. Three Spartans rushed at us, their long oiled braids flapping from beneath their helmets. Their footfalls hammered on the bridge's wooden planks like a shipbuilder's mallet. Mnasyllus and Stachys pushed their shields into my shoulder blades, bracing for the impact. A few steps before reaching us, the obstacle of Drakontios' corpse stole some momentum and cohesion from the Spartans' charge, and they died for it.

The impact of the Spartans on my shield jarred my bones but did not shift me. Mnasyllus clove through helmet and skull with his *kopis,* while Stachys skewered his man through the groin with a thrust under the Spartan's shield. The middle Spartan, suddenly alone, refused to yield and stabbed at me over my shield, but his footing was poor and I crouched low, and his spear-point found only air. It was his only chance, for a second blow by Mnasyllus nearly severed the man's head at the shoulder.

The Spartan gored by Stachys squirmed and moaned next the bodies of his companions as he tried to hold his guts in from the fearsome wound that Stachys had dealt him. With the mewling Spartan at our feet, the three of us cursed Lysander and the remaining Spartans on the far bank, calling their mothers whores and their fathers worse. Our comrades on the western side of the river hurled their own insults over the black water of the river like so many sling-stones at the enemy. Fury radiated from the white-cloaked Lysander like heat from glowing embers.

The Spartans had just seen three of their comrades cut down because of foolish pride. Now there were the three of us as well as a small wall of bodies to hinder any attack. Orchus, donning his helmet, berated the Spartans for their rashness. Shouting commands, the veteran mercenary ordered Lysander's Spartans to lock shields and form a column. Three abreast and six or seven ranks deep, the enemy came at us. On the narrow bridge, the Spartans could not outflank us, but they could push through us with ease.

Slowly, deliberately, the Spartan column advanced. It was a fearsome thing. The front row of lambda-emblazoned shields grew ever closer. The soldiers shouted in unison with each step, like the drumbeat on a trireme. When the mass of men passed the eastern pier and reached the central span of the bridge, the wood under our feet shuddered in warning.

"Step back!" I yelled over the din of the Spartan war-chant. As one, the three of us retreated a step. "Again!" I said and we fell back one more pace.

The Spartans reached the centre of the bridge, trampling over their dead without compunction. As the column came within range of missiles, my comrades on the west bank peppered them with javelins, sling-stones, and arrows. But the practiced Spartan formation was compact and disciplined. Shields and heavy bronze armour left little room for damage, and the rain of projectiles was akin to flies pestering a horse. The failure of the missiles to hinder them bolstered the Spartans' lust for blood, and their rhythmic cries grew louder.

"Step back!" I said. The Spartans were a spear-length away. "Again!" I shouted. Beneath my feet I felt the unmoving mass of stone that was the bridge's the western pier. "Hold!" I called. Stachys and Mnasyllus stopped and once more pushed into my back to brace me.

The distance between the Spartan column our trio of defenders shrank further. Two more paces and the inexorable mass of flesh and bronze and iron would grind over us like a millstone over grains of wheat. My heart pounded in my ears. If my plan failed, death was only a step away from me.

And then the world trembled beneath my feet.

Rope is useful, my friend Lykos had taught me. No patrol should be without it. Besides a hundred uses in camp, rope can help soldiers scale rock faces, pull down obstacles, or hang bandits and traitors at crossroads. Rope is also what gave us victory that day in Thrace.

Sabas and Basti, positioned on either side of the bridge, grabbed the loops of rope lying hidden in the long grass at the river's edge and threw them over the heads of the horses waiting beside them. Sabas slapped the flat of his sword against the rump of his horse and Basti did likewise, and the startled beasts ran in opposite directions.

The ropes joining the horses to the central span of timbers snapped taut in a spray of water as they exploded from the river. The massive boards of the central span jerked askew, causing one Spartan to flail his arms uselessly in an effort to regain his balance before he toppled into the river with a splash. Weighted by his armour, the soldier vanished beneath the black water, his existence erased by the current.

The boards had shifted but not enough. The two horses strained, pulling the ropes so tight I feared they would snap. The timbers grated slowly off the piers. The Thracians and *peripoli* reacted quickly, grabbing onto the nearest ropes and adding their strength to that of the pulling horses. The trapped Spartans on the bridge suddenly realized their peril. My heart pounding, I stared over my shield at the Spartans trapped on the central span. My eyes met those of the Spartan soldier directly opposite me. His eyes widened with the desperate, animal terror that death had come for him. He shouted out, imploring me to save him from the grasping hands of death. I almost reached out to him. But his fate was already woven.

The timbers shuddered and came free.

It was a terrible, wonderful thing to behold. The unsupported struts collapsed under the weight of men and weapons and armour. A few of the Spartans tumbled to the sides but most plunged straight down through the planks and into the icy blackness of the Hebros, their shouts of surprise cut short as the weight of their armour pulled them under the surface and down to their watery tombs. The explosion of wood and water and men lasted for but a few heartbeats and then was done. The Spartan soldiers were there and then they were not, with only a scattering of debris drifting with the current to mark their passing.

A shocked silence settled over the river. Then the quiet air was rent asunder by the cheers of the victors.

My unspent bloodlust and relief flowed out of me in a torrent of anger and scorn. I stood on the edge of the western pier while my comrades and the Thracians jeered at the powerless Spartans on the opposite bank. The *peripoli* and Thracians shouted obscenities and mocked the Spartans' courage. I stood silent, having eyes only for Lysander. I felt the god-man's impotent rage washing over me but it only stoked the furious elation of victory within me.

But I knew Lysander's defeat was not yet complete. *Belief is a strange beast.* The Pythia's words echoed in my mind. Lysander's ambition depended on the belief of others, the belief that the gods favoured him. Then let them see him now. Let them see his failure. Let them see how the gods had abandoned him.

I lifted Whisper, extending her blade and pointing her bloodied tip at Lysander, who stood rigid on the far side. Our eyes locked across the inky span of the Hebros. "Lysander! You are not a god!" I shouted. "YOU ARE NOT A GOD!" The others took up the call and chants of "You are not a god!" shot across the water at the helpless hegemon.

"Let us leave these wretches," I called out, my gaze still on the white-cloaked Lysander. "to contemplate their defeat!" I turned my back on the humiliated enemy and Mnasyllus, Stachys, and I joined my comrades on the western bank. A hearty cheer greeted us as we stepped onto solid ground.

Tibetos blew out a long breath through pursed lips. "Gods, Dammo! I thought you were done for!"

"You left it close," I chided him and we laughed the relieved laugh of those who have faced death and survived.

A pale-looking Telekles gripped my shoulder and I was glad to feel that strength still remained in his fingers. "That tale will be told by the *peripoli* for generations," he said.

"If the *peripoli* survive that long," I said.

"They will if you are there to lead them, Daimon," he said with unexpected seriousness, and I suddenly had no words to respond. Telekles gazed to the south. "It is time to head back to Athens, I think." He gave a gentle smile and left me to my thoughts.

We gathered our gear and mounted the remaining horses. I cast one last look towards the east. Black water flowed past the gaping emptiness in the centre of the bridge. On the far side, the remaining Spartans were readying to depart from the site of their shameful defeat. With a twinge of irritation, I noticed a soaking Orchus was still among the living. The Andrian mercenary was on his hands and knees vomiting water. He was surely protected by some god, for he always managed to evade the death that he had earned many times over. Sooner or later I would catch him and at that time even a god would not be able to save him from my fury.

Lysander did not look back. Without the boy Adaz, Lysander's plan to usurp Delphi's influence lay in ruins. But the greater damage would be to the hegemon's reputation. The loss of a few dozen soldiers would sow seeds of doubt in the minds of those he had led. Word of his defeat in Thrace would spread. Men would whisper a new truth: the god-man Lysander was not a god after all. The true gods, people would say, had punished him for his presumption to count himself among their number and had cast him back down to earth.

At that moment, turning my back on the fallen god and riding west, I did not think about these things. We had abandoned a few horses on the far bank as part of the ruse to lure Lysander into the trap. Sosias rode with me, curiously quiet for a change. I glanced at Adaz, who rode with Basti. The boy's golden curls peeked out from a knobbed Thracian cap that one of the warriors had given him. The boy's once fine tunic was stained and torn. He looked more the Thracian slave than a grand prophet of Apollo.

I allowed myself a smile. Lysander had been denied his prize. We were, I thought, closing my tired eyes, out of danger.

It was the second mistake I made that day.

The gods are cruel.

CHAPTER 40

We had not travelled far before the magnitude of my error began to manifest itself.

"*Narusmanni*," one of the young Thracians said, pointing to the north. *Riders*. Sure enough, a group of horsemen flecked the horizon a mile or so in the distance.

I squinted. I estimated twenty or more horses, almost double the animals we had. "Are they Zyraxes' men?" I asked Basti.

"Could be," he said, peering northwards. "Could be raiders from the east."

"Better not to find out," I said. "Have they seen us?" The question had barely left my lips before the unknown riders turned and began racing towards us. "To the fort!" I yelled, kicking my heels into the flanks of Seuthes' fine stallion.

We had been walking the horses to give them a chance to rest following the race to the Hebros. I could only hope that they had recovered their stamina, for several of them would be bearing two riders. I swore to myself for not having pushed the beasts hard until we had reached the safety of the fort.

Sosias was nestled in front of me, his fingers entwined in the mane of the galloping horse. In a similar fashion, Adaz huddled in front of Basti, nearly obscured by the bulk of his new father's protective body. The terrified slave Klebos clung to his horse's neck for dear life. I thanked myself for putting Iollas and the escaped helot with Thracian riders, otherwise they would have surely toppled from their horse's backs.

Our steeds took up the challenge, their pounding hooves kicking up earth and dust. Periodic glances over my shoulder confirmed that our pursuers were closing the gap. The race to the fort would be a near thing. There was something else. Many of the riders wore the distinctive red cloaks of Spartan soldiers. The thought that Lysander had somehow got some of his men across the river stunned me.

Suddenly a voice made itself heard over the sound of galloping horseflesh. "Look! To the south!" Tibetos shouted.

I followed his line of sight and cursed the gods. Another detachment of cavalry had appeared, similar in size to that of our pursuers from the north. I swore uselessly at them. How had Lysander managed to get his forces to the western bank of the Hebros? Swimming the animals across the cold, fast-flowing current would have been a risky endeavour. But it had been foolish to underestimate the Spartan hegemon's determination to regain his prize. I leaned forward and urged my flagging horse to greater speed.

An excited shout from one of the Thracians renewed my hope, but the feeling was fleeting. The mound of the Thracian outpost beckoned to us in the distance, offering us safe haven if only we could outrace our pursuers. Yet the two bands of horsemen were converging on us like twin wolf packs running down their prey. Flecks of foam flew from our horses' mouths and a sheen of sweat glistened on their coats. The animals were tiring.

Now the enemy horsemen were harrying us on both sides. The red-cloaked Spartans had with them some Thracian allies, who bayed like wolves as they drew near. The black-braided Spartans pointed their spears at us as a promise of the fate that awaited us. The Spartan nearest me cocked his spear to stab at me and Sosias.

Then something astounding happened. As if by magic, the fletching of an arrow appeared in the throat of the grim-faced Spartan. His spear tumbled from his grasp and he clawed at the shaft piercing his neck. His horse veered into the path of other riders, causing chaos among them. Before I could comprehend what had occurred, another arrow skewered the eye of one of the enemy Thracians. The bronze-haired warrior tumbled from his mount directly into the path of one of his comrades, bringing both horse and rider down in a crashing mass of horseflesh.

A hurried glance to my side revealed the source of the shot. Astride her horse like it was an extension of her own body, a centaur-like Nimahe had another arrow nocked and had drawn the string of her small recurved bow to her cheek, a clutch of extra arrows ready in her draw-hand. The arrow sprang from the tautened cord, burying itself in another Thracian's gullet. No sooner had the Skythian loosed the missile than another appeared on the string. She twisted towards the other gang of pursuers, her body remaining strangely level despite the movement of the horse beneath her. Another arrow flew and another Spartan fell. Four lethal shots in almost the same number of heartbeats. Had I not witnessed it with my own eyes, I would not have believed such skill with a bow were possible.

Belatedly the enemy realized their peril. The two groups of horsemen veered away and out of range of Nimahe's bow, but not before her arrows had claimed two more riders. Our horses' chests churned like great bellows as they galloped towards the distant fort. It was still too far. The two bands could merge and block us. A glance to either side confirmed this was the enemy riders' intent.

A squeak from Sosias, barely audible above the pounding of hooves, brought my attention forward. He pointed at the fort. "Look!"

Someone in the outpost had spotted us. A knot of horses from the fort was racing to meet us. The enemy cavalry had likewise seen our reinforcements. In the face of an even fight, the enemy's zeal for pursuit faltered. They peeled away, heading towards the southwest. I squinted against the wind in my face, wondering where they were headed. And then I saw it.

A dark patch stained the plain in the south of the fort, like a shadow cast by a solitary cloud. But there were no clouds to block the sun; there was only clear blue sky. What I spied was no shadow: it was an army. Had Lysander landed another force on the western side of the Hebros river? Perhaps the Thracians had been Seuthes' men? It would explain the unlikely alliance of Thracians and Spartans. In any case, there was little time to reflect on how the hegemon had gotten ahead of us. Our rescuers from the fort were coming.

Dotos led the charge, I could see. The Thracian captain steered his band of horsemen in a wide arc, joining us as we neared the refuge of the fort. The immediate danger gone, we slowed our depleted mounts to a canter. The distant Spartan army to the south grew more clear with every hoof-beat. The shadow resolved itself into a textured mass of armoured men. I reckoned a central phalanx of three or four hundred hoplites and half the number again of skirmishers. That number did not even include the horsemen that had pursued us. I was still puzzling over the mysterious enemy when we finally reached the protection of the fort.

Lather dripped from the flanks of our exhausted mounts. I gave my horse an appreciative slap on the slick wetness of its neck and the animal nickered weakly. The beasts had earned the respite, short as it might be. Sosias twisted to peer back at me. His eyes danced with excitement. His hands, though, trembled. I put a reassuring hand on the boy's shoulder. "You did well to stay on, boy," I said. He nodded vigorously but for once was at a loss for words.

A mass of horses and riders crowded the fort's interior. Dotos was already at my horse's side. "You have brought friends, no?" the Thracian asked, gesturing towards the south.

"Spartans," I confirmed, dismounting. I helped Sosias down.

"And Kikones," Basti growled at from behind me.

I turned to him in surprise. "Not Seuthes' men?" I asked. "From the east?"

Basti shook his head. "I head their accent when they were screaming at us. Kikone weasel-shit, all of them." He spat in disgust. I frowned. Had Lysander enlisted the Kikones as his allies? There was no time to think.

I scanned the shifting throng of Thracians and *peripoli*. There was no one missing from our party, as far as I could see. Nimahe stood protectively near Adaz, who was already surrounded by a clump of curious denizens of the fort. One by one I found the *peripoli*. My growing sense of relief was cut down when my gaze found Telekles. The *peripoli* was slumped over his horse's neck. His pallor was ashen. "Telekles!" I shouted. I barely caught him as he slipped from the animal's back. I spotted Stachys. "Help me!" I called and the two of us manoeuvred the semi-conscious Telekles to a space near the fort's wall. When I removed my hand from his body, it was covered in sticky blood.

The other *peripoli*, seeing their comrade's plight, crowded round as I pulled away Telekles' borrowed Thracian cloak. His tunic was stained red. I cursed, for I knew that the exertion of our flight had torn open the wound from the traitorous Arexion.

"I need some cloth!" I said, cutting through the soaking tunic. The angry gash in his side oozed more scarlet onto his blood-slicked skin. I had seen many wounds. There was too much blood. I knew he would not survive.

Telekles knew it too. He raised his hand and grasped my wrist. "Daimon!" he said, straining to lean up. "The boy — Adaz! — He is safe?"

"He is in the fort, my friend," I said.

Telekles relaxed. "Then I have done my duty as a *peripoli*," he said. He smiled weakly. "I will leave the Spartans outside the fort to you."

"There are many of them, O Telekles," I said. Tears welled in my eyes.

Telekles coughed a laugh. "You will triumph," he said. "Do not fear."

"We will fight to the end," I said.

Telekles nodded. "Do not mourn me, for I have lived well and will die well." His grip on my wrist tightened. "Daimon!"

"I'm here."

He swallowed, gathering his strength. "Lykos would be proud of what you have become," he said. He smiled one last time and closed his eyes. His grip slackened and he was gone. I rose to my feet. Tearful *peripoli* stared down at the body of the fallen Telekles. The Thracians around us fell silent as Mnasyllus bellowed a mournful cry to the sky.

I wanted to howl at the sky and beat at my chest. But I could not. There was no time. Telekles, more than anyone, would not want us to mourn him now, not with the enemy outside our walls.

"Cover him," I said, my throat tight. "And come with me. Prepare for battle."

For the Spartans were coming.

CHAPTER 41

From atop the wall, we peered out towards the enemy. We had gained the refuge of the fort none too soon. A bristling double line of hoplites and Thracian skirmishers now encircled our tiny stone-walled haven. Their considerable cavalry, a mix of scarlet-cloaked Spartans and their Kikone allies, stopped short of the front gate just out of range of our missiles. Silence settled over the space between the defenders ensconced within the fort and besiegers without. I squinted, searching. But the white cloak of Lysander was nowhere to be seen.

Three horsemen detached themselves from the troop and let their mounts approach the fort. Their shields were on their backs and they bore no spears. Halfway across the swath of neutral ground the central rider raised a hand and they halted. I recognized him. It was not Lysander.

And I understood everything.

Pausanias, one of the two Spartan kings, gazed up at us. To the king's left was a Thracian whom I presumed to be the leader of the Kikones. The warrior's copper beard flowed over a chest of bronze scales. The other man on the king's right I knew well enough. "Arexion," Tibetos hissed.

Now I understood who commanded the Spartan warships in the port of Ainos and why Arexion had made such efforts to lead us there. Just as Lysander had corrupted some of the leaders of Delphi, so too had another faction at Delphi sided with the Spartan king Pausanias. It made sense that Pausanias desired to see the boy Adaz dead, for the death of Lysander's young prophet would hinder Lysander's ambitions to usurp the current kings of Sparta. Arexion and his faction had been serving Pausanias all along. Now the Parnassian warrior had come to see his mission finished.

"Let's see what they want," I said to Basti. But I already knew. I pulled Dotos aside. "Tell your best rider to prepare the fastest horse you have," I said. Then I instructed him what to do. "Can it be done?"

Dotos gave me the grin of a condemned man. "It is a mad hope," he said, but hurried off nevertheless.

Once Basti and I were mounted, the Thracian signalled to two of his warriors to open the gates. Together we rode out to parley, stopping a spear-length from the waiting king and his two companions.

While Basti glared at the Kikone warrior, I studied the Spartan king. Pausanias must have been nearly sixty. Despite his age, the king sat with easy strength as he watched us approach, his black-streaked grey beard giving him an air of authority rather than one of physical decline. His burnished bronze armour and crimson cloak were those of a typical Spartan warrior. Only a blue and white striped transverse crest on his helmet marked him out as different from the men he led.

"Daimon, son of Nikodromos," King Pausanias of Sparta greeted me. "It has been a long time." The last time I had seen the king was at a battle outside the walls of Piraeus some years earlier. After the Spartans and the rebel army of Thrasybulus had mauled each other to bloody shreds, Pausanias and Thrasybulus negotiated a truce in which Athens gained back a great deal of her autonomy. The generosity of Pausanias had not come from any desire to see Athens free, but rather to stifle the ambitions of his general Lysander. Little had changed since then.

I did not return the king's greeting. "You find yourself far from Sparta, Pausanias." The king's eyelid twitched at the casual familiarity with which I addressed him. "It is odd that our paths have crossed deep inside the territory of my host, King Medokos," I said.

Pausanias shrugged off my insolence. "Yet I am here."

"Guided by your loyal dog," I said, casting a disdainful look at Arexion.

"I serve Delphi!" the Delphian snapped.

I ignored him. "And you ally yourself with the enemies of King Medokos," I continued, indicating the Kikone leader.

"I take no interest in the petty squabbles of the Thracians," Pausanias said, feigning ignorance. "What tribe these mercenaries come from matters little to me. I pay them in silver and they do my bidding."

"Then why are you here at all, Spartan?" I asked.

"You have something I want," Pausanias said. "Give it to me and we will leave you in peace."

"What would that be?" I asked flatly, already knowing the answer.

"You have the boy Silenus," the Spartan King replied, holding my stare. "You will surrender him to me."

I scoffed. "So that you can execute him?"

Pausanias did not deny my accusation. "You are naïve if you believe that the boy can be allowed to live. The fate of the world could change if that boy ever arrives to speak in Delphi."

"If the boy does not arrive in Delphi before the solstice, then the matter is done," I said.

Pausanias barked a cold laugh. "Do you think that some excuse will not be found to change the day? Prophecy is a fluid thing. Lysander will not stop hunting for him."

"Lysander is done. I have seen to it. The lad is harmless. He will disappear back into the wilds of Thrace. Lysander will never find him," I said.

"I cannot take that risk."

"Then this meeting is at an end," I said, lifting my reins.

Arexion kicked his horse forward. "Give him to us or die!" the soldier of Delphi demanded.

My hand moved to Whisper's hilt. "Step closer and I'll have your head, Parnassian," I hissed. Arexion balked. The Kikone leader grinned, enjoying the exchange.

Basti moved his own horse forward. "Do you find something amusing, Kikone?" He said in Thracian. "Perhaps you just saw an attractive sheep in the distance."

The Kikone's grin vanished. "I will have your woman tonight," he snarled.

"She'll have your balls in her stew, I reckon," Basti countered. With a growl, the Kikone drew his hooked *sica* sword.

The king, sensing that the situation was slipping from his control, lost his patience. "Enough!" Pausanias barked. Basti and the Kikone shot each other baleful glares but held their tongues. The king wrestled down his irritation and turned his attention back to me. "What is the boy to you, Daimon?" he asked, appealing to my logic. "He is nothing. A slave. A piece on the board." He pointed towards the east. "Lysander's piece. And now he must be removed from the game. Why sacrifice your life and those of the men you lead for a game that is already lost? What does it gain you, to die here on this day?"

It was a fair question. But I knew the answer, though I gave no voice to it there on the Thracian plain. For what it gained me was simple. It gained me the right to go to the grey Underworld with honour. It gained me the right to stand with my father, Neleus, Lykos, Telekles – honourable men, all – and count myself among them. Most of all it gained me the right to stand before my wife's shade without my head hung in shame for my actions on this earth. *She* would know me, and that is all that mattered.

The Spartan king awaited my response but was doomed to disappointment. "You cannot have the boy. He is not mine to give," I said, glancing at Basti, who nodded. "Go back to Sparta while you still can."

Pausanias' jaw clenched. "I will not leave Thrace with this matter left undone."

"Then we are at an impasse, Spartan."

"You are a fool, Athenian!" the king said, incredulous at my defiance. A hint of a smile forced itself upon my lips, for the comment amused me. How many times had I been called a fool? As many times as there are stars in the sky, I thought, but surely to be addressed such by the king of Sparta was a bright star indeed. I laughed.

Pausanias took my reaction to be further impudence. "So be it!" With gritted teeth he wheeled his horse around to head back towards his waiting army. "To me!" he commanded his escort.

The Kikone mercenary hurled one last curse at Basti before turning his beast. Arexion, with one last sneer, hauled his own horse around but in doing so brought himself within arm's length of me. It was his mistake.

"Arexion!" I called out.

The Parnassian turned. Whisper hissed like a viper, parting the air in a single horizontal cut that separated the Delphian agent's head from his shoulders. For a heartbeat, Arexion's headless body stayed upright as though unaware of its own death, but a heartbeat later a great mist of blood sprayed upwards like a dolphin's breath and the body tumbled from his mount.

"That is for Telekles," I said.

The Spartan King and the Kikone spun their horses around, their weapons already drawn in expectation of an ambush. "You dare break a truce?" Pausanias sputtered.

I pointed the gracefully arcing blade of my rhomphaia at Arexion's severed head. "He was a traitor," I said flatly. I raised the tip in line with the king's chest. "And I do not recall agreeing to a truce, Spartan."

Pausanias grimaced. He cast a glance at Arexion's headless corpse. "His service to Sparta is noted." The king's eyes met mine. "It is your last chance, Daimon of Athens," he said. "Give me the boy."

A hundred years earlier the Spartan king Leonidas had faced a similar demand from the Great King Xerxes to surrender his weapons. Vastly outnumbered and facing certain death, Leonidas had chosen to fight, answering the most powerful mortal alive with two simple words. Now I threw those words in the face of Leonidas' descendant.

"*Molon Labe.*"
Come and get him.

CHAPTER 42

Before Pausanias could react, I raised my blade and pointed it at the sky. At the signal, horsemen burst from the fort's open gate. The Spartan king's eyes widened in surprise, but he had the sense to spur his own mount and flee the charging horsemen. The surge of Thracians from the fort was already crashing past me. Shouts of alarm spread among the ranks of the besieging Spartan army and their Kikone allies. Basti and I spun our own mounts and joined the charge, shouting our war-cries to the heavens.

During my negotiations with Pausanias, some Kikone skirmishers had wandered closer to the fort so as to taunt their enemies trapped within. Now, caught out in the open, these Kikones paid for their carelessness as Dotos' own Thracians ran them down with glee as they fled ignominiously back to the safety of the Spartan lines.

The Spartans, themselves caught flat-footed, recovered with the brisk efficiency born of experience. Their shields locked together, reinforcing the serried barrier of spears around the fort. In most places the line was two men deep, but only a single rank of men guarded the stretch at the rear.

"There! There!" I shouted, pointing at the vulnerable area. At first the Thracian warriors, caught up in the frenzied slaughter of their hated Kikone enemies, seemed not to have heard me. I feared that my plan would fail, for if the riders forgot their task, they would be easy prey once the Kikone skirmishers and enemy cavalry regrouped.

But to my relief, the Thracians abandoned the temptation of the fleeing Kikones and charged the vulnerable section of the Spartan line. Our numbers were few, only twenty or so horses, but what the Thracians lacked in numbers they made up for in gleeful savagery. The first Thracian drove his steed directly at the locked shields and protruding spears, the screaming young warrior's unbound red hair rippling like flames. At the last moment the warrior's horse balked, unwilling to bull its way through the wall of bronze men, but it was too late, for the beast's momentum brought it crashing into the waiting Spartans, their spears burying themselves deeply into the screaming animal's chest. Thus impaled, the horse toppled over, flinging the flame-haired rider away but crushing two Spartans beneath its fleshy bulk. My heart surged. A gap in the wall had been opened.

"To the gap!" I yelled. But there was no need. Thracian horsemen were already leaping over the thrashing form of the speared horse and slashing at the Spartans as they passed. Suddenly they were pouring through the ever-widening hole in the Spartan line. I spurred my horse forward and with a leap I broke through.

It was chaos. Thracian blades raked the exposed rear of the Spartan ranks like the claws of some great leopard. Among the cries of triumph and death, the intoxicating effect of *aristeia* surged within me. The blood-lust vied with my rational mind to claim my soul. At last I succumbed as the pent-up frustration of the past days breached my inner walls of self-control and I let the battle-madness take me.

I lashed out at the nearest Spartan and Whisper's honed tip sliced through the side of his neck as though it were slashing through water. Hardly had the man begun to fall before the rhomphaia arced around again and chopped deep into another Spartan's unarmoured upper arm. I pulled my weapon back and felt it grate across the screaming man's bone. Beside him, another soldier had managed to turn and jab up at me with his spear but the thrust was hurried and weak and glanced off the black scales of my corselet. I roared at him and Whisper shot out like a scorpion's sting, stabbing him in the face through the gap in his helmet. The Spartan cried out but I was already moving. Whisper spun like a whirlwind at the hard-pressed soldiers as I galloped passed. Sometimes her blue-tinged metal clanged off of bronze helmet and shield rims, but more often fed on flesh. The Furies goaded me on and I gave myself over to them.

A sound stronger than the Furies' bloodthirsty screeches penetrated my consciousness. The serpent-haired demonesses beseeched me to ignore it but the strong, clean note came again. It was like sunlight burning away the mist. The madness ebbed and the Furies' cries echoed into nothingness. The pealing of a horn carried over the cacophony of battle. It was Dotos. He was signalling the retreat, as I had asked him to. From his vantage point atop the rampart, Dotos had read the situation well. Out of the corner of my eye I caught the movement of the enemy cavalry, who had finally reacted to the surprise attack. The telltale hiss of a slingstone shooting over my head told me that the Kikones had regrouped as well. It was time to seek the safety behind the fort's walls.

The Thracians took up the cry of retreat, abandoning the fight and punching through the ravaged Spartan ranks towards the protection of the fort. Not all heeded the call. A female warrior, overcome by battle-madness, continued to chase down isolated soldiers. As my horse broke through the line, I saw her trapped by a throng of Spartans and pulled down to her death by clawing, vengeful hands.

Our horsemen galloped through the open gate. I brought up the rear and the crossbars thudded into place once the gates slammed closed behind me. The red-mist of battle clouded my vision and warped my sense of time. It seemed as though an eternity had passed since the Thracians had burst forth from the fort. But the raid had only lasted as long as it would have taken to sprint around the perimeter of the agora in Athens.

My mind was not so unsettled that I had forgotten the objective of the sortie. I leapt from my horse and hurried up to the top of the wall where Tibetos awaited me.

"Did it work?" I asked, my lungs still heaving with rush of battle.

"Look!" he said, pointing to the west.

I followed the line from his extended finger. A mile or distant, a patch of dust marked the progress of a lone rider fleeing to the west. If the Spartans had seen him, it was of little consequence; the rider, our last hope, had far too great a lead for any pursuit to be worthwhile. We strained our eyes to pick out the receding speck. Then, like hope itself, the horseman faded from sight.

WE HAD LOST FIVE WARRIORS IN THE ASSAULT. The Spartans and Kikones had lost perhaps ten times that number. Yet it was like landing the first punch in a boxing match; it bloodies your opponent's face and bruises his pride, but only serves to stoke his anger and harden his resolve to fight back and drub you into submission.

Inside the fort were forty or so defenders and half that number again in women, children, and slaves. Pausanias fielded ten times that number of Spartans and Kikones, all of whom sought revenge for the casualties suffered in the first clash of battle. Below us the Spartan officers bellowed orders at their men, who hastened to form five phalanxes around the fort. Their strategy was clear. They were preparing to assault the walls, counting on brute force and superior numbers to overwhelm us.

While our Thracian cavalry had been mauling the Spartan lines, those within the fort had not remained idle. The hectic preparations for the siege continued apace. Mnasyllus, his bare torso sheened with sweat, was putting his farmer's skills to work. His great muscles flexed as he tore out the rocks from the foundations of the huts just as though he were clearing field stones from the soil. Every boulder Mnasyllus tossed aside was promptly seized by a Thracian warrior or sometimes two and hauled up to the walkways, ready to be thrown down on attackers assaulting the walls. The piles of stones, though growing, seemed pitiful next to the hundreds of Spartan hoplites assembling outside the fort.

My eyes drifted to the two smaller figures in the compound. Sosias and Adaz stood against the wall, watching the activity. Adaz looked on with frightened fascination. Beside the would-be prophet, his wilder shadow companion Sosias bore an expression of gawping excitement, his gaze darting about like a cat watching birds flitting about in the branches of a tree. Seeing my eyes on him, the javelin-wielding Sosias abandoned Adaz and sprinted over to me.

"*Lochagos,* I want to fight!" Sosias declared.

I blinked at him in disbelieving exasperation. "Don't be a fool, boy!" I growled, tearing the javelin from his grasp. "You'll just get underfoot and get a good warrior killed for it!"

But the boy would not be put off. "*Lochagos*, I want to – "

"Obey me, boy!" I exploded. Sosias flinched at the vehemence in my voice. I pressed on. "You want to kill Spartans?" I demanded. The boy nodded, blinking. "Then start bringing rocks to the ramparts and let the warriors do their work."

Crestfallen, Sosias dipped his chin. "Yes, *lochagos.*"

I bent down so that my green eyes were a hand's breadth from his blue ones. "And if I see you where you don't belong, I'll throw you over the wall myself, understand?"

Withering under my glare, Sosias dropped his eyes. "Yes, *lochagos,*" he mumbled.

"Look at me when you speak to me!" I barked. Sosias raised his face and struggled to hold my stare. "Do you understand?" I repeated.

Sosias did not hesitate. "Yes, *lochagos!*" he shouted.

I straightened up and dismissed him with a jerk of my head. Sosias spun on his heels and dashed to the growing pile of rocks being torn up from the foundations of the huts. I had little time to dwell on the matter, for Tibetos had come down from his perch up on the walkway.

"Dammo, you should see this," he said. His voice was hard.

We hurried up to the platform over the main gate to where Basti and Dotos were waiting. We looked down on the plain. A column of Spartans had assembled a bowshot away. The phalanx was six men wide and twice as deep, a battering ram made of men. Evening was falling fast, and the long shadow cast by the phalanx was like a spear-tip pointed at the heart of the fort. Before the front row of overlapping shields stood two lone figures. One was an elite Spartiate by the look of him. His oiled black braids draped over his shoulders and his open-faced helmet bore the horizontal crest of some higher rank. Beside the Spartan was a young man equal in height but not yet filled in with the bulky muscle that only years can build up.

"Hades," I muttered.

The young Thracian Rhoglos looked up at us, his clean-shaven jaw clenched tightly to combat the fear in his eyes that was visible even from our perch atop the fort's ramparts. His arms bore only a few tattoos that the Thracians earned through acts of valour. My guts knotted at the sight.

There were no negotiations. No threats. No final demands for our surrender. Without a word, the Spartan cut the young warrior's throat and threw him to the ground. The Spartiate spun on his heel and walked back to his phalanx, letting the twitching boy's lifeblood pump out onto the trampled ground. The message was clear enough. The Kikones jeered us and threatened the same fate for those in the fort.

"Bastards!" Basti said. "He was my cousin's boy. Always a hothead, but a good lad." He looked at me with tear-rimmed eyes. "I will avenge him," he stated simply and turned his view back to the plain below.

I could see Pausanias atop his horse with the rest of the cavalry. Beside him a trumpeter raised his bronze *salpinx* horn to his lips and blew three long bursts. The signal for battle given, the Spartans locked their shields and began to chant their paean, a sound that chilled the blood of their enemies, for it was the sound of death. At once the five Spartan columns began to converge on the fort.

At the same time, the Spartans' Kikone allies started twirling their slings. We ducked down just as a whizzing stone passed through the space where my head had been an instant earlier. The stones moved so fast that they looked like shadowy streaks against the sky. Some did not react quickly enough. A Thracian on the far side of the fort screamed and clutched at his shattered face before tumbling off the wall.

"The Kikones will whittle us down!" I said.

"Wait," Sabas replied. The Cretan archer crouched beside me, as still as a statue. Without warning, he popped to his feet, his bow stretched to a full draw. The snapping hum of the string had barely ceased when he dropped back down. "One less Kikone," he said, grinning. Even with hundreds of Spartans attacking, the Cretan seemed to be delighting in the chaos. He was truly mad. He slapped me on the shoulder. "Better to move around," he said before scrambling away.

I ventured a quick peek over the top of the wall. The main column of Spartans was marching on the gate, their shields raised high over their heads to ward off missile fire. The Kikones were more exposed, and Tibetos, Sabas, and Nimehe scurried along the raised walkway, keeping their heads down but popping up to loose a stone or arrow at a vulnerable target.

"Are you ready?" I asked Mnasyllus, who was crouching at my side. The big farmer growled his assent and put his hands under the largest stone on the platform. I adjusted my grip on the leather handstrap of the round hoplite shield on my arm. "Now!"

Mnasyllus and I rose up as one. Sling-stones clattered off my shield as I protected Mnasyllus from missile fire. He rose up like Herakles, the boulder raised above his head and I dropped my shield down. With a grunt he hurled the weight earthwards into the Spartans below. The rock crushed a hoplite as though he were made of wet clay rather than bronze and flesh and bone. The man's shattered body hindered those behind him as they clambered through the ditch towards the gate. Mnasyllus bent over and seized another boulder. We repeated our two-man manoeuvre. But for each Spartan who fell, three more stepped over him and soon they pressed up against the gate.

"Let them push!" Basti laughed. As if in response to the Thracian's taunt, the knocking of axes began to reverberate through the wood. Every splintering bite of the iron blades brought the Spartans closer to victory. There would be only one opportunity to beat them back.

"Again!" I said to Mnasyllus, and we continued the bombardment of the Spartans hacking through the gate below.

On the other parts of the wall, knots of Thracians hurled their own rocks at the Spartans below. Shields and armour offered no defense against the destructive weight of the heavy stones. Screams outside the walls and cheers from inside the fort told me the boulders were causing damage. Sosias, panting with effort, shuffled up the stairs cradling as large a stone as he could carry to replenish our rapidly-dwindling supply. With an exhausted grunt, the boy dumped the rock onto the pile.

"They need stones, too," I said, waving towards the others atop the wall. Sosias sucked in a deep breath and gave a vigorous nod before scurrying back down the stairs. Mnasyllus crouched down beside me, his chest heaving like a bellows. As the big man caught his wind, I looked at our remaining rocks. The largest were already gone and those that remained would hardly keep the Spartans at bay for long.

The lack of stones was almost as dire as our meagre number of defenders. Our number dwindled further as another Thracian, hardly more than a youth, fell victim to the Kikones as a perfectly-hurled javelin pierced his throat and sent him falling to the ground below right where the golden-haired Adaz had sought refuge from the battle.

The false prophet stared wide-eyed at the twitching, dying warrior at his feet. But the boy did not flee from the bloody horror before him. As the frenzy of battle raged around me, I watched in fascination as Adaz knelt beside the quivering warrior. The boy reached out and stroked the man's hair. Adaz leaned close to the doomed man's ear, speaking calming words only he could hear. The Thracian's spasms ebbed and he was still. As if sensing my gaze, Adaz looked up and our eyes met. I had called the boy a false prophet, but his sky-blue stare at that moment seemed more than mortal. I looked away.

There was no time to dwell on it. Around me, the muffled staccato of the Spartan axes echoed around the interior of the fort. The thick timber gate quivered under the assault of the hacking blades, the vibrations shaking loose dust that had lain undisturbed for a generation. The Spartans would break through soon. The fear of defeat crept whispered at me with more persistence, held at bay only by the urgency of battle. My eyes fell on the mules.

The animals' ears were flattened against their heads, their eyes rolling in distress. I had an idea, one born of desperation. I told Basti. He glanced at the mules and nodded, his jaw clenched grimly. "Dotos!" he said. "With me!"

The two Thracian veterans ran down the stairs to where the mules were tied. They freed one of the animals and with much coaxing and pulling led the terrified beast up to the platform. Basti took out his axe from the loop on his belt.

"I'm sorry," I said, for I knew Basti loved his animals more than he liked most people.

The Thracian shook his head. "If it saves us, I will sacrifice an ox to Sazabos in thanks. If not, may the Hero forgive me," Basti said before bringing his axe down. The mule stiffened in a violent spasm, nearly toppling us from the platform. The animal's dead weight threatened to pull us down.

"Lift on my signal!" I said, my jaw clenched with the effort. "Now!" As one we heaved. The mule slid up the parapet but could not reach the top. "More!" I said. My muscles burned with the effort. Men strained and cursed but did not yield. Mnasyllus, drawing from his seemingly inexhaustible well of strength, bellowed with a last push.

It was enough. The beast's body teetered atop the parapet. A final, grimacing shove sent it over and crashing down on the Spartans below. The carcass crushed three hoplites, pinning them in a grotesque scene of animal flesh and splayed limbs. The dead animal was a sudden new obstacle between the attackers and the gate. More critically, the mule's bulk had demolished the cohesion of the first few ranks of Spartans. For the moment, they were exposed.

The Thracians on either side of us did not need any command. Javelins previously deemed too precious to waste on well-protected targets now riddled the Spartans below. I shook off my shield and joined Mnasyllus in chucking rocks down. Suddenly, as though appearing out of nothingness, feathered shafts protruded from legs, arms, and necks as Sabas and Nimahe loosed arrow after arrow into the vulnerable enemy below.

Three distant blasts of a *salpinx* rang over the fort. A signal for another push, I thought, and I bolstered myself for the reinvigorated assault that was sure to follow. But I was wrong. The cracking of axes dwindled to a few random blows and then ceased altogether. A strange, sudden calm took over the fort until a cheer rose up from the remaining defenders, for we were all beholding a rare spectacle.

The Spartans were retreating.

CHAPTER 43

"Dammo!" a voice said, waking me. My eyes flicked open and my hand found the reassuring shape of Whisper's hilt.

"Are the Spartans attacking?" I said, hurriedly pushing myself up from the matted furs.

"No," Tibetos said, extending a hand towards me. I grasped it and he pulled me to my feet. "But you told me you wanted me to get you up before dawn broke," he reminded me.

I grunted in response as my wits brushed away the cobwebs of sleep and I recalled what had happened the previous evening. Following their failed assault on the fort, the Spartans had set up a perimeter of bivouacs just out of bowshot. As darkness fell, a ring of campfires marked each link in the chain that bound us.

"Reckon we could break through?" Basti had asked as we peered out from the fort's walls at the spheres of light.

The Spartans had blockaded the front of the fort so tightly that even a dog was unlikely to slip through their lines. "A few good riders, maybe," I said doubtfully. Leaving the rest to be slaughtered, I did not need to add.

"They wouldn't abandon their comrades in any case," Basti said, nodding towards the young Thracian warriors, who had gathered in the centre of the camp, exchanging tales of the battle and boasts of prowess.

"They fought well," I said.

Basti's chest swelled a touch at the praise. "Would you expect any less from your ancestors? Living in the south has made you soft, I think," he said, cocking an eyebrow.

A hint of a smile pushed through my exhaustion. "It *is* colder here than in Athens," I said, and Basti laughed out loud.

"Those southerners have fires," Basti said, waving a hand towards the enemy on the plain."You could join them!" The half-illuminated, half-shadowy shapes of the Spartans could be seen going about their business around the fires. Their low voices carried well across the flat, bare ground, though not so clearly that we could make out their words.

"They'll come at dawn," I said as we contemplated the Spartan fires.

"Or even a surprise attack at night," Basti offered.

I spat over the wall. It was possible, but I had my doubts. There was no rush for them, and they were as exhausted as we were. But the Spartans could be unpredictable. "We'll stand watch in two shifts just in case," I said. Basti growled his assent.

But first there was the matter of resupplying ourselves. We waited for the sound of activity in the Spartan bivouacs to die down before we lifted the locking beams of the gate as quietly as possible. Our shields raised, we slipped outside.

The shadows outside the fort fought back against the weak illumination of the tight line of campfires beyond the gate. Outside the walls, the dead Spartans lay where they had fallen, the contours of their corpses warped and augmented by the odd half-light from the Spartan campfires. The cloying odor of death pricked the nose, though the cool night air held the stench at bay. Crouching low, we picked out way among the dead, salvaging all that we could.

Spears, rocks, shields, and even spent arrows were passed silently along a human chain back to the fort; everything was of value. Our efforts would have gone on longer had it not been for the unfortunate discovery of a still-living Spartan among the dead. The man had passed into unconsciousness but cried out when Stachys wrenched the javelin from his armpit. Alerted to our presence, a cry arose in the Spartan camp and sling-stones began to thump against the shields of the men who had been hiding our activities from view. We had recovered as much as we would that night. There was nothing but to have some men stand watch while the others tried to snatch some sleep and gather some energy for the renewed Spartan assault that was sure to come with daybreak.

That had been half a night ago. I had taken the first shift along with Dotos and a few other Thracians. Tibetos and Basti had relieved us. Exhausted, I was unconscious almost before I had finished stretching out on the hard ground. A warrior should never miss an opportunity to sleep.

Now, pulled back into the waking world, I rolled my head and stretched the stiffness out of my limbs. Every movement revealed a new pain or ache. Slinging Whisper over my back, I surveyed the camp.

Beside a smouldering fire were the contoured mounds of men asleep under their cloaks. A patterned Thracian cloak covered Mnasyllus' great bulk and it swelled and receded with each of his drawn-out, bellows-like breaths. His face, so fearsome in battle, had softened in sleep to an almost childlike innocence that was a truer reflection of his nature. Tibetos and I looked on him silently like parents gazing upon their sleeping baby.

"He hasn't moved since he lay down there," Tibetos noted.

"Let him sleep," I said. "He's earned every moment many times over. He fought with the power and stamina of Herakles." It did not need saying that we would need his strength come morning.

"I'll go wake Sabas," Tibetos said, jerking a thumb towards the other side of the fort. "Get something to eat. I think there's still some stale bread left," he added with a wink before leaving me standing next to the snoring Mnasyllus.

I moved from fire to fire, greeting any of the young Thracians who happened to be awake. They spoke of this action or that from the previous evening's fight, and I praised them for their prowess. Their faces swelled with pride when I told them of the tattoos they had earned for their brave acts and how their comrades would esteem them for their deeds. Their pride and brave words almost hid the fear in their eyes, eyes of young men who only a few summers earlier had been playing with wooden swords and trying to attract the gaze of the girls in their villages. It was the fear of what was to come with the dawn. I only hoped that my words helped bolster their courage.

Little remained of the central hut, its foundation stones having been torn up for boulders to cast down on attacking Spartans, but the hearth still glowed with embers in the centre of what had been the hut's floor. Nimahe slept on her side, her arms wrapped protectively around Adaz, whose golden curls looked even brighter next to the raven-black hair of his adopted mother. I wondered if I had led them both to their deaths.

As I turned away, questioning the decisions that had taken me to that doomed fort on the plains of Thrace, a voice in the darkness stopped me. "*Lochagos*," Sosias said. He sat wrapped in a cloak just outside the dim ring of light cast by the firepit. He extended a hand towards me, an ill-shapen lump clutched in his fingers. "I have some bread," he said.

I accepted the solid chunk and made a show of weighing it in my hand. "Perhaps we should save this for Mnasyllus," I said, frowning.

"Mnasyllus?" Sosias asked.

"To thrown down at the Spartans," I explained. "It's as heavy as a stone!" Sosias laughed, and I sat down beside him. I had hardly settled when he spoke.

"Were you afraid?" he asked. "On the bridge, I mean. When you fought the Spartan."

I turned the lump of bread over in my hands. "Yes," I said. "Yes, I was afraid."

"Then why didn't you just pull down the bridge right away? Why did you have to fight them?"

Why? Children ask harder questions than the philosophizing windbags that gather in the agora. Because of my pride. Because I was a fool. Because I was willing to risk others' lives so that I could harm my enemy. Because I needed to show the Spartans who followed Lysander that hegemon's infallibility was a myth. But I said none of those things, though they were all true. "Sometimes you have to show your enemy that you are not afraid. Sometimes you must make your enemy fear you so that they will hesitate to attack you in the future." That was true enough, too.

"You always fight," Sosias observed shrewdly.

Now it was I who laughed. "So my father always told me!" I said, suddenly recalling my frustrated father's failure to curb my enthusiasm for getting into fights with any boy who called me "slave" or otherwise taunted me for my barbarian looks. I smiled to myself at the memory.

"Was your father a good man?"

"He was strict and intimidating, but he was a good man, yes," I said.

Sosias leaned over to pick up a pebble. "I didn't know my father," he said, flinging the stone into the fire. "I don't even know my real name. Palus's tavern is the only home I've had."

"Was Palus a cruel master?" I asked, recalling the brawny owner of the tavern in Delphi.

Sosias shrugged. "He beat me sometimes," he said. I did not know many slave-boys who escaped thrashings from their masters, or even boys who didn't get a beating from their fathers. I had certainly earned my share of bruises from my father's punishments.

"Did you deserve it?" I asked.

Sosias flashed his mischievous grin. "Mostly," he admitted. He became silent once more. "What will happen today?" he asked quietly. He turned his head and looked up at me. His characteristic bravado could not mask the fear in his eyes, the fear of a young boy who had seen only thirteen or fourteen summers.

I let out a long breath. "The Spartans will attack, and we will fight them."

"Will they win?"

"Perhaps," I said, lying. We had restocked our meagre supply of rocks and projectiles, but they would not hold Pausanias off for long. And then Adaz and those of us who had the audacity to protect him would die. "But we will fight them, nevertheless."

"But you can't lose!" Sosias protested.

"Everyone wins until they lose. That is the nature of war," I said.

"That is not what Telekles said," Sosias persisted.

I gave the boy a hard stare. "Telekles?"

"He told me that you never lose! He told me that you always find a way!"

My chest tightened at my fallen comrade's words of faith, even if they were just to reassure a frightened boy. I mustered a semblance of confidence that I did not feel. "Then we will test his words today, will we not?"

"Yes, *lochagos*!" Sosias said with a spark that had been absent a moment earlier.

"But you must promise me something," I said.

"Anything, *lochagos*!"

"Should Telekles' words prove wrong, you must deny us. Tell the Spartans that you are a slave. Tell them that you are glad we are dead. Tell them you will serve them."

"I want to fight and die with you, *lochagos*!" Sosias started.

"No!" I said sharply. Sosias flinched at the vehemence in my tone. "No," I repeated less harshly. "You will obey me in this, boy. You will surrender and when you have the chance, you will escape. Make your way to Athens and seek out Thrasybulus, son of Lykos. Tell him your story and that I asked him to take you in."

"I can fight," Sosias objected, but more weakly.

I smiled. "I know, boy. But not today. If I fall today, do I as command and go to Thrasybulus. Do you understand?"

Sosias hung his head. "Yes, *lochagos*."

I was about to rise, but I did not wish to part with him on such terms. Perhaps to give him a thread of hope, or perhaps to bolster my own flagging courage, I wanted to leave us with something to live for, unlikely as that seemed to be. "But if I survive this day −" I started.

Sosias lifted his head and looked at me expectantly. "Yes, *lochagos*?"

"If I survive this day, you will come back with me to Athens," I said.

The boy's eyes grew wide. "Truly, *lochagos*?"

I nodded. "You will be one of the *peripoli*," I said.

Suddenly, Sosias embraced me. I tensed at first, caught off guard by the gesture. But I put my hand on his back. I thought of my son, Nikodromos, to whom I was little more than a fearsome stranger and whom I was unlikely to lay eyes on again on this side of the Underworld. And I thought of something else I could give the slave-boy from Delphi.

We separated and I put my hand on the boy's shoulder. "And you will be more than a *peripoli*. You will be Sosias, son of Daimon," I said. "Or by a name other than Sosias, if you wish."

Sosias blinked at me in disbelief. His mouth was tight with emotion. "I will be one of the bravest *peripoli*!" he declared earnestly. "I will make you proud, *lochagos*!"

I turned my face toward the sky. "Dawn is coming," I said, handing the hard bread back to him. "Share this with Adaz. We will talk later." I rose to my feet.

"Thank you, *Father*," Sosias said, trying out the unfamiliar word.

"Remember your promise," I said. Sosias nodded.

I left him to contemplate his new status, wondering if it had been cruel to grant him a dream that was doomed to remain just that. I had little time to mull over my promise to Sosias, as a shadowy figure awaited me just beyond the edge of the hut. The familiar silhouette fell in step with me as I strode towards the main gate.

"You heard?" I asked the figure.

"You're a good man, despite what everyone says," Tibetos said. I could almost hear his lopsided grin in the darkness.

"And what do they say?" I replied

"That you're a mean-hearted bastard who eats children for lunch."

"Only those that annoy me," I said, and Tibetos laughed. "But I'll gladly eat those Spartans raw. Let's see what the turd-sniffers are up to," I said, slapping my oldest friend on the back.

We joined Basti and Dotos atop the wall. With the hint of approaching day came the first tentative warbling calls of songbirds on the plain, unconcerned with coming battle in their midst. As the sky brightened further, the birds' shrill songs were joined by a steady percussion emanating from the mist covering the Spartan camp.

"What are they doing?" Basti asked as the distant *tock-tock* of banging axes continued.

"It sounds like they're cutting down a tree," Tibetos said.

Basti snorted. "There isn't a tree for miles!" he said, sweeping his arm towards the horizon.

The rising sun burned off the mist, revealing what the Spartans had been up to with their axes. "They made battering rams," Tibetos said. From our vantage point, we gazed at the Spartans' siege weapons in grim silence. The crowns and branches had been cut from two pine trees, save for the bases of some branches that were left as hand-grips. The bottoms of the trunks had been chipped away to form cones so as to better concentrate the force of the impact.

"Where did they get them?" Basti said in amazement. I pointed to the dark line to the north that marked the edge of the distant Thracian forest. Basti scoffed. "It would have taken dozens of men all night to drag that here!" he said in disbelief.

"Never underestimate the stubbornness of Spartans," I said.

"What can we do?" Dotos asked.

I turned to the west, looking for a hope that was dissipating as rapidly as the morning mist. "Hold out as long as we can," I said.

CHAPTER 44

Those who were not awake were hurriedly roused from their slumber. Mnasyllus rose from under his cloak and shuffled off to relieve himself against the wall of the fort. Rolling his head on a neck mostly hidden by muscle, he lumbered back to his fire, taking a moment to drain a skin of *rappa* before strapping on his leather cuirass and picking up his oversized sword. "When can we start killing more Spartans?" he asked.

As if they had heard his challenge, the Spartans sounded their *salpinx*. Two short blasts of the war-horn signalled the start of the attack. The droning chant of the Spartan paean began.

"They're coming!" Dotos shouted down from atop the gate. I bounded up the steps to see for myself and hazarded a quick look over the parapet. What I saw caused the chill of fear to ripple through my bones.

Only the conical tip of the ram was visible, for the rest of the trunk lay concealed in the mass of men hefting the mighty tool of destruction. The central ranks of ram-bearers were protected by the next rank out, whose shield overlapped above the ram as tightly as the plates on a tortoise's back. Two more outer lines covered the flanks of the inner ones, leaving little exposed to missile fire. The assault the previous evening had been hasty and the Spartans had suffered for their rash arrogance. They would not commit the same error again.

Mnasyllus was already beside me. I glanced at the pitiful collection of boulders that we had salvaged. It would not be enough.

Mnasyllus picked up the largest one left and signalled his readiness with a glance.

"Now!" I said.

I raised the shield, sheltering Mnasyllus for as long as possible before pulling the shield away to let him hurl the rock at the Spartans below. The weight hurtled downwards with the same devastating result as the previous day, for no shield could withstand such force. As Mnasyllus bent to grab another rock, I peered down from behind my shield to assess the damage.

It had done little. Another Spartan had already thrown down his own shield and taken the place of his fallen comrade beside the ram. Other soldiers had run forward and were hauling the mule carcass and the corpses of their dead away from the gate, clearing the path for the ram even as Mnasyllus threw down more stones. All the while, the paean continued, the chant growing more insistent as the scent of victory inflamed the Spartans' thirst for vengeance against their tormentors in the fort.

"Last one," Mnasyllus said, picking up the final stone. It was hardly larger than an infant's head and unlikely to break through the shields, even with Mnasyllus' strength behind it. Suddenly the wall trembled beneath our feet. The Spartans had reached the gate.

The timber doors shook under a second impact from the ram. The Spartans swung the trunk back and drove it forward again. With each blow the Spartans shouted in unison, as if they were trying to shatter the gate with the power of their chant alone. Mnasyllus hurled down the last rock.

There was nothing left to do atop the gate tower. "We must go down!" I shouted, seizing a spear. Mnasyllus growled his agreement and we abandoned our perch to join the chaotic last stand unfolding beneath our feet.

My *peripoli* companions and the Thracians crowded up against the gate, pushing into the wood with shoulders and shields, but they bounced off the surface with the shock of each jarring impact of the Spartan ram on the opposite side. The crossbars jumped in their iron fittings but held firm. Mnasyllus and I threw ourselves into the mass of defenders.

I pressed my shield into Basti's back as the Thracian captain roared in defiance at his unseen adversaries. Blow after blow rattled my bones. And still the ancient wood resisted the Spartans' efforts. Until it didn't.

In a splintery explosion, the head of the ram burst through a plank. The Spartans pulled it back for another strike at the weakened area, leaving a gaping hole through which we could glimpse the grim faces of the besiegers.

Something hissed past my ear. I glanced back to see Nimahe and Sabas, their bows drawn. Nimihe's bowstring snapped forward and another arrow flew through the jagged rent in the gate, followed in rapid succession by a shot from Sabas. I turned and pressed forward with renewed vigour.

But the Spartan strategy was proving its worth. Now, each impact of the tree trunk widened the splintery gap in the gate. Then, with a mournful crack, the crossbeam finally succumbed to the repeated blows of the ram. The square beam bent inwards, ripping the iron fittings from their moorings. The two halves collapsed and fell to the earth with a jangling thud.

Now the Spartans hacked and pulled at the shattered wood, tearing away great pieces. Whole planks vanished and suddenly the gate was little more than splintered remnants on either side of the entrance with Lambda-emblazoned Spartan shields spanning the ragged gap. The true battle began.

There was no order, not even the controlled chaos of a phalanx line. From opposite sides of the shattered gate, the Thracians and Spartans shoving in the front ranks screamed curses at each other while spear tips darted back and forth over their heads like serpents' tongues, probing for any patch of exposed flesh. My head jerked to once side as a spear thrust glanced off my salvaged Spartan helmet. Without thinking, I returned the blow at the enemy across the gate. Grace and skill were subsumed by power and endurance. My arm churned in an endless series of spear thrusts, like the drills I had practiced as a youth. Beside me, Mnasyllus' *kopis* rose and fell like a woodsman's axe, its edge driving through wood and metal and bone.

"Daimon!" Stachys shouted. "They're breaching the western wall!"

I spun to see a gaping hole where the second ram had battered through the repaired section of the wall. "Hades!" I growled. A Spartan was already pushing his way through the narrow gap. The

Thracian warriors there stabbed desperately at the intruder with their spears and only after many blows had deflected off the Spartan's armour did they manage to take him down, but a second Spartan was already stepping over the body of his comrade, slashing wildly at the sparse defenders. Sabas took the man down with an arrow through the gullet, and the Spartan's corpse added to the obstacle impeding the soldiers behind him. But the breach had to be plugged before more Spartans came pouring through.

"Mnasyllus!" I yelled, pulling at the collar of the big man's cuirass. Mnasyllus drove his *kopis* down into the mass of Spartans at the gate one more time before casting a glance over his shoulder. Spotting the intruders, he needed no convincing and extracted himself from the melee at the gate, bounding towards the new threat with Stachys at his heels.

"Basti! Can you hold the gate?" I shouted.

"Go!" the Thracian yelled before thrusting his spear into the face of a Spartan tearing at his neighbour's shield.

I sprinted to join Stachys and Mnasyllus just as Mnasyllus clove through a Spartan invader at the collarbone. Stachys grunted as a Spartan spear point pierced his shoulder and he stumbled back. I pushed past him to fill the breach at Mnasyllus' side. "Lock!" I shouted and the edge of the big man's shield slid behind mine like scales on a snake's back. Together our two shields just spanned the gap in the wall.

A familiar voice came from behind me. "I've got you, Dammo!" Tibetos grunted, and I felt the dome of my friend's shield pressing into my shoulder blades. The wounded Stachys joined him and together the four of us stood against a sea of Spartans trying to flood into the fort's interior.

We were beaten. One more push by the Spartans and we were done for. We were not even fighting back anymore. We just dug our shoulders into our shields and pushed with all our strength. My boots began the inevitable slide backwards against the unstoppable force of fifty or more Spartans outside the wall. But then, inexplicably, we were holding our ground.

Outside the fort, almost lost in the cries and clamour of battle, a Spartan trumpet sounded. Again and again the trumpeter blew his *salpinx*, the peals of the bronze war-horn growing increasingly desperate.

Suddenly, we were moving forward again. Soon, the side of my shield knocked against the edge of the wall. I stabbed blindly over the sword- and axe-bitten edge of my shield but found only air. Confused, I peeked over the notched shield rim only to see the Spartans scrambling out of the far side of the outer ditch. I turned back towards the struggle for the gate.

The tide of Spartans assaulting the gate had begun to ebb, drawn away by the *salpinx*'s call. Soon they had retreated completely, and only spears of blinding morning light stabbed through the shattered, tottering remains of the fort's gate. The rhythmic drumming of axes echoing around us let up until it died away in a few last defiant hacks.

The exhausted defenders, facing certain annihilation only a moment earlier, looked at each other in stunned confusion. Mnasyllus, a mess of dirt and sweat and bloody cuts, spoke for all those present. "Where in Hades did they go?" he gasped between heaving breaths. Tibetos grinned at me.

A new energy surged within me. I flew up the stairs to the ramparts to confirm what I already knew. I ventured a peek over the top of the wall, careful not to get picked off by a Kikone slinger, but my fears were baseless, for the Spartans' Kikone allies had forsaken them and were fleeing to the east. The sight of Kikone backs filled my heart with joy, but not as much as the greater sight that greeted me.

In the plain below, beyond the carnage left by their attack on the fort, the remaining Spartans were hastening to form a phalanx, but with a scrambling sense of disorder that was unbecoming of their reputation as the most disciplined soldiers in the world. Then I saw the source of their distress.

In the west, a wall of dust was rolling across the plain towards us like some great wave. A low rumble of thunder heralded its arrival, its power causing the stone under my hand to vibrate. I whooped for joy, a call taken up one by one by my fellow defenders as they joined me on the ramparts.

It was Thracian horsemen. Hundreds of them. Our messenger had succeeded.

Zyraxes had arrived.

CHAPTER 45

Zyraxes himself led the charge, screaming from behind an ornate golden helmet with a towering white crest, his spear held out in front of him. Behind him galloped a baying horde of warriors, many clad in bronze like Greek cavalrymen but many more bareheaded with only leather armour or even no armour at all.

Just as a mother can pick out her own child amidst the throngs in the agora on a festival day, I saw her. Amidst the swarming pack of Thracian riders, Meli's small size marked her out, yet her wiry, diminutive frame and wild, unruly flaming hair somehow gave her a more fearsome aspect. For a moment I was held in thrall by a combination of awe and concern as I gazed down at her. Then I lost sight of her and she was gone, just another among many.

The Thracians sang their war-cries in praise of Pleistor, the Thracian name of Ares. Their song was not the disciplined paean of the Spartans but keening, ancient howls imbued with untamed magic from an earlier age. And now the power of that primal fury was unleashed on the hapless Spartans.

The prince's cavalry parted and flowed around the island of Spartan warriors like rapids breaking around a boulder. Their javelins, augmented by the momentum of the riders that hurled them, lanced into the massed hoplites to the cheers of those watching from the fort. Despite their force, many of the missiles deflected off of metal-faced shields and bronze helmets. Yet not a few punched through breastplates or exposed Spartan faces, and gaps appeared in the phalanx where the men fell.

But where most men might have broken and fled, the Spartans held. Zyraxes' force wheeled around for another pass. A sizable number of Thracians had separated from the main group to run down the fleeing Kikones and scattered Spartan cavalry. As the remaining group of horses began their second charge, a Spartan captain barked a command and the hard-pressed army of Pausanias launched its own javelins. The Spartan volley arced through the air and fell amidst Zyraxes' warriors, mauling the Thracian charge.

Suddenly I feared for my sister. "To Zyraxes!" I called out. "To Zyraxes!"

But there was no need. The survivors of the fort, eager to revenge themselves upon their Spartan tormentors, were forcing open the shattered gate. Dotos and the five remaining Thracians leapt to the backs of whatever horse was nearest and hurried to join their fellows out on the plain. I unhitched the fine grey stallion and pulled myself up to its back, surveying the scene around me.

Mnasyllus and Stachys, preferring to fight from the ground, tore two massive *aspis* shields from Spartan corpses and disappeared through the open gate. Sabas, his arrows spent, ran up to the ramparts with his sling. Tibetos, with a tip of his head my way, hurried after the Cretan.

Not everyone had left. At the mass of Spartan and Thracian dead at the gate, Nimahe knelt on the ground with Sosias and Adaz standing behind her. The bloodied body of Basti lay before her, his head on her lap. The Skythian stroked his matted hair and sang softly to her husband in her own tongue. Adaz stepped close to Nimahe and put a gentle hand on the horsewoman's shoulder.

Sosias, sensing my gaze, turned his hard, blue eyes my way

I pointed my rhomphaia at him. "Stay!" I commanded simply before kicking my heels into the stallion's flanks and riding out onto the plain.

The Spartans had drawn themselves up into a solid ring of impenetrable metal and wood. Their *aspis* shields locked as tightly as planks of a trireme's hull, with the inner ranks angling their raised shields so as to deflect any incoming missiles. The formation bristled with spear-points. The Thracian cavalry circled the phalanx warily, frustrated by the Spartan defenses.

In his golden helmet, Zyraxes was easy to find. Relief filled my heart as I saw Meli beside him. She was flanked by the two female warriors the prince had tasked with protecting her. She spotted me approaching before Zyraxes did. Grinning, they raised their hands in greeting.

"Brother!" Zyraxes said joyfully. He gestured at the shattered fort. "We arrived none too soon, I see."

I leaned over from my horse and clasped his outstretched hand. "It was a close thing," I said gratefully. I turned my eyes towards Meli. "And I am happy to see you, Sister, though I did not know you had become a *hurisa*," I said, using the Thracian title for a female warrior.

The two female fighters on either side of my sister exchanged a sceptical glance, and Meli's mouth curled in a wry smile. "Thruna and Ullana made sure I did not fall off my horse," she said, stroking the side of her mount's neck. Her green eyes returned to me. "But I knew you would call, Dammo. I knew you would need me." I bowed my head in wordless gratitude and regarded her more carefully.

She had changed. Raised skin intensified the effect of the fresh tattoo on her face, a coiled serpent around her left eye whose tail extended down her neck and disappeared under the collar of her tunic. In her Thracian cloak and leggings, there was nothing to betray the fact that she was a child of Athens and not born of the people with whom she now rode. More than anything, it was familiar green *zeira* cloak draped over her shoulders that drew my eye. The meaning of the various beasts and symbols was beyond my ken, but I knew the previous owner well enough.

"And Zia?" I asked, lifting a corner of the cloak.

Meli sniffed. "She tried to steal my power and failed," she said simply. Zyraxes, listening to the exchange, looked uncomfortable in my sister's presence, even a touch fearful, and I wondered who was truly in charge of this expedition.

I changed the topic to more immediate matters. "And what about them?" I asked, looking towards the embattled Spartans.

The prince looked relieved. "We will await their surrender. Where else can they go?" he asked, sweeping his arm across the barren plain.

Zyraxes' Thracians were still circling the Spartan formation, hurling taunts and insults but little else. Some warriors had dismounted to better use their slings and javelins. They darted in close and back, probing for exposed flesh but finding little. It was like a pack of hounds tormenting a trapped but still very dangerous boar. I let go a slow breath. My blood was still hot with the rage of battle, but I could not fault his reasoning. Attacking the Spartans would claim the lives of many warriors that Zyraxes could ill-afford to lose.

"It is the right decision," I conceded.

I had little time to consider the matter, for Mnasyllus had come running over to where Zyraxes and I sat atop our horses. The big warrior's face was filled with some urgency. "Daimon!" the panting Mnasyllus said, pointing towards the fort. I followed the line of his finger and cursed at what I saw.

"Sosias!" I yelled, but my voice was lost among the those of the shouting Thracian warriors.

The boy had disobeyed my order to stay in the fort. He had taken a roan mare and was now riding to join the Thracians circling the trapped Spartans. He held Telekles' sword aloft. His small frame made the weapon seem as enormous as the huge blade wielded by Mnasyllus. Sosias screamed his high-pitched war-cry.

After many battles, there is little to remember. The screaming faces of the men you hack or stab or bludgeon to death are little more than a haze, like a drunken memory. Their whimpering as they try to hold in their guts fades and their last crying words to their faraway mothers evaporate like mist from your mind. And this absence of memory is a blessing from the gods, for without memory of them, their shades cannot haunt your dreams.

But other times it is not so. On the contrary, some deaths are always present, ready to come back in an instant with the lightest touch on the pool of memory. The smell of a man's breath in your face as you drive a spear through his belly. Every word and inflection of a dying man's last curse. The ruined corpse of a youth trampled flat after falling under the crush the feet of his own advancing comrades. They are there in your mind during every waking hour, sometimes in the shadows but never completely gone.

What happened next is one such memory for me. Even so many years later, though my sight is failing, I see it with vivid clarity in mind's eye.

From my vantage point I saw it all. My sight drifted from Sosias to the Spartan phalanx. The blue and white striped crest of

Pausanias drew my gaze. The Spartan king was craning his neck in a risky effort to see something. I followed his line of sight to Sosias, who galloped ever closer to the trapped Spartans. The three of us, Sosias, Pausanias, and I, were three points on a triangle, separated by space but all parts of the same whole.

The king pointed his sword towards Sosias. He shouted furiously, jabbing his weapon in the direction of the boy on his horse. My heart lurched. I could not hear the words, but I knew what Pausanias was saying.

"No! It is not him! He is not the prophet!" I screamed at the Spartans, but it was in vain. I kicked my horse into action to head the boy off. "Sosias!"

But I was too late. At the king's command, a group of ten Spartans broke from the phalanx and sprinted towards Sosias and his horse. The Thracians, caught unawares by the sudden development, reacted slowly, allowing the long-haired Spartans to cut the distance between them and the boy. They would not be able to reach him. The leader of the Spartans shouted a command. As one the Spartans drew back whatever spears or javelins they had and launched them into the air. The iron-tipped shafts arced towards Sosias, who was almost beyond the missiles' range. But not quite.

Some of the javelins fell short. Most buried themselves deep in the chest and neck of Sosias' roan. One hit its mark. It was enough.

Sosias tumbled from his mount and out of sight. I spurred my horse to where he had disappeared. Too late, Zyraxes' Thracians fell upon the isolated Spartans, but it was not my battle.

Sosias lay on the stony ground, a tiny shape among all the stamping horses and armoured warriors. I slid off my horse and ran to him. I knelt beside his crumpled form.

The boy was on his side. The javelin had taken him under the ribs and protruded from his back. I thought he was dead, but then he coughed weakly. Gently I lifted him up so that he was cradled in my arms. His wet eyes were open wide with fear.

"*Lochagos!*" he rasped. "I am sorry!"

I shook my head. "No! You are a brave warrior!" I said through my tears. "You are one of us! One of the *peripoli!*"

The corner of Sosias' mouth twitched into his lopsided grin. He tried to say something more, but no words came. Sosias' face slackened and his sky-blue eyes dulled as his shade left him. With a moan, I pulled him close and held his slight, limp frame tightly to my chest.

There, on the plains of Thrace, in the sight of gods and men, I wept.

CHAPTER 46

My cries shook the heavens. How long I held the boy to my chest I cannot recall.

A voice broke through my sorrow. "Daimon," someone said. "Daimon, come. The boy will be seen to." It was Zyraxes. The sorrow in his face mirrored my own. I stood, unsteady in my grief, and he embraced me like a brother. He was a good man. When we parted, he spoke again. "Come with me."

The Thracian prince led me to a knot of people. Most were familiar to me; Tibetos and the other *peripoli* as well as my sister were there, along with some of Zyraxes' warriors. One face instantly provoked my hostility.

"We captured one of them," Zyraxes said coldly, regarding the Spartan prisoner. "Tibetos knocked him cold with his sling. The others are dead."

The Spartan was held fast by two large Thracians, but he did not struggle. His long, black braids marked him as a true Spartiate, one of the elite warriors of that land. Numerous healed scars on his arms and face attested to a lifetime of battle and war. He sneered at us.

"He is yours," Zyraxes said to me in Greek so that the Spartan could understand. The captive scoffed, though he must have felt fear. The Thracians' reputation for cruelty towards captured enemies was well earned. My father, however, had taught me from childhood that such acts showed weakness rather than strength, and the legacy of those lessons still restrained the worst parts of my nature even many years later.

"I will kill you quickly Spartan," I said. "It is more than you deserve."

The Spartan's broken lips parted to reveal a bloody smile. "Deserve? I have done my duty, that is all," he said.

"To murder a child?" I asked in disgust.

"Was he your whelp?" the Spartan retorted.

Was he? The thought flashed through my mind. But I heard myself saying otherwise. "No."

The Spartan smirked. "Then it is no great thing! Why do you cry like a woman over him? Why do you weep for a worthless barbarian pup? Go to the slave market and buy another boy. They are cheap here!" He laughed at this.

Since I left Athens, I had not succumbed to rage. I had harnessed the icy anger of battle and turned it against Lysander. But such anger is a warrior's tool against his enemies and his own fear. It is controlled and focused, as a bow concentrates its power into an arrowhead. What the Spartan provoked in me was something altogether different. Hitherto restrained emotions snapped the chains that had bound them. Frustration at my powerlessness before the gods and Fates. Resentment at powerful men like Lysander and Thrasybulus, for whom I was but an obstacle to be overcome or a weapon to be wielded. My grief for Sosias, whose body was already succumbing to the chill of death. And the hate I felt for myself at leading the boy to his end. The desire for vengeance was elemental. The Furies screamed their poisoned commands in my ears. And I obeyed.

With a roar, I launched myself at the Spartan. My shoulder crashed into his abdomen, driving him out of the grasp of the two surprised Thracians tasked with guarding him. My arms wrapped around Spartan's torso, and I lifted him off his feet and slammed him into the hard ground in full view of his comrades on the plain.

The Spartan, his eyes wide, lay on his back gasping for breath as I loomed over him. I grabbed his braided black locks and yanked him viciously back to his feet only to drive the top of my forehead into his face, crushing his nose in a spurt of blood. He fell hard, sprawling onto his back in a daze, but I was on top of him in a heartbeat. Instinctively the Spartan's bloody hands came up from his face to ward off the next attack, but my fists fell like hammer blows. I pummelled the Spartan to unconsciousness, but my fury was not yet spent. His face shattered beneath the onslaught of punches, but still I continued, screaming like one of the Furies themselves. Shards and splinters of bone and teeth sliced my knuckles and drops of red pattered my front like rain. But even then, consumed by my rage, I did not stop destroying what was no longer recognizable as human. Only when strong arms seized me from behind and hauled me away did the dead Spartan escape my wrath.

I was bound fast, but still I wrestled to break free. Somebody called my name, as if from a distance. I thought it was my father, calling me from the Underworld, commanding me and imploring me to stop in equal measure. The voice drew closer and my resistance waned. At last it was right beside me, speaking in my ear.

"Daimon," a familar voice said. "There is no honour in this." I ceased struggling. The arms loosened their grip on me and I was free. I turned to see who had torn me away, who has rescued me from my madness. It was not my father. It was Mnasyllus.

I looked about at those around me, hardened warriors who nevertheless could not completely conceal their shock aroused by the viciousness of my assault on the Spartan. When my maddened eyes fell on Meli, for once she yielded before me and turned her gaze downward.

My hands were still trembling. I took three steps towards the Spartans cowering behind their shields on the plain. They had witnessed my wrath and done nothing. The sticky blood of their comrade dripped from my hands and speckled my chest and face for all of them to see. No one moved. I spat at them in contempt. An unnatural silence had taken hold of the battlefield.

Then, from the centre of the phalanx, a spear poked skyward, a scrap of canvas skewered on the point.

Pausanias wanted to negotiate.

THE PARLEY TOOK PLACE WITHOUT CEREMONY under the hard stares of a ring of Thracian warriors. I stood at Zyraxes' side as Pausanias made his appeal. I glared at the Spartan king.

"There is no need to fight, Prince Zyraxes," Pausanias said, ignoring me. "I have no quarrel with you or your father, King Medokos. The reason for my being here no longer exists." The king's tone was steady and measured despite the hostile rumbling coming from his Thracian audience.

I did more than rumble. "You will be wiped out," I said through gritted teeth "Your corpses will feed the crows and your bones will be scattered on this plain forever." I took a threatening step towards the king, my hand reaching for my sword.

The two Spartans flanking the king drew their swords and moved to intercept me. Pausanias raised a hand and the long-haired Spartans froze, their eyes locked on me. The Thracians erupted into angry shouts and not a few weapons came out. A breath away from death, the Spartan king seemed unfazed. He glanced at me, his eyes narrowing. A flick of his hand caused his men to step back and re-sheathe their blades. Their discipline was impressive.

The king could no longer afford to dismiss me. "You can cut me down where I stand, Athenian. The prince," he said with a nod towards Zyraxes, "could kill all of my men. But at what cost? My Spartans will fight to the last man. How many Thracians will die when there is no need?" The Thracian prince's grim silence gave Pausanias the space to push his argument more deeply. "My ships await us at Ainos. When we do not return and it is learned that Prince Zyraxes of Thrace has killed a Spartan king, then King Medokos will find himself at war with all of Sparta. We will aid the Makedonians to your west and Seuthes to your east. It will be the end of your dynasty and will bring suffering to your people," the king finished. He tipped his chin upwards and regarded Zyraxes with kingly hauteur.

The Furies goaded me. Begged me. Ordered me to do it. A step and a sword-thrust. It would have been an easy thing to avenge Sosias. The serpent-haired spirits of vengeance shrieked at me. Every fibre of my soul wished to appease them, but I resisted. For the truth of Pausanias' words rang more loudly within me.

Even if we slaughtered the Spartans on the plain to a man with not a single warrior wounded among us, the price would be high for Thrace. Zyraxes was like a brother to me, yet he had responsibilities to his kingdom that outweighed my personal desire for vengeance. Even so, I could see him struggling with the decision. He glanced my way. With great reluctance, I took a slow step backwards. My hand fell away from the handle of my sword. The Furies' screams of betrayal echoed in my mind. But they had lost their battle. Pausanias would go free. I nodded to Zyraxes.

His burden gone, Zyraxes was free to do what was necessary. "Pausanias of Sparta," he proclaimed in his accented Greek. "You will take your surviving men and leave this place. Should I find you within the borders of Thrace tomorrow, you will not enjoy my mercy a second time." The words stabbed at me, but I held my tongue.

A flicker of relief passed over the king's face. "It will be done," Pausanias replied, perhaps with slightly too much eagerness. How could he not agree? If Lysander's prophet was dead, as he believed, then he had salvaged a victory in his own eyes. The lives of a few hundred men was a small price to pay to thwart the ambitions of his rival Lysander. The king turned to leave.

But Zyraxes had not finished. "Your men," the prince said. Pausanias looked at the taller Thracian royal uncertainly. Zyraxes smiled coldly. "I cannot allow armed soldiers to cross these lands."

Pausanias frowned. "I do not understand."

"Your weapons and armour," Zyraxes said. "You will leave them."

A crack appeared in the Spartan king's composure. "You ask too much!" he hissed.

"Swords!" Zyraxes barked in Thracian. Scarcely had the word left his tongue when blades appeared in the hands of the Thracian warriors ringing the negotiations. Another word from Zyraxes would send the king of Sparta to his death. My own weapon remained sheathed.

Pausanias wavered. The rage of a trapped animal burned in his eyes. For a moment I thought he would sacrifice his army for the sake of honour. But his shoulders sank as his resolve abandoned him. The Spartan king lacked the spine of his royal ancestors. "You will pay for this!" was all he could say.

"I will take that as your acceptance of my conditions," Zyraxes said. He gave a small wave of his hand and his warriors put away their weapons.

Pausanias, seething, pivoted and strode back towards his ravaged army to deliver Zyraxes' terms. The Thracians parted and let him and his men pass.

Yet among those gathered on the plain, no one understood the Spartan king's frustration better than I. Like him, I had achieved the goal of my mission: Lysander was diminished and the boy Adaz was safe. But also like the king, the price of victory had cost me dearly. Telekles. Basti. And Sosias.

It had been a great drama for the gods.

I hate them.

A BED OF SMOKING ASH AND HISSING, POPPING EMBERS was all that remained of the funeral pyres we had built for Sosias and Telekles. The blazing flames that had leapt and danced under the dome of night were no more, their glory already fading to memory as the sun-god reclaimed his domain in the brightening eastern sky.

Tibetos sat beside me, as silent and solid as his nickname, Stone. On my other side was Meli, who leaned against my shoulder. The two of them had stayed with me the entire night, keeping vigil as the boy's shade crossed to the Underworld.

A question had been bothering me. Only now, when my anger and grief had been exhausted, did I dare utter it aloud. "Did you know he would die, Meli?" I asked. The words hung in the air like the smoke from the smouldering pyre. The gentle pressure on my shoulder vanished as Meli straightened up. I turned my head to look at her.

My sister's green eyes peered into mine. "No," she said. "I didn't know. I only knew that if he didn't go with you, you would fail." I believed her. But the hidden consequences of her vision had struck deep.

"Perhaps it would have been better to have failed," I said.

"The Fates would not allow it," she said. "All things are already written." She looked back towards the ash pile. There was nothing I could say, and the three of us returned to our own meditations.

The neighing of horses in the distance made us turn. "Look!" Tibetos said, pointing towards the fort.

Two riders had appeared and were drawing closer. One was a child, the other not much larger in stature. "It's Nimahe," I said.

At first glance, the Skythian horse-woman seemed dressed for war. The deadly recurved bow peeked out from its pouch draped beside her brightly-patterned leggings. From a loop on her silver-plated belt hung her war axe and across her chest were strapped a pair of daggers. The two bulging saddle-bags suspended on either side of her horse's neck told another story. She was going on a journey. She was going home to her people far to the north.

The second animal, a dappled grey pony, bore Adaz. A fox-leather Thracian hat hid the boy's golden hair, and he was wrapped in Basti's patterned cloak. Upon seeing us, the boy gave a small wave. Despite everything, his kind nature persisted. I could not help but wave back. The Pythia had said the boy was a false son of Apollo, but now I was not so certain. I wondered if the god had sacrificed Sosias to protect his own son.

Nimahe's hard black eyes stayed on me as their mounts trotted past. I gave a small dip of my chin, but the Skythian's only acknowledgement was to spur her mount to a canter. Adaz flashed a final dazzling smile before his own pony carried him past us, every hoof-beat taking the boy further away from those who sought to harm him.

"She will take care of him," Meli said as the riders grew smaller on the horizon.

"She will be a hard teacher," I said.

"But she will raise him with love," Meli said. "Like Father and Neleus did for you."

I did not deny the truth of her words. I gazed southward. Towards Athens. Towards home. "I want to leave this place. It is time to go."

I turned to head back to the ruins of the fort, but Meli had not moved. "I am staying here, Dammo," she said quietly. "I have much to learn here. When I am done, when I am myself again, I will return to Athens."

Her declaration should have struck me like a blow, but in truth I had known since I saw the swirling ink tattoos on her face and arms. My sister, a girl of Athens but never fully Athenian, had found her home.

But what Meli did next astounded me. She turned to Tibetos, who was looking at her with quiet intensity. She extended her arm and touched his cheek. "Will you wait for me, Tibetos?" she asked. I blinked in astonishment, not understanding what I was witnessing.

Tibetos held her hand to his cheek and closed his eyes. When he opened them again, he said, "I have waited for you my whole life,

Melitta. I can wait a little longer." My sister's green eyes were ringed with red as she fell into my friend's arms.

With plodding slowness the significance of what had just happened solidified in my consciousness. The two of them separated and still holding hands turned to face me. "I never knew," I said, shaking my head.

"We are often blind to the feelings of those nearest to us," my sister said, casting an affectionate glance at Tibetos. "As I have been."

Tibetos looked at me sheepishly. "I'm sorry I didn't tell you, Dammo. Are you angry?"

I frowned. "There is nothing to be angry about!" I said, putting a hand on my friend's shoulder. Meli, who had gone to the Underworld and returned a broken shadow of her former self, was healed, even if I was not. "You have helped make my sister whole again, Tibo. That is a great thing."

A shadow of sadness crossed Meli's face. "And you, Brother?" she asked, casting my comment back at me. "Are you whole?" The question struck me like an arrow. The Pythia had asked me as much. I looked back towards the south.

"Not yet," I said.

PART FOUR
DEMONS ΔΑΙΜΟΝΕΣ

CHAPTER 47

The town of Delphi had an air of sleepiness about it. Gone were the crowds and the constant din of the vendors hawking their trinkets and black chickens. The settlement around the temple seemed to be taking a collective breath before the world's hopeful converged on the sanctuary for the next consultation in twenty days' time.

The last trace of dusk clung to horizon and the sounds of life were fading with the day. Despite the darkness, my hood was pulled up. The accusations against me still lingered in people's memories, and it would not do to be recognized.

I moved through the laneways with deliberate purpose, for my destination was known to me and I was expected. At the far eastern edge of the town, I stopped before the familiar walls of the Pythia's residence.

"I am here to see Zelarchus," I told the lone guard. "I am Daimon." The guard narrowed his eyes but did not challenge me, and I was admitted to the inner courtyard. The head priest, garbed in the red robes of his office, awaited me.

"Daimon of Athens," Zelarchus greeted me. "Your return to Delphi is welcome." His tone, though not warm, lacked its characteristic hostile edge.

I suffered formality poorly at the best of times. I was in no mood for it now. "The deed is done," I said. "There will be no prophecy. Lysander has failed."

Zelarchus nodded. "Alas, if the purpose of your journey has been to make this report, then I am afraid it has been unnecessary. I have already learned of what transpired in Thrace. You have done well, despite my misgivings. The Pythia's faith in you was not misplaced." The unsettling speed with which information reached Delphi astounded me. But I was reassured that some things remained hidden even from the ears of Delphi, for by now Adaz was with Nimahe in the endless Skythian steppes.

I brushed aside the priest's comment. "I have come for compensation."

"Is it not enough to serve Apollo?"

"Only if he pays me adequately."

Zelarchus' eyes hardened. "You are just another mercenary, then? Perhaps my original estimation of you was correct after all."

"I have never claimed to be anything more," I replied flatly.

The priest sighed. "Delphi is not ungrateful," he said. He beckoned to a slave, who presented me with a cord-sealed leather satchel.

The muffled clinking of the gold coins within seemed unnaturally loud in the lambent courtyard. I hefted the weighty bag in my hand. It was a substantial sum, but nothing but the tiniest fraction of the wealth tucked away in the various treasuries of Delphi. I tucked the satchel of coins inside my tunic and looked at Zelarchus. "I have one more demand," I said.

"A mercenary always overreaches himself, but considering the nature of your service, I will hear your request," the head priest said, emphasizing the last word.

I returned my gaze to the priest. "I want the head of Agasias," I said. I had not forgotten my promise to the handsome young priest.

"Ah," Zelarchus said with a slightly pained expression. "That is a demand that I cannot accommodate."

"You would deny me this?" I said.

"I cannot grant you that which does not exist," he said.

"I do not understand," I said.

"A significant sum of temple treasure was discovered in the home of Agasias, treasure from the temple of Apollo itself!" Zelarchus said, his feigned shock not quite convincing. "He denied any knowledge of the treasure and how it might have ended up in his residence, of course, but the evidence of his sacrilege was incontrovertible. For such a crime, there is only one punishment, as you know; Agasias was thrown from the Hyampeian Rock not five days ago." Zelarchus shook his head. "Such an ignoble end for a promising young man."

I stared at Zelarchus. I reckoned that news of what had transpired in Thrace would have reached the sensitive ears of Delphi not much earlier than five days ago. Zelarchus had moved fast. The priest smiled thinly but it did little to mask the hard cunning in his eyes. He was a dangerous man. I saw in him another Lysander, those soulless men of power who think little of sacrificing others to achieve their own aims. Despite the warm night air, a shiver ran through me.

I glanced towards the upper level of the residence where the Pythia lived with her retinue of slaves and attendants. "And the Pythia?" I asked, wondering what had become of the young girl whom Agasias had said would assume the role of Oracle.

Zelarchus attempted a look of pained grief. "Another unfortunate turn of fate," he said, spreading his hands in a gesture of helplessness. "The poor girl took ill and died not long before young Agasias met his own fate. It is a shame, but who knows why the Disease Bringer took her," he said, using one of Apollo's many names. "The will of the gods is opaque. But Pythias come and Pythias go," he said, echoing the words of Agasias. "And, by the will of Apollo, another will be found before the next consultation day."

His words faded into the night. I did not respond. I had little doubt that the young Pythia's demise had little to do with the will of Apollo. The girl had been blameless. Just another child who became a piece to be sacrificed in the game played by the likes of Lysander and Zelarchus. I could have taken two steps forward and cut the Zelarchus down before he could utter a word. The long-bearded priest, perhaps sensing my thoughts, narrowed his eyes. But what would it have achieved? And, however reluctantly, I owed Zelarchus my life, if nothing else. "I must go," I said, turning abruptly to leave.

"Wait!" Zelarchus said. I looked back at him. "I cannot give you Agasias, but perhaps I can offer you something of equal value."

"What?"

"Information about a certain person's whereabouts have reached my ears. A person over whose fate your interests and those of Delphi coincide. But you must act quickly."

"Tell me," I said, and he did. He had not lied. The information was of great value to me. My return to Athens would be delayed while I attended to the matter.

But not yet. There was one more thing I needed to do before I left Delphi for good.

A DOG BARKED OFF IN THE DISTANCE. After a moment it stopped, apparently having satisfied itself that whatever trespasser had alerted it had moved on. Whoever it had been, they were not the only shadows skulking about Delphi that night.

Tibetos put his foot on the flat surface formed by my interlaced fingers. I heaved as he leapt, propelling him upwards. His hands caught the top of the sanctuary wall and I shifted to push against the soles of his feet. It was enough and he scrabbled over the wall and disappeared.

A moment later a rope tumbled back over the edge. I hauled myself up, my ascent slowed by the extra weight of the tools slung in a knotted cloth across my back. The stubborn daytime heat still clung to the night air and a bead of sweat trickled down my forehead by the time I dropped over the opposite side to join my friend.

Torches dotted the sanctuary, like way-points leading up to the temple. The scattered flames seemed to accentuate the eerie stillness of the forest of statues that filled the grounds like a silent army of stone and bronze.

Tibetos and I skirted edges of the well-trodden paths, staying away from well-lit areas. Tibetos tugged at my tunic and pointed. A pair of sentries had rounded a bend further up the path, a lantern swinging idly by their sides. The temple guards were heading towards us and soon we would fall within the advancing circle light that surrounded them.

I pointed to the phalanx of statues to the side of the path. Tibetos nodded in agreement, and we melted in among the stone sentinels. In their midst, we were just two more frozen, silent figures. The guards passed so close that I could have stepped out and seized them. But the men were not my enemies and I let them continue in peace, their lamps slowly bobbing down the hill until they vanished.

Tibetos and I detached ourselves from the crowd of statues and padded further up the slope. We ascended the final ramp and found ourselves in the forecourt of the great temple of Apollo. The enormous bronze figure of the god towered above us. The light from the torches mounted on either side of the temple doors played over Apollo's divine legs, but the god's head high above was just a dark outline silhouetted against the night sky. It was not Apollo I had come to see. I had come for a reckoning with another god. The proud statue of Lysander awaited us.

The statue's pedestal was almost as high as the sanctuary wall we had scaled earlier. Now, Tibetos boosted me up as I had done for him before and with one final effort I pulled myself up. I rose to my full height, taking a moment to catch my breath. My head barely reached the top of the god-man's thigh. That was about to change.

I unslung the knotted cloth from my back. Laying the bundle beside Lysander's stone foot, I peeled back the fabric to reveal the contents within. The hammer had been easy enough to find in Delphi, where statue-making brought in almost as much wealth as fleecing gullible pilgrims. Tomorrow a worker would wake up to find his tool gone, but he should not have been so careless with it.

I gripped the oak handle with both hands. The weight of the dense iron sledge pushed the wood into my right palm, as if the metal was fighting to escape me. The hammer was for driving wedges into stone blocks and splitting them. It was a crude tool but an effective one. Especially for what I had in mind.

I hefted the sledge in my hands, eyeing my target. The narrow part of Lysander's left leg between the ankle and the swelling of his calf was as thick as my own thigh, but still a weak point. Then, with all my strength, I swung.

The crack of the iron head against the marble reverberated through the temple grounds, like an assault on the silent night itself. Chips of fine stone flew from the impact point. Once again I slammed the iron head of the hammer against Lysander's stone shin, taking out a large chunk of rock. One final blow left a gaping space between the foot and the leg above.

For a heartbeat nothing happened. The echo of the last hit died away. But then the statue groaned in protest against the sacrilege that had been committed against it. There was snapping as a crack propagated through the other leg. Then, giving in to the pull of the ground below, the statue toppled from its perch.

The explosion of shattering stone was like a thunderclap. Marble fragments skittered away in every direction as Lysander's image exploded into a myriad of rocky chunks. The hegemon's severed head lay on its side. Farther away, his disembodied hand still clutched his golden sword, which now pointed at the temple. Internal bars of supporting iron protruded from the severed stone limbs like fractured bones. The god was dead, if not the man.

The commotion had woken every dog in the village and their distant indignant barking floated over the sanctuary. I tossed the hammer to the flagstones below. I let myself hang from the pedestal edge before dropping the remaining distance. I scooped up the tool and looked at Tibetos, who was grinning.

"Time to go, Dammo," he said.

We sprinted across the temple forecourt, away from where we had last seen the patrolling guards. We clambered over the short border wall and into the part of the sanctuary north of the temple. I tossed the hammer into some bushes.

Tibetos turned but I caught his shoulder. "Wait," I said.

We crouched in the shadows just beyond the temple grounds. The two temple guards whom we had seen earlier dashed into the forecourt, their swords drawn. The shattered remnants of Lysander's tribute to himself brought them to a sudden halt. In the torchlight I could see their features well enough as they gaped at the destruction that lay at their feet.

I smiled to myself. "Now we can go," I whispered. Tibetos and I slipped away, swallowed by the night. We were leaving Delphi but not returning to Athens. Not immediately, in any case. There was more task to be completed.

In the months that followed, it was said that Apollo caused Lysander's image to fall that night as punishment for the Spartan hegemon's hubris. Lysander had lost the favour of the gods, people whispered. The desire of some to see him crowned king, always tenuous, had evaporated like mist in the morning sun. Who would dare follow a man whom Apollo had so obviously abandoned?

But it was not the Sun-god who had brought Lysander low.

It was a demon.

CHAPTER 48

Thrasybulus could wait. Before I told the leading man of Athens about Delphi and Lysander's failure, I had another matter to attend to, something the stern Thrasybulus would no doubt disapprove of.

The clay vessel I carried was like those that could be found in almost any house in the city. The pot resembled an egg, but flattened at both the top and bottom, and in size it was a little larger than a hoplite's helmet. The inside was coated with bees-wax to keep the contents fresh, and the lid was similarly sealed shut with wax around the rim. The length of thick rope looped through the ears on either side of the pot, creating a convenient handle. The weight the vessel and its contents made the rope dig into my hand, but not uncomfortably so. In any case, I was not going far.

The plain-looking pot differed greatly from the one that I had brought back from Thrace. That vessel, an urn, was finely decorated with scenes of battle, all painted to my specifications by the finest artist in Abdera. The lid had been affixed with melted wax, sealing the contents within. The ashes of Sosias waited silently in my home but would not remain there for long. When my task was done, I would take the boy to his final resting place in my family tomb outside the Dipylon Gate. The ancient tomb had a spot of honour on the crypt-lined road, for many of my ancestors had been men of great renown. Sosias had earned his space among them. His ashes are still there, awaiting me in that dark, silent place. I will join you soon, Sosias, for I am old and tired. But on that evening long ago, before I delivered Sosias to his final resting space, I had one more mission to complete.

I threaded my way through the familiar lanes and alleys of Athens. My route was not random. With each turn I retraced the steps I had taken as I had pursued the dark-skinned assassin from the home of Thrasybulus so many months earlier. At last I came to the lane where the Pythia's killer had eluded me. Like that night, the doors of the various homes and workshops were shut tight against the encroaching night. But only one of the doors concerned me.

I pressed my ear close to the finely-sanded oak. Muffled voices, along with the occasional burst of laughter, could be heard from within. Satisfied, I took the thick iron ring that served as a knocker and banged it three times against the door.

In due course, the door opened and the clean-shaven face of a light-haired house slave peered out. The young man's face cycled rapidly from anticipation to surprise to confusion to irritation. Clearly he had been expecting someone else, another guest perhaps. "My master is not here," the slave said crisply and moved to shut the door in my face.

It was a lie, of course. Not only could I hear the gathering within, but my own servant, Iollas, had spied on the residence and reported that the man I sought was indeed at home. "I don't have time for this," I said, shouldering through the entrance and into the vestibule beyond.

The impudent slave, grunting in surprise, stumbled backwards. As he recovered himself, his eyes flicked towards the leaf-bladed *xiphos* sword hanging from a loop on my belt. Choosing self-preservation over further protestation, the slave spun and dashed into the interior of the home, shouting for aid all the way.

I followed him without urgency. Even without the slave leading the way, I would have known my destination, for the layout of such homes is quite predictable. In less than twenty paces I was at the doorway of the salon where the master of the house would take his meals and entertain guests. I stepped inside.

The stink of incense hit me first, followed by the indignant stares of half a dozen bearded men. Their tunics bore the wine stains of men already deep into an evening of drinking games and other frivolities. They pulled themselves up from their reclining positions on the cushioned sofas lining the perimeter of the salon. Their hostility morphed into unease as the realization of who it was that stood before them slowly penetrated their wine-addled brains. A pretty youth clad in an undersized tunic looked at me with wide, kohl-lined eyes, his mouth slightly agape. The boy's beauty was accentuated by dark hair perfectly styled into tight, overlapping ringlets. The jug he was holding tilted slightly and wine dribbled out onto the floor. Another bare-torsoed boy sat on a stool with a lyre, whose tune died away with a few pathetic final plucks of the strings. Small tables covered with half-empty dishes of figs, olives, and assorted dainty snacks suggested that the drinking party had already been going on for some time prior to my unwelcome arrival.

The slave who had failed to prevent my entering the house now pointed at me accusingly as he grovelled before his owner. "Master! I tried to stop him, but he *attacked* me!" the slave babbled. Beside him, his master blinked at me furiously with wide eyes, the rest of his body apparently paralyzed by the sight of me.

I broke the silence. "Hello, *Plato*," I said through a false smile.

I could see Plato's mind racing behind his frantic eyes. As was his custom, he decided it best to attack with words rather than force. "How dare you disturb me and my guests in my home!" he blustered, rising to his feet. "The impropriety of your actions goes beyond all decency. I demand you leave at once!" he finished, raising his chin defiantly.

"I only wish to join your circle of friends," I said, indicating the silent audience of fearful long-haired philosophers around us. "Or am I unworthy company for such esteemed men?" I asked, feigning wounded pride. "Do you think my presence would diminish the dignity of your ... discussions?" I said, glancing at the half-naked serving boy.

Plato bristled but managed to control himself. "You know very well why you are not welcome here! State your business and be gone!" The forced disdain did not completely mask the fear in his voice.

"I have come to settle past wrongs between us, Plato. I have even brought you a gift for your celebration," I said, raising the clay pot for all to see. "Or should I say, one more guest for your symposium."

I tossed the clay vessel with an underhand motion. The round pot sailed gently through the air and hung suspended for an instant at the apex of its arc before accelerating towards the tiled floor, where it shattered in a spray of oil and fragments of pottery. Plato's guests recoiled to avoid the splatter of oil, bringing their hands up to shield their faces. When they lowered their hands, they thought first of their own persons, wiping oil from their skin and regarding their sullied robes in babbling dismay. Only slowly did they lay eyes on the object in the middle of the floor, and one by one their bleating died away until there was only silence.

The oil-slicked head, freed from its clay prison, lay on its side facing Plato, who could only blink stupidly at it.

"You know him, I think," I said, pointing at the head. The victim, his eyes shut but lips slightly parted, was recognizable despite the coat of dripping oil. The dark-skinned assassin, murderer of the Pythia, would kill no more. The information the priest Zelarchus had provided me regarding the assassin's whereabouts had proved accurate. Even assassins, it seemed, had homes to which they occasionally returned.

Dread crept over Plato's face. And I knew. I knew that I had been right. "This was his base of operations," I said, nodding at the head. "He and his men waited here for night to fall before going to murder Thrasybulus and his family. This is where he hid when he failed. You are Lysander's agent, Plato, and you will die for it," I finished.

Nervous glances flew about the room. One man with his long hair held back by a leather thong bit at his lip as he considered his options. His eyes widened in panic as I drew my sword and pointed it towards him. "Do you wish to die with your host, philosopher?" I said calmly. The man shook his head vigorously. "And you?" I asked another, who sputtered in a most ineloquent manner. I cut him off with a wave. "If you wish to see another dawn, then be gone from my sight!" I said, my voice rising with each word.

If they had been men of courage, the philosophers could have easily overpowered me, for a single armed man, no matter his strength, is no match for six determined opponents, armed or otherwise. But they were not brave men, practically scrambling over each other to abandon their host to his fate. Plato and I regarded each other as the last of their cowardly footsteps faded into the night.

I was about to speak when Plato surprised me. Showing bravery absent in his companions, he suddenly charged at me with a roar, bending low to take me under the ribs. What the attack possessed in ferocity it lacked in skill. I shifted to the side and avoided the brunt of the impact. I drove my knee into his guts and his breath exploded from his lungs in a hollow whoosh of air. With a growl I spun, heaving him across the salon where he crashed into one of the food-laden tables.

Plato groaned among the scattered delicacies and dishes, finally rolling over onto his knees. I waited patiently. He groped about on the floor and fell upon an overturned cup. With sudden purpose, he scooped it up and hurled it at me, narrowly missing my head. The cup was followed by every plate and dish he could find until his supply of missiles was exhausted. A few hit me, but most were easily dodged. He picked a stool up and ran at me. He put all his strength into a mighty swing. I stepped into the blow and braced my shoulder, and the stool cracked and splintered against me like a wave on a rock.

Plato seemed surprised that the attack had not felled me. Before he could recover his wits, I stepped forward and drove my crown square into his face. I felt the bridge of his nose shatter against the arch of my skull, and he reeled backwards, collapsing beside the overturned table.

My sword sat heavy in my hand. One swing of the blade would remove the traitor Plato from my life once and for all. But I had to know. "Why?" I asked the pathetic, crumpled form on the floor at my feet.

With a groan, Plato pulled himself up and turned around so that he sat leaning against the overturned table, his straight legs splayed out in front of him. He struggled to lift his head up to meet my gaze. Blood from his broken nose had transformed his face and tunic into a sticky red mess.

"Why?" I asked him again. "You are a citizen. You have wealth. You have standing among your peers. Why would you betray your city to Lysander?"

Plato coughed and then hawked a gob of bloody mucous in my direction. He stared at me with resigned anger but did not answer.

"Bah!" I spat back at him. I raised my sword. I would make his death swift.

Plato dropped his chin, awaiting the killing blow. A trembling started in his hands and spread until his shoulders were juddering with great heaving breaths. I loomed over him. I thought that fear of death had taken him, for he was a coward. But I was wrong. Plato was weeping.

And then he spoke, his words choked by sputtering sobs. I couldn't understand. "What did you say?"

Plato jerked his head up. His tear-reddened eyes glared at me. "Because they killed him!" he said, biting each word. "Because they killed him!" he spat once more.

I frowned, not understanding who had been killed nor by whom. "Who?"

Plato coughed. I realized it was a laugh. "Your cell-mate. My master," he said, and I finally understood. Sokrates. "It should have been you," he added quietly.

"Lysander was using you," I said. "He only cares about power."

Plato snorted again. "Perhaps, but Lysander would not be worse than those who rule Athens now: the *people*," he managed to sneer.

"Thrasybulus is a good man," I said. "He can lead Athens well."

"He is a slave to the people's whims as much as you or I," Plato retorted.

"And you are willing to die for Lysander now?"

Plato considered this for a few rasping breaths. He spat again. "Not for him, no. But to avenge my master, yes. For that I would have done anything." He looked up at me. "He was everything to me. I loved him." His head drooped and he began to weep anew.

I looked down on the man who had once called for my execution. The man who had been in league with Lysander. The man who had abetted the attempted murder of Thrasybulus and his family. My enemy. In the shadows of my soul, the Furies goaded me to fulfil my duty of vengeance. But at that moment I felt only pity for the pathetic, weeping Plato.

The howls of the serpent-haired Furies receded and vanished into the ethereal night as I denied them. I lowered my sword. "Up!" I ordered. Plato raised his teary, bloodied face with a look of utter incomprehension. "Up! It is a simple enough command, philosopher!" I barked. Plato tottered to his feet.

I have slain many men, some good, some evil, but always my enemies in war. I did not execute unarmed men who cowered before me in their own homes. To Plato, I merely said, "I am not a murderer."

"I do not understand," Plato said.

"Sokrates saved my father's life long ago, and he saved mine. I owe him a debt, which I am repaying now," I said.

"You will spare my life?"

"My debt is paid, but yours is not," I said. "For your crimes, you will go into exile. If you are still in the city at sunset tomorrow, you will not enjoy my mercy a second time."

Plato acknowledged my condition with a reluctant nod. I pushed past him, but his voice stopped me at the threshold of the debris-strewn salon. "Daimon!" he called. I looked over my shoulder at him. "I will not forget this," he said.

I left Plato there, standing among the ruins of his symposium. I have thought back on that moment many times during my life, reflecting on my decision to spare him and all that was to pass between us in the following years. One thing is certain.

I should have killed him.

EPILOGUE

The slave Xanthias admitted me to the house of his master, Iasos. "The master is teaching the children. Do you wish me to fetch him?" the ancient slave asked.

"No, I do not want to disturb his lesson," I said. "I will watch until he is done."

Xanthias shrugged. I followed him into the courtyard, and the slave shuffled off to carry out this duty or that. At the far end of open space, Iasos watched over his charges, who were absorbed in scratching out their letters on tablets of wax. My old tutor saw me across the courtyard and smiled warmly. He did not speak but indicated one raven-haired boy with a gentle nod.

I moved quietly to one side of the courtyard to see my son more clearly. In profile he looked so much like his mother. He was beautiful. Iasos looked my way once more, and Niko, sensing his shift in attention, turned to follow his teacher's gaze.

Seeing me, Niko flinched ever so slightly. I did not grimace or frown, but smiled, for I loved him. I knelt down on one knee and held my arms out to him. "Come here, my son," I said. My tears came easily, unrestrained after so long.

Niko did not move, but then his eyes widened in joyful comprehension. He leapt from his stool and ran to my embrace, his tablet and stylus clattering on the ground behind him.

My son's small frame disappeared in my arms. "I'm sorry," I said. "I'm sorry for everything." Niko tightened his hold on me. We remained that way, weeping, for a long time.

And then I let go.

Author's Note

The most improbable plot point of the preceding story is ironically the part that is best supported by historical documentation, if Plutarch is to be believed. In his *Life of Lysander*, Plutarch writes: "There was a woman in Pontus who professed to be pregnant by Apollo, [...] and when she had brought forth a man-child, several not-unimportant persons took an interest in its rearing and bringing up." Among these "not-important persons" was Lysander, who concocted the plot to use the boy and the prestige of Delphi to legitimize his planned usurpation of the Spartan throne, more or less as the Pythia describes for Daimon in the depths of the Temple of Apollo at Delphi. Plutarch also notes, vaguely, that the plot failed and remained a secret until after Lysander's death. This was the incident around which I built the rest of the story for God of Sparta.

For my research on Delphi, my primary source was *Delphi: A History of the Center of the Ancient World* by Michael Scott. Over its long history, Delphi has been destroyed, rebuilt, renovated, and plundered numerous times. Many of the most notable sights one sees today at Delphi did not exist at the time of Daimon's story, so Scott's work was a tremendous help in my recreation of Delphi circa 400 BC. Many other details are my own additions, but that is the license of a writer of historical fiction…

Another perhaps less traditional resource was *Stephen Biesty's Ancient World*. Biesty does tremendously-detailed, thoroughly-researched exploded views of historical subjects. A picture is worth a thousand words, and Biesty's vision of Delphi and other Greek sites have given me a fabulous visual framework to work with. Biesty's works (I own most of them) are ostensibly for young readers, but I would recommend them to history fans of any age.

One point that kept appearing in my research on Delphi was the idea of Delphi being a kind of "information hub" of the ancient world, something I played up in the story. People of all stations came to Delphi from all over the Greek world and beyond, such was the renown of the Oracle. With them they brought news, rumours, and sundry tidbits of information that the priests of Delphi could collect and archive, perhaps even using their knowledge to provide more prescient and insightful oracles to the suppliants who came to put their questions to the Pythia.

Another consideration is the source of the Pythia's visions. It was long believed that subterranean gases of some sort worked their way up through cracks in the rocks of Delphi and caused hallucinations. The idea was dismissed by modern scholars, but more recent research has suggested that we should place more faith in the ancient writers who reported the phenomenon. Were Daimon's fears in the Pythia's lair induced by such gases, or was he merely the victim of the power of suggestion? It is up to the reader to decide.

As for the Thracians who play such an important role in history and Daimon's story, relatively little is known. At the time of this story, there was indeed a rift between the real King Medokos and his renegade general Seuthes (known to history as Seuthes II.) For this book, *The Amazons* by Adrienne Mayor was an invaluable resource and the direct inspiration for the character of Nimahe. The Greeks had some hazy notions of the barbarian pants-wearing peoples north of the Aegean, and the customs and appearances of the Scythians and the Thracians often blurred together. In Scythian society, especially, men and women seemed to be equally fierce horse-riding warriors, something I hoped to convey in the story through Nimahe's martial prowess.

For Plato, a book I read very early on in my research greatly informed my portrayal of the great philosopher and his relationship with perhaps the most famous philosopher in history, Socrates. *Plato at the Googleplex* by Rebecca Goldstein is not only a fantastic introduction to Plato's ideas, but contains many historical nuggets about Plato and his times, many of which found their way into the book. The book helped me understand what might motivate Plato as a person, and hopefully to give his character more depth and nuance, if not always sympathy.

Finally, I would like to briefly touch on the situation in Athens in the years following the end of the Peloponnesian War. When the oppressive Thirty Tyrants of Athens were defeated and democracy restored, Thrasybulus declared an amnesty for those who had supported the Tyrants, an understandable decision as the supporters made up a large proportion of the population. Nevertheless, it could not have been easy for those who suffered at the hands of the Tyrants to live side by side with collaborators or informers of the former regime, something that we have seen repeated in our own times. Suspicion lingered and sometimes manifested itself in more concrete actions. The conviction of Socrates was in no small part due to his connections to figures such as Critias and Alcibiades. For similar reasons of self-preservation, Plato seems to have gone into exile soon after the execution of Socrates, but I could not resist having Daimon be directly involved in Plato's decision to leave Athens.

As Daimon suggested, his fraught relationship with Plato has not ended, but that part of the tale lies in future stories. For, after a short period of relative peace brought about by the Spartan hegemony, the Greek world is about to once again explode into decades of open warfare. And Daimon, gods willing, will soon be back to tell of his own part in those chaotic times…

ACKNOWLEDGMENTS

I would like to thank all the people who asked me, "When is Book 2 coming out?" It really encouraged me to keep going. I would like to thank my mother, Judy, for correcting my more egregious grammar and spelling errors. I would also like to thank my uncle, Peter Dalziel, for giving me valuable feedback on how I could tighten various aspects of the story. It was very much appreciated.

A REQUEST...

I hope you enjoyed this story. If you did, I would really appreciate it if you could leave a review on Amazon or Goodreads. It is really important for the Amazon algorithm-y things, and it is also good for the author's fragile ego... Thank you!

M.S.

ABOUT THE AUTHOR

Martin Sulev graduated from the University of Toronto with a degree in Palaeontology but now wishes he had studied Classics. He has worked as a freelance writer in the ESL industry and has contributed translations of Chinese short stories to two anthologies published by Cornell University. He currently lives in Toronto with his wife and son.

More information on upcoming Demon of Athens novels can be found at:

www.martinsulev.com

Follow on Twitter @MSulev

Facebook: @MartinSulevAuthor

COMING IN AUTUMN 2021

SHADOW OF THEBES
Demon of Athens Book 3

For almost ten years, Athenians have bowed to their Spartan overlords, but there is a glimmer of hope for the once mighty city. Lysander has been humbled and his power greatly diminished. Spartan forces are spread thin across the Aegean and Sparta itself has grown decadent with the wealth and power of empire. Thrasybulus, *strategos* and first citizen of Athens, deems that the time for rebellion has come. But first, Daimon, Thrasybulus' most trusted agent, must accompany a secret shipment of Persian gold to Athens, money that will convince reluctant cities such as Thebes to join Thrasybulus in his uprising against Sparta. But enemies, known and hidden, seek to thwart Daimon at every turn, and only with old friends and unexpected allies can Daimon accomplish his mission. The fate of Greece hangs in the balance.

Printed in Great Britain
by Amazon